"Strange, isn't it, how we've traveled across two countries, but this is the first time we've ever truly been alone," he said.

Her heart quickened. It was pounding, about ready to burst. He drew closer still. "If you don't want me to kiss you, tell me to stop. A pity, though, after I went to all this trouble to get you alone."

She felt so warm, so protected—how could this be wrong? "Just one kiss?"

"One kiss," he said softly, "just one. And after, we shall become our noble selves again, virtuous to a fault, dutifully tending to our moral obligations."

"All right," she said, wrapping her arms around his neck. With an intake of breath, he clasped her body tightly to his own, one hand exploring the hollow of her back. She gave herself up to him completely, savoring the heady sensation of his lips pressed against the pulsing hollow of her throat, then her cheek, across her forehead, down to her nose, then at last, urgently demanding, her mouth. . . .

The
Irish
Upstart

Shirley Kennedy

A SIGNET BOOK

SIGNET
Published by New American Library, a division of
Penguin Putnam Inc., 375 Hudson Street,
New York, New York 10014, U.S.A.
Penguin Books Ltd, 27 Wrights Lane,
London W8 5TZ, England
Penguin Books Australia Ltd,
Ringwood, Victoria, Australia
Penguin Books Canada Ltd, 10 Alcorn Avenue,
Toronto, Ontario, Canada M4V 3B2
Penguin Books (N.Z.) Ltd, 182–190 Wairau Road,
Auckland 10, New Zealand

Penguin Books Ltd, Registered Offices:
Harmondsworth, Middlesex, England

First published by Signet, an imprint of New American Library,
a division of Penguin Putnam Inc.

First Printing, April 2001
10 9 8 7 6 5 4 3 2 1

Dedicated with heartfelt thanks to my many friends on the Internet who helped me with my research for *The Irish Upstart*.

They include Paddy Kavanaugh of Athlone, Ireland, who supplied me with information on Clonmacnoise, as well as Ireland's early coaching days.

They also include the learned gentlemen of a certain maritime history group who went out of their way to supply me with details about the ships that sailed between England and Ireland in Regency times. Among others, they are:

Norman Napier Boyd, Suffolk
Dr. Ian Buxton, University of Newcastle, Newcastle upon Tyne
Jon Godsell, Wallasey
John Guard
Colin Hague, Curator, Naval Museum at Portsmouth
Alan Hardy
Malcoln McRonald, Heswall
Lincoln Paine, Portland, Maine
Alan Pritchard
Jeffrey Bennet Smith
Frank Pierce Young, Annapolis, Maryland

MANY THANKS!

Chapter 1

Dublin, Ireland, 1807

Evleen O'Fallon took one last look around the drawing room of her Dublin town house and choked back tears. In all her fifteen years, this was the worst day of her life. She thought again and quickly corrected herself. *No, not quite the worst because the worst was five years ago when Papa died. That would make today the second worst...*

No—the second worst was the day Mama married the Englishman.

So today was third worst, no question. It was the day she must say good-bye to the only life she had ever known and face a life of ... what? She had yet to see their future home, that small farm to the west, near Galway Bay. "It's going to be fine," her mother had assured them, but Evleen knew better. How could anything in the world be as good as the life she had now? What could replace her come-out into the glittering Dublin society that she'd so looked forward to? Nothing. And her mother knew better than to promise there would be the same balls and soirees on the other side of Ireland in barren County Clare, which, as far as she was concerned, might as well be on the other side of the moon.

And all this thanks to the Englishman. Bitterness filled Evleen's heart as she thought of Randall, Lord Montfret, whose lies and slick charm had fooled her mother completely. Despite all the warnings, she had married him. Then, just as friends and family predicted, he squandered her money, practically down to the last farthing, and then had the gall to up and die. Typhoid, the doctor said.

As a consequence, her mother had been compelled to sell

their elegant town house on Lower Fitzwilliam Street, directly across from Merrion Square. Although the sale of the town house had fetched the tidy sum of eight hundred pounds, citing the family's poverty, she sold most of their possessions as well. "Don't for a moment think we're rich," she warned. "We will no doubt have to stretch those eight hundred pounds for years to come." As a consequence, there were no more jewels, baubles, and pretty clothes; no more servants, no more lady's maid to help them dress and fix their hair . . .

Evleen squeezed her eyes shut. *Oh, I must stop this. I'm the oldest. I must remain strong, not only for Mama, but for Darragh, Sorcha, Mary, and Patrick.*

Wrapped in misery, Evleen watched as two indifferent draymen removed the few fine things of her mother's she'd decided to keep to the wagon outside. At least she had kept her needlework boxes, and all the books they owned. Still, there were so many lovely things that, of necessity, would be left behind. Evleen glanced at the fireplace and called, "Mama, are you not taking the pole screen?" A lump rose in her throat as she remembered the countless evenings her mother sat by the fire with her needlework, her pretty face shielded from the heat of the flames by the elaborately carved mahogany screen.

"I think not, Evleen. I'll have no use for it, not where we're going."

Evleen felt her spirits plunge even lower, if that was possible. "But we'll still have a fireplace. And you'll still be sitting beside it."

Sinead O'Fallon entered the room, sighing deeply, on her hip the baby, redheaded Patrick, who was just one year old. "That screen was used mainly to keep the wax in my makeup from melting. I won't have much use for makeup now." An ironic smile crossed her face. "Not unless I want to impress a bunch of sheep." She lowered her voice and continued, "Lord and Lady Aimsberry are here." At Evleen's questioning gaze, she continued, "Don't you recall? They're the English couple who bought the house. They're looking around in the library. Go ask if they'd like tea."

Evleen bit her tongue, but the words burst out anyway. "I still don't see why you had to sell our beautiful home to an Englishman."

"Because he has the money," Sinead answered in her usual blunt fashion. *Just like Mama,* Evleen thought. Even in the midst of adversity, she remained strong, accepting her unfair fate with wondrous equanimity. She even looked as beautiful as ever, despite everything, with her thick red hair pulled into a bun atop her head, her white skin flawless, her figure slender still, despite five babies. This new trouble had taken its toll, though. Lately, fine lines had appeared at the corners of her eyes. Strain showed on her face, and her shoulders slumped, although ever so slightly.

I, too, Evleen thought as she caught a glimpse of herself in the looking glass. She much resembled her mother, tall and slender, with the same fair skin and blue eyes, although her hair was black, not her mother's flaming red. With dismay she noted the rosy glow that usually brightened her cheeks had disappeared. Now her face, like her mother's, was drawn tight by worry and strain.

"I shall go ask if they would like tea," Evleen said and made her way to the library door.

Inside, she heard voices and immediately identified those unmistakable, lofty accents so characteristic of the English *ton.* She was about to enter when she heard a woman, no doubt Lady Aimsberry, ask disdainfully, "How long must we stay in this miserable, godforsaken country?"

A man's voice, no doubt Lord Aimsberry's, replied, "But surely you find Dublin quite civilized."

His wife retorted peevishly, "Dublin would be all right if it were not filled with the Irish, whom you know are inferior. Not far above savages, if you want my opinion."

Evleen heard a patient sigh, followed by Lord Aimsberry's voice again. "Our stay will be two years at the most, until I see my bank safely established. Meanwhile, you must admit this town house is every bit as elegant as ours in London. Note the magnificent ceiling plasterwork. And this chandelier. Magnificent! Genuine Waterford crystal, don't you agree?"

"I suppose, but really, Edward, I cringe at the thought of residing where some shabby Irish family once lived. It's all just so distasteful."

"But my dear, the O'Fallons are not shabby," protested Lord Aimsberry. "Mrs. O'Fallon is most cultured and refined. Quite knowledgeable, too, and with an appreciation of fine literature and art. In talking to her, I learned the family is descended directly from the kings of Ireland who were descended from . . . er, the first Milesian king, Ollam Fodla, or some such thing."

"Such rubbish. Who gives a fig for Irish nobility?"

"But her second husband was English."

"Really? Well, if the second husband was English, what is she doing with that dreadful Irish name?"

"From what I understand, the marriage was quite hush-hush. I heard the fellow fled England and was disowned by his family. Debts, apparently. Not long after the rascal arrived in Dublin, he married Mrs. O'Fallon, ran through all her money in no time flat, then up and died. And that, my dear, is why she is compelled to sell this town house."

"So where are they going?"

"To a piece of property that belonged to the scoundrel—his only legacy, apparently. I don't envy them. From what I understand, it's a wretched farmhouse and a bit of rocky land, enough for a sheep or two, I suppose, located on a desolate hillside overlooking Galway Bay."

"Am I supposed to feel sorry for her? Far as I am concerned, it serves her right. She should have known better than to rise above herself and marry an Englishman."

The gall. Tea indeed. Evleen turned and fled back to the drawing room, unwilling to hear another word. *How could they talk about Mama that way!*

"What's wrong, Evleen?" Her sister Darragh stood forlornly by the fireplace. She was pale. Her eyes were red from crying.

"It's that wretched English couple who bought the house," Evleen replied. "Fools. You should hear them talk—going on and on about how superior they think they are to us Irish. I didn't like the way they talked about Mama."

"Mama," repeated Darragh, seizing upon the word with that ominously incensed tone that warned Evleen she was about to start again. "How could she have married that man? She has ruined our lives, she—"

"That's enough," Evleen interrupted, kind but firm. "I'll not hear one more bad word about our mother." Her heart went out to poor Darragh. It was hard enough being fourteen under the best of circumstances. She was still a child in so many ways, yet wanting to be treated like a grown woman. Not so very long ago, Evleen, herself, was fourteen, and she could well remember her own feelings. Still, she didn't think she'd been as rebellious as Darragh, nor so sullen and resentful. At least she hoped she hadn't. "What's done is done—try not to make Mama feel worse than she already does."

Darragh's blue eyes narrowed in resentment. "Everyone told her not to marry him. Everyone warned her. Well, she did what she wanted and look what happened. Now we're poor and my life is over. Oh, I shall never forgive her."

Issuing a silent prayer for patience, Evleen gripped her sister's shoulders. "What you say is true, Darragh. You have every right to be angry and upset. Mama made a terrible mistake, but it was out of love, don't forget, so you mustn't condemn her."

"Love? Ha! How could anyone love an Englishman?" A corner of Darragh's upper lip curled with contempt. "Mama was a fool. That scoundrel never loved her. He was only out to rob her of her fortune."

Evleen answered softly, "That may very well be, but the man is dead now. There's no sense in nurturing a grudge. He won't know, and it certainly won't do Mama any good. You must think of the good things about our mother—all she's done for us, all—"

"It's time to go, girls," called Sinead, entering the dining room, carrying Patrick, followed by her two youngest daughters, Sorcha and Mary. All were dressed in warm clothes suitable for travel.

Time to leave. A lump rose in Evleen's throat. "I'll get my coat," she said, and softly added, "and have one last look around." *I shall never do this again,* Evleen thought as she lifted her skirts and sped up the three flights of stairs that led to her room. Her heart wrenched as she thought, never again would she ever climb these stairs, or stand by the window of her room and gaze down at bustling Merrion Square, or lie in bed of a morning and drowsily gaze at the flowered wallpaper while she daydreamed of all the parties she'd attend and beaux she would have when she turned eighteen.

Oh, it was so hard to keep from crying.

By the time she was downstairs again, dressed in a warm redingote, she had regained at least a part of her usual composure. "This might even be fun," she said brightly as they piled

into the old wagon packed with their belongings, a far cry from
the smart barouche they used to own. *At least we're all together,* Evleen thought as she looked at Sorcha and Mary, near
tears and huddled together; at Darragh, a mass of quivering indignation and despair; and rosy-cheeked Patrick, bundled up
and safe in their mother's lap. He was only her half brother, son
of the hated Englishman, nonetheless beloved by them all. She
must try to be cheerful, Evleen reminded herself, and pasted a
careful smile on her face. "Just think, we'll get to live near the
ocean, and milk the cows and feed the chickens, and herd the
sheep."

"Have you lost your mind?" Darragh asked in an anguished
voice. "We are but peasants now, just poor Irish trash. Oh, it
makes me ashamed. We can never hold our heads up again."

"Ashamed to be Irish?" Sinead squared her shoulders; her
chin lifted with dignity; pride blazed in her clear blue eyes.
"You must never forget, my children, that your father was Ian
O'Fallon, son of Daniel O'Fallon, eighth Earl of Dunkerry,
who was directly descended from the Duke of Connaught, who
was a direct descendent of Euchaid, one of the ancient kings of
Ireland who reigned over one of the earliest Gaelic kingdoms
many centuries ago." She turned to Evleen. "Can you tell us
more of Euchaid?"

Evleen promptly answered, "Euchaid was a great king,
Mama, descended from the first Milesian king, Ollam Fodla,
who was a true father to his people, and an able statesman."

Sinead nodded proudly and looked back at Darragh.
"Ashamed to be Irish? You, all of you, should be bursting with
pride that the blood of Irish kings runs through your veins."

Tears glistened in Sinead's eyes, a sight Evleen had never
seen, not even when her father died, most assuredly not when
the Englishman drew his last breath. "We know," she said gently and clasped her mother's hand. "We're proud to be Irish.
Darragh, too, no matter what she says, and we'll never forget,
no matter what happens or how poor we are."

"Always hold your head high," Sinead said, calmer now,
and smiling.

"Yes, Mama."

"And never love an Englishman."

"Yes, Mama."

The wagon began to move. Evleen turned her head for a last glimpse of their elegant red brick town house with its tall sash windows, wrought iron balusters, and intricately carved wooden front door. Tears sprang to her eyes, and she had to turn away, knowing in her heart she would never see it again.

Chapter 2

Hertfordshire County, England, 1816

The medieval towers of Northfield Hall, the ancestral home of the Marquess of Wythe, rose majestically through December's evening mist as a lone horseman turned into the long, winding driveway that led to the front portico.

Lord Thomas, second son of the fifth Marquess of Wythe, smiled as the beautiful old mansion came into view. A flood of pleasant memories struck him at the sight of the home where he'd spent his happy childhood. He had been away three long years. Despite his fatigue after his journey from London, he was elated to be home.

At the marble steps of the portico, Thomas, a man of medium height, with dark good looks and a sinewy build, swung from his horse with the graceful, fluid ease of a man much accustomed to the saddle. He looked toward the entryway, half expecting his father to burst forth at any moment. In the past, his father, a florid-faced, blond bear of a man, had always greeted his sons with a warm hug and a booming "Welcome home!" Apparently not today, though. Instead, Thomas's sister, Penelope, swung open the door. When she spied him, a look of delight spread across her pretty face.

"Oh, Thomas, you're home." She flew down the steps and threw her arms around him.

"You've grown up," Thomas laughingly remarked when they finally broke apart. He held her at arm's length, his eyes admiring as he looked down upon his slender, blond-haired sister. "Why, Penelope, what a beauty you've become. How old are you now, eighteen?"

"Nineteen."

"And not yet married."

She tossed her head. "Hardly. And I warrant I shan't be if I don't find the right one."

He grinned and said, "Independent as ever, I see. You were never one of those bubble-headed girls dead set on finding a husband."

"And what about you?" she asked. "Has some young belle lured you anywhere close to the altar?"

"Not a chance," Thomas replied, eyes twinkling. "That's one of the many joys of being a second son. Nothing's expected of me, including heirs. Which reminds me, I don't suppose Montague is here?"

Penelope made a little moue. "Of course not. Our dear brother is firmly ensconced in London. If you're expecting he's mended his ways by now, you're doomed to disappointment."

"He's still drinking, gambling . . . ?"

"And whoring." Penelope grinned impishly at her use of the naughty word. "Worse than ever. Poor Papa is so disappointed."

Thomas's gaze flicked toward the door. "And speaking of Papa—?"

"In his room, in bed." A shadow crossed Penelope's bright, young face. "It's the gout. He suffers terribly."

Papa not well? It took Thomas a moment for his sister's words to sink in. His father was never sick. Thomas could not remember a time when his vigorous, burly father was not a robust picture of health. "Why didn't he let me know?"

"What good would it have done? You were all those many miles away in the West Indies. What could you have done except worry?" Penelope frowned. "And speaking of that, we received your letter telling us you were coming home, but you didn't say why. Is something wrong? Will you be returning to Jamaica?"

"I've come home for good, for reasons I shall discuss with Papa first. Reasons that . . ." Thomas shook his head ruefully. ". . . good Lord, it never occurred to me he might not be well." He bit his lip. "That makes telling him all the more difficult."

Penelope eyed him accusingly. "He won't like this, whatever your reasons."

"I know." Thomas felt a heavy weight descend on his

shoulders. His father was not going to like what he had to say, not at all. "Let's go inside, shall we?"

As Thomas ascended the main staircase to see his father, he reflected that in all his thirty years on earth, the one thing he'd learned for certain was that things never turned out exactly as he expected. But even knowing that, in all the agony of indecision he'd gone through, all that torturous soul-searching, he had assumed that when he announced his decision, his father might bellow and stomp around, as always, but then, as always, would forgive and understand. Never did Thomas expect his father might be ill. An illness meant weakness, disability. He could not even imagine his father an invalid.

At the door to his father's room, Thomas knocked and was admitted by Whitney, the valet. He had expected to find his father in his bed, but instead, the Marquess of Wythe was sitting in an armchair, his right foot heavily bandaged, propped in front of him on a plump pillow resting on a low stool. For a moment Thomas was stunned. Where was the strong, barrel-chested father he had known? The man in the chair seemed a stranger, shrunken somehow, hunched over, wan. "Papa, I'm back," he said, and started across the room to embrace him.

His father's eyes lit. "Son!" Instantly he raised his hand. "Stop. Don't come close."

Momentarily abashed, Thomas stopped abruptly.

"Sorry, my boy," his father went on. "Welcome home, but keep your distance. I cannot abide anyone near me. 'Tis this abominable toe of mine. I live in fear it might get jostled. Whitney, bring wine," he called in a muted voice far from the booming one Thomas remembered. "Sit down, son. By God, it's good to see you. Now, tell me why you're here and not seeing to my sugar fields in Jamaica."

Thomas seated himself, keenly aware the moment he dreaded was at hand. What he was about to say would be a blow to his father. Worse, now that he was sick. Still, Thomas had made up his mind. Nothing on this earth could make him change it. "I shall not be returning to Jamaica."

His father's eyebrows raised. "Damn. And why is that? And who's watching over the plantation?"

"Don't worry, I found a reliable overseer, so you're safe on that score. But . . ." Frowning, Thomas laced his fingers and earnestly leaned forward. "I could not stomach it another minute."

"Stomach what?" his father asked, genuinely confused.

"Slavery. It's not right. I refuse to be a part of it anymore."

"But . . . but . . ." Astounded, his father could do nothing but sputter. Finally, he gathered his wits enough to say, "How else do you expect to run a profitable plantation in Jamaica but for slaves?"

"I don't," Thomas declared, and added firmly, "and neither should you. You should see the cruelty. For three years I tolerated it, but no more. Men are meant to be free, not treated like animals."

"So what would you have me do?"

"Sell the plantation."

"Are you out of your mind? Why, the rum alone turns a tidy profit, and the sugar—"

"You're rich. You don't need the money."

Wide-eyed, the marquess stared at his son. "This is so unexpected. By God, I . . ." All at once, to Thomas's astonishment, the marquess threw back his head and let out a great peal of laughter. "Ah, Thomas," he finally said, wiping a tear from his eye, "I always wanted a son who would be his own man. Well, you are, and every bit as tough and independent as I could ever hope for. If only . . ." The marquess heaved a heavy sigh before he shouted, "Whitney, where's that wine?"

Thomas had no need to hear his father's finished thought. Over the years, he had heard the same diatribe many times before:

If only you, Thomas, had been born first instead of Montague.

Why must Montague lead that profligate life in London?

What a sore disappointment.

If only your mother were still alive, she might have had some influence on the boy.

Thomas said softly, "Montague's the first son, Papa. That's the way it is, and nothing will change it. Besides, he might come to his senses one of these days and become the son you've prayed for."

"Not likely," the marquess said with a scowl. "He'll get it all, you know. This house, the land, the money, which he'll immediately toss away with both hands on the tables at White's, or is it Brooks's these days?" He heaved another deep sigh. "Montague's my first son whom I dearly love, but—"

"What about the plantation?" Thomas had interrupted purposely. He hated to see his father brood about a matter that was beyond his power to change. "Will you sell?"

The marquess immediately snapped out of his doldrums. He thought a moment, then judging from the sudden, crafty light in his eye, some sort of solution occurred to him. "I take it you're quite serious about wanting me to sell."

"It's a matter of principle."

"Then I have a proposition. I shall sell the plantation in Jamaica on one condition."

"And what is that?"

"I want you to take a little jaunt to Ireland."

Chapter 3

"Ireland?" Thomas's voice rose with surprise. "Why on earth would I want to go to Ireland?" Accepting a glass of wine from Whitney, he sat easily back in his chair. "Do tell me. I am all ears."

"Surely you recall I have property in western Ireland," the marquess replied.

"It was presented to the second Marquess of Wythe by James the Second, was it not?"

"Very good, Thomas." The marquess beamed approvingly. "You always did have a keen grasp of our family history, as opposed to . . . ah, well. I'm sure you recall the second marquess was an illustrious warrior, a hero of the Battle of Sedgemoor in 1685. King James was most grateful for his services."

"And thus awarded him the land." Thomas then continued, "Good farmland, as I recall. In County Mayo, is it not?"

Papa nodded. "It's all rented out, of course, to tenants who raise corn, barley, God knows what else. Till recently, I never had a problem, but lately receipts have fallen off. Since there's a new overseer, I suspect there might be some sort of chicanery going on. I would go see for myself, but"—he cast a resentful look at his bandaged foot—"you see how it is."

"What about Montague?"

The marquess let out a snort. "You would never catch my illustrious son and heir that far from St. James's Street. He has no intention of prying himself away from his dissolute life in London, not even for a brief trip to Ireland." He regarded his younger son with brooding eyes. "Perhaps it's fortunate you returned home, after all."

Thomas said, "You mentioned a *little jaunt* to Ireland. Are you aware it takes a week to get there at the very least?"

Papa scowled impatiently. "Will you go?"

"Did you ever think I might have plans of my own?"

"Knowing you, I'm sure you do." Papa sighed in resignation. "So tell me your plans."

"As you know, I have always been keen on raising horses. You remember Tanglewood Hall?"

"That small manor near Abingdon your mother left you?"

"My grand estate," said Thomas, raising his eyebrows in self-mockery. "The house is satisfactory, and the land is ideal for raising thoroughbreds. That's where I'm going." Ruefully, he added, "I would have started sooner, had I not gone to Jamaica."

"I didn't force you to go. Matter of fact, need I remind you, it was your idea?"

"I went of my own free will," Thomas quickly replied. "In fact, I insisted."

"Indeed, you did, and I, well aware how obstinate you've been since the day you were born, had no desire to stand in your way. I will admit, though, I did nothing to discourage you because at the time I thought running the plantation would be for your own good. You did a fine job of it, too, until you found you had a conscience."

"Don't condemn me."

"Oh, surely not. But what was I to do with you, Thomas?" His father shrugged his shoulders in mock resignation. "I would have been more than happy to buy you a riding, but you had no desire to enter the clergy. I would have gladly bought you a commission in the Navy, but you refused. Then I tried—"

"Ah, the trials of having a second son," Thomas interrupted, casting an amused glance at his father. "Stop fretting. Obviously I'm doing fine on my own. I am quite capable of taking care of myself and making my own decisions, as you well know."

"Fine, son. Breeding thoroughbreds is an admirable ambition, and I shall give you considerable help in that direction, upon your return from Ireland."

Thomas felt an urge to throw up his hands. Although he loved his father dearly, years before he had rebelled against his forceful nature. The escape from paternal domination had not been easy. He could have remained the obedient second son, subject to his father's bidding, but instead had chosen to face his father's wrath and declare himself his own master. The marquess, to put it mildly, had not been pleased, and yet, when he saw that his son would not back down, he gave in, actually most graciously. After making his stand, Thomas most certainly would not back down now.

He refrained from mentioning that on the long journey from Jamaica, he'd been hard-put to contain his eagerness, so anxious was he to reach England, hasten to Tanglewood Hall, which sat on a lush piece of land, and begin preparations for the breeding of thoroughbred horses. He had every confidence he could succeed, and was wise enough to recognize a certain nagging disappointment with himself for having, in essence, given up on Jamaica and come running home in defeat. His reasons for leaving were altruistic, and most valid—he truly could not stomach the slavery—but still, he recognized that some would call him a failure, no matter what the noble reason. "Sorry, Papa, but I most definitely do not want to go to Ireland."

Annoyance flashed through his father's eyes. "So once again you chose to disobey me."

"Is that anything new?"

"God's blood," declared Lord Wythe, his voice raised. "I need you to go to Ireland."

Thomas didn't bother to react, so accustomed was he to his father's bellowing, which, when all was said done, amounted to all bluster with no substance behind it. In a gesture that Thomas well remembered, his father stabbed an accusing finger at him and was preparing to speak again when, accidentally, he moved his ailing foot, winced, and cried out from the pain.

Thomas felt an immediate rush of sympathy. In a flash of keen self-observation he realized that whereas fear of his father would not cause him to capitulate, sympathy surely would. He must not convey this newfound feeling of pity to his father, though. If he capitulated, and he was about to, it must appear to be out of filial loyalty; otherwise, his father would be hurt and highly insulted. "If you want me to go to Ireland, I suppose it's my duty," he said with a reluctant shrug. "Although I do think Montague should go. When would I leave?"

"You'll not regret it, son."

The flash of relief in his father's eyes told Thomas he'd

made the right decision. He returned a lopsided grin. "I regret it already, but that's beside the point."

"Excellent," his father exclaimed, and nearly slapped his hand to his leg before he thought better of it. "Now, there's just one other small matter."

Uh-oh. What was his wily father up to now? Thomas was suddenly alert. "And what might one more thing be?" He braced himself.

"You're to go to Aldershire Manor to see Lord Alberdsley. Matter of fact, I'll send a message over. He'll no doubt want you for dinner tonight."

"The devil," Thomas exclaimed as memories of previous, utterly woeful dinners at Aldershire Manor came to mind. The food was always excellent, of course, but not the company. Lord Alberdsley's brother, Walter, was all right, though rather on the meek side, but Walter's wife, Lydia, fancied herself superior to the rest of mankind. She was also much given to dominating a conversation with her iron-clad opinions, pontificating in a superior tone that indicated she knew everything while her listeners knew nothing. As for the three daughters . . . Ah, well, he mustn't be ungentlemanly. Three years had passed. Perhaps they'd changed, although he doubted it. Thomas laughed and slowly shook his head. "If you keep this up, I shall wish I was back in Jamaica, toiling under a hot sun."

Lord Wythe had the decency to look regretful. "I know how you feel about Alberdsley's nieces, Thomas, but remember, Alberdsley has been a good friend to me over the years."

"Are they married yet?"

"Er . . . no, not any of the three. Matter of fact, I'm still waiting for Montague to do his duty and propose to Charlotte. Bettina is waiting for *you,* Thomas"—Papa raised his brows significantly—"but then there's Amanda, who's sixteen now and pretty enough, although not a beauty. I should think Montague would want Charlotte, since she's the eldest, as well as the most beautiful, although I allow he could pick Bettina or even Amanda, if he chooses."

The words *some choice* rushed to Thomas's lips, but his gentlemanly instincts suppressed them. Instead, he sighed, reflecting not much had changed in the three years since he'd left for Jamaica.

"Oh, I know what you're thinking," the marquess said with a perceptive nod, "and you'd be right. Things have gone from bad to worse at Aldershire Manor, starting years ago when Alberdsley lost his only son."

"A real tragedy." Thomas clearly recalled Lord Alberdsley's troubles had begun when Randall, Viscount Montfret, Alberdsley's one and only son, a wastrel if ever there was one, had got himself in debt and fled England. "Randall went to Ireland, did he not?"

"Yes, and died there at an early age, after his father disowned him. Don't know of what. He was completely out of touch with his family those last years of his life."

"A pity," Thomas remarked, recalling that after Lord Alberdsley's only son died, he allowed his younger brother, Walter, and Walter's unpleasant wife, Lydia, to move into Aldershire Manor along with their three daughters. From all appearances, Walter, prodded by his domineering wife, had just about taken over the estate. "Has the situation at all improved?"

"It's gotten worse. Alberdsley's grown quite feeble of late and seems to have lost his grip. His brother and his wife pretty much run the estate and do what they please, although I allow the chicanery is more hers than his." The marquess scowled. "No backbone, that Walter. I don't much care for him, but, still, he's now the heir." His countenance brightened. "As you know, it's been a dream of mine to conjoin our two estates. Think of it. Montague will marry Charlotte, you will marry Bettina. Thus, Northfield Hall with be forever joined with Aldershire Manor. A grand idea, what?"

Picturing the three daughters, Thomas smiled wryly. "A lofty ambition, Papa. What does Montague say?"

The marquess's eyes hardened, reminding Thomas that when occasion warranted, his father could be as unyielding as a stone. "Montague will do as I say. I have put him on notice. He will marry one of Trevlyn's daughters, preferably Charlotte, and soon."

Poor Montague, Thomas thought, feeling a rare pang of sympathy for his prodigal older brother.

His father continued, "And it wouldn't hurt, Thomas, if you considered marrying Bettina sometime soon."

"Not likely," Thomas said with a smile. "I've told you before I'm not the marrying kind, but if I ever do, it will be for love, not because it's expected of me." He raised a sardonic eyebrow. "One of the few advantages of being a second son."

The marquess breathed a wistful sigh. "Ah, Thomas, if only . . ."

"Give Montague more time, Papa," Thomas said softly. "Who knows? Some day he might tire of brandy, women, and White's every night. Then he might surprise you."

The marquess returned a skeptical sniff. "I no longer delude myself. Montague will never change. What a travesty that he will inherit my estate, whereas you—"

Thomas raised his hand. "Say no more. I live my life with no regrets. So should you."

Love and pride filled his father's eyes. "You're a son to be proud of."

Thomas arose and smiled. "Send the message to Lord Alberdsley. I shall be happy to see him, for dinner, or whatever he likes. If it's dinner, perhaps he'll invite Penelope, too. Then I won't be totally bored. I don't suppose you . . . ?"

"Dear God, no." He gazed ruefully at his foot. "I'm a prisoner in this room until my gout improves." After a pause, he said, "I appreciate your doing this. Bear in mind there are worse hardships in life than dining with Trevlyn's daughters."

"Of course there are," Thomas assured him. *But at the moment I cannot think what,* he thought but didn't say.

Bored, bored, bored.

Thomas had never been so bored in all his life. No, take that back. He hadn't been so bored since the last time he'd come to Aldershire for dinner and the Honorable Miss Bettina Trevlyn, Lord Alberdsley's niece, had deigned to describe to him, in the most excruciating detail, her latest triumphs in the world of needlework. How much longer must he sit now, he wondered, regaled by a stitch-by-stitch description of her Europa-and-the-bull pillow cover? Where was Lord Trevelyn? When would dinner be served? How soon could he politely leave? How was it possible that one human being could talk incessantly, without end, about petit point?

Parliament should pass some sort of law.

Across the ornate drawing room, he caught a furtive

glimmer of amusement in his sister's eyes. He would get no sympathy there. Penelope dearly loved to see him suffer.

"Lord Thomas? Are you listening?"

"Hmm? Oh, yes, of course, Miss Trevlyn." He focused his attention upon another thickly embroidered pillow cover she was now displaying. "You were saying about the stitches? Fascinating. Do tell me more."

"You will note the seven rows of flat and French-knot stitches done in silk chenille thread," Bettina continued in her humorless voice, running her finger lovingly over her latest triumph. "Note they're done in various shades of pink. I almost made them red, though. In fact, I started to stitch them in red and then I thought, I might like them better in pink. A most perplexing dilemma, as you can see. So then I decided I really did like them better in pink, so I pulled out all the red stitches and put in the pink."

God save me, thought Thomas. Actually, the girl wasn't that bad-looking. Nice figure . . . brown hair piled stylishly atop her head . . . pleasantly rounded face, although rather on the bland side, but with eyes that held not one iota of spark or humor. He must try to be kind.

He was saved when Bettina's mother, purse-lipped, pinchnosed Mrs. Walter Trevlyn, sitting grandly on the settee across, called sharply, "Bettina, I do believe Lord Thomas has heard enough about your needlework." She regarded Thomas with avid curiosity. "So tell me, Lord Thomas, what of your dear brother, Lord Eddington? Did you see him in London upon your return from the West Indies?"

Thomas was not surprised at her question. For years, it appeared Lydia Trevlyn's main goal in life was to marry off her eldest daughter to Montague, or if not the eldest, one of the other two. Obviously nothing had changed. "I didn't have a chance to see my brother. I came straight from the docks to Northfield Hall, stopping only long enough to hire my horse."

Charlotte, the eldest daughter, always a model of elegance, beauty, and propriety, awarded him a tight smile. "A pity, Lord Thomas. Of late, we have seen little of Lord Eddington. Do you suppose he's been taken ill?"

Not likely, Thomas thought, but tactfully answered, "If he is ill, I haven't heard." He had noted an edge to her voice, and no wonder. Miss Charlotte Trevlyn's beauty was without imperfection. Her deportment was impeccable. She could sing like a lark and play piano with amazing skill. She spoke French like a native. Her watercolors were superb. She was, in essence, everything a young lady of the Polite World should be, but up to now, despite her best efforts, and her mother's, she had not managed to trap old Montague.

Thomas knew the reason. "The girl is like a beautiful doll," Montague had once complained. "Such perfection. But it's all just for show. Underneath she's hollow, except for greed and vanity, just like her mother."

Thomas could not have argued with the truth. "All that aside, Montague, Papa expects you to marry her. He'll be keenly disappointed if you don't."

Thomas remembered his brother's grim look of resignation as he replied, "I know, and someday I'll propose, as soon as I can stomach the thought of marrying that block of ice." Montague had made a face and added, "You don't know how lucky you are to be a second son."

But Charlotte's a beautiful block of ice, Thomas thought as he turned his attention to the eldest daughter, admiring her white skin, blond hair piled high, her figure stunning in her low-cut satin dinner gown. *What a pity . . .*

"Thomas, my boy, how good to see you."

To Thomas's relief, Lord Alberdsley entered the drawing room. His father was right. His lordship had aged since Thomas last saw him. His hair was completely white; deep lines etched his face; his shoulders were stooped, as if in defeat, and he now walked with a cane. Thomas stood, bowed, and remarked, "And it's good to see you, sir." He stopped himself from adding, "You're looking fit," because that would be a lie. He had always liked Lord Alberdsley, who was one of his father's best friends, despite their being almost exact opposites, both in temperament and interests. His father was a big, burly man, noisy and outgoing—or at least he had been before the gout. He liked fishing, hunting, and all outdoor sports. Alberdsley, on the other hand, was a reclusive man, who spent much time in his study, reading the classics in their original Greek and Latin. He had turned even more reclusive after his only son died, and now foolishly allowed his brother, Walter, and his family full run of his estate.

Lord Alberdsley gazed at Thomas with his soft, kind eyes. "Did your father tell you I wanted to speak to you?"

"Yes, he did, sir."

"Then after dinner, eh?"

"Of course," Thomas replied, at a loss to know what Alberdsley could possibly want to discuss.

Despite his misgivings, Thomas enjoyed dinner. Perhaps, he thought wryly, it was because he'd concentrated on his meal, saying little, while Mrs. Trevlyn and her daughters jabbered nonstop about that most exciting event, the upcoming London Season. As always, Lord Alberdsley was a gracious host. Even his brother, Walter, who usually remained almost silent, was congenial tonight.

When dinner was finished and the ladies had adjourned to the drawing room, Lord Alberdsley settled with his guest in the library, each with a glass of fine brandy in his hand. "So you're going to Ireland," Alberdsley observed.

Curious, Thomas sat back in his chair. "I am indeed, sir, at my father's behest. He owns land in County Mayo, as I'm sure you are aware."

"Did you know that I, too, own land in Ireland?"

"No, I did not."

Alberdsley appeared to be musing as he swirled the brandy in its glass. "My land is not nearly so fruitful as your father's. Fact is, it lies in County Clare, near Galway Bay. Full of rocks, I've been told, and not good for much of anything but growing potatoes and grazing sheep."

"That's interesting, sir." *What on earth did Alberdsley want?*

"As long as you're going to Ireland, I would be most grateful if you'd check on my land as well as your father's."

More delay. Thomas felt an instant's squeezing disappointment. But this was his father's best friend, so there was only one possible response he could make. "I would be most happy to, sir." *But why?* he wondered.

"You're curious, aren't you?" asked Lord Alberdsley with a knowing smile. "You cannot fathom why a man as rich as I, owner of countless tracts of land here in England, could possibly be concerned about one small, barren patch of land in Ireland."

Thomas sipped his brandy. "That did occur to me."

"I hardly know myself," came Alberdsley's surprising reply. "I lost interest after Randall—" A look of sorrow crossed Lord Alberdsley's face, and he cleared his throat. "It has to do with my son, I think. Randall has been gone these many years now." He sighed, then continued, "I disowned him, and for good reason. Yet, as the years have gone by, I find myself thinking of him more and more. It's as if . . . I find it impossible to explain, but I have the feeling Randall wants to tell me something, that there's something unfinished, there, near Galway Bay, something I should know."

"Have you any idea what?"

"Try not to think me a fool, Thomas." Alberdsley uttered a self-deprecating laugh. "Although I am one, I suppose. Before he fled England, Randall talked about that piece of land. There was a cottage that overlooked the sea, and a bit of land for raising sheep. He showed an interest in it, although I have no idea if he ever actually visited the place or not. It's just that . . . I simply . . ."

The poor old man was floundering. Thomas hastened to put his mind at rest. "Say no more, sir. Of course I'll go. If there are people living on your land, what shall I say?"

"Tell them . . . well, I suppose you should try to collect the rent," said Lord Alberdsley, growing thoughtful. "Not the back rent, which I fear would be too great a hardship, but in future, tell them they'll have to pay. That's only fair, don't you agree?"

"I do indeed, sir."

"Well, then, I am most grateful." A gleam of relief lit the old man's eyes. "Lord knows, there's not much joy left in my life, although it's a consolation knowing my estate will be left . . . in good hands."

That pause before *good hands* gave the old man away. It was a bitter pill to swallow, Thomas mused, that Alberdsley's only child, once his pride and joy, was dead, and now his brother and his greedy, tiresome family would inherit his beloved Aldershire Manor, and all the rest.

Later that night, as Thomas drove their curricle the short distance home, he asked his sister, "Where is Galway Bay anyway?"

"On the west coast of Ireland, I believe." Penelope patted

his arm affectionately. "It's most generous of you. You did not have to say yes, you know."

Thomas remained silent. No need to explain that in the study, after Alberdsley had finished his poignant request, Thomas had easily, almost eagerly, said yes, not only because he felt sorry for Lord Alberdsley, but because he, too, felt a compelling curiosity to see that rocky plot of land near Galway Bay.

Chapter 4

Evleen O'Fallon could not understand the feeling of discontent that had just swept over her. *What's the matter with me?* she wondered. Wasn't it Sunday afternoon and a balmy spring day? Wasn't she out for a pleasant stroll with Timothy Murphy, the man she would probably marry? She should be bursting with joy at the very thought of marrying jolly, handsome Timothy, whose fleet of fishing boats made him one of the richest men in County Clare. No matter that she didn't think she loved him. *Of course I'll be happy*, she told herself. She would learn to love him later on. Other brides had doubts, yet after their weddings seemed content.

She and Timothy were taking their usual Sunday stroll along a promontory that jutted into Galway Bay. Usually her heart lifted when they came to this particular spot in the narrow dirt road, where suddenly a grand view of both the ocean and sparkling Galway Bay lay revealed below, and it seemed she could see the entire Connemara Coast of Western Ireland, as well as practically clear across the ocean to lands far away. She felt no special thrill today, though. Timothy was pressing. She must give him her answer soon. And she would, too, even though a nagging feeling within her said she was making a mistake. But she must make the best of it. Timothy Murphy was a "catch," everyone said so. And besides, her needy family was sure to benefit from her marriage to Timothy.

So there is no way out, she told herself firmly. Besides, her troubles were nothing compared to some, and she should stop vacillating.

Evleen stopped, shaded her eyes, and peered to the northwest. "It's so clear you can see the Aran Islands today, and Connemara and North Clare." She turned to the east, where the extensive sand and mud flats of Ballyvaughn lay exposed at low tide. It was springtime, when migrating birds stopped to feed before heading to their breeding grounds. Evleen pointed overhead at a majestic V-formation of geese flying out to sea. "Look, Timothy, those are Brent Geese going home. Just imagine, they're flying all the way to arctic Canada." Her heart lifted and she smiled. "Wouldn't it be wonderful if we could grow wings? We could fly all the way to Canada . . . China . . . South America . . . any place we pleased."

"Are you daft?" Timothy asked, his usually cheerful face furrowed in a frown. "I've fish to catch and a business to run. Sure an' I wouldn't have time for such foolishness."

"But I didn't mean literally . . ."

Why finish? she thought. *What was the use?* She must learn to overlook Timothy's shortcomings and concentrate on the good things. He was, after all, a pleasant man, not half bad-looking with his open, smiling face, full head of curly dark hair, broad shoulders and impressive height. He was well educated, too, at least compared to most of the men in County Clare, and had even attended Trinity College in Dublin for a year. Still, Timothy was a simple man, engrossed in making a living with his fishing fleet. Evleen had long since discovered he had little interest in poetry, art, or music, in other words, all the things she loved.

Marriage with Timothy Murphy would be dull, indeed, but at least she would be secure.

And it was what her mother wanted.

"Where would you find a finer man than Timothy Murphy?" she asked but yesterday. "Isn't he the vicar's son? Doesn't he earn a good income with those fishing boats he owns? Doesn't he go to church like clockwork every Sunday? Doesn't he stay home with his dear old mother every night instead of drinking himself blind at the Shamrock and Thistle?" She wagged her finger. "Young ladies of twenty-four had best not be too choosy."

"But in Dublin . . ." Evleen stopped herself and said no more. Nothing was to be gained by another futile recollection of happier days long gone.

Her mother didn't let Evleen's words go unnoticed and said softly, "Ay, you could have had your pick of society's finest, back when we were rich. But we're not in Dublin anymore, and we're not rich anymore."

You're right, Mama, we're poor—oh, so very, very poor, thanks to the Englishman. Evleen smiled up at Timothy. She would make herself love him—she would try very hard. After all, he was a hard worker, honest and trustworthy, who would gladly help her family. They needed help desperately, now that the eight hundred pounds was nearly gone.

If only he had a bit of wit. If only he could see when she was only joking or when her imagination took flight. But perhaps in time she'd learn to love him, especially when he became father of the children she expected to have.

As she stood gazing pensively at the sea, she sensed Timothy's gaze upon her, no doubt with that puppy-dog, full-of-love expression in his eyes. *Stop that,* she chastised herself. That he loved her, there could be no doubt, and she shouldn't be thinking unkind thoughts about him.

"What are you thinking?" Timothy asked. No doubt he'd seen the faraway look in her eyes.

"I'm thinking it's a beautiful day," Evleen replied. He needn't know what else she was thinking. "I should get back. Mama's not well, as well as . . . there are other problems."

As they strolled home, Evleen still could not shake off the feeling of something not being right. Perhaps it wasn't Timothy. Perhaps it was the state of the family finances that was causing her woeful state of mind. To say the least, their lives had not gone as her mother had expected when they moved from Dublin to the little stone cottage that overlooked the sea. She had expected the eight hundred pounds she received from the sale of the town house to last forever, supplemented by the lessons in deportment, French, and watercolors she would give the local gentry. What a rude awakening she'd received! What her mother had failed to realize was that in this barren county with its rock-hard, unyielding soil, there was no local gentry, not to speak of, anyway. The vast majority of the citizens of County Clare lived a hand-to-mouth existence, eking barely enough sustenance from the sea and poor soil to stay alive. The ladies of County Clare did not spend their time planning balls, nor did they spend hours on fittings for fancy clothes or conduct "at homes" with liveried servants serving tea. Few had servants. There was hardly time to be a lady, either, because the women of County Clare were occupied with such matters as digging potatoes, cooking meals over an open fireplace, hauling water from the well, and cutting peat in the nearby bogs.

Evleen and Timothy approached her family's cottage. Built of stone, with lime-washed walls, it faced directly west, high on a hill that provided a magnificent view of the sea. The view was the only good thing about the cottage. Evleen would never forget that awful day nine years before when, during a rainstorm, their wagon had pulled to a stop in front of the Englishman's small, bleak plot of land. Nothing green was to be seen—no shrubbery, flowers, or trees, just coarse brown grass broken here and there by low stone walls, the stones not cemented but just piled up. The walls were not laid out in neat squares, but instead slanted this way and that, acting as wind breaks to retain the thin layer of arable soil. For no apparent reason, two walls ran far up the hill behind the cottage where a few sheep huddled to protect themselves against the rain and cold. To Evleen's relief, the house itself was a cut above most of the cottages they had passed, some of which were constructed of mud with only one room and no windows. The floors were of dirt, and the roofs were made of sod and earth laid on timber rafters and covered with a thatch of straw. At least this cottage was of a fairly good size, two stories, and six rooms altogether, limestone painted walls, several windows, and a reed-thatched roof, which was better than the straw. Still, it could hardly compare with their Dublin town house. The big room—one could hardly call it a drawing room—had simple, plastered walls, one of which consisted totally of a huge fireplace, where the cooking, and most of the living, was done. Evleen had been shocked when she saw it. Her sisters were in tears, and her mother was appalled.

"We cannot stay here, it has no kitchen," she declared, her face grim. "We can surely afford better than this. We'll stay here the night, and then tomorrow we'll go back to Ballyvaughn, where I shall seek something better."

That was nine years ago. They had yet to move. Sinead, always frugal, had realized early on they could not afford a better house, especially when she discovered that few of the poverty-stricken citizens of County Clare had the least interest in the lessons in deportment, French, and watercolors she intended to teach. For the most part, they were more concerned with the constant struggle to keep themselves and family from starving to death. Her only salvation came from the Gaelic-speaking citizens of County Clare who wished to learn English. The small sums she earned from her English lessons, combined with her prudent management of the eight hundred pounds from the town house, had enabled the O'Fallons to eke out a meager existence for nine years. Now the money was almost gone.

At least Sinead had added a kitchen and spent some of their precious money for a stove. Evleen, in particular, was grateful. After her mother, who had never prepared a meal in all her life, cooked one disastrous dinner, Evleen took over the kitchen. For these past nine years, while Sinead taught her lessons, Evleen had been in charge of the cooking, as well as the housekeeping and care of the younger children.

When someone asked why she hadn't married, she could honestly answer she hadn't found the time.

But now the children were of an age to take care of themselves. At twenty-three, Darragh was ready to marry, if any man would have her. Sorcha was fifteen, Mary fourteen, and Patrick a very wise ten. Evleen had thought more than once with some amusement that her excuses for not marrying were wearing thin. She had been putting Timothy off for years, but it was time she made up her mind.

When Evleen and Timothy arrived back at the cottage after their stroll, they found Evleen's half brother, Patrick, outside taking feed to his rabbits, kept in hutches at the back of the cottage. His face lit when he saw Timothy, and he called, "You're stayin' for dinner, are you not?"

"If I'm invited."

It was a ritual. Of course, Timothy was invited. He came for dinner every Sunday. *And I'll be having Sunday dinner with him all the rest of my life, and the rest of the days, as well.* The prospect did not fill Evleen with delight. *What's the matter with me?* She reached to ruffle Patrick's red hair that was so like their mother's, or, to be more accurate, the color Mama's hair used to be before it faded and finally turned white. "Timothy's staying for dinner, Patrick. Why don't you show him your new baby rabbits?"

As an enthusiastic Patrick led Timothy away, her mother came to the door. *How wan she looks,* Evleen thought. *She used to stand straight as a board, but now her shoulders slump and she leans against the door.* But then her mother smiled, and when she smiled, she lit up the world. "Did you have a nice walk with Timothy?" she asked.

"Yes, we did."

Sinead lowered her voice. "Did you talk about a wedding date?"

"Not yet."

Sinead crossed her arms and sighed. "Evleen, you have been the best daughter in the world. You've had little fun these past nine years. Hard work is all you've known, never thinking of yourself, but sacrificing for the family." Sinead drew herself up. "Well, that's an end to it. You must put yourself first now. Darragh will be marrying soon, I'm sure. It's time you got yourself married and had your babies. It's time—what on earth?"

Sinead was looking beyond her, down the steep, rutted driveway that led to the cottage. Evleen turned to see what her mother was staring at. To her astonishment, a coach with a fancy seal emblazoned on the side, drawn by four matched bays, came rolling up the narrow, bumpy driveway. There appeared to be one male passenger inside, an elegantly dressed gentleman in a polished beaver top hat. He was slender, dark-haired, and dark-skinned, and appeared to be thirty or so.

Evleen frowned in puzzlement. How utterly out of place the elaborate coach looked in this godforsaken little part of the world where rough-hewn oxcarts were more the vogue. Not that they had many visitors. What few they did have arrived either on foot or in a cart drawn by a donkey or some nag of a horse. Never had a coach or carriage even half as fancy as this one come up that hill, not even the vicar's. "Whoever can it be?" asked Evleen.

A look of foreboding came over her mother's face. "I don't know who it is," she replied. "I can only hope my scoundrel of a second husband hasn't come back to haunt us."

Good God, so this is Alberdsley's Irish estate?
As his coach rolled along the narrow road overlooking the sea, Thomas had looked out in increasing disbelief at the

barren landscape, broken only here and there by low stone walls and sparse trees that had somehow managed to survive the salt air and winter storms. His disbelief increased as the coach turned up a steep driveway to a small, two-story cottage that sat halfway up the barren, windswept hill. A few sheep grazed on the hillside behind the cottage. Two moth-eaten donkeys grazed directly alongside. At least there was a small, low-walled garden in front, but still, the sprinkling of daisies, delphiniums, and lupines hardly began to relieve the bleakness. Thomas leaned his head out the window to have a word with the coachman he'd hired, as well as the coach, in Galway.

"O'Grady, are you sure this is the place?"

"Positive, sir," the coachman called back in his thick Irish brogue. " 'Tis the land owned by the Englishman, Lord Alberdsley." Almost under his breath he muttered, "Another blasted Englishman who's never seen the place." He raised his voice again. "A widow and 'er flock 'av been livin' there a good nine or ten years now. Two girls, grown, two in their teens, and a boy of ten or so. Never been ta school, they say. She's an educated lady and teaches 'em at home."

With a thanks, Thomas sat back as the coach, harness jangling, horses snorting in the midst of rising dust, came to a halt in front of the single doorway of the cottage. *I've gone far out of my way for this?* he asked himself. What was Alberdsley thinking of, sending him to check on this worthless piece of land?

Two women were standing in front of the doorway. One was somewhere in her middle fifties, he would guess, tall, white-haired, with the strained look of poverty on her tired face. She wore a plain cotton gown that had seen better days, covered with a white apron. She'd been leaning against the doorjamb in a tired sort of way, but now she'd pulled herself straight and was regarding him with wary eyes.

Thomas was about to speak when his gaze fell upon the younger woman. Something about her immediately gripped his attention. She was deucedly attractive, he thought, as he gazed at her slender white neck, milk-and-apricot skin, delicately featured face with its firm chin and pert, up-tilted little nose. As Thomas watched, a brisk breeze from the sea lifted her raven black hair so that it streamed back from her face, long, wavy, and shining. The breeze caught hold of her skirt, too, and pressed it tight against her tall, slender body, molding to nearly every enticing curve she possessed. He wondered if she had any idea what a fetching picture she presented with that tiny waist, those full, high-perched breasts, slender hips, and shapely thighs.

But this was not the time to be distracted, Thomas thought as he sprung lightly from the coach. If these were indeed tenants who had not paid a pittance toward their rent for the last nine years, his mission was indeed a delicate one and so he must be the soul of tactfulness and diplomacy. Thomas addressed the older woman, who stood seemingly composed, yet he detected increasing wariness in her eyes. "Good afternoon," he said, smiled, removed his beaver hat with a flourish, and bowed.

"You're English," she replied, not returning his smile.

What is that supposed to mean? "Indeed I am English, madam. My name is Thomas Linberry"—no need to throw in the title—"from Hertfordshire County, England, a town near—"

"Hatfield," she replied in an unfriendly tone.

"Er . . . yes." Her frosty reception had thrown him off stride, but he gathered his wits and continued, "And might I ask to whom I am speaking?"

"First, why don't you tell us why you've come, sir?" asked the younger woman, just barely polite.

He could have been offended, but instead found himself captivated by the soft silkiness of her voice, coupled with the potent appeal of her melodious Irish brogue. He turned to answer her and was immediately struck by the beauty of her deep, wide-set eyes that were a stunning sapphire blue, fringed with an abundance of thick, dark lashes. His breath caught. He was hard put not to let his feelings show, but managed a slight, grave bow. "I have come on the behalf of the Earl of Alberdsley, who owns this land."

A small gasp escaped the mouth of the older woman. She stiffened and placed a hand over her heart.

"Mama, are you all right?" asked the younger woman, casting a withering glance at Thomas.

If looks could kill, thought Thomas, *I'd be lying dead as a herring on this rocky ground.*

"I am fine." The older woman proudly brushed back her white hair and stood tall. "I must say, it took the earl a while."

"A while for what?" he asked.

The younger woman narrowed her eyes at him. "She means it took a while for the earl to give a thought to his dead son."

Thomas still did not understand. Who were these women? They dressed like peasants, lived in a simple farmhouse, yet their speech was so refined they would be at ease in London society . . . except for the Irish accents, which the *ton* would no doubt scoff at. Had the older woman somehow been acquainted with Randall? Perhaps she'd been a servant . . . one of the upper servants . . . Yes, he thought, that had to be it. She had worked for Randall, perhaps as a cook or housekeeper, and now, through some arrangement, lived upon his land, or rather, now Lord Alberdsley's land. "Might I ask your name?" he inquired.

The older woman proudly lifted her chin. "I am Sinead O'Fallon, widow of Randall, Viscount Montfret."

Widow? Thomas was thunderstruck. He had a hard time keeping his mouth from dropping open. "Do you mean you are the widow of Randall, the son of the Earl of Alberdsley?"

The younger woman placed a protective hand on the older's shoulder. "Of course that's what she means," she firmly stated, regarding him with those amazing deep blue eyes that at the moment were full of accusation. "What reason would you have to doubt her?"

"I didn't mean, I . . ." Thomas cursed himself. In polite society, he was known for his suave demeanor. Now he was bumbling about like some half-wit. And it wasn't simply the shock of discovering that Randall had been married. It was also the effect those blue eyes were having on him. "Of course I do not doubt you. Rather, I'm surprised. I was not aware Lord Montfret had ever married, nor was his father aware of it, I'm sure."

An ironic smile crossed Sinead O'Fallon's lips. "I'm not surprised. You are aware Randall was estranged from his father?"

"I am." *Not estranged, the man was disowned*, he thought, but decided not to say.

"Then you can understand why Randall felt under no obligation to inform his family he had wed. I never knew exactly why, but he had compelling reasons for keeping our marriage quiet."

Thomas knew better than to ask what she meant by compelling reasons. Doubtless they were all in the form of those angry creditors who had hounded Randall until he was forced to flee to Ireland. Thomas's thoughts were churning. This wasn't what he expected. "Do you suppose we could talk, Lady . . . er . . . Montfret? Or did you say your last name was—?"

"O'Fallon," said the younger woman, stepping forward protectively. "My mother goes by her first husband's name"—she wrinkled her nose—"most assuredly not the second's. I am her daughter, Evleen. So, sir, do you know enough about us now that you can state your business?"

Before he could answer, Sinead O'Fallon gave a warning nudge to Evleen's shoulder. "Let us not be hasty."

Evleen ignored her and continued to glare at Thomas. "You've come about the rents, haven't you?"

Sinead frowned. "Daughter, we must remember our manners. It's nearly dinnertime. Our guest must be hungry. After dinner will be soon enough to hear what he has to say." She looked at Thomas. "Will you stay?"

"I am honored."

Thomas smiled to himself when he saw the thundercloud descending over Evleen's face. But no doubt remembering her manners, she had the grace to quickly smile and say, "So it appears you are invited to dinner, Mr. Linberry." She placed a hand on her hip and cocked her head appraisingly, her gaze sweeping him up and down. "Or perhaps it's Lord Linberry, judgin' from that elegant coach and the fine clothes that you're wearin'. We'll be having a bit of fresh salmon, poached, I think, along with cabbage and potatoes. A simple meal, I'm afraid, not like those fancy banquets you must be accustomed to at home."

He could tell the girl was seething underneath all that ridiculous chatter. She knew full well he'd come about the rents, but no doubt for her mother's sake, she had dredged up the decency to maintain a facade of politeness. He would set her straight about the titles. "Not that it matters, but I am known as Lord Thomas. I'm the second son of a marquess, you see, and so—"

"We are well aware of all that English folderol about titles," Evleen interrupted with a disdainful sniff.

He answered wryly, "I can see how I've impressed you."

She tilted her chin, thus revealing the sweet curve of her neck, which, to his chagrin, he found himself wanting to touch and explore with his fingers. "If you want titles," she declared, "this family has them in abundance. My father was Ian O'Fallon, son of Daniel O'Fallon, who was the eighth Earl of Dunkerry, who was directly descended from the Duke of Connaught, who was—"

"Enough, Evleen," said her mother. "I doubt Lord Thomas is interested in our family's history, no matter how much royal blood runs through your veins." She looked toward the coach, and the coachman waiting patiently atop. "Greetings to you, O'Grady. You'd best come in for dinner, too."

After O'Grady had climbed down from his perch on the coach, and Sinead had shown him inside, Evleen said airily, "What a pity it's the cook's day off."

"A pity," Thomas remarked with caution. He had detected her gritty undertone.

"It's also the butler's day off, as well as the footman, the parlor maid, the scullery maid—"

"I do get your point," Thomas interrupted dryly. He wanted to tell her he didn't give a groat for titles, that they didn't mean a damn thing, but he stopped himself. Why should he defend himself? Why did he want to impress this girl? The bubbly young belles in London were mostly docile creatures who deferred to his supposed lordly presence with much manipulating of fans and fluttering of eyelashes. He had never given much thought to it, but wasn't that the way girls were supposed to act? But this Irish lass was different.

Never had he encountered a girl quite this bold, who didn't care one whit about impressing him and apparently said anything that came into her head, no matter how outrageous.

Now she had tilted her head to the side and was looking at him quizzically. "I can hardly wait to hear why you've come so far out of your way to this godforsaken corner of the world." She smiled wryly. "If it's a dip in the ocean you want, shouldn't a fine gentleman like you be in Brighton?" She made a show of shading her eyes and gazing up and down the distant coastline. "I don't see any fancy resorts around here."

"I'm not looking for a resort, I—"

He was distracted by a tall, pleasant-faced man and a freckle-faced boy with bright red hair who were rounding the corner of the cottage. They were speaking in a strange language, he guessed Gaelic, when they spied him, and both stopped in surprise. "We have a guest," Evleen called. "Lord Thomas, this is my good friend, Timothy Murphy, and this is my brother, Patrick O'Fallon."

Startled, Thomas took a second look. There was something about the boy . . . something around the nose and the eyes that reminded him of . . . Lord Montfret. Even though Thomas had been but sixteen or so at the time, he clearly remembered when the debt-ridden rascal had fled England, creating a juicy local scandal, causing his family great pain. Could Montfret be this boy's father? No, that was absurd. Except for that uncanny resemblance, this boy looked as pure Irish as his name. O'Fallon suited him perfectly, what with his red hair, eyes as blue as Evleen's, and open face covered with freckles. No doubt the boy and Evleen shared the same father, as well as mother, and unless Patrick had an older brother, he most certainly was the tenth earl of . . . whatever that Irish title was. Thomas knew little of Ireland's nobility. In England, it carried little esteem.

With a graceful bow, surprising in one so young, Patrick said, "I am most pleased to meet you, sir. Are you from England?"

There's a surprise. The boy knew his manners, as opposed to most of the Irish Thomas had met on this trip. Likeable all of them, and most friendly and helpful, yet their speech and manners were far from the polished perfection of the *ton*. Evleen had spoken like a lady, too, except for the brogue, of course, but it was a melodious sound that touched off something inside him that made him yearn to hear more. Thomas bowed to Patrick in return. "I am indeed from England," he replied.

"That's too bad, sir. My mother doesn't like the English."

"Patrick!"

"But it's true, Evleen," the lad told his sister earnestly. "She hates everything English. You've heard her say so many a time." Patrick made a face. "You hate them, too."

"We must remember our manners, Patrick," Evleen chided her brother. "We must be polite"—she cast a disdainful glance at Thomas—"even if he is one of *them*."

Amused, Thomas returned an easy laugh. "I admire a streak
of independence in a child. He speaks his mind, an admirable
quality as far as I'm concerned. He's very bright, isn't he? I am
amazed at how well he speaks."

"For an Irishman?" Evleen asked, lifting her eyebrows.

The devil. I cannot get it right. "For anybody," he answered
smoothly. "He would do well among the most prestigious gathering of the *ton*, as would your mother—" he paused slightly
for effect—"and you."

"Well!" she said, and seemed at a loss as to what to say in
answer to his flattering words. *Rude creature.* She could not
imagine why he found her so fascinating.

The tall man she'd addressed as Timothy spoke up. "Sure
an' he's a bright lad"—he placed a protective arm around
Evleen's shoulders—"as is this colleen."

Ah, so she's his, thought Thomas, recognizing the age-old
male sign of possession. "If your mother hates the English, then
I am indeed most flattered she has asked me to stay."

She replied, "My mother is a generous soul. The devil himself could appear at her door, and she'd invite him in for tay."

Tay? Of course, she must mean tea. Thomas was silently
amused. Despite Evleen's well-educated speech, still and all
she was Irish and it was bound to show. "Your mother is most
charitable."

"Patrick's right, you know," she went on. "My mother does
hate the English. We all hate the English, and with good reason."

He executed a slight bow. "Then I am most grateful for her
tolerance, as well as yours." He wondered if, despite Evleen's
obvious prejudice, he might somehow persuade her he wasn't
such a bad sort, despite being English through and through. His
spirits dipped as he realized his chances were slim. She'd been
right about the rents. After dinner, when she knew for a certainty why he was there, she would dislike him all the more.

Chapter 5

"Why have I never seen this tablecloth before?" asked Patrick as they all sat down to dinner. His bright eyes darted curiously about the long table. "Why are we burning candles when there's still daylight? What's that funny thing you put in the middle, Mama?"

Sinead frowned at her son. "We have a special guest, Patrick." She ran her fingers lovingly over the Chantilly lace tablecloth and looked around the table at Evleen, Darragh, Sorcha, Mary, Timothy, O'Grady, and the honored guest, Lord Thomas. "I have not laid this lace cloth on a table since we left Dublin." She laughed ironically. "In this cottage, somehow it never seemed to fit. Patrick, someday you'll learn candles aren't always meant for simply casting light. As for that thing in the middle, it's the epergne that sat on its silver platform in the center of the table at our Dublin town house." She cast a wistful glance at Evleen. "Do you remember our dining room, all done in shades of pale gold? Do you remember my Chinese vases?"

Evleen nodded. "Of course I remember. They were displayed on that giltwood console table from Limerick you were so proud of."

At Sinead's deep sigh, Evleen felt guilt that ever since Lord Thomas had arrived, she had been upset with her mother for being so nice to him. Her mother certainly did not deserve her hostility. She had suffered greatly these past nine years and yet, despite their hardships, had been a pillar of strength. Still, worry nagged Evleen. How could her mother have invited the Englishman to dinner when she knew full well he had come to see about the rents? Evleen had a sick feeling in the pit of her stomach. No wonder she'd had an uneasy feeling earlier today. Didn't her mother realize they could be facing total disaster?

Evleen was sitting directly across from the Englishman, who, she had to admit, had been the epitome of charm and graciousness since he arrived. Still, for all she knew, he could be just as iniquitous as that other Englishman, who also had exuded charm and graciousness by the bucketful. She had no doubt this Lord Thomas from Hertfordshire had come to cause them grief. But how much rent would he want? The only reason her mother was able to make the eight hundred pounds last so long was that they had paid no rent since they moved here. Evleen shuddered to think that Lord Alberdsley's emissary might be bent on collecting every penny they owed for the past nine years. Or worse, what if it wasn't a question of making up the rent? It was well within the realm of possibility that this pleasant young man—and quite handsome, too, she had to admit—was waiting for the right moment to announce they were being evicted. Sudden panic gripped her. *Where would we go? What would we do?* The money was almost gone. They'd be out in the cold with no food, no shelter, and no place to go but—she shuddered to think of it—*the workhouse*. And all because of *him*.

Well into dinner, Evleen, her trepidation rising, could not help but glare at their visitor. She didn't care if he knew she was staring. Besides, how could she avoid him? Sitting directly across from Thomas—oh, she thought, *Lord Thomas,* she'd been hard put not to notice every move he'd made. So far, the dinner had been quite congenial. She'd watched when their visitor had taken his first bite of her poached salmon and smiled with delight, pronouncing the salmon the best he had ever eaten. For some unfathomable reason, she'd felt inordinately pleased, then wondered why she should care if the man who was about to toss them out of their home liked her salmon or not.

Darragh's conduct was disgusting. Evleen couldn't help but note that since the moment her flirtatious younger sister had met Lord Thomas, she'd been fluttering her eyelids at him, making silly, featherbrained remarks. Of course poor Darragh didn't realize what was going to happen, Evleen thought charitably. She would be changing her tune soon enough.

Even Sorcha and Mary, in their adolescent fashion, were taken by Lord Thomas, who had been charming throughout dinner, Evleen had to admit. *But how he must pity us.* Evleen looked about the room. It was cozy enough with its many pictures on the walls, her mama's beautifully set table, the air filled with the fragrance of peat burning in the fireplace. Still, it was obvious they were just another shanty-poor Irish family, hardly better than dirt, in the eyes of the haughty English. She wondered if he was comparing what must be his own fancy estate in England to this pathetic hovel.

Timothy seemed to be the only one at the table besides herself who was leery of the Englishman, although she doubted his dislike stemmed from fear Lord Thomas might evict them. Rather, she'd found over the years that Timothy, despite his good nature, tended toward a jealous disposition. No doubt he harbored some farfetched fear that Lord Thomas might be a rival for her affections.

No chance of that.

At the end of the meal, when all were full and in a relaxed mood, Lord Thomas laid his fork on his empty plate. "A delicious meal," he announced. "I have never tasted better."

Sinead nodded her appreciation and smiled wryly. "We have Evleen to thank. She learned how to cook when we came to live in this cottage. And speaking of this cottage . . ." She looked Thomas square in the eyes. ". . . had you something to say to us, sir?"

Evleen braced herself. The blow that would change their lives was about to fall. She waited tensely, trying to read Lord Thomas's concerned expression. Obviously he was aware that any reference to the family's fall from riches to rags must be handled delicately.

Lord Thomas glanced around the table, especially at O'Grady. "I wonder if we might talk in private, Mrs. . . . or is it Lady O'Fallon?"

"Mrs. O'Fallon will do," Sinead answered briskly. "And let us not worry about privacy. I have no secrets from friends or family. Anything you wish to say can be said right here."

"Then . . ." Lord Thomas paused, no doubt forming his words carefully. "As you already know, I have been sent here by Lord Alberdsley to check on his property. I was to find out why no rents have been forthcoming for these many years, and, if possible . . ." Lord Thomas cleared his throat, for the first time seeming unsure of himself. "I was to arrange to collect the rents, but that was before I knew of Lord Montfret's marriage."

"That does put a different slant on things," Sinead said flatly. "You must realize, sir, it was my husband's wish that we move here. This was after he had gotten into . . . shall we say, certain financial difficulties in Dublin."

Evleen spoke up, unable to hold her tongue a second longer. "What my mother means is that Lord Montfret squandered her modest fortune after telling her I-don't-know-how-many lies. By the time he died, all she had left was the town house my father left her. Because of Randall's debts, she had to sell it, which left us with nothing. There was no place to move but here."

Sinead sighed. "I never heard a word from any of Randall's family, until now. So I . . ." She bit her lip. A look of near panic crossed her face. "What does Lord Alberdsley want? If he wants me to make up the rents for the past nine years, there is no possible way I—"

"No, madame," Lord Thomas interrupted, at least having the decency to look disturbed. In fact, his eyes were filled with concern. "Alberdsley was not aware his son had ever married. This, of course, puts a new light on things. Were you not aware of the reason Randall left England?"

"I was never sure."

"Then he never told you he fled from debtors and that he'd been disowned."

"That comes as no surprise." Sinead gave him a grim smile. "I know now that Randall was an expert at deceit. He told me his father would be sending money any day. It never arrived, of course."

"Ah, I see. Then rest assured, I shall do nothing now. I shall return to England and present the facts to Lord Alberdsley. He's a kindly man, and quite reasonable. One wonders how he could have had a son so irresponsible . . . so reprehensible—"

"Don't you talk about my father that way!"

Everyone at the table gasped as young Patrick, eyes blazing, leaped up so fast he knocked his chair over and it clattered to the stone floor. He was trembling. His eyes glistened with tears as he cried hoarsely to his mother, "He was my father. I don't care what he did. How can you let that man talk about him that way?"

Sinead immediately rose from the table and hurried to put her arms around her son. "I am so sorry, Patrick. That was completely thoughtless of me. There were good things about your father, too."

After a stunned silence, Lord Thomas, shaking his head contritely, spoke again. "I, too, am terribly sorry, Patrick. I didn't know. I thought O'Fallon was your father."

"It seemed simpler to have Patrick carry the family name," Sinead explained, still cradling Patrick in her arms. "I never thought to tell you he's the son of Lord Montfret."

Evleen watched as their guest actually seemed to turn a bit pale. He started to speak, then stopped. Finally, he arose from the table and stood there, blank, amazed, and very shaken. "If you will excuse me, I feel the need for a breath of fresh air," he said in an odd voice. He turned and left the cottage.

It had turned dark, but a half-moon was shining. The air was brisk, moist, and there was a slight breeze blowing as Evleen, upon the request of her mother, stepped outside to find Lord Thomas. She spied him immediately. He was standing, deep in thought it appeared, at the end of the cottage, an arm cocked upon his hip. He was staring out at the blackness that was the sea.

She could not see him clearly, but saw enough to marvel at how handsome he looked, standing there in that most masculine way, his jacket pulled back by the hand on his hip, revealing a trim waistline, powerful chest and shoulders, and a stomach as flat as the back of her hand. She could hardly see his profile, dark in the moonlight, yet already the fine features of his face were etched in her mind: skin bronzed by wind and sun, generous mouth, aquiline nose, touches of humor etched permanently around his mouth, and deep-set brown eyes.

She walked up to him and said, "It appears something is bothering you."

He started, not having heard her approach. Now, with a wry laugh, he turned to her and replied, "Bothered is hardly the word. I received quite a shock in there."

"I don't understand," she said, truly bewildered. "We were not trying to hide that Patrick is Randall's son. Really, does it matter?"

"Matter?" Thomas asked with incredulity. "Of course it matters. It matters a good deal."

"I don't see why."

"Of course you don't, and it's my fault for not fully explaining. Were you not aware that Randall's father is the fifth Earl of Alberdsley?"

"Not really. We hardly gave it a thought, but even if we had, of what significance is it?"

"Can't you see?" She could tell Lord Thomas was trying to control his patience. "Randall was his only son, the heir apparent. His first son, and that would be Patrick, became the heir apparent when his father died."

"That may be, but surely by now Lord Alberdsley has made other arrangements."

Lord Thomas took a deep breath. He appeared to be trying to control a certain agitation. "As it stands now, there's an heir presumptive, Alberdsley's brother, Walter. But can't you understand? When Randall died, Lord Alberdsley should have been notified at once and told Randall had a son. As matters stand, the brother is first in line to inherit the title, the estate, the entire fortune, which is considerable, I assure you."

"Fine, let him." Sinead had come outside to join them. Wrapping a shawl about her thin shoulders, she continued, "I don't care if Patrick stands to inherit the crown of England. I don't care how poor we are, he'll be better off right here in County Clare than he'd ever be in England." Even in the darkness, Evleen could see her mother proudly lift her chin. "My son is Irish born and bred, sir. This is where he belongs. As long as I have a breath in my body, he'll not set a foot across the Irish Sea."

Shoulders set in a resolute manner, Sinead spun on her heel and marched back inside.

"Then that's the end of it," said Evleen.

"So it would appear." He sounded regretful.

She had to admit to herself that Lord Thomas was not at fault. His genuine concern had been for Patrick, not himself. "I appreciate your interest," she said. "It appears you have nothing to gain from this. I must say, you're not a bad sort for an Englishman."

He laughed. "I'm glad you don't find me the complete villain. Lord Alberdsley is my father's best friend. I was simply doing him a favor, seeing to his land. Had I known I'd discover he had a grandson—"

"But you won't tell him, will you?" She was suddenly

concerned, aware this might not be the end of it. She waited for his reply, but he was silent. "Will you?" she repeated suspiciously.

"I . . ." Thomas paused, as if in deep thought. "In all good conscience, I cannot promise I won't inform Lord Alberdsley he has a grandson."

"But why?" she asked, suddenly alarmed. "What good would it do? My mother told you what she thought, and I agree. Patrick is Irish through and through. He's done without Lord Alberdsley and . . . and . . ." Sputtering, she continued, ". . . all those English relatives all his life. Why would he want anything to do with them now?"

"Perhaps you should ask Patrick."

"I don't need to ask Patrick," Evleen replied, her anger mounting. And just when she was beginning to like this man. "Patrick is very bright, I grant you, but he's still a child. He will do what his mother thinks best for him. And what's best for him is to stay here in County Clare and not be torn from the arms of his loving family."

"I'm sorry. I didn't mean—"

"Is there something wrong, Evleen?"

It was Timothy, come to check on her. *Good.* His timing was perfect. "There's nothing wrong, Timothy. Lord Thomas and I were having a discussion, but now we're almost done." She raised her chin, having only one more thing to say to this troublesome Englishman. "You English look down upon us Irish. Don't deny it. You think because we're poor, we're ignorant. You think our children are all illegitimate and we find the ultimate solution to all our problems at the bottom of a glass of Guiness."

Even in the darkness she could tell Lord Thomas was taken aback. "But I hardly think—"

"Let me finish," she declared, her brogue growing thicker as she talked. "We may not be rich, but we are just as good as you are, sir. Just as smart, and just as capable of guiding our own lives. The O'Fallons are a happy family, and that includes Patrick, despite this business you're tellin' us now about bein' an heir apparent. Saints preserve us. He's an O'Fallon through and through, so think about what I said, and don't be causin' any more trouble than you've already caused." She bobbed her head to signal the end of her pronouncement. "Let's go inside, shall we, Timothy?"

Thomas watched as Timothy, his arm protectively around Evleen, led her back into the cottage. *I should be insulted,* he thought, *angry.* But despite himself, his stomach clenched with a feeling he had never, in all his thirty years, experienced before, jealousy. He had a sudden, totally unreasonable urge to punch the big Irishman square in the nose and grab the girl away. *How totally uncivilized.* He could hardly believe it of himself. Despite being a second son, he had never been compelled to lift a finger to attract any woman he chose. Strange, but her words had not stung him in the least. Instead, as he'd listened to her ranting, all he could really hear was the entrancing sound of her melodious voice, her words becoming more and more Irish, flowing from her sweet mouth in that beautiful, lulling brogue.

When he returned to the cottage, not sure of the welcome he'd receive, Sinead O'Fallon greeted him graciously and apologized. "You must understand how we feel, sir, and it's nothing personal. You and O'Grady must spend the night if you don't mind makeshift beds in front of the fireplace."

He had said nothing more, and in the morning, after a near sleepless night full of O'Grady's snoring and his own tossing and turning, they left amidst a chorus of friendly good-byes. Even Evleen shook his hand, but her words were a final plea. "Leave us be. Please don't tell."

"I cannot promise."

For a moment, she seemed to pause and reflect, and then smiled gently. "Then I can but wish you *siochain leat,* sir," she answered softly. "That means peace be with you."

He left, deeply affected by the young woman's graciousness in the face of his intractability. No truer lady could be found anywhere in England, he thought, and he knew that although he would never see her again, he would have a most difficult time forgetting Evleen O'Fallon.

Despite the warm weather, the return journey from Ireland to England was not a comfortable one. The easiest part was his trip across Ireland, via Bianconi Coach, to the port of Ringsend, called by all a "vile, filthy, disgraceful-looking village," which, despite its poor reputation, was the busy port from which Thomas took the packet that crossed the Irish Sea to Holyhead in Wales. The seventy-mile journey took the better part of a day. *What a miserable boat ride,* Thomas glumly reflected more than once. For the fare of ten and six, he was given the great privilege of taking passage on a ship in which facilities were primitive and minimal, the air was confined and nauseating, and for most of the unfortunate passengers, seasickness was a constant misery. At least he'd been spared that final indignity, Thomas reflected, as the ship approached Holyhead. Still, his journey had been a discomfiting one. He could easily tolerate the physical discomforts, but ever since he'd left that little cottage in County Clare, his usual serenity had been shaken to the core. Up until now, his well-ordered life had contained few dilemmas, but over and over, he now wondered, should he tell or should he not tell? Sinead O'Fallon and her daughter Evleen had been adamant in their plea that Lord Alberdsley not be told he had a grandson. With good reason, too, Thomas mused. Despite his family's poverty, the boy was bright, healthy, and obviously happy right where he was. *Why chance fate?* If Alberdsley knew of the grandson, he would not only want to see the boy, he would no doubt seek custody. After all, Patrick could live a life of ease and luxury, waited on hand and foot, with everything he could possibly need.

But what does he need he doesn't have right now?

And that wasn't all. To his great chagrin, Thomas could not get Evleen off his mind. *You will never see her again,* he kept telling himself. He had done his duty, both to his father and Lord Alberdsley. Of a certainty, he would never make this unpleasant trip again. All memories fade, given time, but again last night the beautiful face of Evleen O'Fallon glimmered before his eyes, keeping him awake far past the time he should rightfully be asleep. There was absolutely no future in thinking about her, he kept telling himself, but he did just the same.

And then there was Patrick. What should he do? Thomas mused. He despised indecision.

The ship was delayed by the tides for hours. Finally, as it slipped into Holyhead Harbor, he made up his mind. He would not say a word to Lord Alberdsley. The boy was happy where he was, in County Clare, Ireland, and there he should remain.

Chapter 6

"So, Thomas, how was your journey?" asked Penelope. In the drawing room of Northfield Hall, Thomas, who had just arrived home, made a wry face as his sister poured from a silver gilt pot and handed him a delicate bone china cup of tea. "The journey was wonderful," he replied, "if you like tossing about in a filthy boat for a day, then waiting for hours at Holyhead until the tides are favorable enough for you to get ashore."

"You seem to have survived," Penelope remarked dryly. She stirred daintily. "I take it things did not go well?"

"Well enough." Thomas described the first part of his journey, wherein he visited their father's lands in County Mayo and assured himself they were in good hands. "And then I went to County Clare . . ."

Knowing his sister was the only person in the world in whom he could confide everything, or at least almost everything, Thomas related the story of his visit to the cottage at Galway Bay and his astonishment at finding that Montfret had a wife and child. He told everything, omitting only his turbulent feelings concerning the Irish girl. "Afterward, I struggled, trying make up my mind what was best to do. It was not an easy decision, but I've decided not to tell Lord Alberdsley he has a grandson."

"But that's wrong," Penelope firmly declared. "Think of the wealth, the title. At the very least, shouldn't the boy be allowed to decide for himself?"

"His mother is adamant," Thomas explained, "and who can blame her? Being pure Irish, she has always disliked the English, but now, after her experience with Randall, she hates everything about us. Ask yourself—why would she want to send her one and only beloved son to the very land she detests?"

"Hmm . . . you have a point, I suppose." Penelope's bright eyes flashed with excitement. "Good grief, just think of the stir this would cause. Wouldn't tongues be wagging! If Patrick were to be proclaimed the true heir, then that little worm Walter Trevlyn and his family would be deposed." An impish grin crept over her face. "Wouldn't we love to see Lydia and those stuck-up daughters of hers taken down a peg or two."

"What an uncharitable thought," Thomas admonished, although he could not suppress an answering smile. "But despite the shortcomings of the heir presumptive and family, I have made up my mind." He frowned. "Now I must ride to Aldershire Manor and inform Lord Alberdsley of my return."

"But if you conceal the news he has a grandson, won't you be forced to lie?"

"I should hope not."

"So do I. Really, Thomas, you're not a very good liar."

"I take that as a compliment."

Penelope wrinkled up her nose. "You are not as clever as you think, brother dear. According to the London dandies, lying is an art. Well, you're no artist. Your problem is, to be a first-rate liar, you must possess some finesse, and you have none." With sisterly derision, she continued, "You are much too blunt."

"I still take it as a compliment. I've never been a London dandy, as you well know. If you mean I always speak my mind, then I plead guilty." Thomas spoke lightly, concealing his concern. He, who held liars in the lowest possible esteem, was about to become a liar himself, if only by omission. *But it's for the greater good,* he told himself, his mind drifting once again to that proud Irish family who dearly loved Patrick and would be devastated if he were sent away, especially to hated England. "I shall tell Alberdsley as little as possible. It's for the best. The boy looks Irish, acts Irish, sounds Irish. He would be a fish out of water here, and no doubt completely miserable. How could he possibly fit into this tight, bigoted world of ours?"

Penelope made a moue. "Is that what we are? I had no idea you had such a low opinion of the *ton.*"

"I don't see you chomping at the bit to get to London again. You've gone through—how many?—two Seasons now? All I

hear is complaints, complaints about how frivolous and superficial everyone is, and how odious are those shallow, vainglorious London dandies."

"Touché," Penelope replied, lifting a knowing eyebrow. She
thought a moment, and her face brightened. "Enough of this.
Whatever the problem with Lord Alberdsley, I'm sure you'll
handle it. This evening we celebrate your return. You'll be
pleased to hear Father and I have invited the Trevlyns, and, in
particular, Miss Bettina Trevlyn for dinner."

Thomas tried to hide not only his surprise but his displeasure. Since the moment he'd laid eyes on Evleen O'Fallon, he
had not given a thought to the girl everyone expected him to
marry.

"So, my boy, have a seat. How was your journey?" asked
Lord Alberdsley.

"Fine, sir." Thomas sank into one of the Louis XV yellow
velvet chairs in his neighbor's mahogany paneled library and
with great caution began a description of his trip to Ireland.
When he found himself including every boring detail he could
think of concerning his father's estate in County Mayo, he
chided himself. *Get on with it. Stop prolonging the inevitable.*
Lord Alberdsley had listened patiently, but Thomas perceived
by the watchful look in his eyes that he was anxious to hear the
report on his own land. *Drat.* "And then, per your request, I
went to County Clare."

"And?" Alberdsley sat straight, hardly able to contain his eagerness.

"Actually, there's not much to tell. The land is poor, not
much more than dirt, grass, rocks, and a few sheep. Hardly
worth bothering with. A widow and her five children presently
occupy the place."

"Tell me her name," Alberdsley said quickly.

"Sinead O'Fallon. She's been a widow for quite some time.
She's a well-educated, refined woman, not the type you would
expect to find living in that miserable cottage, but it seems in
recent years she's fallen on hard times. The cottage is quite
small, and the land suited for nothing more than a small garden
and a few sheep. Frankly, I wouldn't bother collecting rent. It's
hardly worth the effort."

Looking crestfallen, Alberdsley asked, "You found nothing to tie this Sinead O'Fallon to Randall?"

Damnation. Thomas wondered how could he lie to a direct question. He could not. There was no way around it; he was bound by his own honor to tell the truth . . . the partial truth anyway. "There is a connection. O'Fallon was Sinead's first husband. Her second husband was—brace yourself, sir."

"I'm braced. Go on."

"Your son, Randall." It was out, and no harm done unless Alberdsley asked details of the children. Thomas paused to let his news sink in, but Alberdsley's face had become a mask. He seemed to be taking the news with equanimity, but it was hard to tell. Thomas continued, "From what I understand, she was quite well-off when they married, having inherited a small fortune from her first husband, who was some kind of an Irish earl, by the way, the eighth earl of something-or-other. You know how those Irish titles go. She and Randall weren't married long before Randall died of typhoid, I'm sorry to say, but before that, he'd managed to run through her fortune."

There was a long pause. "Typhoid," bitterly remarked Lord Alberdsley. "Good Lord, how could I have had a son who . . . ah, well." He looked inquiringly at Thomas. "And the children? Tell me about them."

God help me, thought Thomas. If only he'd learned to lie as well as Montague. He squirmed uncomfortably in his seat—something he never did—crossed one smart nankeen-covered leg over the other and paid meticulous attention to a piece of lint on the sleeve of his short frock coat. "The children," he repeated.

"Yes, Thomas, the children." Alberdsley was regarding him strangely.

"Well, let's see now. There are four girls . . . Evleen, who's about twenty-four, Darragh who's twenty-three, Sorcha, who's around fifteen I'd say, and the youngest, who's fourteen. All pretty, by the way, and well educated, and quite—"

"You said five children," interrupted Alberdsley, his voice brimming with impatience.

Damnation again. "There's a son, Patrick."

"And how old is Patrick?"

Trapped. Why hadn't he realized Alberdsley was no fool and could add as well as anyone? "Ten, sir."

"Randall died nine years ago." Alberdsley's voice had gone sharp. His gaze pierced Thomas's as he asked, "How long was he married to Sinead?"

"Two years."

For a time, the room was heavy with silence as Lord Alberdsley first shut his eyes, as if absorbing the shocking fact, then opened them and gazed at Thomas with an expression of incredulity, followed by pure joy, followed by a look of dawning disbelief. "You were not going to tell me?" There was a faint tremor in his voice.

"I was not." A war of emotions raged within Thomas. He was relieved because in his heart he had wanted Alberdsley to know the truth, but on the other hand, he could only begin to imagine the grief and turmoil his truthfulness was bound to cause.

Alberdsley could not contain himself. "By God, I've got a grandson," he exclaimed, rising to his feet, eyes gleaming with excitement. "Tell me what he's like, Thomas. Tell me . . ." Suddenly he frowned. ". . . no, first, you must tell why you were going to remain silent. Not like you. Why would you not tell me such glorious news? You must have had what you thought was a good reason." He sank in his chair again and sat tensely, awaiting Thomas's response.

Thomas decided to start with the good part first. It would fit with what he had to say. "I'll tell you my reason, but first I'll tell you about Patrick. He's tall for ten, on the skinny side, as young boys are, yet I can tell from the proportions of his chest and shoulders he'll grow into a fine, strong man. He's well spoken in Gaelic, English, and French, and possesses excellent manners. He has bright red hair, which he gets from his mother, and freckles. He raises rabbits and takes great interest in the world around him. Altogether your grandson is a bright, fine-looking boy."

Alberdsley countered, "All well and good, and I'm happy to hear it, but you must tell me why on earth did you not want me to know about my own grandson."

"Because . . ." It was Thomas's turn to shut his eyes a moment, to think. The straight-out truth would be best, he decided.

"His mother is Irish through and through, sir. She detests the English, just like many of her countrymen, and for a variety of reasons, most of which I am sure you know. Your son Randall . . . well, there's no other way to say this . . . caused her no end of grief. It appears he threw away her entire fortune, with both hands, so to speak, then died and left her destitute. Need I add, the fact that Randall was English did not raise her estimation of the English as a whole."

"So you're saying . . . ?"

"What I'm saying, is that I have talked to Sinead O'Fallon, so I know you must not get your hopes up. She is adamant. Never would she allow Patrick to have anything to do with anything English, let alone send her only son to England."

"Patrick belongs here with me," burst Alberdsley. "Just think what I can give the boy."

"Sinead O'Fallon is a strong, determined woman. I can assure you, she would never relent. Never," Thomas added for emphasis. He was determined to make sure the old man understood and never got his hopes up. "Perhaps when Patrick is grown—"

"The boy belongs to me," Alberdsley said with quiet but obdurate firmness. "Think who he'll be, Thomas. I shall bestow all Randall's titles upon him. He shall be Patrick, Viscount Montfret. *Lord Montfret*. Doesn't that sound grand?"

"Lord Alberdsley, you're not listening to me." Thomas felt as if he were talking to a stone wall.

"But why would his mother want Patrick to stay in Ireland, digging potatoes, catching fish . . . whatever those poor Irish do?" Alberdsley clenched his jaw. His eyes narrowed. "I don't care what it takes. I want my grandson."

Thomas released a weary, defeated sigh. "And how do you propose to get him?"

"I shall direct a letter to his mother immediately, of course. Once she sees in writing the advantages Patrick will enjoy here in England, I am sure she will relent. You say the family is poor?"

"Very."

"Then I shall offer her a stipend. How does forty pounds a year sound?"

"A fortune by Irish standards."

"Well, then." Lord Alberdsley smiled with satisfaction. "The matter is settled, is it not?" As he spoke, he walked to his walnut desk, sat down, and took up his quill pen. "This will go out with the next post."

Thomas knew he shouldn't ask, but couldn't resist. "Had you considered your brother? He was to inherit the title, was he not? I should imagine—"

Alberdsley interrupted with a snort. "Walter," he said, wrapping the word in contempt. "You think I am not aware how that weak-kneed brother of mine and his silver-tongued wife have been robbing me blind these past few years? If you think I care one whit that Walter won't inherit my title and my fortune, then think again."

"Of course," Thomas replied. No need to add his own opinion of Walter and his wife, or that surely there was trouble ahead if Patrick came to England. Walter was no problem, but with her greed and devious ways, Lydia Trevlyn could be a formidable foe. She could cause endless difficulties if her husband was done out of his inheritance by one redheaded Irish lad.

But that wasn't going to happen, Thomas thought. He watched with sympathy as Lord Alberdsley dipped his pen in the ink stand and started diligently writing his letter. *It won't do you any good, sir. You don't know Sinead O'Fallon. Never in a million years will she allow her son to come to England.*

It was the beginning of summer when Evleen, who had been working in the garden, entered the cottage and knew immediately something was wrong. "What is it, Mama?" she asked in alarm, seeing the grim, tight-lipped look on her mother's face.

"A letter has arrived," Sinead replied. She was sitting at the table, staring at a piece of folded parchment lying before her, fastened by a large red wax seal.

Lord Thomas, Evleen immediately thought. Since his visit, he had been much on her mind. "I would guess it's from England. Aren't you going to open it?"

Mama's lips pinched even tighter. "The letter is from Lord Alberdsley, Patrick's grandfather. I have no need to open it. I know what it says."

Evleen's heart sank. *He told.* She sank into the chair across from her mother and tapped a firm finger on the letter. "It won't go away, you know. You'd best open it. You'll never know what he has to say if it's just sitting there."

Sinead took up the letter, broke the seal, unfolded it, and skimmed the contents. Her face grew grim as she remarked, "Just as I suspected," and began to read aloud.

My Dear Madame,

Lord Thomas has just returned from Ireland and has informed me I have a grandson, product of your union with my son, Randall.

I cannot begin to express what joy this news has given me and how much I now regret my reluctance to discover more about the life Randall led in Ireland before his tragic death. I had no idea Randall had married and that you had borne his son. In my own defense, my only explanation for my derelict behavior involves the unfortunate circumstances surrounding Randall's hasty departure from England. His disgrace left me devastated, angry, and keenly disappointed in my only son. Still, I am at fault for disowning him. I regret my hasty, ill-thought-out decision never to mention his name again, or my demand that no news of him ever reach my ears and that I never see him again.

Now, having heard the wonderful news that I have a grandson, I am anxious to make amends. It is my devout and humble wish that you send Patrick to me, here in England, where he will lead a life suitable for a young lord. Thomas has given me a glowing description of Patrick and tells me what a fine young lad he is. It would be impolitic of me to compare his potential future here in England with his future in Ireland. I can only assure you that should Patrick come to live with me, he would be accorded all that is rightfully his. That includes the best of tutors until he is old enough for Eton. After Eton, he will be sent to Oxford, then on to Europe for the grand tour. As heir apparent, he will inherit my entire estate, which includes several homes and vast tracts of land throughout the country, including Aldershire Manor, this most beautiful country home in which I, my brother, and his family reside. He will also inherit my fortune, which is considerable, I can assure you.

To sum up, if Patrick comes to England, he will live a life of privilege and luxury, his future assured. Naturally I am not unaware of the considerable sacrifice I am asking that you make. I understand you have four unmarried daughters. With that in mind, I propose to compensate you and your family with the sum of forty pounds a year, payable your entire lifetime and beyond, if necessary, until your last daughter marries. To this purpose I will arrange to set up an account through a solicitor and bank of your choosing. Naturally, I trust you realize my offer is made in good faith, as just compensation for the loss of the company of your son.

I trust you will let me know as soon as possible of your decision in this matter. Rest assured, Patrick will be treated not only with due consideration and respect, but I will love him with all my heart and see that he has a good, happy, and rewarding life here in England.

> Respectfully yours,
> Alberdsley

"How dare he!" Sinead, fire in her eyes, dropped the letter on the table as if it were a hot coal. "Never in a million years shall I send my boy to England."

"Of course," Evleen answered absently. Her mind was on the dark, handsome man with the graceful stride who had so charmed her when he was here. He had told. How could he, when she'd practically begged him not to? She felt an odd twinge of disappointment, even while telling herself she really shouldn't care. After all, what could she expect of an Englishman? Besides, she most assuredly would never see him again, so why give even one tiny thought to him?

Sinead, in a state of agitation Evleen had never seen before, arose from the table, nearly overturning her chair, and strode to the small front window, where she stood, hands jammed on hips, looking out at the sea. "How could Lord Alberdsley even think of taking my son away? By what right has he to—"

Suddenly, she clutched her heart, turned, and staggered. Her face turned gray, and she cried, "Evleen, my heart. Help me."

With a cry, Evleen leaped up. Minutes later, she had helped her mother to her bed and was hovering over her. "I'll send for the doctor—"

"No, I'm all right." Sinead grasped her wrist. "I do get pains in my chest every now and then, but I'm better now. I'm sure it was just the agitation caused by that terrible letter, but I'm fine, really I am. Just let me rest awhile."

"But—"

"No doctor. We can't afford it and I don't need one."

Evleen knew better than to disobey her strong-willed mother. She concealed her fear as she replied, "All right, I shall just sit here as you rest awhile, then you'll be as good as new."

Sinead managed a rueful smile. "I had better be. Else, how would we live?"

"I don't care about that, Mama," cried Evleen. Sinead had always been so well. Evleen had never had to face the unbearable thought that someday she would lose her beloved mother. And yet, death was inevitable. And what if it happened soon? She herself would be all right, since she might be marrying Timothy soon . . . she guessed, although she still hadn't completely might made up her mind. But what of her sisters? Darragh was old enough to marry, but with her prickly personality, no one had asked her. But Patrick? For the first time, the thought crossed her mind that her brother might indeed be better off in England, where he would live in the wealth and luxury that were rightfully his. She would not dream of mentioning such a thought to her mother, though. That would be a betrayal of all she held dear.

Sinead clasped her hand. "I'll get up soon. Really, I'm fine. Run and find paper. As soon as I get up, I shall give Lord Alberdsley his reply."

In the late summer sunshine, Thomas and Penelope were standing in front of the ivy-covered stone stables of Northfield Hall. "What do you think of him?" Thomas asked. He ran a brush over the shining brown coat of his new Irish thoroughbred. "A fine bit of blood, wouldn't you say?"

"He'll make a good addition for your breeding farm," answered Penelope, nodding approvingly. "I shall hate to see you leave. It's been wonderful having you home."

"I won't be too far away."

"I know, but . . ." A wily expression came over Penelope's face. "Such a large house you're moving to. I hate to think of you there, all alone. A pity you can't share it with someone."

"There you go again," Thomas answered with a grin. "Do you really expect me to marry Miss Bettina Trevlyn? I would soon expire of boredom. Murder by petit point, you could say."

She laughed appreciatively, but quickly grew serious. "But you must marry somebody, sometime."

"I'm thinking about it." Thomas determined that was all he would say. Although he confided in his sister more than anyone, during the entire time he'd been back from Ireland, he had mentioned Evleen only briefly, and only in conjunction with his brief description of the O'Fallon family. Despite its being utterly insane, he kept wishing he could see her. But no matter how many times he told himself he would never again make that miserable trip to County Clare, let alone Ireland, her bright blue eyes and enchanting smile stayed as vivid in his mind as the day they'd met. There was nothing he could do about it, though. Evleen O'Fallon would remain an unfulfilled dream, the kind he supposed all men had at one time or another in their lives. What was there to do except resign himself that he would never see the beautiful Irish girl again?

"Who is that?" asked Penelope, looking over Thomas's shoulder.

Thomas turned to see a rider approaching, an older man, he gathered, riding slowly and somewhat stiffly in his saddle. As the man drew nearer, he recognized who it was. "Why it's Lord Alberdsley. It must be important. One hardly sees him on a horse anymore."

Lord Alberdsley dismounted so slowly and painfully Thomas was sorely tempted to offer his help, but refrained in deference to the old man's pride. He almost changed his mind when Alberdsley's knees buckled as he hit the ground, but the old man recovered himself by gripping the saddle and quickly pulling himself erect.

After a greeting accompanied by a courtly bow to Penelope, Alberdsley reached into his pocket and pulled out a letter. "From that Irish woman. You will never believe what it says."

"I believe I can guess, sir," Thomas replied, careful not to sound too cocksure.

"Read it."

Thomas took the letter and read aloud.

My Dear Lord Alberdsley,

 I am in receipt of your letter requesting that I send you my son, Patrick O'Fallon. Please be advised that although I appreciate your concern for your grandson, never, not while there is breath in my body, will he ever set one foot upon the soil of England.

Yours in good health,
Sinead O'Fallon

Sounds just like her, Thomas thought, but in deference to Alberdsley's obvious perturbation Thomas hid the wry smile that flew to his lips. He'd been right. The letter was exactly the sort he would expect Sinead O'Fallon would write—uncompromising, intractable, and to the point.

"It sounds as though she has most definitely made up her mind," Thomas remarked. "I'm afraid that's an end to it, then. Perhaps when the boy is older—"

"I want my grandson," Alberdsley declared, voice shaking with intensity. Confusion filled his eyes as he continued, "I don't understand. How could that woman defy me after I offered her son the kind of privileged life few can have? Why would she want Patrick to stay on, leading a deprived existence on that . . . that . . ."

"Barren, rocky piece of land?" Thomas softly supplied.

"Precisely. Well, it simply won't do. That woman can defy me all she wants, but she'll not get her way."

"What do you intend?"

The old man's eyes gleamed with determination. "I want you to return to Ireland. I want you to threaten, beg, plead, cajole, bargain—whatever it takes to get me my grandson."

"No," cried Thomas, his ever-present, stern composure for once forgotten.

"Yes, Thomas, you must."

"Have you any idea how difficult it is to get to Ireland? How much time the journey takes? As it is, I am so far behind now on the my plans for—"

"I don't care about all that." Lord Alberdsley flicked a gaze toward the house where the marquess was still indisposed, still suffering from the gout. "Your father would want you to go, Thomas."

"He's right, Thomas," said Penelope, who'd been listening, wide-eyed. "Don't forget Lord Alberdsley is Papa's oldest friend. Of course he'd want you to go."

Unfair, Thomas wanted to shout, feeling utterly dismayed. That little jaunt to Ireland had greatly delayed his plans for breeding horses. Now, since he'd returned from Ireland, he'd made great strides, not only in making several trips to Tanglewood Hall, where he had already renovated the house and hired servants, but also in starting to purchase his horses. He reached to pat the withers of his new thoroughbred. This latest addition was only one of several of the finest horses in the land. "What about your brother?" he asked Alberdsley. "Can't you send him?" Up to now Walter and his family had done nothing to earn their keep.

"Are you daft?" Alberdsley replied with a sniff. "Walter stands to lose everything if Patrick comes to England. I can imagine his enthusiasm should I send *him* to County Clare."

"Of course, I hadn't thought." *That was utterly stupid,* Thomas chastised himself. *Born of desperation.* Was there nothing he could do? "What about Montague?"

This time Penelope sniffed. "Montague take time from his precious life in London? Thomas, you belong in Bedlam if you think he'd agree to go. And besides"—she slanted a knowing gaze at him—"only you have the tact to deal with this . . . this Sinead, or whatever her name is, and the girl you said was feisty, that Evleen."

Evleen. At the sound of her name, Thomas felt a jolt in the pit of his stomach. To see her again . . . how he yearned to see her again. But he had set his course. His sole purpose in life right now was breeding horses. His carefully planned future most certainly did not include a girl from Ireland who would fit into his well-run existence like water into oil. Everything about such a relationship would be wrong, dead wrong. "I'm sorry," he told Alberdsley. "To go to Ireland now . . . I simply cannot. Perhaps in a year or so—"

"Quite all right, I do understand," Alberdsley broke in briskly. "On second thought, I'll go myself." He gave a hollow laugh. "A bit of brisk sea air might be just the tonic for my rheumatism." He grabbed the reins of his horse, placed his foot in the stirrup, and attempted to swing onto the saddle, but he fell back down, too weak to give himself the proper boost. "Wretched animal won't stand still," he muttered. He tried again, grunting from his all-out exertion, but failed a second time. "Damn." Biting his lip, obviously chagrined, he said, "Well, Thomas, my groom had to help me when I left. I had hoped I could gather enough strength not to make a spectacle of myself, but obviously not. Come, give me a boost."

As Thomas helped his old neighbor into his saddle, he remarked, "Sir, don't even think about going to Ireland. Believe me, it's much too strenuous a trip for a man who . . . "

"Say it, Thomas. For a spindle-shanked old man with the strength of a gnat." From his mount, Lord Alberdsley regarded Thomas with a look of grim determination. His jaw jutted out as he announced, "I shall go to Ireland. Nothing can stop me."

"Not a good idea, sir. The journey is a nightmare, and gets worse now that winter's coming. Perhaps in the spring—"

"I shall leave immediately." With a great show of wheeling his steed around, Alberdsley started away, but Thomas grabbed the reins and brought him to a stop.

"Please reconsider, sir. Conditions aboard those packets are abominable. The air is confined and suffocating. There's nausea . . . the food is disgusting. If you cross from Holyhead to Ringsend, you're obliged to pay a shilling to the boatman to row you ashore. If you can find a boatman. Otherwise, you'll wait on a rolling boat for hours, cold and hungry, no doubt heaving your dinner, that is if you were able to keep any of that rotten food down. And then—"

"I'm going. I want my grandson. I have little time to waste."

Thomas was weakening, despite all his plans. Despairing, he realized a journey to Ireland at this time of year could well mean the end of this old man, who, after all, was not only his father's best friend but had treated the whole family with the utmost care and consideration over the years. *One more try.* "She won't give him up, sir, take my word on it."

"Then . . . I shall bring the mother to England, along with her son. Make it well worth her while."

"She would die before she came to England."

"One of the daughters, then . . . that Evleen, the oldest one."

Evleen in England? What an astonishing thought. He was about to give in anyway, but the thought of the Irish girl put him well over the edge. "I'll go."

Lord Alberdsley loosed his reins. "You will?"

"I will."

"How soon?"

"The sooner the better before winter sets in. Tomorrow if you like."

Lord Alberdsley appeared to be having second thoughts. "Not that I wanted to pressure you . . ."

Ha. Thomas nearly choked, but got the words out. "It's my pleasure, sir, now that I know how important this is to you. Besides, what's a few weeks? I'll still have a lifetime to pursue my own plans."

Penelope, trying to stifle a laugh, said, "How suddenly noble you are, Thomas," her lips twitching.

Not so noble, Thomas thought privately. He remembered Tanglewood Hall and a flash of keen disappointment ripped through him. *But enough.* From this moment on he would set all regrets aside. Most assuredly he would not dwell on yet another delay of his plans. "You took me by surprise, but I'm happy I can be of help, sir."

"Wonderful." The old man's face was wreathed in a smile. "You can do it, my boy, with that charm of yours. Use every power of persuasion you can think of. Money . . . I'll set some aside, whatever you need. And be sure to tell the mother she can come along . . . Bloody hell, tell her to bring the whole family if she likes. If not the mother, then the sister, that Evleen. Does the boy get along with her?"

"Famously."

"Well, then tell this Sinead O'Fallon that if she sends the daughter along with the boy, I'll see that the daughter—how old did you say she is?"

"She's twenty-four."

"Hmm . . . a bit old, but still . . . Tell the mother I shall give the girl a Season. Find her a good match, don't you see? I'll have her presented to court if she likes—brought out. She'll have new gowns, as many as she pleases, and hats, shoes, gloves—all those baubles so dear to a pretty girl's heart. Er, that is . . . she is pretty, isn't she? I trust she's not one of those sturdy peasant girls with rough hands."

"She's beautiful."

"Well, then. A few baubles to win her over, don't you think?"

"I'll do what I can, sir." *A few baubles?* Thomas recalled that first moment he'd laid eyes on Evleen O'Fallon, standing by the door of her humble cottage, the wind playing such devilish tricks with her gown he'd felt a tug of excitement just watching from a distance. Later, when she'd been fixing dinner and he'd watched fascinated by her every move, he'd been struck not only by her beauty but by her competence, maturity, and the proud, sure, no-nonsense way she'd carried herself.

A few baubles?

He tried to picture Evleen in the midst of her London Season, her bosom half exposed in her low-cut gown, giggling behind her fan, fluttering her eyelashes at some cravat-choked, simpering, superficial dandy.

Never. Ludicrous. Utterly impossible.

Chapter 7

With a heavy heart, Evleen left the pot of soup she'd been stirring and went to stare moodily at the sea from the small cottage window. There would be rain soon. The sky was dull and leaden, a perfect color to match her mood. Actually, all the family's mood now that Sinead wasn't well.

Darragh, who had been sitting by their mother's bedside, came into the kitchen, huddled in her shawl. "Mama's sleeping now," she said. "I think she's a mite better."

"Do you?"

"I suppose it's wishful thinking." Darragh's brows drew together in a frown. "It's that Englishman's fault. She was fine until his letter arrived."

With a shake of her head, Evleen answered, "Let's be fair. Mama has not been feeling well for ages, long before the letter. Don't you remember all those times she was breathless, all the times she felt faint?"

"I suppose," Darragh answered tartly, "but you must admit her condition has worsened since that day. If you ask me, she's sick with guilt. She knows very well she's done Patrick out of his rightful inheritance." Her face clouded. "And us, too. Just think what forty pounds a year could do." She glanced down at her light calico gown, her lips thinning with irritation. "Look at this old thing. No wonder I haven't a husband. We could have new clothes, live in a halfway decent house, if only Mama would relent and send Patrick to England."

Evleen felt a sudden urge to inform her sister it was not the lack of pretty clothes that was turning her into an old maid; it was her waspish tongue and selfish attitude. Such a chastisement would be most unkind, though. Unjust, too. Despite her faults, Darragh worked as hard as anyone and worried as much as anyone about their mother. Evleen replied gently, "Don't be hard on Mama. Can't you see why she loathes all things English? Surely you understand why she could never send Patrick to live with his grandfather."

It came as no surprise when Darragh gave her a look that said she'd never understand.

Later, after everyone else had gone to bed, Evleen sat by her mother's bed and smiled down at her. "All the chores are done, Mama. You see? We're surviving, hard though it is without you." She noted with sorrow that her mother, once the picture of health, now lay on her bed, pale, hollow-eyed, and exhausted, a mere shadow of her former self.

"I hate this," Sinead said with a deep sigh. "Where has my strength gone? Why can't I walk a step without panting as if I'd just run a mile uphill?"

"You know it's your heart, but the doctor says if you keep taking your tonic you'll get better. In a while I'll fix you some chamomile tea."

Mama turned her face to the wall. "Chamomile tea won't fix what ails me. Nothing will."

At her mother's embittered words, Evleen felt a chill around her own heart. She had made a valiant effort to remain optimistic, but had known from the start that her mother's ailment was not likely to get better and could only get worse. It was almost too much to bear, to see her once proud, once strong mother reduced to being a near helpless invalid.

"It's time we talked about the future," said Sinead. It was as if she'd read her daughter's mind. She sighed and took Evleen's hand. "I shall be leaving soon."

"Don't. You mustn't say it."

"It must be said." A look of despair filled Sinead's eyes. "I confess, I've thought and thought, but I don't know what to do. The eight hundred pounds is gone. As you well know, what little money we have comes from the English lessons I give . . . gave, I should say. I cannot teach anymore."

"Then I can do it, Mama. My Gaelic is as good as yours."

"True, daughter, and I'm relying on you, but the money from the lessons won't be nearly enough."

"There's the sheep."

"They bring in but a pittance."

Evleen said firmly, "Somehow we'll make do."

"I wanted my daughters to find good husbands. I wanted Patrick to go to Trinity College in Dublin." Sinead laughed with bitter irony. "Well, he won't now, will he? He'll likely end up just another poor fisherman while you girls, unless you marry, will be forced into service where you'll spend your days scrubbing hearths and emptying chamber pots."

"What a dreadful future," Evleen replied, wanting to make light of Sinead's dire prediction. She smiled and squeezed her mother's hand. "In the first place, you're going to get better. In the second, somehow or other, we'll scrape by."

"Scrape by," Sinead repeated mockingly. "I wanted better things for you."

"I can always marry Timothy, you know."

"Saints preserve us. After all these years you're finally admitting you'd be best off with Timothy Murphy? Will wonders never cease. What brought on this change of heart?"

"I'm twenty-four, time is passing, and I know Timothy would be good to our family." Speaking humorously, she went on, "I used to think someday a knight in shining armor would come knocking at my door. He would be handsome, wealthy, kind, tender, and—"

"Irish."

"Very Irish. We would fall in love, and he would carry me off to a life of bliss. That's what I used to think. Lately I'm not so sure."

"Now you're getting some sense in your head."

"I know I could be happy with Timothy, at least reasonably so."

"That's wise, especially since the chances of your prince's finding his way to our humble cottage are rather slim."

A sudden pounding on the door caused Evleen to jump in alarm. "Who could it be at this hour?" She went to the one small window and looked out, but it was dark outside and raining, and she couldn't see a thing. "One of the neighbors must be in trouble," she surmised as she flew to the door and swung it open.

Lord Thomas.

She gasped and stiffened. There he stood, completely unexpected, drenched and looking miserable. He bowed low, water pouring off his beaver hat. In an unconcerned voice, he said, "Ah, good evening, Miss O'Fallon. Lovely weather we're having, wouldn't you say?"

"You."

"Yes, 'tis I." He glanced over his shoulder at two horses and a curricle, barely visible in the black night. "I would have arrived at a more decent hour, but it seems I got lost and ran off the road in the dark." He smiled wryly. "Actually, I am wet and close to freezing. You have no idea how much I'm hoping you'll allow me into your warm abode, despite my being an Englishman."

"I wouldn't let a dog stay outside on a night like this." Evleen swung the door wide, pleased with herself for finding an apt riposte despite her shock at seeing him again.

"First, my horses," he said. "Your stable—?"

"The stable's in the back," Darragh said over Evleen's shoulder. "There's plenty of room." In an excited voice, she added, "How lovely to see you again, Lord Thomas."

Lovely? thought Evleen. Dread filled her heart. Lord Thomas could be here for only one reason.

Minutes later, the cottage was bustling as Darragh made tea and Evleen threw an extra lump of peat into the fireplace. Lord Thomas, finally warm after standing shivering for a time by the fire, sank into a chair and remarked, "Ah, warm at last. I would not recommend such a journey to my worst enemy."

"Can we assume, sir, you were just passing by?" Evleen asked, tongue in cheek.

"No, you cannot assume."

Evleen had to take a moment to gather her wits. Her emotions were mixed, to say the least. Her mother's words lay heavily on her heart. Not only was she still in a state of astonishment over Lord Thomas's unexpected arrival, she found his presence most disturbing. Over the months, she had never been able to clear his handsome image from her mind. Now here he was again, looking more handsome than even she remembered. Despite what must have been a grueling journey, he sat at ease in his chair, his well-formed, muscular legs stretched out before him, a glint of mockery in those marvelous flashing dark eyes. "I suppose I do know why you're here," she said frankly. "Lord Alberdsley sent you."

"Exactly so."

Darragh asked, "He would not take no for an answer?"

"He wants his grandson. You can understand why."

"Well, he's doomed to disappointment," Evleen adamantly replied. "My mother would never, under any circumstances send Patrick to England. My mother—"

"Your mother will speak for herself," came Sinead's voice from the doorway. She had thrown a dressing gown over her nightgown and now stood clinging to the doorpost, looking deathly pale.

"You should not be out of bed," exclaimed Evleen.

Lord Thomas leaped to assist. "Let me help you back—"

"No," Sinead answered firmly. "I shall sit at the table, if you please." With a grand wave she indicated the chairs arranged around the table. "Kindly join me, Lord Thomas . . . Evleen? Darragh? We shall let the younger ones sleep."

When they were settled at the table, Sinead asked Lord Thomas, "Are you here for the reason I think you are?"

"Lord Alberdsley wants his grandson," Lord Thomas replied. "To that purpose, he's sent me to inform you in person of what he now proposes."

Sinead eyed him with suspicion. "Did I not make it clear I would never allow Patrick to set foot in England?"

"Your letter was extremely clear. A mind can be changed, though, can it not?"

"Why even listen to him?" Evleen interjected, addressing her mother. "What could he say that could possibly make you change?"

A corner of Lord Thomas's mouth lifted in a smile. "I've come a long way, Miss O'Fallon. Kindly hear me out."

"You should at least hear what he has to say," said Darragh, who was listening with rapt attention.

Sinead replied, "Very well, tell us, but I warn you, it won't do you any good. Patrick is my *son*, sir. Have you any children?"

"I am not married."

"Then how could you even presume to know how I feel?"

"I don't presume."

Sinead sat back and looked him squarely in the eyes. "It's good that you don't presume because you won't know what matters in this life until the day you have children of your own. Then you will realize how the bond between you and your children is more precious than any amount of money."

Oh, dear God, thought Thomas. How he wished he were anywhere but here. His reluctant journey had been extremely arduous, but nothing compared to now. Darragh seemed pleased to see him, but the wrathful eyes of Sinead and Evleen burned into him, as if he had horns and a tail and had just arrived via his hired curricle through the gates of Hell. Perhaps he should give up, go home, and explain to Lord Alberdsley that nothing in the world would move Sinead from her dogged position. Still . . .

Honor must prevail, Thomas realized glumly. Lord Alberdsley had entrusted him with a vital mission. He would see it through to the bitter, and no doubt, unsatisfactory end.

Sinead spoke again. "As you can see, Lord Thomas, I am not well."

"I am terribly sorry," Thomas said sincerely. He had been shocked when he first saw Sinead. In but a few months the woman's health had obviously declined, and she was now but skin and bones.

"So am I sorry, sir," answered Sinead, a grim smile touching her lips. "At a time like this, I need my family around me, all my daughters, and, of course, Patrick. I assume Lord Alberdsley has sent you with additional persuasions, but you will find I cannot be persuaded, no matter what."

Thomas could tell by the firm set of Sinead's jaw that, indeed, she meant what she said. Still, he would try. "I can see you mean your every word, madame, but I've come a long way, so at least hear me out."

After a pause, Sinead answered sharply, "Go ahead. Since you've come all this way, I am curious to know what additional enticements Lord Alberdsley has in mind. Although, I can assure you, you're wasting your breath."

"Mama," cried Evleen, "why even listen to him? You said you would never—"

"Quiet, Evleen." Sinead, her jaw set, leaned resignedly back in her chair and addressed Thomas again. "So begin, sir."

At least she'll listen to me, thought Thomas with some relief, although he still didn't hold out much hope. "To begin with, Patrick will have everything—wealth, position, power."

Evleen sniffed disdainfully. "Jonathan Swift said, 'Power is no blessing in itself, except when it is used to protect the innocent.' "

Blast the girl. At least she's literate. "Well, then, if you are against Patrick's going to England alone, then Lord Alberdsley invites you and your entire family to come to England. He will see that you are more than amply compensated for this major adjustment in your life and will provide a home of your own choosing, as well as an ample income to last the rest of your life. Your new home would be close to your son, of course. Or, if you prefer, you are welcome to come live with Lord Alberdsley at his home—"

Sinead burst into laughter. "My, my, he must be desperate. But no, that's going too far. I could never go to England." She eyed Thomas intently. "What else?"

"Then . . ." Thomas flicked a quick gaze at Evleen before he continued, "If you are concerned about Patrick's going to England alone, Lord Alberdsley has suggested one of your daughters could accompany him."

"And how would she be treated?" asked Sinead. "For all I know, Lord Alberdsley would make a servant of her, force her to share a cold, tiny room in the attic with a scullery maid."

Lord Thomas drew in a patient breath. "If you would allow it, the daughter, whichever one you chose, would be accorded every consideration, every luxury. She would have a Season, as well as clothes, jewels, and, as Lord Alberdsley put it, 'baubles to her heart's content.' "

"Baubles," Sinead repeated, her voice oozing with contempt. "You ask a true daughter of Ireland to trade her beloved land for baubles?

Blast. Thomas had known this would be difficult, but nothing like this. It was obvious that despite her illness, Sinead was still a willful woman, tenacious in her beliefs. He would treat her as such and lay down the hard facts. He'd not patronize her because of her present condition.

"From what I understand, aside from your two adult daughters, you have a girl of fifteen, one of fourteen, and then Patrick, of course, who is ten."

"That is correct, sir."

"May I be brutally frank?"

"By all means."

"I do not pretend to know your finances, but I would surmise, since you're not in good health, these are difficult times for you." At Sinead's bare nod, Thomas proceeded. "Then think, madame, of what forty pounds a year would do. Fifty. I am sure Lord Alberdsley would be happy to raise the amount."

"And in return I lose my son."

"You don't lose him. England isn't that far away. You'll see him from time to time and—"

"I'll lose him," came Sinead's anguished cry. "He'll turn into a bloody Englishman."

Thomas could almost smile at the unexpected use of such a forbidden word coming from a lady—and Sinead O'Fallon was a lady, despite her poverty. "I assure you, Patrick will never forget his Irish heritage. Take my word—Lord Alberdsley is a reasonable man with great sensitivity. He'll not turn Patrick into an Englishman, not ever. To make doubly sure, I would make him aware of your feelings."

"Would you?"

Sinead sat thinking so long that Evleen, who had been listening with obvious growing concern, now spoke up. "Mama, you're not seriously entertaining the thought of relenting, are you?"

"I'm old and I'm sick," Sinead answered. "Until this moment I never considered letting Patrick go, but the future of all you children is at stake. Lord Thomas has helped me see that perhaps, considering the wretched state of my health . . . I hate even to think it, but perhaps sending Patrick to England would be the right choice after all."

Evleen was flabbergasted. "You're not thinking of going to England?"

"Of course not. I shall never leave Ireland." In deep thought, Sinead bit her lip and pondered. "Evleen, would you go with Patrick if I asked you to?"

Before Evleen could answer, Darragh, her face reddening, spoke up. "Why does it have to be Evleen? I'll go, Mama. I would love to go."

"Be quiet, Darragh," Sinead commanded. "Well, Evleen?"

Thomas watched as Evleen's heavy lashes flew up in surprise, followed by a mixture of confusion, bewilderment, and downright astonishment spreading across her face. "I can't believe this, Mama. That you would even consider—"

"Would you go, daughter?"

"Ireland is my home," Evleen declared. She flashed a glance at Thomas that well displayed her indignation.

"Mama, I would gladly go," cried Darragh. "*She* doesn't care, but I do. I—"

"Silence," Sinead declared, her voice stronger than Thomas had yet heard tonight. "I'll not hear one more word." Pushing with both palms flat on the table, she shakily arose. "Help me to my bed, girls. Good night, Lord Thomas. You must stay the night. The girls will make a bed for you by the fire. Meantime, I shall think on Lord Alberdsley's proposal and give you my answer in the morning."

Thomas couldn't sleep. In his makeshift bed in front of the fireplace, he thrashed about this way and that, his mind in a scramble. *What have I done?* he wondered. His arrival had created a turmoil that would affect the O'Fallons for the rest of their lives, no matter what Sinead's decision might be. If she said yes, Patrick would be given a chance at a privileged life, but the family would be torn apart. If she said no, who knew what bitter recriminations might emerge in the future? Darragh's feelings already were obvious. But might not Patrick someday resent his mother's denial of his inheritance?

And then there was Evleen . . .

Earlier, when he arrived, he had to catch his breath when the door swung open and he saw her standing there, a surprised light vivid in her sapphire blue eyes, her hair hanging loose and like a wavy cloud around her delicate face. For a moment he allowed his gaze to drop to her tiny waist and those enticing rounded curves he'd been seeing in his dreams ever since he first laid eyes on her. He was loathe to admit it, but Evleen O'Fallon disturbed him in every way. Her slim, wild beauty haunted his thoughts, yet he must be sensible. Sinead would reject Lord Alberdsley's request, he was sure of it. But what if she said yes? And further, what if she decided Evleen should accompany Patrick to England? That would mean . . .

Good God. The journey back to England would take at least a week. He was faced with being in close proximity to a woman who'd dwelled in his thoughts since the moment they had met. Driving a drafty carriage across Ireland . . . sailing across the Irish Sea in a flimsy ship . . . they would be thrown so closely together he would be hard put to keep his hands off her. He must not touch her, of course. Judging from those gritty looks she'd given him, she was in no mood to be civil to him, let alone entertain any modicum of friendship, let alone affection.

I would be better off with Darragh, Thomas thought grimly. The younger sister's whiny attitude was so off putting, he would have no trouble keeping his distance.

An errant flame sparked in the fireplace, then died down until the snug room was wrapped in complete darkness. Thomas inhaled a sweet whiff of peat. *How different from home,* he thought, where his valet would have laid out his nightclothes, turned down his bed, and warmed his sheets with a warming pan if the air held the least chill. Strange, but despite the humbleness of this cottage, he felt just as comfortable and at ease as he had ever felt in his own bedchamber at Northfield Hall. The O'Fallons had made him feel at home.

He wished he could fall asleep. Why was he still wide awake? He thought of Evleen. She must be in her bed by now, only a few feet from where he lay, those long, lithe thighs, that full, curved bosom all tucked snug, warm, and beguiling beneath the covers. And her shiny raven hair spread over her pillow. She was probably asleep already . . .

Which, dammit, I am not.

Wide awake, Thomas thrashed about in his makeshift bed, rearranging covers that needed no rearranging. He'd be lucky if he got but a jot of sleep before morning.

The sun had not yet risen when Evleen, hearing her mother's faint call, threw a shawl around her voluminous white nightgown and went to her mother's bedchamber. "You're awake early, Mama," she said as she sank to a chair by the bed.

Sinead sat straight in her bed, fully awake. "I've hardly slept. I lay here thinking most of the night, and then I went to speak to Patrick."

"Have you decided?"

Darragh entered, shivering in her nightgown. "Yes, Mama, tell us. I'm dying to hear."

"Go build up the fire and heat the porridge, girls. Wake Lord Thomas, if he isn't already awake. Wake Sorcha and Mary. Patrick's already awake. When we're all at breakfast, I shall tell you my decision."

At the table, Evleen found herself holding her breath as they all sat waiting for Sinead to speak. Patrick had a strange look on his face. Sorcha and Mary did not appear concerned, but then, Evleen concluded, they hardly knew what was going on. Not so Darragh, who sat with eyes alert, so eager to hear her mother's decision she could hardly contain herself. And Lord Thomas . . .

He was up and dressed already when they came to rekindle the fire. Now he sat, seemingly at ease, yet Evleen perceived a certain tautness of his body and an alertness in his eyes.

Somehow Sinead had found the strength to drag herself to the table again. Although she looked as pale and wan as ever, she sat straight, a look of serenity upon her face as if her decision, whatever it was, had given her great peace of mind. She was about to speak. *Please, Mama, let Patrick stay*, Evleen pleaded silently. *Let me stay, too, because you need me.*

Sinead addressed Lord Thomas. "I have a question for you, sir, but first—" she looked at Patrick—"tell Lord Thomas your feelings about becoming an Englishman."

Patrick stood, squared his shoulders, and fervently declared, "Even though my father was English, I shall never be an Englishman."

"Tell Lord Thomas who you are, son."

Patrick proudly lifted his chin. "I am Patrick O'Fallon, son of Sinead Coneeley O'Fallon, daughter of James Coneeley, Duke of Dormonde, whose roots can be traced back to Macha Mong Ruad, the red-haired queen who reigned over the land nearly three hundred years before Christ."

Sinead nodded her approval. "That's enough, Patrick. I do believe Lord Thomas can see what your background is. Now tell us what you know of the part England has played in Irish history."

Without hesitation, Patrick continued, "After King James

the Second landed in Ireland, to try to regain Britain from William and Mary, he was defeated at the River Boyne. Then the Irish who had not rallied to his cause, both Catholic and Protestants, were punished severely."

"By measures from which we suffer to this very day," Sinead interjected with a meaningful glance at her visitor. "And that, Patrick, is one of a plethora of reasons why we do not like the English, is that not correct?"

The boy nodded enthusiastically. "Indeed it is, Mama."

Sinead turned to Lord Thomas. "There you have it, sir. Does it appear to you the boy would, under any circumstances, ever forget his Irish heritage?"

"No, it would not appear so," he replied. Evleen noted that if he was the least perturbed by Patrick's words, he showed no sign of it.

Sinead smiled faintly. "I know what you think of us in England. The Irish are sinners, you say, and that's true enough, but we're much more. We are a mix of sinners, saints, gamblers, gentry, peasants, priests, rebels, heroes, and villains, but we're all Irish, and proud natives of this emerald isle. Lord Thomas, I must make it plain to you that Patrick is Irish through and through. If he lives to be a hundred, he will never be an Englishman."

Lord Thomas nodded solemnly. "I cannot argue."

Sinead continued, "Then my question is, do you honestly believe Lord Alberdsley would want a grandson who is so thoroughly Irish? Who could never be molded into an Englishman, no matter what measures Lord Alberdsley employed?"

Lord Thomas took his time in answering, seeming to mull his answer carefully. Finally he said, "You understand I cannot speak for Lord Alberdsley."

"I am aware of that."

"I can only tell you what I think Lord Alberdsley would say, an assumption I would never dare make if it weren't that he sent me here to represent him."

"Understood."

"Then it's my strong belief Lord Alberdsley would say Patrick will do very well in England." Lord Thomas smiled at Patrick. "Your grandfather is old now, and somewhat feeble, but all his life he has been a man of strong character who

believes a man must have a purpose to his life. He would ap-
plaud your Irish independence. To his mind, a tenacious belief
in oneself and one's principles is a virtue. Never would he try,
as your mother puts it, to mold you into something you are
not."

Lord Thomas paused to reflect, then said to Sinead, "Patrick
is the heir to a vast estate. As such, his grandfather will be more
busy instilling in him the virtues of honor and hard work, rather
than the rather dubious advantages of being an Englishman. I
cannot imagine any circumstance in which Lord Alberdsley
would allow his grandson to dissipate his time, wealth, and
health, as I regret to say, many of my fellow Englishmen do."

"Well said, sir," answered Sinead. Evleen thought so, too.
Their visitor had been forthright, and she admired that quality
in a man. She suspected Lord Alberdsley's lofty virtues might
be Lord Thomas's virtues, too.

"If Patrick should go to England, I have one condition," said
Sinead.

"Which is?"

"That if, after a reasonable length of time, he's not happy in
England, he may return to Ireland, no recriminations, and his
return passage paid."

"I am sure I speak for Lord Alberdsley when I say he'll happily agree to those terms."

"It's settled, then." Sinead looked around the table. "Patrick
shall go to England," she announced in a voice that brooked no
further argument.

"No, Mama you cannot," cried Evleen, feeling her throat
close up.

"No," cried her sisters.

Sinead firmly set her jaw. "It's for the best."

Looking cool and detached as ever, Lord Thomas spoke up.
"Will you come also, madame?"

"Did I not make it clear I would never leave Ireland?"
Sinead turned a piercing gaze on Evleen. "My eldest daughter
shall accompany Patrick to England and stay as long as she
likes." She looked to Thomas. "As with Patrick, if she decides
she doesn't like it there, will Lord Alberdsley pay her passage
back?"

"I guarantee it."

Despite her own shock, Evleen's attention was diverted by Darragh's wail, which doubtless could be heard clear to Dublin and beyond.

"No, Mama. How could you send Evleen when she doesn't want to go and I do? How could you—?"

"That's enough, Darragh," Mama sternly interrupted. "Evleen is the eldest, and therefore the most entitled to go. She deserves to travel, see a bit of the world. Besides, I need you here, not only to take care of Sorcha and Mary, but, quite frankly, me."

Evleen felt like crying out her protest, too, but if she did, she would sound as whiny as Darragh. In an agony of doubt, she shook her head. "You talk of my seeing a bit of the world, Mama, but I have no wish to. I have what I want right here. Let Darragh go."

"Yes, let me go." Darragh eagerly bobbed her head. "I would love to have a Season. I would love the clothes, the parties, the baubles. I would love to be a part of the Polite World. After all, isn't that where we belong? And besides, what of Timothy?"

Sinead had listened patiently. "We won't worry about Timothy. Besides"—a corner of her mouth lifted wryly—"Evleen has never appeared to be in any great rush to marry him."

Evleen could not help casting a quick glance at Lord Thomas, although why she should need to see his reaction, she wasn't sure. "Darragh has a point, Mama. Timothy will most certainly disapprove."

Sinead replied, "I am not the least concerned with what Timothy Murphy thinks, and I suspect that deep down, neither are you. I have made up my mind and you shall go. At least give it a chance. Then, if you really want to come home, you may do so. Meantime, if Timothy loves you, he'll gladly wait."

"It's not—" Evleen began, then stopped abruptly. The granite set of her mother's chin told her further argument was futile. She had been going to tell her mother it really wasn't Timothy who concerned her, that she wanted to remain at home because of Sinead's health. Besides, for some unfathomable reason, she felt uncomfortable discussing Timothy in front of Lord Thomas.

Sinead turned fond eyes to Patrick, who looked dazed by the

news. "Patrick and I have already talked. He agrees I've made the right decision."

"You had better talk to me, too, Mama." Evleen had to speak over a lump in her throat. She turned her eyes to Lord Thomas. "It appears your visit has changed our lives." She spoke the words flatly, yet the bitter accusation in her voice was unmistakable, and she made no attempt to hide it.

Lord Thomas was silent a moment. It was as if he was keenly aware of the roiling emotions he had caused and knew he must choose his next words with the utmost care. "I can make no apologies, Miss O'Fallon," he began softly. "I am only the messenger, don't forget. But need I point out that henceforth Lord Alberdsley will be furnishing your family fifty pounds a year? I am sure you will admit it's an amount that will provide your loved ones with a much more comfortable life. And need I point out that Patrick will soon be receiving every advantage a young boy could possibly receive? And you, too, actually."

"You need not point those things out, sir." Evleen stood, inwardly reeling from this shocking turn of events in her life. "When would we leave, Mama?"

"How much time do you need?"

"Enough to say good-bye to my friends . . . and Timothy."

"Day after tomorrow then? I shall immediately direct a letter to Lord Alberdsley, telling him you're coming."

"Fine," Sinead replied, finality in her voice. She slanted a glance at Evleen. "If it turns out Lord Alberdsley is an ogre, you are to bring Patrick home immediately, fifty pounds a year or no."

"Rest easy. Lord Alberdsley is no ogre," Thomas assured her. With a look of the utmost admiration, he continued, "You're a brave woman, Sinead O'Fallon."

She returned a small smile and remarked, "I trust you can stand one more night on that makeshift bed."

"I've slept on worse." He shrugged dismissively. "And so will Patrick and Miss Evleen, I fear. The journey to England won't be an easy one."

"I'm not worried about their journey," said Sinead. "It's what happens after they get there that causes me concern."

And well it might, Thomas thought but wisely didn't say.

*   *   *

It was morning and time to go. Outside the cottage, dressed in a coarse blue flannel gown covered by a yellow and pink shawl, Evleen took one last, lingering look at the far shining sea, the sparse, bent trees that stood on the cliffs below, and, closer, the cottage and its small walled garden. Her heart swelled with the pain of parting as she said, "Oh, Mama I shall miss you all so very much."

Sinead, supported by Darragh, gently pressed her palm to Evleen's cheek. "My prayers go with you."

"Mine, too," Darragh said sincerely. She could not contain herself and burst, "Mama, how could you just let her go off with that man?" She looked over at Lord Thomas, who was hitching the curricle. "Evleen should have a chaperone."

"Don't be silly, Darragh," Sinead replied. "Leave chaperones to those pampered English young ladies who must be treated like children. You should be grateful we don't live in such an artificial society. Besides, Lord Thomas is not a monster. Even if he were, Evleen is quite capable of taking care of herself."

"You realize I shall soon be living in your so-called artificial society," Evleen declared.

Darragh pounced on Evleen's words. "It will be the ruination of her, Mama. Evleen won't know how to handle herself amidst the *ton*. All those rules, those fancy manners. She won't have the least notion what to do."

"Ah, yes she will." Sinead regarded her eldest daughter with proud eyes. "I have every faith that wherever she goes, whatever she does, she'll remember the lessons I have taught her. She will at all times act courageously, and with fortitude. She will always see the best in people and ignore the worst. She will always do what she knows is virtuous and right. Those are rules that will keep her safe, not only in Ireland but wherever she goes."

"But what if my head is turned by the clothes, the jewels, the baubles?" asked Evleen, her lips twisting into a wry smile.

"To be sure, you will find yourself in difficult situations, my daughter, but I have no doubt you will stay the course, see it through. Just one thing more."

"And what might that be?"

"Never love an Englishman."

Evleen started to laugh. "You've said that before, I don't know how many times. If you're thinking of Lord Thomas—"

"As I have said, he appears to be a kind man, and I'm sure you'll travel in safe hands. Still, he's English and not to be trusted."

"You have my word."

"I had better have your word. Forget what I said before. I want you to enjoy your life in England. Go to the parties, the routs, the balls. Find a rich, titled Englishman and marry him."

Evleen stared at her mother, astounded. "Marry an Englishman? But you said—"

"I am only being practical," Sinead answered. "What I said was, never *love* an Englishman because if you do, he'll break your heart. But I never told you not to marry one, not so long as he can offer you wealth and a fine title."

"But this is so unlike you. I never thought I'd hear you say these things."

"I lay awake the night, reflecting," answered Sinead. "At dawn, it all came clear. My love of Ireland has clouded my thinking. Don't you see? Much as you don't want to face it, I shall be gone soon. The girls will marry and be gone, too. So what is there for you to come back to? Timothy Murphy and his fishing boats? No, Evleen. You, with your beauty, your warmth and wit and charm were made for better things."

"But Ireland is my home," cried Evleen. "I want to come back. I want—"

"Men will adore you in England." Sinead gripped her daughter's arms. "Listen to me. There's nothing for you here, child. Nothing except poverty and want and a marriage with a man you could never love. I know what's best for you, and I know you must make a fine marriage in England. Just don't do anything foolish. Always listen to your head, not your heart, and you'll do fine."

Still shaken from her mother's astonishing turnaround, Evleen asked, "What if I don't find a rich and titled Englishman?"

With an amused smile, Sinead answered, "You will. Promise me you will. Before I die, I want to know your future is secure. It's what I want for you more than anything else in this world."

A thousand objections crossed Evleen's mind, but one thing she knew—she could never deny her mother. "I . . . suppose. Yes, I promise I shall try."

Sinead shaded her eyes and looked down the road. "Ah, speaking of Timothy, here he comes to say good-bye."

In the lower corner of the garden, Timothy, resentful and confused, looked down on Evleen, his brows pulled together in an affronted frown. "I cannot see why you are doing this," he said.

"It's for Patrick," Evleen informed him for at least the third time. She felt terrible. Timothy had dressed in his Sunday finest to come and say good-bye. He looked his very best in his grey wool coat, linen shirt with the collar fastened by a black ribbon, and corduroy trousers with a bunch of ribbons floating at the knee. She wished with all her heart he would understand, but so far nothing she said seemed to penetrate. "I must go with Patrick. He's too young to go alone."

"Ah, Evleen, why must you go so far away?"

Why wouldn't he listen? "It's not so very far—only across the Irish Sea to Holyhead, then we take a coach to London, and then another to Hertfordshire, near Hatfield, to an estate called Aldershire Manor."

"Names I never heard of."

"But you will. I shall write as often as I can."

"But when shall we be married?"

She knew it was going to be hard, but with her future as uncertain as it was, she knew she must be truthful. "We are not betrothed, Timothy. It would be unfair of me to promise I'll marry you when the future is so unsure." She expected he'd be deeply hurt, but to her surprise, Timothy didn't appear wounded in the least. It was as if he hadn't heard her.

"I'm buying another fishing boat," he said, "and by the time you return I'll have built our new house."

"Didn't you hear me?"

Before Timothy could answer, Sinead called, "Evleen, are you ready?"

"In a moment, Mama." Evleen gazed up at Timothy and thought how strange it was that now she was leaving she felt fonder of him than she ever had before. And he *did* look handsome in his Sunday clothes. "I must go, Timothy. I pray you understand."

"Kiss me good-bye." As Timothy pulled her into his arms, she felt self-conscious. This was no time to be pulling back, but despite herself, she sneaked a glance to where Lord Thomas had been hitching the two bays to the curricle. *Good.* His back was practically to her, and he was examining the harness, not paying the least attention. Timothy's arms encircled her. She raised herself on tiptoe and brushed her lips across his.

"Sure and you can do better than that." He crushed her against him and brought his lips hard against hers. They swayed for a long moment. She felt a ringing in her head, until finally he let her go.

"Oh," she said, quite surprised. In the few times they'd kissed, he had never been this passionate.

Timothy stepped away and looked down on her, his honest face shadowed with concern. "You won't forget me now." He cast a resentful glance at Lord Thomas. "And promise you'll be careful of himself over there. I don't trust the man any farther than I could throw that fine carriage of his."

Evleen realized Timothy was bound to be jealous, and hastened to reassure him. "The only duty Lord Thomas has right now is to escort Patrick and me to England. I hardly know the man, but he seems dependable. Mama likes him, anyway. He mentioned he plans to breed thoroughbreds at his estate near Abingdon. I'm sure he'll leave for there immediately after we arrive at Lord Alberdsley's, so I doubt I shall ever see him again."

That said, Evleen could not prevent herself from sneaking another peek to where Lord Thomas was still busy checking the harness, oblivious to her and Timothy. *A good thing,* she thought. She would not have wanted Lord Thomas to witness hers and Timothy's parting kiss and close embrace.

Thomas had to grip the harness and look out at the sea an extra moment to steady himself. He was shocked at the roiling wave of pure jealousy that had surged through him when he observed Timothy Murphy slide his arms around Evleen O'Fallon. Never had he been a man to pry into the private affairs of others, yet, unable to prevent himself, he had surreptitiously watched as Timothy's hand intimately caressed the small of Evleen's fine, straight back as he pulled her closer, ever closer, then crushed his lips to hers.

He must be crazy, but the sight of that Irish oaf kissing Evleen had made him want to rush to the bottom of the garden and punch the fellow out. An absurd notion, of course. Timothy Murphy was not an oaf. He was a fine, upstanding, honest Irishman who would make Evleen a fine husband. *You had better remember that*, Thomas warned himself. If this surprising spurt of jealousy struck again, he must guard against acting the fool. In fact, he would have to exercise the utmost control if he was to accompany this tantalizing woman and her brother clear back to England and hang onto the cool detachment he had always maintained when dealing with women.

But I will, he vowed, despite hardly being able to keep his eyes off Evleen O'Fallon. *How ironic,* he mused, thinking of the many beauties of the *ton* who had thrown themselves at him to no avail. He could not have cared less, despite their elaborate coiffures and beautiful gowns. Now here was this Irish girl, her hair worn simply, dressed in a gown that was hardly the height of fashion. He felt a pang of concern, thinking how the women of Aldershire Manor would scoff at Evleen's coarse blue flannel gown and the yellow and pink shawl she had thrown over her shoulders with such artless grace. But what mattered fashion? What man would not be enchanted by her melodious Irish voice, the wealth of dark hair that swung with such allure about her slender shoulders, the knowing light that twinkled deep in those sapphire blue eyes? Yet, he must contain himself and never let his attraction show. For all her fire and beauty, Evleen O'Fallon could play no part in his future plans. If he married anyone, it would be Miss Bettina Trevlyn. Not now, of course, but some faraway day when and if he could get past the embroidery stitches. His father not only approved, he expected Thomas to marry her. Not that Thomas did not have a mind of his own, but he, too, recognized that Miss Evleen O'-Fallon was from a different world. Besides, she was betrothed to Timothy Murphy, was she not? Actually, despite the conversation at the table last night, he wasn't sure.

Darragh had come to stand beside him. He nodded to the couple still standing at the bottom of the garden and asked, "Are they betrothed?"

Darragh seemed to hesitate before she answered, "Indeed they are. Evleen is madly in love with him. They plan to marry as soon as she returns from England."

*   *   *

"Good-bye, Mama," said Evleen, trying unsuccessfully to hold back her tears. "I hate to go."

Tenderly Sinead gripped her arms. "Go to England. Keep an open mind. Yes, I hate the English, but I'm not so blind I cannot see how much more England has to offer than impoverished County Clare."

"But if you feel that way, why don't you come to England and bring my sisters, too?"

Sinead smiled sadly. "Your sisters and I belong here, but you, with your strength, your wit, and keen intellect, were meant for better things. In England you will flower. Embrace every bit of it—the poetry, music, books, art. The glittering social life, the brilliant people. Learn. Enjoy every minute of your life. Never feel guilt and never feel obligated. And most of all, make me proud, Evleen." She looked toward Lord Thomas. "He's not a bad sort."

Evleen shrugged. "I suppose."

"You'll be thrown together on this journey. I worry." Her brow furrowed. "Don't you be falling in love with Thomas Linberry."

"I?" Evleen asked skeptically, "fall in love with an Englishman?" She laughed derisively. "I grant you, he's handsome enough, and rather charming, but he's English after all, and I shall never forget what one Englishman did to you and all our family."

"Good, and if you find yourself attracted to him, remind yourself he possesses neither wealth nor significant title."

"But find an Englishman who does," Evleen replied warily. She still could hardly believe what her mother had told her a while ago.

"I meant what I said, Evleen."

Evleen's heart wrenched at the thought of leaving Ireland forever, yet if it was what Mama wanted . . .

"I shall try," Evleen said over a growing lump in her throat.

Sinead hugged her tight. "Don't be afraid. If worse comes to worse and all else fails, you can always come home and marry Timothy Murphy."

Chapter 8

L *oughrea . . . Ballinasloe . . . Athlone . . .*
The melodious names brought a flood of memories to
Evleen as she, Patrick, and Lord Thomas began their trek. It
had been nine years since she and her family had traveled
across Ireland along this very same Dublin-to-Galway Mail
Post Road. Not much had changed. The village names might be
as beautiful as ever, but the sad irony was, the countryside was
still barren, the mud huts along the wayside still among the
poorest she had ever seen. *I have changed though,* she thought
wistfully. When she'd left Dublin she'd been a girl of fifteen,
full of hope for the future despite the loss of her mother's fortune. But now . . .

A flash of wild grief ripped through her. To leave her mother
and sisters was bad enough, but Ireland, too. How she wanted
to cry, but she couldn't, not only because of Patrick, but she
would not give himself the satisfaction.

She flicked a glance toward Lord Thomas, having to admit
that since they'd been on the road this morning, he had been
courteous, kind, and most patient with Patrick, even when the
child asked a dozen questions all in a row.

"Lord Thomas, do we get the horses for free?" Patrick was
asking now. They were heading for Athlone, having just started
down the road again after a stop at a posting station for fresh
horses.

"No, we must pay for them," he answered, his eyes attentive
on the narrow, bumpy road ahead as he guided the two bays.
Noting the easy, self-confident way he handled the reins, she
had to admit he had a ruggedness and vital power about him,
and a toughness that could not have been gleaned from leading
a dandy's frivolous life in London. So far on this journey, he

had been rather distant, which was as it should be. She didn't
want to get too close. Still, she was curious about the man and
couldn't resist remarking, "You look as if you've spent much
time with horses."

He glanced to where she sat on the seat beside him. "I've
just returned from managing a sugar plantation in Jamaica for
three years. I practically lived on the back of a horse."

"How you must have missed the delights of London."

"Hardly." He gave her an odd glance, raising an eyebrow. "I
leave the delights of London to my brother."

Surprising. She wanted to ask more, but Patrick spoke up
again. When *would* he be quiet? "Lord Thomas, how much
does it cost for the horses?"

"One shilling sixpence a mile, paid for the horses, and sixpence to the postboy."

"Why didn't you hire a coach?"

"There's only the three of us. A curricle is sufficient."

Thomas was forced to veer to the side of the narrow road as
a coach and four came thundering by, the coachman, whip in
hand, riding high and haughty in the seat box atop.

"I think I should like to be a coachman when I grow up,"
Patrick announced. "I think it would be great fun. I'd feel like
the king of all I surveyed."

Evleen and Thomas exchanged amused glances. "That's an
admirable ambition, Patrick," Thomas said thoughtfully, "but
you had best wait to decide. You might find being a lord and
managing a vast estate will take much of your time."

"Will we get clear to Dublin today?"

"I think not," Thomas replied patiently. "Tonight we shall
stay at an inn in Athlone."

An inn. Evleen felt definitely uncomfortable at the thought.
In all the excitement and agony of parting, she had not given
any thought to the journey itself when she would be alone, except for her little brother, in the middle of nowhere with this
tough, attractive man and he . . . what? Timothy had warned
her about his intentions, but as far as she could tell, Lord
Thomas was treating her with politeness and that was all. *No
wonder,* she thought glumly. This man comes from a world
where women adorn themselves in satins, silks, and laces;
where they have lady's maids to coif their hair and iron their

gowns; where they would consider themselves disgraced if ever they had to lift a finger to do for themselves. *What must he think of me?* Evleen uncurled her strong, slim fingers and surreptitiously examined her hands. True, they were tidy and neatly kempt, yet they didn't have the pampered softness of a lady's hands. *Tending the garden most definitely did not help,* she thought, bemused, *nor did cooking or scrubbing the floors.*

No wonder Lord Thomas was being only merely polite. He must think of her, if he thought of her at all, as just another poor Irish peasant, so totally beyond the realm of his privileged world that he hardly recognized her as a genuine human being. Doubtless he was counting the hours until this onerous favor he was doing for his father's friend was completed and he could get back to . . . his betrothed, perhaps? Or, like so many men, did he have an arrangement? Perhaps not, if he'd just returned from Jamaica. She smiled to herself, thinking how she would love to ask, *Oh, by the way, Lord Thomas, do you have a mistress?*

She caught herself, and wondered why on earth she was bothering to speculate upon the love life of an Englishman. *He can have a dozen mistresses—it's fine with me,* she thought, glaring at him. She caught herself again and silently laughed. If the man had seen the resentful glance she'd thrown him, he would not have the faintest idea what she was thinking.

Lord Thomas pointed to the south. "Patrick, there's an old monastic site not far from here called Clonmacnoise. It dates clear back to the sixth century."

"Can we see it?" asked Patrick, instantly alert.

Lord Thomas glanced at Evleen. "Shall we? It should not take long. We can take the Marconi Coach Road that passes close to Clonmacnoise. The boy would enjoy seeing the old ruins and so might you."

"Why, I . . ." Evleen hesitated and bit her lip. The idea of doing something pleasurable had not even occurred to her.

"Why not?" Thomas asked. "How long has it been since you did something purely for enjoyment?"

She replied flatly, "I haven't had time for enjoyment."

"That's evident, Miss O'Fallon," he said, gazing at her with his dark, probing eyes. "You've done nothing but work and worry about your mother these past few months, haven't you?"

"So what if I have?" She spoke defiantly, yet inwardly she was touched by his unexpected perceptiveness.

Thomas appeared to ignore her, and addressed Patrick. "I believe a bit of sight-seeing is in order, don't you agree?"

"Yes, sir." The boy added earnestly, "My sister used to laugh a lot, but she doesn't anymore."

"Well, then, we're off to Clonmacnoise." Lord Thomas gave a smart flick to the reins. "See just ahead? There's where we turn."

A short time later, Evleen stood with Patrick and Lord Thomas on the bank of the River Shannon, all taking in the breathtaking view of a green, quiet valley where stood the ancient stone tower and the ruins of the nine churches that made up the monastic site of Clonmacnoise. The site was overgrown and neglected, but beautiful, nonetheless.

"It's very old, isn't it?" asked Patrick.

"Founded by Saint Ciaran in 545 A.D.," Lord Thomas replied.

Evleen was surprised. "I would not have guessed you had an interest in ancient history."

"I once had a tutor who delighted in pounding ancient history into my skull." Thomas shaded his eyes and smiled as he took in the view. "Imagine, Patrick, a weary pilgrim in the year 800-something, walking across the Midland bogs to this mystic place. Or a merchant boating his way down the mighty River Shannon, bringing goods."

"I can see it," Patrick eagerly cried. He looked down upon the many ruins of old churches and the vast graveyard with its tall crosses exquisitely carved of stone. "Evleen, can I go explore? I want to see if I can climb inside that big tall tower."

"If you're careful—"

Patrick darted away before she finished. Evleen exchanged amused glances with Lord Thomas again, then both watched until the boy disappeared behind the ruins of an old church. In the silence Evleen became aware that except for an old caretaker in the distance, she and Lord Thomas were alone. An awkwardness came over her, she could not imagine why, for she was usually at ease with people. Not this man, though.

"Shall we stroll?" he asked with great politeness.

"I don't see why not," she cautiously replied. They made

their way down a gentle slope and for a while strolled upon the emerald green grass in comfortable silence amidst the stone crosses and clusters of ruined churches.

In the distance, Patrick reappeared. "I'm going to climb inside the tower now," he called, then disappeared again.

"What a fine lad," remarked Lord Thomas.

She asked, "Is he not driving you daft with his questions?"

"On the contrary. I greatly admire an inquiring mind. He'll do well in England, mark my words."

"Will he?" A flood of doubts coursed through her. Her mother's decision and their departure had all happened so fast that until this very moment she had hardly given a thought to exactly what the future held. "What kind of a family will we be living with?" she asked.

"You will find Lord Alberdsley most amiable and kind," Thomas responded.

"And the rest? You said there was a brother and his wife?"

"Yes, Lord Alberdsley's brother, Walter, his wife, and their three daughters." They came to the arched entryway of an old stone church. "Shall we go inside?"

Evleen started through the entrance, then stopped in her tracks, jolted by a startling realization and quickly turned to face him. "They were not aware of Patrick's existence, were they?"

"No, they were not."

"So the brother presumed he was the heir?"

Thomas stopped, too, and turned to face her, nodding reluctantly. "'Presumed' is correct. Up to now he's been the heir presumptive, not the heir apparent."

Suddenly, she understood. "Be that as it may, can you honestly say that Patrick will be welcomed with open arms by the brother and his family?"

Thomas exhaled, then shut his eyes a fraction of a moment before he replied, "I don't suppose he will. Naturally, Walter and his family will not be particularly pleased when they find out about Patrick."

She was horrified. "You mean they still don't know?"

"If they don't, they soon will."

This is getting worse and worse, thought Evleen, her spirits plunging. Bad enough Patrick had been wrested from the only

home he had ever known, but worse, he was bound to meet
with hostility at this utterly foreign place where he was going
to live. *And what of me?* she wondered. How would the women
of the family deal with a strange young woman from one of the
poorest counties in all Ireland? "Tell me about the family."

Although Lord Thomas was obviously striving to appear unconcerned, she perceived the gleam of solicitude that had
flashed in his eyes. "The daughters are of a marriageable age,"
he began, and went on to describe how Mrs. Trevlyn was a
"forceful individual albeit truly a grand lady," how Charlotte,
the eldest daughter, was "indeed a great beauty, both refined
and delicate," how Bettina, the middle daughter, excelled in
embroidery, and how Amanda, the youngest, was "rather on the
shy side but extremely well-mannered." Having said all that, he
added, "I shall be blunt. Neither you nor Patrick are likely to be
welcomed with open arms." He looked down at her, his dark
eyes keenly assessing, yet admiring, too. "But doesn't the
blood of Irish kings run through your veins, Miss O'Fallon? If
there's anyone who can handle them, it's you."

Although she had mixed feelings, her spirits lifted at his reassuring words. She was beginning to realize he was not just
another dissolute Englishman. In fact . . .

As they stood close in the archway of the ancient stone
church, the midday sun shining down upon them, a bird swoop-
ing low overhead, she found herself intensely conscious of how
drawn she felt toward Thomas Linberry, and how keenly she
was aware that this was a man to be reckoned with, who, if she
judged correctly, possessed a fierce virility but thinly veiled.
Lord Thomas most certainly had no place in her future plans,
though. She would be a fool if she allowed herself to be attracted to him. *He thought of her as strong? Well, strong she
would be.* She tilted her chin and said, "How right you are
about my Irish blood. No matter what, I'll not let them plague
me."

He smiled and was about to speak when the wizened old
caretaker they had seen in the distance came limping around
the corner of the church. "Ah, I see 'tis visitors we have," he
said in his thick brogue. " 'Tis not many who make their way
to Clonmacnoise."

"It's most beautiful," said Evleen.

"Ay, beautiful it is. Do ye know where ye be standing?" When both Evleen and Thomas shook their heads, he continued, "Ye be standin' by the cathedral, largest of the churches, built in 909. This be the north doorway, carved in limestone. They call it the Whispering Arch. Courtin' couples 'ave been comin' 'ere for centuries. They stand, one on each side, whisperin' their words of love to one another."

"We're not courting, I'm afraid," said Evleen.

"Ye must be cousins then, or mayhap brother and sister."

When Thomas told him no, the old man cocked his head and regarded them appraisingly. "Well, from the looks of ye, ye should be courtin'," he announced abruptly, then hobbled away.

When he was gone, Evleen and Thomas broke into laughter, but it was not an easy laughter and was soon stilled. "What a funny little man," said Evleen. She felt self-conscious and had groped for something to say.

"Very," Thomas echoed. He seemed perfectly at ease, and yet some strange force seemed to be preventing him from moving from the spot, just as it was preventing her from moving, too. As they stood staring deep into each other's eyes, a current of something intense flared between them. Evleen quickly looked away. Her pulse was racing, and she felt dizzy. This man had just made her senses spin. He also was affected, she could see. She could tell from the sudden tenseness of his shoulders and the way he'd pulled in his breath just now that he had also felt this . . . this . . . what? *Deep attraction,* she supposed. *Yes.* Foolish, impossible though it was, that look they had just exchanged had been full of unspoken desire. She had felt a vibrant excitement that made her forget herself for one tiny moment and want very much to fling herself wantonly into his arms.

"Lord Thomas, Evleen! I climbed inside the tower. Come see."

Patrick again. What a welcome interruption. "Did you now, Patrick?" she called, collecting herself posthaste. The look she cast Lord Thomas was as cool and indifferent as she could make it. "Would you care to go see the tower, sir?"

"Indeed," he answered, bowing slightly, equally composed. "I cannot get enough of ancient monasteries."

Disgusted with himself, Thomas could hardly believe what

he had almost done. Despite his stern resolve, during that dizzying moment with Evleen at the Whispering Arch, he had been sorely tempted. The woman was betrothed, spoken for. Honor alone would prevent him from touching her, yet he had let his guard down enough that he'd come close to pulling her soft, tempting body tight against him and crushing her soft, rosebud lips with his own. And then . . .

A quiver surged through his veins, but he commanded himself to ignore it. He must stop all thought of her except as her escort to England. Had he gone mad? What was the matter with him? Not only was Evleen betrothed, but eventually he, himself, would be committed to Miss Bettina Trevlyn, who was far better suited to him than this bold-spirited Irish girl.

"Shall we go find Patrick?" she asked.

"Indeed, time is flying," he answered, forcing himself to sound brusque. From now on, he must not dare allow himself to become too friendly again, or he would . . .

Would what? Flout society's rules? Thomas laughed to himself. If that were the case, he would have done far more than kiss Miss Evleen O'Fallon there, under the old man's Whispering Arch. *God, what a tempting woman.* If he'd had his way, society's rules would have been more than flouted, they would have been ground into dust, much like some of the ruins of Clonmacnoise. He spotted Patrick. "Ah, there he is, Miss O'-Fallon," he remarked, noting with satisfaction how cool he sounded, how very aloof.

And he would remain aloof from now on. Evleen had enough on her hands right now. Their recent conversation concerning Walter and his family had reminded Thomas of the inevitable problems that lay ahead. He wondered if Lord Alberdsley had informed Walter he was not the heir presumptive anymore. A black premonition of impending trouble came over Thomas as he realized Walter might go quietly, but most assuredly not greedy Lydia and her three daughters.

Surprised, yet not overly upset, Walter Alberdsley stepped from the mahogany paneled library of Aldershire Manor, where his brother had just delivered the supposedly ghastly news. "I know this comes as quite a blow," Charles had compassionately added at the end, "but I could wait no longer. I have just received word from Lord Thomas that he, Patrick, and his half sister, Evleen, will be arriving any day now."

Walter knew he was supposed to be stunned, devastated, and outraged. Instead, more than anything else he felt a vast sense of relief that he would not be compelled to become the sixth Earl of Alberdsley. He had never fancied being addressed as "His Lordship," with people bowing and scraping to him as if he had just descended from Heaven and was a touch above the rest. He was comfortable as he was, and most certainly did not need a vast fortune when he already had his books, his bird-watching expeditions to the woods, his sketch pad and paints. What more could he ask for? After all, he'd had no expectation of inheritance during Randall's lifetime. Then, as now, his life was happy and complete, except . . . *oh, Lord, Lydia.*

Oh dear, oh dear, oh dear.

He pictured the look on his wife's face when informed her dream of ruling over Aldershire Manor as "Her Ladyship" would never be fulfilled. Now she would never assume the title she coveted, which was very bad news indeed. Over the years, how many times had he heard Lydia lament her lack of a title? If she told him once, she told him a thousand times the dreaded day was coming when the husband of her arch rival, Mrs. Drummond-Burrell, would inherit his mother's title. When he did, Mrs. Drummond-Burrel, esteemed patroness of Almack's, would become Lady Willoughby de Eresby. Who knew when this woeful event would actually occur? All he knew was that when it did, if Lydia was still plain Mrs. Trevlyn, her life would be ruined. Never could she hold her head up or appear in polite society ever again. Not that she wished Walter's dear brother ill, of course, but after all, he was quite old, and getting feeble, and how much longer must she wait to be called "Her Lady-ship," a title she justly deserved?

And then there were the girls . . .

Oh dear, oh dear, oh dear.

The more Walter thought, the more he realized this whole affair was nothing but trouble no matter how he looked at it. Lydia would doubtless have a fit when she found out. Daughters, too. Although . . . *Good grief.* How could he marry them off now? It had been bad enough before, despite the large dowries.

The butler encountered him in the hallway. "Dinner is served, sir. The family is waiting."

The remains of Walter's brief spell of euphoria fast disappeared. He heaved a sigh and heartily wished he could just go to his rooms and read Euclid. But no, he must face his family and give them the devastating news. Truth be told, he would rather face Napoleon's army than dinner tonight.

"Is something the matter, Walter?" asked Lydia when he entered the dining room. She and the girls were already seated at the dining table, engaged, as usual, in their lively discussion of suitors and the coming London Season, which they were about to attend.

Lydia asked, "Lord Alberdsley is dining in his bedchamber this evening?"

"As usual." Walter seated himself at the head of the table, a habit Lydia insisted he pursue since his brother seldom came down to the dining room anymore.

"Cook has fixed Westphalian ham tonight, Walter, your favorite as I recall." Lydia frowned and peered closer. "Are you all right? You look . . . strange."

He smiled, discovering that despite his kindly nature there existed a tiny part of him that anticipated with keen delight the horrified expression that would soon occupy his ambitious wife's face. *Must be the devil.* He should be ashamed of himself, but he would save his remorse until later.

"I have something to tell you, m'dear. Something you won't like."

He proceeded to relate the news, noting as he talked his wife's slow change of expression from mere interest, to incredulity, to now, as he finished, pure horror. He ended his discourse saying, "So there you have it. Nothing to be done, I'm afraid," and sat back in his chair.

There was a moment of stunned silence. They all sat round-eyed, forks suspended in midair. Charlotte was the first to recover. "You cannot mean this, Papa."

"You heard correctly. I shall not be the sixth Earl of Alberdsley after all. Much as you may dislike the idea, Randall's son is next in line."

Until now, Lydia had resembled a sleeping volcano, quiet but gathering steam. Now, much as he anticipated, she erupted.

"Do you mean to tell me some scrawny little whey-faced urchin from Ireland is to inherit Charles's estate?"

Walter shrugged. "It would appear so."

She glared at him, transmitting a mixture of incredulity, rage, and stupefaction. "Well, don't just sit there. Do something."

He felt a nudge of guilt because that tiny part of him that was enjoying this debacle refused to be squelched. He shrugged again, fully aware his seeming indifference would drive her mad. "Not much I can do."

"But what of us?" she asked, gesturing dramatically around the table. "Are we to be thrown out into the cold and snow?"

The devil got the better of him again. With great deliberation he peered toward the window. "I do believe spring has arrived. I don't recall it snowed once this past month. Now, last month—"

"Oh . . . oh." Lydia's little pursed mouth kept opening and closing, but nothing came out.

At last, feeling a modicum of guilt, Walter hastened to say, "Charles won't throw us out. We are welcome to stay as long as we like, although of course after his demise, I cannot speak for what the new heir might do. But do remember, Lydia, I do have an income of my own. Small it might be, but enough to sustain us, although not anywhere near"—his gaze swept around the luxurious dining room—"this grand a fashion."

She glowered at him. "Don't even bother to mention that paltry sum."

Oh, dear. He glanced at each of his stunned daughters and remarked, "Also, Charles has assured me those generous dowries will remain the same." He could not resist adding—the devil again—"*If* the need ever arises, which it has not thus far."

Lydia rose to the bait. "You know full well the girls have so many proposals they don't know what to do with them."

"Oh, do they now?" He ventured a slight raise of one eyebrow.

Lydia turned beet red. "This is not to be borne. If you think for one minute I'll give up my rights to this house for one of Randall's by-blows, you are much mistaken."

"Not a by-blow, madam. He and Patrick's mother were legally married."

"Oh, Mama," Charlotte suddenly wailed, "I wanted to be called Lady Charlotte and now I cannot."

"And I wanted to be the daughter of an earl," cried Bettina.

"But we still have one another," Amanda near whispered, but no one except her father heard.

"Oh, one more thing," said Walter, acting as if he'd forgotten, but really he hadn't. Knowing how this next would be received, he had wanted to delay the revelation of the additional outrage as long as possible.

Lydia regarded him with eyes that gleamed like glassy volcanic rock. "And what might one more thing be, Walter?"

"The boy is not coming alone."

There was a chorus of *"What?"*

"My brother has informed me the young lad will be accompanied by his half sister. I believe her name is Evleen."

Another shocked silence. *Oh dear, oh dear.*

"Irish trash in *this* house?" asked Lydia in a voice like ice.

"Er . . . the boy is only ten. He needed—"

"The Irish are low and common," said Lydia, "no better than savages, the lot of them."

"I have heard they live in mud huts and eat dirt," Charlotte contributed.

Bettina giggled. "Then it won't cost much to feed them, will it?"

Charlotte grimly smiled. "Perhaps we can clean her up and make a servant of her."

Lydia spoke again. "This Evleen . . . Walter, does she even speak English?"

"Er . . . I'm not sure. Charles did mention, however, that her family on her father's side is descended directly from the kings of Ireland. Her mother is descended from royalty, too."

Lydia sneered. "Who gives a fig for Irish royalty?"

"Oh, I know," proclaimed Bettina with another giggle. "We shall call her the Irish princess."

"Quiet, all of you," commanded Lydia. "This is no time for frivolity, Bettina. Walter, you must do something."

"But—"

"I mean it. I'll not have this. There's nothing you can do at the moment, but after Patrick arrives, we shall wait and we shall see. And as for the half sister . . ." Lydia's small eyes squinted in concentration. "How old did you say she is?"

"I didn't say. She's a grown woman, apparently."

"Grown, eh? Well, mark my words, I shall not be outdone by the likes of some greedy, grasping little peasant from Ireland."

"On the contrary, Charles told me Lord Thomas spoke quite highly of her."

"She'll be after Thomas if she isn't already."

"Perhaps even Montague," Charlotte chimed in alarm.

Walter threw up his hands. "Please, ladies. You must not pass judgment on someone you haven't even met."

"I don't have to meet her to know what's going on," said Lydia, glowering. "At this very moment she's no doubt sashaying herself across Ireland, throwing herself at Thomas's head, having herself a marvelous time thinking of the fortune she's about to get her claws into." Lydia's expression grew hard and resentful. "We'll not have it, will we, girls? Irish princess, indeed."

Chapter 9

O n the rolling deck of the *Countess of Liverpool,* Evleen leaned over the bulwark and heaved again. Never in all her life had she been so miserable.

"Are you all right?" Patrick asked. He stood beside her, red hair whipping wildly in the northern gale, his face pinched with concern. Through some miracle, he remained unaffected by the rolling and tossing of the ship, as did Lord Thomas. She was far from being the only pitiful soul hanging over the side, though. Many of the other passengers were suffering the same as she.

The bow dipped into a deep trough formed by the churning waves and abruptly rose again, leaving her stomach behind. "Ah, Patrick," she moaned, "if the sea should open up and swallow me, I wouldn't mind."

Patrick patted her arm. "But you were feeling so fine."

"That was an hour ago," she gasped, "in Ringsend, before we sailed." Another attack of nausea struck her. She bent nearly double over the bulwark, stomach wrenching as she heartily wished she were dead. Up to now, she had, to her surprise, enjoyed the journey immensely. Last night they had stayed at the Raven Inn at Athlone, which she'd found to be much more comfortable than expected. The rooms were clean, and the food! Oh, she shouldn't think of food at a time like this, but she remembered how she and Patrick could hardly believe their eyes at sight of a table laden with boiled round of beef, roast loin of pork, peas, parsnips, a roast goose, a boiled leg of mutton, plum pudding, and more. She had been hard put to take dainty bites instead of stuffing her mouth. Patrick, though, had been unencumbered by concern about good manners and how it would look in front of Lord Thomas. He dug with gusto into all that delicious, unaccustomed food which now, just the thought of it was making her even sicker than she already was. Not long after dinner, while a fiddler played lively Irish tunes, Patrick had fallen asleep at the table and Lord Thomas was obliged to carry him to bed. Thus far, she reflected, Timothy had been mistaken about Lord Thomas. Up to now, he had been most solicitous and kind. And when he'd said good night at the door to her room after putting Patrick to bed, he had been gracious but remote. It was as if that enthralling exchange of glances at the Whispering Arch never happened. *And it probably didn't*, she mused darkly. It must have been all her imagination. How could she possibly think a man with as high a rank as Lord Thomas could have any personal interest in a poor Irish girl? Not that it mattered. She shivered in the cold, biting wind and drew her shawl closer about her. A wave of dizziness and nausea swept over her again. *Not that anything matters.*

Thomas arrived, having obtained a blanket from somewhere. "Here, let me wrap this around you," he said, and draped it around her shoulders. "Are you sure you don't want to go below?"

"Mercy, no." The very thought made her stomach heave again. "It's so dark and confined and suffocating down there. It's fresh air I'm wanting."

Patrick spoke up. "I guess the boat isn't so enjoyable after all, is it, Evleen?"

"No it is not," she gasped back, remembering—was it only a few hours ago?—how she had stood on the shore of the port of Ringsend and caught her first glimpse of the *Countess of Liverpool* rocking gently in the harbor. As she recalled, she had remarked how eager she was to set sail across the Irish Sea. At the time, it had seemed like great fun—an exciting adventure. Ha. Little had she known.

"What kind of boat is it?" Patrick had asked, equally excited and eager as he looked across the water toward the *Countess of Liverpool*.

"It's a mailboat, cutter rigged," Lord Thomas answered. "One hundred and five tons, a beam of nineteen feet or so, draught of ten feet six inches, mast of sixty-eight feet. Very strongly built."

"There's a comfort," she had lightly remarked, impressed by

Lord Thomas's broad knowledge of ships. *In fact, what didn't he know?*

He hadn't known she was going to get deathly sick on the Holyhead packet, she thought morosely as another wave of nausea hit her. How could anything be left? But, alas, there was. To her chagrin and utter humiliation, she realized Lord Thomas was holding her, gently rubbing her back as she hung over the side. She managed to say, "I feel so embarrassed I could die."

"But you won't," he replied, all matter-of-fact, as if he saw young ladies toss their breakfast every day.

"I . . ." A wave of dizziness overcame her. Little black dots started dancing before her eyes. She felt herself start to sink, but then a strong arm went around her from behind and with the other, he half lead, half supported her across the pitching, rolling deck.

"Patrick, get the blanket where it's dragging," she heard him say.

"What shall you do with her?" she heard her brother ask.

"Get her out of the wind. There's a sheltered spot on the poop deck aft, since she does not deign to go below."

She felt an urge to snap, *Of course I don't want to be in that awful, smelly hold,* but could not sum up enough energy even to open her eyes, let alone her mouth. Gradually, she felt warmer. There was no cutting wind anymore. When she finally raised her eyelids, she found he'd brought her to a sheltered part of the ship and set her upon a hollow coil of line. Not only was it holding her in place, it was much softer than the hardwood of the deck.

Thomas knelt in front of her, still half holding her in his arms. "Feeling better?" he asked, then glanced up at Patrick, who looked deeply concerned. "Run get some water, lad. And stop worrying, your sister will be fine."

"Will I?" she weakly asked.

"You've had a bad case of the seasickness, but of course you'll survive."

"I'm not sure I want to," she said, managing a very small smile.

She struggled to stand, but he held her fast. "Don't try it."

"I don't want to trouble you."

"You're no trouble." He smiled. "This way I can hold you in my arms and everyone will think I am but a good Samaritan."

She managed to gasp, "What other reason might you have?"

He gripped her tighter and brought his face to within inches of hers. "You know very well the reason, Evleen O'Fallon."

Sick though she was, his meaning did not escape her. *He likes me,* she thought in great surprise. At another time she would have found his remark challenging, perhaps even thrilling, but she was too sick to care, too weak even to form an answer. Patrick returned with the water. With Thomas helping hold the tin cup steady, she drank her fill and asked, "How much longer?"

"Hard to say this time of year," Thomas answered. "In bad weather, with adverse winds, it could take up to thirty hours, but today I should wager we'll arrive at Holyhead in another ten."

When she groaned, he reluctantly added, "I should warn you, it could get worse."

"What do you mean, sir?" Patrick asked.

"Berthing at Holyhead's port is sometimes hazardous. Pray the tides are favorable or we might not be able to get ashore."

"Not land?" she cried. "But then what would we do?"

"Return to Ringsend, then be obliged to wait several days until the tides are right."

The thought of sailing back to Ringsend over the storm-tossed Irish Sea was so horrifying, she could not find words. *Better I don't find the words,* she thought.

He gave her an encouraging smile. "But that's not likely to happen. You've been very brave. Persevere, for just a while longer. We'll be in Wales before you know it."

Although she took some comfort in his words, at that moment, more than anything on earth, she yearned to be back in the cozy cottage overlooking Galway Bay with her dear mother and Sorcha and Mary, and even prickly Darragh. Such was not to be, though, and she realized she must be brave for Patrick's sake.

And, oh, will we ever get there?

Finally, the miserable journey was over. They were not compelled to turn back at Holyhead and return to Ringsend after all.

Instead, they landed without incident, Evleen's health remarkably restored the moment her foot touched shore. Lord Thomas had been remarkably proficient at hiring a fine coach-and-four for their journey through the mountainous country from Holyhead to Shrewsbury. She worried at the start because the motion of the coach felt exactly like the *Countess of Liverpool* as the ship rocked and beat itself against the heavy sea. Evleen hadn't got sick again, though, and they'd moved along at a fine pace.

After a change of horses at Shrewsbury, Lord Thomas planned to continue on in the hired post-chaise. Patrick had a better idea, though. He had been watching when one of the crack "flying machines" came rolling grandly into the posting station, announced by the guard riding atop sounding his horn. Before the coach had even come to a full stop, the passenger sitting next to the coachman had unbuckled the ends of the leads and wheel reins. The coach still moving, the guard got down and ran forward to unhook the near leader's outside trace, and then draw the lead rein through the terrets or metal rings. Next, he changed the near horse and finished by running the near lead rein while the horsekeeper on the offside unhooked the remaining lead traces, uncoupled the wheel horses, and changed the offside horses.

"All done in but two minutes," Lord Thomas said with approval as the coachman finished changing the leaders.

Patrick had watched in awe. "Can't we ride in the mail coach, Lord Thomas?" he cried, round-eyed with excitement. "I'd like to sit next to the coachman and be the one to unbuckle the ends of the leads and the wheel reins."

Lord Thomas cast a fond glance at Patrick. Evleen could tell he had thoroughly enjoyed seeing the child so full of awe at the swift and exciting change of horses. There was nothing that exciting in County Clare, and, in fact, she, too, was fascinated by the clattering hooves, clanging of bugles, slamming of doors, and stamping of feet on splash boards, and through all this din the raucous voice of the ostler continually sounding, like the cry of a medieval herald with a cold in his nose.

Lord Thomas ruffled the boy's hair. "I know exactly what you mean, Patrick. I doubt there's a man among us, no matter what his rank, who wouldn't have a go at being a coachman."

"Really?" she asked. "I would have thought a nobleman such as you would be above such things."

" 'Noble' is a term I abhor," Thomas answered somewhat vehemently, to her surprise. "I am not noble; I am a second son. Even if I were the first son, I would never consider myself a cut above the rest simply because I owned a fancy title. Nor would I be wasting my life indulging in debauchery. I would never—" He seemed to catch himself, making her wonder if he was about to mention Patrick's father as a shining example of debauchery, but realizing the boy's presence, thought better of it. "Suffice to say, Miss O'Fallon, I live by my own rules, not society's. Long ago I stopped caring what other people think."

She answered a bland "Indeed," covering her sudden admiration. He seemed sincere. Could it be not all Englishmen were alike? She had never thought about it, but perhaps they weren't all scoundrels like Randall.

Thomas looked at her inquiringly. "Well? Shall we take the mail coach?"

"Why not? I'd like it, too."

The warmth of his smile echoed in his voice as he replied, "You're a woman after my own heart."

"Good show," cried Patrick, his eyes sparkling with excitement. Evleen gave Lord Thomas a grateful glance. *How kind and thoughtful of him.* Surely a man of his high station would not enjoy riding with the riffraff in a public coach, and yet, on second thought, she supposed he would. His eyes, too, had been full of excitement when he'd seen that flying machine.

Daventry . . . Dunstable . . . St. Albans . . . The trip was as thrilling as Patrick expected it would be. Evleen enjoyed every moment, despite being crammed in a coach with strangers. Also, like Patrick, she loved the grandeur and elegance of the inns where they stopped to eat, as well as the excitement of the stops at all the chief posting stations. And like Patrick, she openly expressed her enthusiasm at the sight of the splendid horses, as well as all the crack "flying machines" that came in many different shapes and sizes, their doors emblazoned with the names of the places where they started and the places they would end.

And always, she sensed Lord Thomas's attention upon her.

More than once, she caught him regarding her with warmth and amusement in his eyes.

"I suppose you don't think I'm being ladylike," she said once, when she and Patrick had exclaimed over the immense size of one coach's back and front springs.

"No, I don't think you're being ladylike," he answered equitably, "but that's a compliment. Some ladies I know are so stiff and proper they would not deign to show an interest in anything as lowly as carriage springs. That you do only shows what a bright young woman you are."

Despite herself, she found herself glowing from his praise. Most certainly, Lord Thomas wasn't so bad as Randall.

The exciting journey ended in London, where Lord Thomas stopped off at his family's town house long enough to appropriate the family coach and coachman. After a quick trip, they were about to arrive at Aldershire Manor.

At last she was going to meet the Trevlyns. Evleen felt vast relief mixed with trepidation as the coach-and-four turned into a long driveway and the stone turrets and grey stone walls of Aldershire Manor came into view.

"Look, Evleen," Patrick called, "have you ever seen such a big house in all your life?"

As the coach rolled to a stop, Evleen looked down at herself and bit her lip. How crumpled she looked. Early this morning she had washed and dressed, aware she must look her best, but after six days of traveling, even her Sunday gown looked downright dowdy. At least her straw bonnet hid her hair, which was, she had concluded, a hopeless mess. *Patrick also looks bad*, she thought as she examined the rumpled child. That morning in London she had made sure he dressed in his best jacket and trousers, but she suspected his appearance fell far short of the high standards of the Polite World.

As she brushed at her skirt, she realized to her disgust that her knees were shaking. "Look at us," she said to Lord Thomas. "Lord Alberdsley will take one look and send the two of us straight back to Ireland."

Lord Thomas laughed as he sprung from the carriage, then handed her down as if she were a queen. The moment their hands met, she felt a tingle, as she had every time they had accidentally touched since that moment on the boat that she could not stop thinking about. *You know very well the reason, Evleen O'Fallon.* What had he meant by that? And here she'd been so seasick she couldn't even ask, just moan and groan like a fool. But then, she reasoned, if she hadn't been seasick, he wouldn't have said what he said because his remark was doubtless out of pity and nothing more. And yet . . . there were those glances he kept giving her, as though he couldn't keep his eyes off her. *But on the other hand?*

She knew her reasoning had to be correct because ever since they had disembarked from the *Countess of Liverpool,* he'd not said another personal word and had, in fact, conducted himself with the utmost politeness, bordering on remote.

"You look fine, Miss O'Fallon," Lord Thomas said gravely. "I've no doubt Lord Alberdsley will be ecstatic to see you both and more than grateful you've come clear from Ireland."

"And looking like the Irish peasants we are," she glumly remarked.

"I do not want to hear you talk that way," he said, then added with a smile, "No matter what happens, don't ever forget you're descended from the kings of Ireland."

No matter what happens? What did he expect? She was about to ask what he meant by that, and also tell him the kings of Ireland were of no help to her now, when a white-haired old man with a cane hobbled onto the marble-columned portico. His eyes lighted up at his first glimpse of the young boy now springing down from the coach. "Patrick," he exclaimed in a voice filled with joy and wonderment. "I am Lord Alberdsley, your grandfather."

Without hesitation, Patrick stepped forward and held out his hand. "I am delighted to meet you, Grandfather."

The old man's eyes misted with joy. He seemed nearly overcome. "You look just like your father," he said, his voice choked with emotion.

"Did my father have red hair, too, sir?"

An expression of delight crossed Lord Alberdsley's face as he bent to hug the boy. "I suspect your red hair comes from your mother, Patrick, but you greatly resemble your father just the same." Over Patrick's head, he regarded Thomas. "Ah, my boy, how can I thank you? And you must be Evleen," he remarked, making her instantly feel welcome with his kind, warm eyes. "You are most welcome. From now on I shall consider you one of the family, as much as Patrick." He raised his arm in a broad gesture of welcome. "Come, the three of you, shall we go inside?"

Lord Thomas demurred, saying he was anxious to see his father.

"Of course, Thomas. Your father still suffers from the gout and will indeed be happy to see you. Also, Montague is home. I know you'll be anxious to see him, too. But come to dinner tonight, won't you? You, Penelope, and Montague." When Thomas nodded affirmatively, Lord Alberdsley placed an arm around Patrick's shoulders. "My brother and his family are out visiting this afternoon, but you'll meet them soon enough. Now come inside and I shall show you your new home."

"Evleen, I think I'm going to like it here," Patrick called over his shoulder as he was led away.

Lord Thomas spoke up. "Miss O'Fallon will be right along, sir. I want to tell her good-bye."

They were alone, still standing beside the coach. One of the horses pawed the ground and whinnied softly as Lord Thomas took both her hands in his and gazed down on her fondly. "So it's good-bye."

"But won't I see you at dinner tonight?"

"You will, but by then we'll be two different people." He smiled ruefully. "We shared the intimacy of a journey, you and I. God knows, it wasn't all fun, but still, we did what we pleased and had many a laugh, didn't we? But it's over now. Tonight we return to society's rules. I shall be Lord Thomas, all bows and elegant manners. You will be Miss O'Fallon, dipping curtseys and fluttering your fan."

"I don't own a fan," she said.

"Ah, but you will." He stepped closer and looked deep into her eyes. "I have never enjoyed a journey as much as this one."

"I, too . . . well, except for crossing the Irish Sea. That I could have done without."

"I thought you were magnificent. You never complained."

He stepped even closer, and there it was again, that mystic force between them that caused her heart to race. "I try never to complain," she said, shrugging and trying to look as if she didn't notice how close he was standing when all the time she felt overwhelmed by his presence and hardly knew where to look. He was right about the intimacy of their journey. They had formed a close bond, laughing together, sharing a parents' kind of joy over Patrick and his antics and bright remarks. They had shared the grueling voyage over the Irish Sea when Thomas had done all he could to ease her suffering, not too proud to hold her in his arms, comfort her, assure her she shouldn't be embarrassed. Now, a feeling of emptiness swept over her. In all the excitement she had not fully realized until this very moment that from now on their relationship could never be the same. Of course, it was obvious she would see him again, but how different would be the circumstances.

"I shall never forget your kindness to Patrick and me," she said.

A long silence followed. They seemed locked in each other's gaze. He looked as if he was about to speak, as if he was on the brink of saying forbidden things he shouldn't say. *That would be wrong, though. Anything between us would be wrong. Never love an Englishman.* That was her mother's good advice, which she most assuredly must heed. Breaking the spellbinding moment, Evleen stepped away. "I like Lord Alberdsley already," she said, striving to sound casual. "Now that we're here, I'm sure all will be well."

A shadow of doubt crossed his face before he said, "I hope it will." Fondly, he touched his finger to her cheek. "But be careful." One corner of his mouth quirked into a half smile. "Never forget you're descended from the kings of Ireland." Before she could answer, he pulled her close and kissed her, only a brief kiss, but it was full on her lips, then she heard the intake of his breath as he quickly thrust her away.

"Good-bye and good fortune," he called, then was in the coach, signaling to the coachman, and gone.

When Pierce, the dignified, white-haired butler, showed Evleen to her bedchamber, she was astounded at its size and opulence. Beside her, Patrick exclaimed, "All of this room just for the two of us?"

Pierce concealed a smile. "No, Master Patrick, this is Miss Evleen's. Your bedchamber is right next door."

Evleen could not believe it. After Pierce left, Patrick eagerly trailing behind, she wandered about the spacious bedchamber, admiring the plush Administer rug, the fine damask draperies. She flung herself with abandon on the high four-poster bed, first delighting over its luxurious softness, then feeling a touch of guilt, wondering how she could possibly be enjoying herself when her mother and the girls slept on straw mattresses. Still, she realized she may as well enjoy herself while she was here, for who knew what might happen? She might very well find herself back in County Clare.

A quick knock sounded on the door, followed by the entry of a pretty young woman in a maid's uniform. In a thick French accent she said, "I am Celeste, ma'am. Lord Alberdsley sent me to assist you in dressing for dinner tonight."

In confusion, Evleen sprung off the bed. Years ago in Dublin, her family had servants. Now, though, the idea of having a lady's maid to help her dress was so foreign she could hardly comprehend. "I . . . thank you, Celeste, but I can do for myself."

"Oh, no, miss." Celeste grew round-eyed. "Dinner at Aldershire Manor is always a very formal occasion. Mrs. Trevlyn insists. She would have my head if you were not properly attired." Celeste picked up Evleen's small portmanteau, set it on the bed, and opened it. "We shall see what you have brought to wear."

With a sinking feeling, Evleen replied, "Not much I'm afraid."

"*Mon dieu.* Is this the best you have?" Celeste pulled out Evleen's Sunday gown, a not-so-new bishop's blue calico, and held it high. Nose pinched with distaste, she regarded it as if it had just been used to clean the stalls.

Evleen tried to cover her embarrassment, but felt herself blush. "That is my very best."

"*Déplorable.*" Celeste paused, appearing to ponder. Her eyes lit. "You and Miss Charlotte are about the same size. She has a gown she never wears that I am sure would suit you. It is perfect for you."

"But do you think I should?"

"Miss Charlotte won't care."

"Are you sure?"

After a noticeable pause, Celeste replied, "I'm sure she

won't, and even if she does, I have strict orders from Lord Alberdsley to make you look your very best tonight."

Although Evleen was suspicious, she decided not to argue. If Charlotte resented her wearing the dress, then she would explain and apologize later, and surely Charlotte would understand. "All right, Celeste. Now what do you think my brother should wear?"

"We don't have to worry about clothes for Patrick. He will take his dinner in his bedchamber tonight, and every night."

"But we're accustomed to eating together."

"Never. The English say children should be seen and not heard, most especially at dinner."

Parents eat separate from their children? What a strange, heartless notion. Evleen remembered all those family dinners in County Clare when the air was filled with laughter and bright conversation with her lively little sisters and Patrick's incessant questions. She could not imagine eating separately.

Ah, well. She realized she must keep reminding herself she was in a different country now and should stay silent, going along with whatever were the customs. Still, what strange habits these English have!

"Magnifique," exclaimed Celeste when Evleen had finished dressing.

Evleen turned this way and that in front of the mirror, examining herself. She loved her new upswept coiffure, as well as the borrowed gown. "I like the dark orange color," she said as she admired the sleeves, covered with a network of satin, and the hem trimmed with white satin rouleau.

"Not orange, miss, *capucine.*"

"Whatever you call it, it's not bad."

Celeste brought clasped hands to her heart in admiration. "The color is perfection for your dark hair and fair skin."

Evleen agreed, although in modesty, didn't say. Actually, she was feeling better by the hour, for a myriad of reasons. Not only did she feel she looked her best, but her fears had mainly been allayed. Lord Alberdsley, whom she feared might be some sort of ogre, was most pleasant and kind. Patrick could not ask for a better grandfather. Also, Aldershire Manor was a beautiful mansion, not nearly so formidable as she had expected. She laughed to herself, remembering how her mother feared she

might be given a small, cold room in the attic, shared with a
scullery maid. Instead, here she was in this beautiful bedchamber, dressed in this beautiful dress after—miracle of mira-
cles!—she had luxuriated in a long, pleasurable bath. *Imagine!*
Maids scurrying up and down the back stairway, hauling buck-
ets of hot water, just so she could bathe. How wonderful it had
felt to scour herself all over and finally wash her hair, all with
a lady's maid to assist. It was a good thing Darragh couldn't see
her now, she would be green with envy. Leaning closer to the
looking glass, Evleen tweaked the tiny curls that Celeste had
arranged around her forehead. Never had she looked so elegant,
at least not since she was fifteen and they had lived in Dublin.
Now she felt more confident, sure that despite those veiled little warnings from Thomas and that funny hesitation of the
maid, she had nothing to fear.

*The grand, sweeping stairway is a perfect way to make an
entrance,* Evleen thought as she glided down the steps, head
held high. Over her protests, Celeste had insisted she carry a
white plumed fan, which she held regally high in one white-
gloved hand, the gloved fingers of her other lightly touching
the polished mahogany railing. *Except there's nobody to see
me,* she thought when she got to the bottom. *Where am I supposed to go?*

Pierce appeared and sensed her dilemma. "They are in the
drawing room. Follow me." He led her to a set of double doors,
partially open, and said, "Through there, Miss O'Fallon," then
withdrew.

She started to enter, eager to meet the whole family, then
heard voices, and stopped upon hearing her name.

"But it's *my* dress," wailed someone young and female, "not
that . . . whatever is the girl's name?"

"Evleen," said another voice, equally young and female. "I
hear from the servants she's quite beautiful." There was a giggle. "You'll have to watch she doesn't get her claws into Montague. Thomas, too, especially since he's just traveled clear
from Ireland with her."

"Over my dead body. I shall snatch my dress right off her
back."

"But Charlotte, you didn't even *like* the dress," said another female voice, a sweeter one this time. "You always said the color didn't suit you."

"I don't care about that. Celeste had no right to give it to her."

Saints preserve us. Evleen's spirits plunged like the bow of the *Countess of Liverpool* dipping into a trough. Suddenly, the gown she adored was now but a mere garment, and worse, a garment its owner did not even want her to have. She considered turning on her heel and retreating to her bedchamber, but only for a moment. Since when did a true daughter of Ireland let the English get the better of her? She was here, and here she would remain, for Patrick's sake, not her own, so she must at least attempt to make them like her. If they didn't, perhaps they could at least get along.

Evleen squared her shoulders, took a breath, and swept into the drawing room. The first person she saw was a man with thinnish hair, standing by the fireplace. Although he was elegantly dressed, his small frame, slumped shoulders, and pinched face were not impressive. He smiled when he saw her and said, "Ah, this must be Evleen. I am Lord Alberdsley's brother, Walter. Come in, meet my family."

"I would be delighted." Evleen forced a smile, keenly conscious of four pairs of female eyes sharply assessing her.

"My wife, Lydia," said Walter, nodding toward a thin woman seated grandly upon an Empire mahogany *fauteuil-de-bureau.* "These three young ladies are my daughters," he went on. "Charlotte"—he nodded toward a pretty blonde girl of twenty or so. "Bettina"—he indicated a round-faced young woman working on her embroidery. "And my youngest, Amanda."

Only Amanda, a plumpish girl with nondescript brown hair and the look of a frightened deer about her, returned Evleen's effort at a smile. "You are most welcome, Evleen. I—" She appeared about to continue, but suddenly wilted, as if she had caught a signal that she should shut her mouth.

"So," Lydia said loudly and sharply. "Won't you sit down, Miss O'Fallon?" Evleen did as requested, seating herself upon a striped green silk settee. "I hear you are from Ireland. Do tell us about yourself." It was not a request; it was a command.

Sitting squarely in the center of the settee, her back as

straight and stiff as she could make it, Evleen could feel the resentment aimed in her direction, not from timid Amanda, but from Lydia and the two older daughters. There was more than a bit of rancor. She felt enveloped by a deep, thick cloud of hostility and hard feelings. She gulped a deep breath and determined to make the best of it. "Well, I'm from Ireland," she began.

"We *know* that," said Bettina, seeming to suppress a titter.

"From County Clare."

Lydia interjected, "We know that, too. County Clare," she repeated, seeming to muse. "That's one of Ireland's poorest counties, is it not?"

"All rocks and mud, from what we hear," Charlotte volunteered.

In a voice chill as the wind over the Irish Sea, Lydia continued, "Is it true you and Patrick are descended from the kings of Ireland?"

What is this, some sort of Spanish Inquisition? Evleen felt her temper rise, but determined to control it. "Patrick is my half brother. As I'm sure you know, his father was Randall, Viscount Montfret." She enjoyed the gritting of teeth that seemed to occur after her remark and could not resist tilting her chin and parrying, "So if he's descended from kings, we most likely should include the kings of England."

"I see. Hmm." Mrs. Trevlyn's fighting spirit seemed quashed for a moment, but she quickly recovered and inquired, "So do tell us of *your* heritage."

"We are so impressed," said Bettina.

Evleen was not sure if they were jesting or not. Perhaps she was being overly sensitive because of the remark about the dress, but that was minor and they truly wanted to make her welcome. "You're sure you want to hear?" They all nodded. "Well, then . . ."

She told them of her father, who was Ian O'Fallon, son of Daniel O'Fallon, eighth Earl of Dunkerry, and how he was descended from the Duke of Connaught, who was a direct descendent of Euchaid, one of the ancient kings of Ireland who reined over one of the earliest Gaelic kingdoms many centuries before. "So that's why I'm descended from the kings of

Ireland," she concluded. "Would you like to hear about my mother's side?"

All were silent a moment. Then Bettina giggled, trying to conceal it by bringing her hand to her mouth.

"Bettina!" admonished her mother.

"I cannot help it, Mama, she really is an Irish princess."

Evleen hastily began, "Oh, please, I don't think of myself as a princess. I—"

Her abrupt halt was caused by the sudden realization that they were making fun of her. Not Walter Trevlyn, who still stood by the fireplace, now with a pained expression. Not Amanda, who looked downright stricken. But it was clear Mrs. Trevelyn, Charlotte, and Bettina were most definitely not her friends.

"What were you going to say, Miss O'Fallon?" asked Mrs. Trevlyn, faking a solicitous concern. "You were going to tell us about your mother's lineage?"

Never in a million years. Evleen answered softly, "I make no pretense at being a princess. I am plain Evleen O'Fallon from County Clare, Ireland, no better, no worse than anyone else on God's green earth."

"Well, we cannot fault her for that, can we, girls?" Lydia asked with a forced laugh. Her eyes drilled into Evleen's. "And what will you be doing while you're here?"

"Looking after Patrick, of course. Until he grows accustomed to his new life."

"Then you intend to return to Ireland?"

"I am not sure of my plans. Much depends on how well Patrick fares here in England."

"Ah." Mrs. Trevlyn made no attempt to hide her relief, nor did Charlotte and Bettina. "So you'll be acting as sort of a governess, then."

"I suppose . . . yes, you could say that." Evleen was bewildered. What was Mrs. Trevlyn getting at?

"Not a governess," came Lord Alberdsley's voice from the doorway. He entered, and despite the slight trembling of his limbs and his heavy dependence on his cane, Evleen sensed from the way all in the room quickly came to attention, his very presence commanded respect. "I thought I had made it clear Evleen is no governess."

Looking embarrassed, Walter replied, "Of course, Charles." He cast a warning glance at his wife and daughters. "We understand that."

Lord Alberdsley sank with a weary groan into an armchair. Regarding Evleen fondly, he declared, "You look beautiful tonight, child. Have they been treating you well?"

She smiled brightly. "Of course. I've been made to feel wonderfully welcome."

Lord Alberdsley smiled. "You will all meet Patrick tomorrow. Wait till you see him. A fine big lad."

"We can hardly wait," said Mrs. Trevlyn, her daughters all eagerly nodding their heads.

Beaming with delight, Lord Alberdsley launched into an ecstatic description of his newly found grandson. ". . . and he's an extremely bright boy. Runs in the family, you know. Already the lad knows Greek and Latin, thanks to his mother who has done an outstanding job in educating the child." He cast an admiring glance at Evleen. "That also applies to Miss O'Fallon, who is a bright, as well as most beautiful, young lady. Is that not so, everyone?"

Evleen could have sworn she heard the sounds of gritting teeth again as the Trevlyns all eagerly nodded their heads affirmatively. She noted that although Lydia retained a fixed smile on her face, she had slightly flinched more than once as Lord Alberdsley praised Patrick to the skies.

Lord Alberdsley continued, "Now what is this nonsense about Evleen being a governess? She will be no such thing. She is to be treated like one of the family, and when it's time for the London Season, we shall all go, and that includes Evleen and Patrick. I want Patrick to enjoy the sights of London. As for our Evleen"—he cast a warning glance at his sister-in-law—"she shall have a Season, just like your daughters, madam. I shall see to it she has the proper clothes, jewels, furbelows, and whatever else that warms the hearts of young ladies."

Evleen sat stunned. *A London Season?* She had not realized. Even in supposedly unenlightened Ireland, she had heard of the London Seasons, in which young girls "came out" and had to exhibit the kind of decorum and elegant deportment that would crown a successful Season with marriage.

"But Lord Alberdsley, I cannot," she protested.

"Why ever not?"

"In the first place, I'm twenty-four, which is much too old. Besides, I have not 'come out' and at this late date, I'd look ridiculous."

"Nonsense. Everyone will know you're from Ireland. No need for you to officially 'come out' as they say."

"But then, I don't know if I can . . ." Evleen struggled to find the right words ". . . I mean, I've led a simple life in Ireland. I don't know if I'm ready for the dances, the fancy manners, the elegant clothes—"

"The girl has a point," interjected Mrs. Trevlyn. "In my opinion it would be cruel to foist her upon a society she knows nothing about. She simply doesn't have the training."

"Shouldn't be a problem," Lord Alberdsley firmly replied. "I trust, Lydia, you and your daughters will take Evleen to your collective bosoms, teach her everything she needs to know."

Lydia started to protest, but Lord Alberdsley raised his hand. "Enough. Evleen shall have a Season, and that's final."

Evleen could see further arguing would be futile. And now that she was thinking about it, *really, what would it hurt?* They had passed through the awesome city of London yesterday, just long enough for her to get a taste of how exciting life must be there. How she would love to go back, stay awhile and see all the sights, and no harm done. Perhaps she might even stumble across that rich and titled Englishman her mother wanted her to find.

Further conversation was cut short when Pierce announced the arrival of Montague, Lord Eddington, his sister, Penelope, and his brother, Lord Thomas.

Chapter 10

"How I detest these affairs," declared Montague as he, Penelope, and Thomas waited in the entry hall to be announced.

Thomas snorted. "How my heart bleeds for you. I am all sympathy."

Montague lowered his voice. "You know I cannot abide that dreary woman and her daughters."

"Oh, come now," said Penelope, looking lovely in a white bombazine dinner gown trimmed with blue lace. "I can see why you don't like Charlotte and Bettina, but Amanda is not all that bad."

"Granted, Amanda is a harmless enough creature, but that boring Bettina. That shallow Charlotte—"

"Whom you're going to marry, and soon," Penelope declared. "It's time you made the best of it, Montague. It's Papa's wish."

"Oh, I suppose." Montague sighed, obviously resigning himself to a dull evening. "You say the Irish girl will be here?" At Thomas's nod, he brightened. "Then we'll soon see if she's truly as beautiful as you say she is."

Thomas glared at his brother, heartily wishing he had not even mentioned Evleen, but when he'd arrived home, his thoughts had been so full of her that he couldn't help describing her in the most glowing terms. "Beautiful or no, Montague, you're to keep your hands off."

"There's a strange bit of brotherly advice," Montague declared triumphantly. "Could my stalwart younger brother actually be jealous? Damn, if I haven't hit a vulnerable spot in his psyche."

Thomas was long past the stage when anything his brother said could make him angry, though he did find himself slightly annoyed. He should not even be that, however. More than ever lately, he had felt concern for his brother, who, with his drinking and debauching, was throwing his life away with both hands. "Leave my psyche out of this, Montague. Evleen O'-Fallon is a fine woman, as you shall soon see. I have nothing but the utmost respect for her."

Montague laughed scornfully, but before Thomas could retaliate, Pierce invited them into the drawing room.

Stunning. That was all Thomas could think when he saw Evleen. Even when she wore her simple Irish garb, he had known she was beautiful, yet he had hardly been prepared for this elegantly coiffed and gowned creature who returned his bow with a graceful curtsey. How striking was the charming contrast of her snow-white skin against the deep orange of her low-cut dinner gown. *Capucine,* he thought the ladies called it. Whatever the color, just looking at her caused a lurch of excitement.

This is ridiculous. He realized he must stop acting like a green schoolboy. Fresh in his mind was the conversation he'd just had with his father, still confined to his room with the gout.

"So you like and admire this young woman," the marquess had commented after Thomas's detailed description of his journey.

"Very much so," Thomas had answered. "I find her witty, intelligent, and charming." He had felt like adding, *and intensely exciting,* but thought better of it.

"Surely you have not forgotten Miss Bettina Trevlyn," the marquess had reminded him, wincing from the pain of his gout.

"No, I have not, but bear in mind I have not yet proposed to Miss Trevlyn. However . . ." Thomas had carefully formed the words to explain. "Marriage is not a consideration. Miss O'Fallon is betrothed to an Irishman named Timothy Murphy."

His father had nodded. "There you have it, then. Honor decrees—"

"I know about honor, Papa," Thomas had testily replied, in no mood for a lecture.

"Even Montague would not deign to dally with a married woman or one betrothed."

"One of his few virtues." Thomas knew differently, but his father had been disappointed enough without knowing the whole truth about Montague.

Thomas had proceeded to inform his father how happy he

was his journey to Ireland was over and how eager he was to get about the business of breeding Thoroughbreds. He found he was feigning part of his eagerness, though. To his growing chagrin, since the day he'd returned to that small cottage in County Clare, nearly every waking thought had been of Evleen O'Fallon. How could he forget her bravery crossing the Irish Sea, deathly ill, yet still joking? Or, when he was trying to comfort her, how the wind caught her shining dark hair, lashing its softness against his face, taunting him, making him want to thrust his hands through its luxurian softness. How could he forget that moment at the Whispering Arch when their eyes had locked and deep in his belly he'd felt the hot stirrings of desire?

"Why if it isn't Lord Thomas."

Bettina Trevlyn's shrill voice swiftly brought him back to cold reality. Seated on a rose-colored satin settee, she patted the cushion beside her. "Come, do sit down," she said, her many curls bobbing. "I cannot wait to show you my newest pillow cover."

Oh God.

Smiling pleasantly, Thomas settled himself beside Bettina. Evleen sat straight across, her dark, lively beauty contrasting with the pale blond, washed-out coloring of the Trevlyn sisters. A rose among the thorns as far as he was concerned. At least he could surreptitiously feast his eyes upon her while being led, yet again, on another tedious journey through the land of needlepoint. As he watched, Montague sat next to Evleen and engaged her in conversation. A long conversation, and then he led her into dinner, where he managed, by a swift exchange of place cards, to sit next to her.

He might have known. Thomas knew the meaning of his brother's every movement, every nuance of his voice, so no doubt existed. As the evening wore on, it became crystal clear that Montague was becoming increasingly infatuated with Miss Evleen O'Fallon.

"Not an altogether unpleasant evening," Montague remarked as he, Thomas, and Penelope journeyed the short distance back to Northfield Hall in their curricle. "Fine dinner . . . a few hands of whist . . . I was not as bored as I thought I would be."

"Who cares if you were bored or not?" snapped Penelope. "Besides, I know you weren't bored because you spent the

evening peering down the bodice of Miss O'Fallon's gown.
Don't deny it, I saw you."

"So what if I was? Besides being quite beautiful, the girl possess a magnificent bosom. So white, so soft, so full . . . umm,
whah!" Montague brought a hand to his lips and made a kissing
sound that so infuriated Thomas he balled his fists. But before
he could act, Penelope swiftly rapped their brother's knuckles
with her fan. "Stop that this instant! How could you be so crass?
Miss O'Fallon doesn't need the likes of you drooling over her.
She has enough problems of her own."

"What do you mean?" Thomas asked.

"Isn't it obvious? Charlotte and Bettina were green with
envy. And did you not notice their mother? I swear, her claws
came out when our dear brother here arranged to sit next to
Miss O'Fallon at dinner." ·

"Granted, they're a bit jealous," Montague remarked, "but
isn't that natural, given the circumstances? Miss O'Fallon is indeed a remarkable young woman. Bright, lively, full of charm.
Surely they'll like her once they get to know her."

"Montague, lusting after women does not mean you know
them very well." Penelope thought a moment. "I hate to think
what might happen when they go to London for the Season."

"Why do you say that?" Thomas asked. Silently, he agreed
with all that Penelope had said.

"Evleen is all the things Montague just described, and I like
her very much," replied Penelope. "She's obviously well educated and possesses infinite amounts of charm. Still, I fear
she'll have a difficult time in London."

"What do you mean?" asked both Thomas and Montague.

"First, there's a rawness about her. Granted, her station in life
is far above that of some dairymaid. Her manners are good
enough, but she's a country girl, not accustomed to the *ton*. She's
simply not so polished as she should be. I fear she'll be like a
lamb led to the slaughter. When she's tossed into the middle of
that cutthroat society of ours, every little gesture, every little
thing she says will be measured, weighed, scrutinized, and dis-
cussed. Mark my words, at the very least, they'll laugh at her."

"And at most?"

"I fear she might be cut."

"And the second reason?" Thomas asked grimly. He had not wanted to hear this, yet somehow he had known.

"She's Irish. Personally, I adore that Irish brogue of hers. When she talks, it's like a poem set to music."

"True of all the Irish," granted Thomas.

"But you know how the English look down their noses at the Irish. How can Evleen possibly escape the derision and snubs that are bound to be heaped upon her?"

"But she's strong," protested Thomas. "She'll overcome whatever criticism might come her way. Besides, Lord Alberdsley will be of great support."

"It does not bode well," said Penelope sadly shaking her head. "I know women. The Trevlyn sisters and their mother will not only not help, God only knows what they might do to undermine Evleen's position."

Thomas heartily declared, "They would not dare, especially when they know she has Lord Alberdsley's support one hundred percent and is under his protection."

Penelope broke into unexpected laughter. "My dear brother, don't you know that so-called protection will make Miss O'Fallon's problem even worse?"

Montague said musingly, "Perhaps I should take her under my wing."

"You'll do no such thing," Thomas remarked, his voice icy.

Montague snickered. "Whatever is the matter? Not jealous of the little Irish chit, are we?"

In the moonlight, Thomas made out Montague's thin, aristocratic face and wanted very much to plant his fist full in the middle of it. *Bad idea.* He did love his brother, despite everything. Besides, Thomas recognized his own ridiculous and uncalled-for jealousies. He must set his brother straight about Evleen, though. "I believe I mentioned Miss O'Fallon is betrothed."

"So?"

"So she is *taken,* Montague." Thomas's anger was rising. "An honorable man does not dally with a married woman or one betrothed."

"Oh, grow up, Thomas. You're living in a dream world. Above all, an honorable man is discreet, not some sort of chaste idiot. If I should tell you of my dalliances, some with married women of the highest rank, you would be amazed."

Thomas gritted his teeth. "I would not be amazed, I would be sickened. Actually, I don't care what you do, Montague, except for two things."

"And what might those be, Thomas?" Montague asked.

"First, never let Papa know about your dalliances. What he does know is bad enough and hurts him considerably. Don't make it worse."

"And second?"

"Stay away from Evleen O'Fallon."

"Your jealousy is showing, Thomas. You were alone six days with her. What happened on that journey from Ireland? Did you—?"

"That is none of your affair," Thomas snapped, losing his cool facade despite himself. He regained his composure quickly and continued, "For God's sake, Montague, did you not see the looks on the faces of Charlotte and her mama tonight? They were livid when you so much as bowed to Miss O'Fallon. They think they possess you, and with good reason, since we know how desirous Papa and Lord Alberdsley are of uniting their estates. You are putting Evleen to a great disadvantage when you show an interest in her." Thomas glowered at his brother, even though he knew full well Montague could not see him in the dark. "In words you can understand, those feral females will tear the girl apart if you continue with your attentions."

"But perhaps I find myself already growing fond of her," Montague playfully protested. "What if I fall in love with her?"

"You will never love anyone but yourself."

"She's accompanying them to London, you know, for the Season. I sensed the others weren't too keen on it."

"Of course they weren't. Montague, please—" Thomas stopped himself, damned if he would beg. *Besides,* he thought, *what is the use?* His brother would do what he pleased, no matter the consequences.

"Just go tend to your horses, Thomas," Montague remarked.

"I plan to do just that," Thomas answered, hard put to quell his anger. But Montague was Montague, and he was right on one score: Thomas should indeed tend to his horses and forget Miss Evleen O'Fallon. Even so, Tanglewood Hall was not so very far from London. After all, he would have need to attend Tattersall's occasionally, and in so doing, would it not be the courteous thing to drop in on Alberdsley's London town house from time to time?

Thomas smiled with satisfaction. *You've not seen the last of me yet, my sweet Evleen.* Of course, his interest was only that of a concerned friend. Anything else would be ungentlemanly and quite without honor.

And you are nothing if not a gentleman, Thomas told himself grimly, knowing he would be kept awake tonight by visions of Evleen O'Fallon and how delectable she looked in that low-cut gown. How she would deal with the Trevlyns, he wasn't sure. There was bound to be trouble, but perhaps Evleen, being the feisty Irish girl she was, could handle all the petty jealousies that were bound to arise. He could not help but feel concern, though. Personally, he would rather face a pack of lions than Mrs. Walter Trevlyn, now forever bereft of a title, and her unmarried daughters.

The next morning Evleen awoke feeling both tired and discouraged. The strangeness of a new place—the Trevlyns' hostility—the unsettling presence of Lord Thomas—all contributed to her restless tossing and turning most of the night, and in the process her not getting much sleep. She wished she could avoid going downstairs to breakfast, even though when she'd arrived, she had looked forward to getting better acquainted with the family. She had even envisioned the sisters, and perhaps the mother, showing her and Patrick around the estate, a gay, friendly little group exploring the house and grounds. How deluded she had been! Now she wondered if she might just stay in her bedchamber and have the maid bring her breakfast on a tray.

That wouldn't do, of course. Never had she been a coward, and she wouldn't be one now. For Patrick's sake, she must make the effort. It was just . . . last night had been such a disaster. It hadn't taken long for the true feelings of Mrs. Trevlyn and her two elder daughters to emerge. Amanda, she wasn't sure. And then there was Montague. What an odious man! How could Lord Thomas, who was everything wonderful and kind, possibly be the brother of that egotistical fop who actually had the nerve to assume she liked him?

Evleen dragged herself from bed and had just finished

dressing in her old calico gown when Celeste came bustling in, took one looked, and exclaimed, "Miss Evleen, you cannot wear *zat*."

"Why ever not?" Evleen perversely asked, knowing the reason full well.

"Because . . . because . . ." Evleen could see Celeste was trying to control herself, but she finally burst forth with "*Zat* is the ugliest gown I have ever seen."

"I know that, Celeste." Evleen feigned the utmost indifference. "But I chose to wear it anyway."

"Never. I shall borrow another gown from—"

"No you won't," answered Evleen in a voice that brooked no argument. "Lord Alberdsley says he's already sent for a seamstress. Meanwhile, I shall wear what I brought."

Despite that last, Celeste's eyes lit up. "Marvelous. I am so glad, miss. If you are going to London, you will need gowns for morning, afternoon, dinner, walking, riding. You must have several ball gowns, as well as the shoes, hats, jewels—"

"Don't overwhelm me, Celeste," interrupted Evleen, laughing. "Where I come from we put one gown on in the morning and take it off at night. No one has the time to be constantly changing clothes."

"But you are not in County Clare now, miss," answered Celeste with a sly smile. "And you do want to look your best, for many reasons."

"Heed what I say, Celeste. From now on, I shall not borrow so much as a handkerchief from anyone. Have I made myself clear?"

Impressed by Evleen's obvious determination, the lady's maid said not another word on the subject, but asked, "And Master Patrick?"

"Patrick, too. And furthermore . . ." Evleen was about to voice a subject she'd been thinking about and just now had made her decision. "I am not going to London."

"But you must," exclaimed Celeste. "You cannot miss the Season. It is all that counts in the *ton*."

"Well, I'm not a member of the *ton,* am I now? Better I stay here."

Her brother chose that moment to burst in, dressed in his old clothes. "I'm hungry, Evleen. Let's go down and eat and then we can explore."

Celeste took one look and rolled her eyes. "He should not go downstairs now, Miss Evleen. Here it's customary for the children to take all meals in the classroom with their tutors, or in their rooms."

"Not this child." Evleen took Patrick's hand. If ever she was going to assert herself, it must be now. "Come Patrick, we shall go downstairs and eat. If Lord Alberdsley disapproves, he'll have us both to deal with."

When they walked into the dining room, Evleen discovered the family already there, including Lord Alberdsley. "Patrick is going to eat with us," she announced boldly. "I don't believe in children being isolated in their rooms." Ready for an argument, she stood waiting for Lord Alberdsley's answer, noting the startled expressions of the sisters and their mother.

"But of course," came Lord Alberdsley's reply. "I shall enjoy having the boy share my eggs and sausage." Amidst audible shocked intakes of breath from nieces and sister-in-law, he continued, "I have a lovely surprise for you, Evleen."

"What is that?"

"I am arranging to open my London town house early." He looked fondly at Patrick. "I cannot wait to show my grandson the sights of London. In a few days we shall leave for London. How does that sound?"

But I do not want to go, a little voice within Evleen screamed, but the words would not come out. Patrick was in his grandfather's custody now, so she had no authority to forbid him anything. Besides, how could she stand in the boy's way when he had expressed a great desire to see London? *And so do I,* she thought miserably. Despite the problems she knew she'd find there, she very much wanted to see all the sights of the huge city. *That settles it, then.* There was only one answer she could give.

"How lovely, Lord Alberdsley. Sounds fine to me. I can hardly wait to get there."

Chapter 11

"Hst! Evleen, get up."

"Patrick?" Evleen rolled over in her bed, still half asleep.

"Time to get up, Evleen."

"But it's hardly dawn." Evleen half opened her eyes. "Where am I?"

"London, silly."

"Well, how am I supposed to know? I've awakened in so many strange beds lately it's hard to tell." Evleen propped herself on one elbow and regarded her clear-eyed brother, who was already dressed. "Why are you waking me so early?"

"Because at last we're here in London and I want to explore." Patrick tugged at her bedcovers. "Please, I cannot wait."

Evleen sighed, wishing she could think of some fine excuse for putting Patrick off. She was tired. Lord Alberdsley's creaking oak coach had arrived from Hatfield long after dark last night. It had been an uncomfortable ride, what with the coach being of an ancient vintage and not well sprung. Then, too, she'd had the Trevlyn ladies to contend with. Curbed by the presence of Lord Alberdsley, they had been polite, but underneath she could sense the seething resentment, with the exception of Amanda, of course, who pretty much sat silent in her corner. At least Patrick had kept her distracted, asking at least a million questions about the post road they were traveling on, and the coaches that occasionally thundered by. Exhausted, the whole family had turned in not long after arriving at the earl's large town house in what appeared to be the heart of London. "Can't you wait a little while?" she asked, eyeing her pillow.

"Come on, sleepyhead, don't you want to see London?"

She thought a moment. "As a matter of fact, I do."

Minutes later, Patrick and Evleen, who had hastily dressed in the old calico dress and straw hat, were in the downstairs entryway when Pierce, who had accompanied the family to London, regarded them askance. "You are not going out at this hour, Miss Evleen?"

"Why not? Morning is the best part of the day."

The butler's eyebrows shot up. "But alone? Unchaperoned?"

"Unchaperoned," Patrick repeated, bursting into laughter.

Evleen laughed, too. "Not to worry, Pierce. I am quite accustomed to taking care of myself."

"Might I inquire where you intend to go?"

"To see London," Patrick called excitedly. "Come on, Evleen."

In a flash they were out the ornately carved double doors of the Alberdsley town house, into the sunshine, suddenly confronted with the bustle of the street.

She sniffed the crisp, early morning air as they bounded down the scoured-clean steps, and inquired, "You're the chief explorer, Patrick. Which way shall we go?"

"Any way. I want to see it all." Patrick held out his palm and uncurled his fingers, revealing a gold half guinea. "See what Grandfather gave me? He said an heir apparent should never be without a bit of blunt."

They started walking, she wasn't sure which direction, until they reached a street called St. James's. Although the shops and businesses that lined the street were closed at this early hour, they still enjoyed looking into shop windows that were bright with color, as well as savoring the delicious aromas of fresh buns and tarts that wafted from the pastry shops. The diversity of the shops was intriguing. "What's a bagnio?" Patrick asked, glimpsing a sign that announced, PERO'S BAGNIO.

"Those are baths, I believe."

"Can't people take a bath at home?" he asked, but before Evleen could answer, he had spied another shop. "Oh, look, Lauriere, the jeweler. Is that where they sell diamonds?"

"I suspect it is, Patrick," she laughingly replied, "and there's the Bunch of Grapes, which I should wager is a tavern, and there's Sam's Library, which no doubt is full of books." *How wonderful,* she mused, *to have a huge bookstore close by. There is nothing nearly this big in Ireland, not even Dublin.*

"Why must gentlemen have clubs?" asked Patrick after they had passed by White's, Brooks's and Crockford's.

"So they can play cards, I suppose." She remembered her mother's low opinion of the British aristocracy. "And so they can be exclusive and fancy themselves above the rest."

"Do you think Lord Thomas belongs to a club?"

"No." She thought of that wastrel, Montague. "But I'm sure his brother does."

"Oh, look, Evleen, a palace."

And so the day went. After duly admiring Saint James's Palace, they wandered past a place called Almack's on King Street, as well as the Golden Lion public house, where they stopped for refreshments, paid for by Patrick's half guinea. They found the Haymarket, in which stood a grand opera house, but more exciting was the market itself with its produce of every description, performing dogs and monkeys, a fire-eater, and all manner of entertainment.

Toward the end of the day, they found themselves on a street called Piccadilly. Had she been here before? Evleen felt weary, her feet were tired, and she began to worry. "How do we get home from here, Patrick? I cannot recollect which way we came."

"What street does Lord Alberdsley live in?"

Heaven help us. Why had she not made note of the street the Alberdsley town house was in? "I don't know the name, but we'll find it," she said with a confidence she didn't feel.

Lost in London. Such a big city, and so confusing. As the minutes wore on, and they kept wandering, Evleen fought back panic. She must remain calm for Patrick's sake. "We'll find it, so don't worry. I do hope they haven't missed us at home."

With eagerness and more than a modicum of annoyance at himself, Thomas mounted the steps of Lord Alberdsley's town house. If someone were to ask why he was here, he would say he came to London to view the horses at Tattersall's. He, however, knew otherwise. His concern for Evleen was such that despite himself, he could not stay away. Patrick would be fine. Thomas smiled, knowing that bright, likeable lad would get along well wherever he went, especially now, with a doting grandfather to watch over him. Those female dragons of the Trevlyn household would not dare harm Lord Alberdsley's heir apparent, but Evleen? He would not put any sort of chicanery past Mrs. Lydia Trevlyn and her two older daughters. Evleen was bright, as well as perceptive, but in many ways she was still a simple country girl from Ireland and could hardly be a match for three selfish women who had cut their teeth on the deviousness and duplicitous scheming that went on every day in the *ton*. He and Evleen had parted only a few days before, yet he was thinking of her constantly, not only with that strange longing he could not seem to shake, but with a feeling of unease.

The moment Pierce opened the door, Thomas noted the expression of distress that covered the butler's usually impassive face and knew something was amiss. Inside, there appeared to be some kind of controlled chaos, what with servants scurrying about and the raised voice of Lord Alberdsley clearly audible. When Thomas was ushered into the drawing room, he noted the whole family gathered there, all solemn-faced, the ladies not their usual simpering selves, shy Amanda excepted, of course. Lord Alberdsley, standing by the fireplace in a great state of agitation, greeted him precipitously.

"Ah, my boy, glad you're here. My word, what a fix we're in. You must help with the search."

"What search, sir?"

"My grandson and Evleen have gone missing. Left early this morning. Haven't heard a word." Forehead furrowed with concern, Lord Alberdsley started pacing the drawing room. To Lydia he said, "Tell me again, what did they say to Pierce when they left this morning?"

"Something about wanting to see London," Lydia replied with a shrug, looking more annoyed than concerned.

"To see London, indeed. Where is my grandson?" In desperation, Lord Alberdsley addressed Thomas. "I've sent two footmen out to search. If they don't come home soon, I'll turn out this entire household to join the search, servants and family both."

"Surely not us, Uncle," protested Charlotte, who sat primly next to her mother on a settee. "It's nearly time for tea, and after that we must get ready for the routs we are attending this evening. Lord and Lady Beckford's in particular—"

"Confound it," burst Lord Alberdsley, "here I am beset with worry and you talk of routs? They've been gone all day.

Thieves swarm the streets of London. Cutthroats! Murderers! God only knows what dire fate has befallen my grandson."

"But why did they go out so early?" asked Bettina, who sat quietly embroidering. "Everyone knows it's not fashionable to go out before three o'clock."

"God's blood." Lord Alberdsley turned beet red. He started to sputter, groped for a chair and sank into its depths. "I . . . I . . ."

"I shall go look for them, sir," Thomas said quickly. "Chances are they're only out 'exploring' as Patrick would put it." He placed a comforting hand on Lord Alberdsley's tense shoulder. "Do relax. Have some tea, or better yet, a splash of brandy."

"There's the Irish for you." Lydia picked up her petit point and stabbed it vehemently with her needle. "Not here a day and already causing trouble."

Thomas would have liked to reply in kind to such vitriol, but he had no time. After a hasty good-bye, he was out the door and into his curricle, urging his two matching bays into a trot down Arlington Street.

Now where would they go first? he wondered, his head craning this way and that. Ah. Chances were, they would have been attracted to all the hustle and bustle of St. James's Street.

Thomas turned into St. James's Street. Slowly, continually searching, he drove to Pall Mall, over to Regent Street, then Haymarket, and surely, if they'd been out to see the sights of London, they would have strolled along there. "Have you seen a boy of ten with red hair?" he occasionally called to vendors and passersby, using the most identifiable mark of the two. "He would be with his sister, who's tall, and both of them Irish."

At last a fish peddler called back, "Seen 'em this morning, sir, a pretty young lass and a bright little lad with red hair. Kept asking questions."

Patrick, indeed. "Which way did they go?"

"Haven't the foggiest."

Dammit, where were they? It would be dark soon. Lord Alberdsley was right to be concerned. What if they wandered into those pitch-black, narrow streets where thieves roamed, carrying knives and bludgeons loaded with lead?

He must keep searching.

Back to Saint James's Square . . .

Over to Piccadilly Circus . . .

Traffic was getting heavier. Now the streets were full of well-dressed gentlemen on the backs of fine-blooded horses; dashing, beautifully dressed ladies driving their own vis-à-vis; elegant equipages pulled by horses matched with precision and groomed to a high gloss. All seemed to be heading toward Hyde Park, and suddenly it struck him. *Of course.* This was the fashionable hour of five P.M. Where else would those two be but at the grandest show in London?

Soon, Thomas was carefully driving along Rotten Row, amidst the press of countless horses and fine carriages, when he spied two bedraggled figures on the footpath, both dragging their feet as if they had been walking for a very long time. *Thank God, Patrick and Evleen.* The relief that nearly overwhelmed him was an awakening experience that left him reeling. He had not realized until this moment how much he cared. Patrick, of course, but . . . *Oh, Evleen, my sweet Irish beauty, if anything had happened to you, I would never have been the same.*

He had to laugh. What if his father knew what he was thinking? What would his sister, Penelope, say?

At least he could keep such a sentiment to himself. *And you will,* he thought as he drew the curricle to the side of the road, reined in his horse, and arranged his mouth in a casual smile. "Fancy meeting you here, Miss O'Fallon, Master Patrick. Out for a stroll?"

Patrick was the first to spy him. "Look, Evleen, 'tis Lord Thomas," the boy called, tugging at his sister's sleeve. She turned. He saw a quick light of recognition in her eyes, followed by vast relief, then, as he watched, her face took on an expression of indifference.

"Why, Lord Thomas, what a surprise." She tilted her chin in that snippy way she had. "Somehow I would never have guessed you would be enamored of the Fashionable Hour, but on second thought, why not? You're one of the *ton,* after all." She gestured at the passing throng. "Quite a sight, isn't it, the *ton* parading themselves and their mounts about? Don't any of them work? Have they nothing better to do with their time?"

Her perceptiveness amazed him. It was the rare woman who could look beyond the seductive glitter of the Polite World, into the selfishness and hypocrisy that lay beyond. Galling though it was, he ignored her uncalled-for remark about his being enamored of the Fashionable Hour. "Work is anathema in the *ton.* You'll soon learn."

"I don't know that I care to," she answered, raising her head high, as if she were Lady Jersey herself.

He sprung down from the carriage, swept off his hat, and bowed. "I'm relieved I found you. Your family is concerned. They've been looking for you."

She looked surprised. "How strange! We were merely out taking in the sights of London. We were about to return home."

"But how could we, Evleen?" asked Patrick. "We were lost, remember? You said so yourself. You were worried because you forgot what street Grandfather lives in."

"Patrick," she began, but when Thomas started to smile, she could not suppress a smile of her own. "Oh, very well, I admit it. We had a lovely day, up until I realized we were lost." Her smile deepened, revealing dimples he'd not noticed before. They made her look even prettier than he already thought she was. "It would appear we are in your debt again, sir. That is, if you could kindly take us home?"

"My pleasure."

He's being so gallant, thought Evleen, *even though I just came close to insulting him.* She decided she had been much too shallow, much too glib, and she had best be honest and set him straight. "In truth, I was overjoyed when I saw you. What started out as a lark was turning into a nightmare."

"I can imagine," he replied. "In a strange city, not knowing your way home."

"And getting hungry, too," said Patrick.

She hardly heard him. Something was passing between Lord Thomas and herself again. Their gazes locked, just as they had that day at the Whispering Arch. *I shouldn't be, but I feel so drawn to him,* Evleen thought as she finally got control of herself and shifted her gaze away. "I trust we are not imposing." Chagrined, she realized that last remark had sounded stiff and contrived, which in actuality it was, since she'd been trying to conceal her inner turmoil.

He, too, seemed compelled to make a deliberate effort to set the spellbinding moment aside and motioned toward his curricle. "Come along, it's not as far as you think. Patrick, you can ride in the groom's seat in the back." He added playfully, "You can be my 'tiger.' You're just the right size."

"Excellent, sir," Patrick called and eagerly scrambled into the small seat.

"Let me hand you up," said Lord Thomas. Quelling her first response, *I can help my own self up,* Evleen obediently took his hand and allowed herself to be assisted to the high seat of the curricle. When she was seated, arranging her skirt about her, he went round, climbed in beside her, and took up a light blanket. "It's chilly," he said, and started tucking the blanket in around her. At once a feeling of security and contentment flowed over her. She was accustomed to taking care of herself, yet how snug and warm she felt in the care of a man whose strength and character she respected and admired. She had another feeling, too, which had nothing to do with security but, rather, with her keen awareness of the gentle pushing of his hands against her thighs, remote though they felt through the blanket. His head was bent directly in front of her. If she leaned but a few inches forward, she could kiss that spot by his ear where a tendril of his dark hair fell casually. Suddenly, he looked toward her, his gaze a soft caress, so full of words unspoken she could hardly breathe. Thus they remained, until he finally looked away, sat straight, took up the reins, and urged the horses into the crowded roadway. After a silence made almost unbearable by the unspoken emotions swirling around them, he, not turning his head, softly asked, "Evleen O'Fallon, is there something between us?"

Her heart pounded. Never had she been so physically affected by a man. But what was the sense of it?

"You know what Mama says," Patrick called from the back. *Patrick and his big ears!* She might have known. She squeezed her eyes shut. *Not another word, Patrick, please, please.*

"Evleen, you must never love an Englishman."

She twisted around and glared. "Patrick, without doubt I shall kill you the moment we get home." She noticed Thomas's shoulders shaking with suppressed laughter. "You're laughing?" she asked, feigning high indignation.

"Patrick is absolutely right, you know. We Englishmen are conceited, overbearing, and exceedingly selfish. Highly unsuitable as husbands. Better a handsome Irishman."

"I most certainly agree," she answered lightly. The emotion-filled moment was over. She positively must see it did not happen again. To further her resolution, she had a question of her own. "And what about you, Lord Thomas? Surely there must be a woman in your life. You never said."

He took his time, seeming to concentrate on maneuvering his curricle around a slower-moving coach before he answered. "It is my father's wish that I marry Miss Bettina Trevlyn. Eventually, I probably shall."

Her spirits plunged. So ridiculous, but she could not let go. "Do you always do what your father tells you?"

He cast her a lopsided grin. "Actually, no. Since I'm only a second son, my father leaves me to my own devices. However, in this instance—"

"Do you love her?" *Oh, how rude.* She fought the urge to clap her hand to her mouth, astonished at what had just popped out. "Sorry. You don't have to answer that."

"Love and marriage do not necessarily go hand in hand," he commented dryly.

So he did not love Bettina. Even knowing the futility of it all, Evleen felt greatly relieved.

"What street do we live on, Lord Thomas?" Patrick called.

"Arlington Street, a most prestigious address, by the way. Many dukes have lived on Arlington Street."

"Which ones?"

"Well, let's see—the Dukes of Hamilton, Beaufort, York. Matter of fact, the Duke of York died quite suddenly in his arm-chair while living on Arlington Street. His body was removed to St. James's Palace, where it lay in state."

Evleen listened, her admiration for the man growing all the more. How considerate he was to take time to explain. Most men would have ignored Patrick, or told him to keep quiet, but not Lord Thomas. Despite herself, she sneaked a peek at his profile, so clean cut with that firm chin and straight nose. *I must stop this,* she thought, thoroughly disgusted with herself.

Lord Thomas spoke again. "Before we arrive home, I must warn you, you might be in for a difficult time."

"Lord Alberdsley is angry?"

"He was sick with worry, but it's not Lord Alberdsley I'd be worried about, it's . . ." He hesitated, as if keenly aware a gentleman must never defame a lady.

"You don't have to say it," she responded. "I know whom you're talking about, but don't say." She cast a swift glance behind her.

He said softly, "Be aware they are not overly sympathetic and might cause trouble."

"I know. But there's nothing I can do about it, is there?"

From behind, Patrick asked, "What are you two talking about?"

Laughing, Evleen turned to look at him. "Some things are none of your business, little boy."

"Fair enough," Patrick answered equitably, sounding very grown up for a ten-year-old. "But I think I already know. You're supposed to go with them to a rout tonight, and then next week, when your ball gown is made, you're going with them to Lady Claremont's ball, and you hope they'll be nice."

"Well said, Patrick," commented Thomas.

Patrick asked, "Are you going, Lord Thomas?"

He shook his head. "Routs and balls hold little interest for me, although I always receive an invitation. But I consider them a waste of time." He glanced at Evleen. "So will you, I'd wager, after you've attended a few, but for now you may as well savor the so-called delights of London."

"You sound old and jaded."

"That's better than young and naive."

She ignored the barb and inquired, "What exactly is a rout?"

"They are absolutely dreadful affairs. You're in for a rude awakening. In fact, it would almost be worth it to see you there, fighting for air, crushed in the crowd." He smiled, thinking about it.

"Does that mean you're coming?" she asked archly.

He looked back to see if Patrick was listening. Apparently he wasn't. "Who knows? Perhaps I shall be there. You needn't worry. At a rout you would not have to fear I would get you alone."

Instantly, she knew his meaning. "I don't fear you, Lord Thomas, no matter where we are or what the circumstances."

"Perhaps you should," he said simply, then turned his attention to driving the curricle.

Chapter 12

Misery sat on Evleen's shoulders like a huge iron weight. She wished she could sink from sight when Lord Alberdsley called her into his study and chastised her for what he referred to as her "ill-thought-out escapade."

"I cannot express to you how concerned I was." He gazed at her with saddened eyes. "You'll not do that again?"

She assured him she would not, feeling terrible that she'd caused this kindly old man such great distress. She explained that in Ireland she was accustomed to roaming about as she pleased, with nary a thought for the hour of the day or the need for a chaperone.

"Say no more, I understand." Grateful to have his grandson back, Lord Alberdsley could not bring himself to be too harsh. "The incident is forgotten." He glanced at the jeweled ormolu clock on the mantel. "Aren't you ladies planning to attend a rout tonight? You had best get ready."

"Must I go?"

Alberdsley's shaggy white eyebrows rose in surprise. "You would rather not?"

"Isn't it obvious I don't fit in with your so-called cream of society? After today, I should not even try."

"But, my dear, I promised your mother you would be treated like one of the family. Bear in mind, when Patrick becomes the Earl of Alberdsley, he'll hold a position of high rank and prominence. I shall do all within my power to ensure he's educated for the position and feels at home among the *ton*. As his sister, you must feel at home, too. Please, for Patrick's sake, won't you give it a try?" He gave her a warm smile of encouragement. "You can do it. You have the looks, the charm, the brains. You could be the most popular belle in London, if you cared to."

"Me, a London belle?" Evleen asked, laughing. "I don't think so. All I want right now is to look after Patrick."

"Won't you humor an old man?"

There was such a pleading in Lord Alberdsley's eyes she could hold out no longer. "All right, I shall go to the rout. I can only hope I don't commit another faux pas."

"Mon Dieu," muttered Celeste. Lips pursed in disapproval, she stepped back to view the result of her efforts to dress Evleen for the rout.

Evleen turned this way and that in front of her full-length mirror. *How ugly,* she thought, regarding the newly borrowed dark brown dress with distaste. It fit well enough, and the simple style with its modest neckline could not be faulted, yet something was wrong. "Why is it I look so drab?" she asked.

"Mud is most definitely not your color," replied Celeste.

Of course! That dark brown did look like mud. "It makes my skin look dull and lifeless."

"Not like *zee capucine.*" Celeste frowned. "Too bad Miss Charlotte said she might want to wear it soon herself. It would have been perfect for you." Her frown deepened. "Before she wears it, hell will freeze." She cast Evleen's gown a look of aversion. "No one has ever liked that mud-colored atrocity. For years it's hung at zee back of Miss Charlotte's wardrobe."

"Beggars cannot be choosers, Celeste." Evleen perceived exactly what the lady's maid was hinting at, yet after her transgression today, she had no wish to find fault with anyone.

"You will need a fan," said Celeste. "I shall go borrow—"

"I don't need a fan. I carried that silly plume thing to dinner the other night, and found it nothing but a bother. All it did was tickle my nose."

Celeste persisted, but Evleen was adamant. Shortly, wearing the mud-colored dress, not carrying a fan, Evleen descended the stairs to the drawing room, wishing heartily that she could just stay home.

Evleen was relieved Lord Alberdsley had forgiven her, but now, as she sat in the drawing room with the Trevlyn ladies, waiting for their carriage to come around, she felt like an accused prisoner in the Old Baily docks. Except for Amanda, they looked formidable, all dressed to the nines for the rout. Lydia Trevlyn was a study in mirthless severity in severe black; Charlotte looked more like a beautiful wax doll than a real person in her peach satin gown, her blond hair perfectly arranged; Bettina was all frills, lace, and tiny bouncy curls. Only Amanda, unattractive in a plain dull-colored gown, did not have that accusing gleam in her eyes. Evleen realized that Amanda would actually be pretty if she sat straight, not hunched over with her shoulders slumped.

Lydia spoke to Evleen, her lips pursed in disapproval. "What I cannot understand is what possessed you to go wandering about the streets, especially at that indecent hour of the morning."

Evleen wondered how she could possibly explain that at the time, she had not given her and Patrick's little stroll a thought. And how was she to know whether an hour was "indecent" or not? There was no such thing as an indecent hour in County Clare since most of its citizens arose early in order to do their work. She would try to explain. "You see, in Ireland—"

"It simply is not done," interrupted Bettina, looking down her nose. "A lady on the streets alone? Whoever heard of such a thing?"

"And on St. James's Street," Charlotte contributed, her expression properly horrified. "Everyone knows a lady must never show her face on St. James's Street."

"Yet there you were," Lydia went on, "wandering alone, with only a little boy for company—hardly a chaperone—going wherever you pleased for the world to see."

"I could not see the harm," Evleen answered, knowing in advance they wouldn't like her answer.

"You cannot see the harm?" repeated Lydia in horror. "We are only concerned for your welfare, Miss O'Fallon, and can only hope the people who count didn't see you on St. James's Street alone. If they did, your reputation is in shreds before you've hardly started."

Charlotte bobbed her head in agreement. "And furthermore, you have endangered the reputation of the entire Trevlyn family."

And just who were "the people who count"? Evleen wondered. *Best not to ask.* "Perhaps I should be drawn and quartered," she murmured, seeing the humor despite her discomfit.

Only Amanda caught the whimsy in her remark, and to
Evleen's surprise, threw her a fleeting smile. Alas, her mother
caught it, and demanded, "What is funny, Amanda?"

"Nothing, Mama." Amanda pulled herself straight, obviously gathering her courage, and burst out, "But perhaps we
should remember that Evleen just arrived from Ireland, where
things are different, and she cannot possibly be expected to
learn all our customs at once."

The sound of Lydia's sigh of exasperation filled the room. "I
am surprised at you, Amanda. Henceforth, I suggest that you,
not being knowledgeable of the situation, would do well to remain silent." Lydia turned back to Evleen. "You are not in Ireland now, are you? I trust you'll know how to conduct yourself
at Lord and Lady Beckford's rout tonight."

"Also called an 'at home,' Evleen," Charlotte loftily informed her, "just in case you didn't know."

Evleen heartily wished she had not promised Lord Alberdsley she would go to the rout, or at home, or whatever it was
called, but she had promised, and there was no getting around
it. "I shall do my best, Mrs. Trevlyn. That's all I can do. You
may as well know, I am not keen on going."

Lydia gazed pointedly at the mud-colored gown. "You don't
wish to attend? After we took all the trouble to find something
suitable for you to wear?"

"Don't mistake me. I promised Lord Alberdsley I would go
and so I shall."

Not appeased, Lydia heatedly continued, "You disgraced us
all today with your thoughtlessness and unthinking behavior.
Oh, don't think I don't sympathize. Coming from a country as
uncivilized as Ireland, you simply don't know any better. I fear
you'll be dreadfully out of place. Quite frankly, if it were up to
me, I would most readily grant your wish not to attend the at
home tonight, or any events of the Season. However, Lord Alberdsley insists you go. Imagine. He actually thinks you can
learn the social graces overnight and become an accepted member of our Polite World."

Bettina whinnied. Charlotte burst into a gale of giggles and
exclaimed, "Our Irish princess will never fit in. You know that
yourself, don't you, Evleen?"

"I'm not so sure of that," said Amanda, boldly speaking up

again. "Did you not see Lord Thomas when he brought her home? He seemed quite taken with her."

All laughter ceased abruptly. A silence followed, during which Evleen could almost see the waves of resentment wafting in her direction.

Lydia finally responded, "Lord Thomas is a most compassionate man, Amanda. You would be wise not to mistake charity for affection."

Charlotte glared at her younger sister. "Anyway, you're mistaken. Lord Thomas harbors a secret affection for me, and always has. A pity he's only a second son, or I might have considered him, especially since he is rather handsome, and most charming. However"—she shrugged a shoulder in mock indifference—"Montague will be proposing soon."

Bettina sniggered. "The way things are going, you'll turn into a dried-up old ape leader waiting for Montague."

"Girls," Lydia said sharply. "Not another word. We all know Montague is on the brink of proposing."

"What if he doesn't?" asked Amanda.

"Then there are other first sons in this world," declared Lydia.

Bettina said, "If you ask me, *I'm* the one Lord Thomas holds a special affection for. Just look how he dotes on my embroidery. He'll be proposing soon, too."

"I'm sure he will, Bettina," Lydia said fiercely, "and your father and I shall approve, even though he's only a second son." She sighed wistfully. "I would have wanted first sons for all of you, but apparently that's not to be."

Pierce announced their carriage had arrived at the front entrance. Accompanying the Trevlyns from the drawing room, Evleen wondered, *first son? second son?* How could a man's station in life so totally depend on the order in which he was born? Apparently it did, though, and she thought it very strange.

"So this is a rout?" Evleen murmured, incredulous.

Despite Lord Thomas's warning, she had pictured a dignified evening in which elegantly dressed men and women would dance, congenially converse, take refreshments, and play cards. Her first indication that her expectations were woefully wrong came when the Trevlyns' carriage became caught in a horrific jam of horses, coaches, and carriages, all waiting to approach

Lord and Lady Beckford's front portico. At least fifteen minutes
passed before they reached it, then had to fight their way through
a crowd to obtain entrance. After a hasty greeting by their
harried-looking hostess, they fought their way up the packed
staircase to a series of rooms on the first floor, where everyone
seemed to be milling about with no purpose. There appeared to
be no place to sit. "Where are the chairs?" asked Evleen.

"Nobody sits," whispered Amanda.

"But what on earth are we supposed to do? Where's the conversation, the cards, the music? Where's the food?"

"You don't understand. All we're supposed to do is elbow
our way through the crowd, and then, after a quarter of an hour
or so, we leave."

"But how could they enjoy this?" Evleen asked, gazing at
Lydia, Charlotte, and Bettina, who despite the crush, were smiling brightly, appearing to be having a delightful time.

"We come to see and be seen," answered Amanda. "It's es-
sential in high society. We have to entertain and be entertained
to maintain our standing. That's just the way it is."

Standing indeed. Evleen refrained from voicing her opinion
of what utter foolishness she thought this all was, or how she
could make better use of her time staying at home with a good
book. She breathed a sigh of relief when, after she'd been jostled and her toes trampled several times, they finally reached
the street again. As they waited amidst the milling crowd for
their carriage, Evleen took a gulp of fresh air and said softly to
Amanda, "Thank the saints, that's over. Now we can go home."

Charlotte overheard and arched an eyebrow. "We have just
begun. Lord and Lady Beckford's was only the first. There are
several more at homes we plan to attend this evening."

Trapped. Evleen considered walking home—it was not very
far—but she could well imagine how such a course of action
would be perceived, considering the heinous crimes she'd already committed this day. She could imagine, too, how short a
time it would take for news of her latest transgression to reach
Lord Alberdsley. Not a good idea. She wouldn't want to hurt
him again. They continued waiting, jostled by the crowd.
Would the carriage never come? She stepped back, then felt
herself shoved away from the rest just as she heard a voice pro-
claim, "Why Miss O'Fallon, what a delightful surprise."

Montague. She recognized his oily voice and immediately felt repelled, remembering his salacious attitude toward her that night at Lord Alberdsley's country estate. "Good evening, Lord Eddington," she said as coolly as she dared. He was a handsome man, almost pretty with his extremely pale complexion—did he never venture into the sun?—and flattering brown ringlets encircling his thin, patrician face. Even so, she sensed the debauchery that dwelt behind that beauteous facade. Determined to say something polite and then move on, she gathered her shawl more closely around her and politely inquired, "Have you just arrived, or are you leaving?"

"Leaving," Montague answered with a relieved smile. "I have done my duty for tonight. Now it's on to White's."

His breath reeked of alcohol, bringing Evleen a fleeting memory of the men of County Clare, quaffing their glasses of Guinness at the Shamrock and Thistle of a Saturday night. "Delightful to see you again, sir," she said, pulling away. "Now I must get back to my—"

"Don't go yet." He took hold of her arm and drilled her with a gaze of blazing intensity. "Where are you going next?"

"To another rout, but I don't know which one. Now I must get back."

She tried to pull away, but, staggering slightly, he held her fast. "I should think it's Lady Fanshawe's." He appeared to hit upon an idea and glanced toward the curb. "Ah, I see my carriage has arrived. One more rout won't hurt me. Come, I shall give you a ride to Lady Fanshawe's rout."

She would as soon ride with a tangle of writhing snakes. Besides, what would the Trevlyns say if she rode merrily off with this object of their desperate pursuit—this ultimate prize, a first son? The thought was too horrible to contemplate. "Thank you, but I most definitely think not."

"Oh, come now, where's your spirit of adventure? Go inform the old dragon if you like. She cannot object."

"If you mean Mrs. Trevlyn, she most certainly can object." How stupid could he be? Evleen had no intention of prying into Montague's personal affairs, but still, something must be said, albeit tactfully. "I am aware you're not yet betrothed, but I believe there exists some sort of commitment between you and Miss Charlotte Trevlyn."

"Nonsense, I am committed to no one," declared Montague. His eyes raked her boldly. "When we met, I was immediately impressed not only by your beauty but by your independent attitude—your spunk, if you will. Was I right? Or are you simply a poor peasant girl from Ireland, too awed by this noble assemblage to break a rule?" He raised a mocking eyebrow. "My dear Miss O'Fallon, I dare you. Come ride in my carriage." A lecherous smile played on his lips. "I assure you, you'll be perfectly safe—on my word as a gentleman."

Does he think I am daft? She was certainly not frightened—after all they were standing in the midst of a crowd of people—but she was thoroughly disgusted. She tried to break free, but he gripped her arm tighter.

"I have heard about you wild Irish girls," he murmured in her ear. "Are you one? How I yearn to find out."

"Is my brother bothering you?"

Thomas. Just the sound of his voice caused her anxiety to drain away.

Montague instantly released his grip on her arm. "What is the matter with you, Thomas? I am not bothering the young lady. We were simply having a chat."

Thomas smiled. "Of course you are, Montague. As always, you're a paragon of virtue."

Montague said, "Er . . . I think I shall be going."

"Have you not paid your respects to the Trevlyns?" Thomas asked in mock astonishment. With pointed words, he added, "Most especially to Miss Charlotte Trevlyn, to whom you will soon be betrothed."

Looking exceedingly discomfited, Montague backed away. "We'll talk later, Thomas. White's awaits. Good evening, Miss O'Fallon, perhaps another time?"

Evleen stared after Montague as he made a hasty retreat. In Gaelic she muttered, *"Go nithe an cat th is go nithe an diabhal an cat."*

"I take it you were not wishing my brother a pleasant evening?"

"It's an old Irish saying. I said, may the cat eat him and may the devil eat the cat."

Thomas looked amused. "What a fitting end for Montague."

Evleen smiled up at him, noting he looked more handsome

than she had ever seen him in a double-breasted frock coat with claw-hammer tails, long trousers, a fine linen shirt, and an "Oriental" tied cravat. "You came along at the right time. Sure and I'm happy to see you."

"Sure and I'm happy to see you, too," he said, mocking her Irish brogue, but in an endearing kind of way.

"I thought you never went to routs."

"I don't."

"Then why—?"

"Your fault. I couldn't stay away."

Her pulse quickened at his startling reply. But what could she answer? She would take the wisest course and find another line of conversation. "I had best go find the Trevlyns. They're waiting for their carriage to"—she could not keep from wrinkling her nose in distaste—"take us to another rout."

"So at last you're getting a taste of life in the *ton*," he said pleasantly. "And how are you enjoying hobnobbing with society's finest?"

"So far, I am not enjoying it at all, what with this ridiculous rout, and then Montague—" She cut her sentence short, wise enough to realize she had said enough about his brother. Besides, it was hardly politic to keep disparaging the esteemed Lord Eddington, destined to be the Marquess of Wythe someday. "Sorry, that slipped out. I didn't mean—"

"Have you read *Childe Harold*?" asked Thomas, growing serious. "It was written by—"

"Lord Byron. Does it surprise you we have books in Ireland? But we do, and, yes, I've read the poem."

He ignored her barb. "The poem concerns a debauched young nobleman, the weary survivor of many a love affair and many a night of riotous living. One line reads, 'Apart he stalked in joyless reverie.' That's Montague, miserable in his debauchery. The line suits him perfectly. I suspect Byron used him as a model."

Ah, so Thomas does perceive his brother's shortcomings. Even so, politeness decreed she should search for something complimentary to say. "But Montague has his charms, certainly."

"I love my brother, but he is an arrogant, joyless man, drugged with pleasure and hell-bent on self-destruction." Thomas grinned unexpectedly. "But enough of such a grim subject. Come, I shall escort you back to the Trevlyns."

Lydia scowled when she saw them. "Good evening, Lord Thomas. You should not have wandered away, Evleen. Where have you been? Come, our carriage has arrived."

Lord Thomas asked, "Are you going to the rout at Lady Fanshawe's?" Lydia nodded. "Then your carriage must be crowded. I have the family coach tonight. Kindly allow Miss O'Fallon to ride with me."

"Well, I . . ." Lydia looked discomfited, obviously wondering what rule she might break if she consented.

"You have nothing to worry about, Mrs. Trevlyn," Thomas said, amused. "My coach will follow so closely behind yours you would instantly be aware of any . . . shall we say, foolishness?"

To Evleen's surprise, the dour woman actually managed a small laugh as she declared, "Oh, Lord Thomas," and playfully tapped his chest with her fan. "You know we trust you. It's just that I am always mindful of my duties as a chaperone."

"Let Evleen go with him, Mama," Charlotte said indifferently. "He's right about our carriage being crowded."

Lydia shrugged. "Oh, very well, she may ride with you, Lord Thomas." It was obvious the matter was of little concern to her. With careful eyes, she surveyed the crowd. "I don't suppose your brother . . . ?"

"I am afraid not, madame. I believe he has gone off to White's." Thomas bowed slightly to Evleen. "Shall we find my coach, Miss O'Fallon? I am wild with anticipation at the very thought of the next at home."

"As am I," Evleen declared, doing her best to keep a straight face.

When Evleen sat back in Thomas's closed coach, she remarked, "You could have asked me."

Thomas settled next to her. "Would you have said no?"

"Of course not, but you could have asked."

"Point taken, but you needn't be so fractious." He leaned out the window and called to the coachman, "On to Lady Fanshaw's." Reaching for a blanket, he regarded with distaste the thin, inadequate shawl that only partially covered her gown. "It's cold tonight. I don't know why you women insist on dressing as if it were the middle of summer."

"I have learned already that in London it's not fashionable

to be warm." Evleen looked down at herself and shivered. "If I had my way, I'd be bundled to my ears. I'd be laughed clear out of Ireland if I wore this ridiculous outfit on a chilly night like this in County Clare."

As he began to tuck the blanket about her lap, she was again reminded of that day they'd started their trek across England. Earlier, he'd done the same, only it was daylight, and they were in an open carriage. Now, in the cozy darkness, she felt more than warm and snug, she felt secure and safe in the hands of a man she could completely trust. "Sorry if I was . . . did you say fractious? Now there's a big word." With a laugh just loud enough, and impudent enough, for him to hear, she settled back in the darkness, where she was instantly lulled by the rhythmic clip-clop of horses' hooves and the gentle sway of the coach.

"I see your fiery Irish spirit is still alive and well," he said softly, not the least perturbed. "Which I greatly admire, by the way. Timothy Murphy is a lucky man."

Curious, she asked, "In what way?"

"He'll have you for a wife, won't he?"

"Not that I know of," she answered briskly.

He sat back. In the dimness she could just see his shocked expression. "But I thought . . . someone told me . . ."

"They were wrong, whoever they were. I am not marrying Timothy. I made that clear to him before I left."

"But . . . ." All at once he threw his head back and let out a great peal of laughter. "And all this time I've been acting the honorable gentleman."

"I don't know what you mean," she said, puzzled. He leaned close again. His face, only inches away, was lit at intervals by the flickering glow cast by the gas streetlights. Ordinarily she would be annoyed with anyone who got this close, but the intimate proximity of Thomas Linberry was causing a strange stirring in the pit of her stomach.

"But this puts a new light on things." He took her hand and clasped it in both of his. "Strange, isn't it, how we've traveled across two countries, but this is the first time we've ever truly been alone."

"Does it make a difference?" Her heartbeat quickened. She sensed what was coming, but could not bring herself to draw away.

"Of course it makes a difference. I could hardly kiss you in the middle of St. James's Square, now could I?" He slid his hands around her shoulders.

"But you think you can kiss me here?" Now her heart had more than just quickened, it was pounding, about ready to burst.

He drew closer still, his face only inches from hers. "Be warned, my dear Miss O'Fallon, I had an ulterior motive when I offered my coach. Timothy or no Timothy, my honor as a gentleman was wearing thin."

Her rational thought was fast fading, but she managed to quote, " 'Men are happy to be laughed at for their humor, but not for their folly.' Jonathan Swift said that. He——"

"The devil with Jonathan Swift." He pulled slightly back. "If you don't want me to kiss you, tell me to stop. A pity, though, after I went to all this trouble to get you alone."

"But this *is* folly. You know there are all kinds of reasons why we shouldn't."

"Ah, the obstacles." Thomas leaned close again and murmured, "There are four ladies in the carriage directly ahead who would be utterly scandalized if they could see us now." They passed a streetlight that briefly illuminated his devilish grin. He gripped her shoulders tighter. "I warn you, there's every reason in the world why you shouldn't kiss me, but you're going to do it anyway, aren't you?"

Although his words were half in jest, there was a tremor in his voice, and she could feel his body trembling. She said lightly, "Mama would not approve."

"She's not here."

"Just one kiss?" She felt so warm, so protected. He was such an exciting man, how could this be wrong?

"One kiss," he said softly, "just one. And after, we shall become our noble selves again, virtuous to a fault, dutifully tending to our moral obligations. Eventually you will either marry a rich Englishman or return to Ireland and doubtless marry that fine, outstanding Irishman, Timothy Murphy, no matter what you say. Eventually, I shall marry . . . I forget her name, but I shall think of it in time."

She started laughing softly. How could she help it? And how could she say no? "All right," she said, wrapping her arms around his neck, "but just one, and we had better pray Lydia Trevlyn doesn't have eyes in the back of her head."

With an intake of breath, he clasped her body tightly to his, one hand exploring the hollow of her back. "You don't know how much I've been wanting to do this," he murmured.

She gave herself up to him completely, savoring the heady sensation of his lips pressing against the pulsing hollow of her throat, then her cheek, across her forehead, down to her nose, then at last, urgently demanding, her mouth.

The feel of his lips against hers caused a delicious, warming sensation. She kissed him in return, lingering, savoring every moment. She forgot Timothy Murphy, Montague, Lydia Trevlyn. There was no outside world. Nothing existed beyond this hot, tight space within this gently swaying carriage and this witty, charming man who was passionately embracing her.

"Almost there, sir," called the coachman.

Thomas lifted his lips and murmured, "Damn. We've got to stop. God knows, I don't want to, but we must." His voice was hoarse, his breath coming hard.

She had felt transported on a soft, wispy cloud, but came down to earth in a hurry. Though his kiss had left her dazed and breathless, she managed to say, "Indeed we must. This was not in my plans. I—"

"I want you, Evleen," he said in a ragged whisper. Tenderly, he brought his trembling fingers to her cheek. "I have wanted you from that minute I first saw you. Ah, how beautiful you are. I think of you night and day, my Evleen."

Totally undone by his words, she was searching for an answer when the bright lights from Lady Fanshawe's mansion suddenly illuminated the carriage. They broke apart and slid to sit circumspectly in opposite corners. Thomas's usual charming smile reappeared, yet his eyes drilled into hers with burning intensity. "It won't end here."

"It must," she said before he swung from the coach and reached to help her down. The Trevlyns were upon them as she stepped into another milieu of horses, carriages, and a swarming crowd.

Lydia flashed an artificial smile at Thomas. "How kind of you to take our little Irish princess under your wing. We're all aware how difficult it must be for her to suddenly find herself in an enlightened society such as this." She shook her head in mock sympathy. "So very different from the simple life she knew at home."

How dare she. Evleen was about to speak her mind when Thomas intervened.

"How kind of you to be concerned over Evleen's welfare. From what I've seen, though, she's more than a match for any young lady of the *ton.*"

If Lydia caught the underlying reproach in Thomas's remark, she did not let on. Instead, she wagged a finger under his nose. "You tell Montague he's been a naughty boy tonight, running off to White's. Tell him we expect his presence at Lady Claremont's ball this coming Friday."

Thomas bowed. "I shall convey your message, although I cannot guarantee—"

"You tell him our patience is running short and he had best be there." Lydia's smile had disappeared.

"I understand," Thomas said quietly. He turned to Evleen. "A most delightful ride, Miss O'Fallon. I most thoroughly enjoyed our discussion of the poets." He bid good night to everyone and disappeared into the crowd.

"Such a charming man," remarked Lydia. "It's a pity Montague did not inherit more of his virtuous deportment and high moral character."

Evleen was still so wrought up from the interlude in Thomas's coach, she had to suppress a peal of near hysterical laughter. What would Lydia and her daughters think if they knew that from Waverton Street to Berkeley Square she had nestled in the arms of that charming young man with the "virtuous deportment and high moral character"? *Willingly, too. Perhaps even wantonly,* she admitted, as she thought of their kiss, a delicious shiver running through her.

Ah, if they only knew.

Chapter 13

When Thomas arrived at his family's London town house, he found Penelope awake and waiting up for him.

"I cannot believe you, of all people, went to all those silly routs tonight," she said as he joined her in the drawing room.

Thomas slung himself into a chair. "And where were you?"

"Need I remind you this is my third Season? I'm no longer thrilled with milling about in a mob to no purpose other than it's the *thing* to do."

"Poor Penelope," he said with mock sympathy. "Nineteen and already jaded."

"Speaking of jaded, did you see Montague?"

"Only briefly, before he took himself off to White's, where he assuredly is now, throwing God-knows-how-much of the family fortune away on the faro tables. By the way, he did a fine job of ignoring Charlotte Trevlyn this evening. Her mother is less than pleased."

"Papa won't be pleased, either," Penelope answered regretfully. "You know how grouchy he's become of late, what with his gout. I can only imagine his fury if Montague doesn't propose to Charlotte, and soon."

"Even though Walter is no longer heir to the estate?"

"She's still a Trevlyn, is she not? All Papa wants is for our two families to be forever united, into eternity. All dependent on Montague, of course."

Thomas sighed. "Well, it's Montague's problem, not mine. I have enough else to concern me."

Penelope regarded him thoughtfully. "You're not your usual lighthearted self tonight. You seem distracted."

Distracted was hardly the word for the mood he was in. "I'm

leaving London tomorrow. Time I got back to my thoroughbreds. It's best I leave before I . . ."

"Before you what, Thomas?"

"Nothing." Since that kiss in the coach, his emotions had
lurched back and forth between hot desire and disgust with
himself for allowing his feelings to get out of hand. Penelope
was his closest confidante. No doubt she knew more about him
than anyone, yet how could he explain his feelings when he
hardly understood himself?

"How can you possibly leave now?" inquired Penelope.
"Lady Claremont's ball is next Friday night. Surely you'll want
to stay for one of the most important events of the Season."

His eyebrow lifted sardonically. "I suppose everyone who
counts will be there?"

"How did you guess?"

"Since when did I ever care about who counts and who
doesn't?" Feeling restless and irritable—all his own doing, of
course—Thomas arose from his chair and headed for the door.
"I'm off to bed."

Penelope called after him, "It's Evleen O'Fallon, isn't it?"

Curse her perceptiveness. He turned as Penelope remarked,
"I heard what you did today. How noble, rescuing the damsel
in distress and her adorable little brother."

"I would have done as much for a stranger." *Why was I bur-
dened with a sister so skilled at reading my mind?*

Worse, she wasn't through.

"*On-dit* has it that the two of them were wandering the
streets unescorted." Penelope pursed her lips and tilted her nose
in a fair imitation of Lydia Trevlyn. "Simply not done, my
deah," she mocked, and went on, "and letting herself be seen
on St. James's Street, where everyone *knows* a lady would not
be caught *dead*."

Thomas could not help laughing at his irreverent sister, but
quickly sobered. "It's such hypocrisy, isn't it? The truth is,
Lydia Trevlyn is not so much concerned about her family's reputation as she is about marrying her daughters off."

"Exactly," said Penelope, "and she sees the Irish girl as a
threat."

"And well she might, considering Evleen O'Fallon has more

beauty, brains, and charm in her little finger than the Trevlyn girls possess—"

Uh-oh, now he'd done it. Judging from that sagacious little grin playing on Penelope's lips, Thomas suddenly realized he had just revealed far more than he had intended.

"I knew it," Penelope declared triumphantly. "After all these years, the high-and-mighty Thomas Linberry has finally fallen in love. Don't bother to deny it. It won't do you any good."

That uninvited vision of Evleen and Timothy embracing again arose before his eyes. He said harshly, "I had thought Evleen O'Fallon was betrothed to that Irishman."

"She's not."

"So I found out. Up to now, my feelings were of no consequence. Now I . . . This puts a new light on things."

"Oh, Thomas." Penelope started slowly shaking her head in sympathy. "You were using Evleen's so-called betrothal as a defense, weren't you? It didn't matter how fond you grew of her. She was betrothed, and that made you feel safe, didn't it? No action on your part was necessary."

"That's absurd."

"Is it? Then why are you so agitated? I think you've fallen in love with her, and now, all of a sudden, you find she's available and you don't know what to do."

Thomas neither affirmed nor denied his sister's shrewd observations. Instead, closemouthed, he bid his sister a hasty good night and retreated to his bedchamber. Now, safe from Penelope's penetrating questions, he reflected upon her words. "Fallen in love," she'd said. No, that wasn't possible. Never in his entire untroubled, well-ordered existence had he been so foolish as to lose his heart to a woman. Some of his friends had been struck by Cupid's arrow, and what a result! Their ensuing conduct had caused him to marvel at how an intelligent, reasoning, and heretofore tough-minded man could turn into a quivering mass of erratic emotions, writing abominable love poems, mooning about like some lovesick schoolboy, claiming his life would be ruined unless the object of his newfound love consented to marry him. And all because he'd been brought down by some bubble-headed chit. *Not Thomas Linberry. Indeed, no.* He'd had his share of Cyprians, and though he had to admit he'd been fond of them and treated them with courtesy—

more than he could say for some of his friends—he had never lost his heart, even to the most seductive and beautiful of them. Nor had he lost his heart to Miss Bettina Trevlyn, which was exactly as it should be. Although he fully expected to develop some sort of affection for her when and if they married, love hardly mattered. Love was a handicap. Love interfered with one's well-ordered life. Love made a man look foolish, and that's why he, a man totally in control of his emotions, could not possibly be in love with Evleen O'Fallon.

True, he'd been unable to stop thinking about her, or shake off the strange sensations that rushed through his body when he did. Especially now, after that kiss. There went his sleep tonight, again. Positively and without fail, tomorrow he would get a grip on himself and put her out of his mind, but not tonight. Tonight he would lie in his bed and picture how she had nestled into his arms, a perfect fit, as if she belonged there, all soft and warm, and how she . . .

Perhaps he would stay in London, at least for a while. But that was wrong. Penelope was right about his defenses being down. The sooner he left for Tanglewood Hall, the better.

"Evleen, what is the lady doing?" asked Patrick. He had come to her bedchamber, and now sat upon her bed, feet dangling, watching curiously as she stood on a chair, still as a statue.

Evleen glanced at the middle-aged woman kneeling on the floor. "This is my new dressmaker, and she's measuring a hem. Do you like it?" She spread her arms, showing off her new ball gown. "Your grandfather has insisted I have some gowns made so I shall be fashionable."

"Mama says to be fashionable is to be vain."

"She's absolutely right, but I like being fashionable all the same."

"Shall you wear it to the ball tonight?"

"No, it won't be ready in time, but I shall wear this to a ball next Friday night."

"Shall you dance with lots of men?" asked Patrick with a frown.

"Of course I shall."

"But what of Timothy?"

She could tell this wasn't an idle question. Patrick had always liked Timothy and expected her to marry him. She'd have to set him straight. "First, I am not betrothed to Timothy," she said gently. "Second, your grandfather wants me to grow accustomed to the glittering society you're going to be living in the rest of your life. Dancing with other men is quite acceptable."

"I've finished with the pinning, miss," said the dressmaker.

Carefully holding up her skirt, Evleen stepped down and went to her mirror. "Oh," she said with a gasp, unable to contain her delight. Her nearly completed gown was of white silk, high-waisted, low-cut, and adorned with clusters of pink roses around the hem, accompanied by wide bands of white lace trim. Best of all, this gown was practically all her own creation. She had chosen the pattern and fabric herself, and if she did say so, it had turned out perfectly. *Wait until Thomas sees me,* she thought, then caught herself. These past few days, she'd had great difficulty keeping her mind off Thomas and their hot, breathless, totally unexpected kiss in the darkness of the coach. *So utterly wrong.* "Highly improper," Lydia would say, but for the life of her, Evleen couldn't work up any guilt. Instead, she felt deliciously wicked. If Lydia could have seen into the back of that carriage, she would be so scandalized! But there was something else, too, that kept her thoughts on Thomas, something beyond a frivolous kiss. She'd felt it when, trembling, he'd taken her in his arms, and when his lips found hers, she could have sworn there was more than lust on his mind, something deeper, as if he meant his kiss to tell her something. Oh, it was so hard to know what he was truly thinking.

But this was wrong, thinking so much about him. If her mother wanted her to marry a rich, titled Englishman, she would try, and in the process forget about Thomas.

Lydia entered as the dressmaker was leaving. "Well, Evleen, I see your dress is nearly complete. Let me look at you."

Evleen dutifully turned and stood quietly as the older woman examined her with a critical eye. "Hmm, that should do for the ball next week." Her remark carried all the warmth of a frost-covered tombstone.

"If only it were ready for tonight," Evleen said wistfully.

"Charlotte's gown is perfectly suitable for tonight," Lydia

replied, her voice devoid of sympathy. "I trust you're aware Lady Claremont's ball is one of the most important events of the Season. Everybody who is anybody will be there, and I advise you to act accordingly."

Evleen stiffened, sensing immediately the implied insult.

"Just what do you mean by 'accordingly,' Mrs. Trevlyn? That I not spit on the floor? That I not rip my clothes off and dance in my chemise? That I—?" *Oh-oh.* She had gone too far. She could tell because Lydia's mouth had dropped open and her face was turning purple.

"You know what I mean," snapped Lydia. That she was annoyed was an understatement. "You would be wise to stay away from Montague. And might I suggest you say as little as possible? That way, no one will know you come from Ireland."

I've done it now, thought Evleen, regretting her impudent answer. She must keep reminding herself of her vow to maintain good relations with the Trevlyns, no matter what. She didn't want to apologize, but knew she must. "I am truly sorry for my frivolous answer, Mrs. Trevlyn. Have no fear, I shall be as circumspect as a nun."

"That's good to hear, Evleen."

Hearing a trace of softening in Lydia's voice, Evleen decided to go a step further. "I want you to know how sorry I am about . . . well, everything. It must have been very difficult—I mean, expecting your husband would be the heir to Lord Alberdsley's estate, and then here came Patrick, without so much as a warning."

After an awkward moment of silence, Lydia's face twisted with emotion. "You have no idea how difficult. We've lost our fortune. If we're not careful, the girls won't marry nearly as well. And I . . . I . . ." She gulped, rigidly holding tears in check. "All these years I expected that someday I would have a title. My dear friend, Mrs. Drummond-Burrel, expects a title. Someday she'll become Lady Willoughby de Eresby, but will I ever become *Lady* Alberdsley? No! Because of Patrick, I am doomed to being nothing more than plain Mrs. Trevlyn"—her voice began to rise —"for the rest of my life."

How amazing. Evleen found it hard to believe Lydia's main concern in life appeared to be the loss of a title she never had. How shallow to put such value on a mere word in front of one's name. And yet, it was clear her anguish was genuine. Evleen had never expected she'd feel sympathy for this bitter, mirthless woman, but now she did. "I am so sorry," she began, but Lydia raised a hand to silence her.

"Don't. There's nothing you can do about it, is there?" In complete control of herself once again, Lydia squared her shoulders. "Was there anything else, Evleen?"

After allowing that one brief crack in her armor, Lydia was obviously back to her old self again. To say anything more on the subject would be useless. Instead, Evleen decided to voice a small fear that had been nagging her. "In Ireland, we did the country dances. Is it the same here?"

For a fleeting moment, Evleen could have sworn she saw a tiny glitter of triumph in Lydia's eyes, but she must have been mistaken because the older woman smiled and said, "You'll do fine. You shouldn't have a bit of trouble with the dances. They are all quite easy, and you can simply learn as you go along."

"Then I shall do my best," Evleen said, greatly relieved.

"I'm sure you will." Lydia's jaw tightened. "Remember, our family's reputation is at stake. We cannot tolerate another of your little escapades."

"Now you've done it," said Patrick after Lydia had left. He had listened silently, still perched on Evleen's bed.

"Yes, I've made her angry, haven't I?" Evleen answered thoughtfully. "It's my own fault, too."

"You shouldn't have been so impudent."

"That's quite perceptive of you, Patrick," she answered, not happy hearing the truth from a ten-year-old. Hands on hips, she advised, "Well, let that be a lesson to you, my future Lord Alberdsley. It's usually best to hold one's tongue."

"I don't want to be Lord Alberdsley. I want to go home."

Surprised, she said, "But I thought you liked it here."

"Yes, I do like it. Grandfather has been wonderful to me, but I . . ." Patrick bit his lip. He appeared to be on the verge of tears. "I miss Mama, and Darragh, and all of them. I want to go home."

Patrick's tears started to flow as Evleen, fancy ball dress and all, knelt and took him in her arms. " 'Twill be all right, dear," she crooned as she rocked him, "we must not give up. Mama wants you to stay, remember? Her last letter said she's much

better. I, too, want to go home in the very worst way, but we'll
stay and see this through, won't we?" Patrick nodded, wiping
tears away. "And we won't let the English get the better of us,
will we?"

"No, Evleen, we won't." Patrick smiled through his tears.
"If I stay, you must stay."

"Of course." She forced a bright smile. "And I shall marry a
very rich and ever-so-titled Englishman, just as Mama said."

Patrick eyed her with suspicion. "Mama said you should
never love an Englishman. You wouldn't, would you?"

"Of course not. Are you daft?"

As Patrick smiled, relieved, Evleen asked herself, *How does
the child know?* He sensed the doubt that had begun to cloud
her thinking these past few days, and especially since Thomas's
kiss. But that was nonsense. She knew what she had to do, and
she, honorable woman that she was, would do it.

"You look pretty, Evleen," said Amanda, who had just entered Evleen's bedchamber.

They were about to leave for the ball. Evleen looked down
at the mud-colored gown and knew she didn't look pretty at all.
She hated the gown. Worse, Celeste, occupied with the sisters'
demands, had no extra time, so Evleen had been compelled to
do her hair herself. *Adequate* could best describe her up-swept
coiffure, she thought with dismal certainty.

"You look pretty, too," she said to Amanda. And indeed, the
girl looked charming in a lavender lace gown, her hair caught
up in a mother-of-pearl comb.

Amanda shook her head. "Charlotte and Bettina say I'm too
fat."

"Not at all." Evleen had heard with her own ears the outrageous manner in which Amanda's sisters constantly criticized
her. Truly, she wasn't fat. She simply wasn't as scrawny-looking
as her mother and sisters. She was very pretty, in fact, and if she
hadn't been so browbeaten all her life, she could easily be popular and sought-after. "You're not too fat. You're just right, and
you mustn't let others convince you otherwise."

Amanda remained unconvinced. "I wish I could be more
like you, Evleen. You are so beautiful. And you have such
spirit, and you always seem so sure of yourself."

"Perhaps on the surface." Evleen sighed, thinking of the enmity directed at her from the elder Trevlyns. "Underneath I worry as much as anyone. I must be on my best behavior tonight. Heaven help me if I do anything wrong."

"You won't," said Amanda, regarding her with admiring eyes. She noticed Evleen's empty hands. "But where is your fan?"

"I don't have a fan. It's chilly tonight. I shall have no desire to stir up a breeze."

Amanda giggled. "Silly, you don't carry a fan to really fan yourself. I noticed you didn't carry one at the rout, but tonight you absolutely must have one for the ball."

"Well, I don't. I shall go without."

"You can't." For once, Amanda appeared to take a firm stand. "The fan is a most important fashion accessory. I shall loan you one of mine, and I shan't take no for an answer."

Without another word, Amanda left and shortly returned with a satin-lined fan box made of finely polished wood, filled with fans. "Take your pick, although I think the lace-and-ivory is the perfect match."

"If I must, I must, but it still seems silly." With reluctance, Evleen selected the small lace-and-ivory fan. "They'd be laughing their heads off in County Clare if they saw me waving this around."

"You don't just wave it, you must learn the language of the fan," said Amanda, ignoring Evleen's complaint. "If you carry it in the left hand, thus, that means 'desirous of an acquaintance.' If you carry it in the right hand, that means—"

"Never mind," Evleen interrupted with a smile. "I shall do my own speaking tonight, and not through a fan. Carrying it will be more than enough." She tugged at one of the long white gloves she was wearing and grimaced. "I'm not accustomed to these. Must I wear them all evening?"

"Of course you must." Amanda giggled again. "There's also a language of the gloves. If you bite the tips that means, 'I wish to be rid of you very soon.' If you drop both of them, that means—"

"I don't want to hear it," Evleen replied, laughing now. "Suffice to say, I'll wear the silly things, but I won't be speaking through my fan or my gloves."

Amanda's expression grew solemn. "Evleen, I . . ."

It seemed as if she wanted to say something, but couldn't get the words out. Evleen asked, "What is it, Amanda?"

The girl started to blush. "I want more than anything to be just like you."

Evleen was taken aback. "I?" she asked, pointing at herself. "I am not exactly your mother's ideal of female perfection."

"I don't care what Mother thinks," said Amanda. "I admire you because you don't simper. You're strong and independent, and you think for yourself." She sighed. "I would give anything to be like you."

"Then be like me," said Evleen.

"How?"

"Well, it's very easy. You hold your head high, keep your shoulders back, and do what *you* think is right, not what other people want you to do."

"I shall try."

"Good. That's all there is to it."

Evleen was proud of herself for sounding so completely confident. Underneath, all she could hope for was that her insecurity didn't show, not only to Amanda, but later tonight, to "all those people who count" at Lady Claremont's ball. Would Lord Thomas be there? She should not be thinking about him, but, all the same, she was.

The ball was well under way when Evleen and the Trevlyns stepped into Lady Claremont's ballroom. At first, Evleen felt overwhelmed. Never had she seen so many tiers of lighted candles flickering on crystal chandeliers, heard such stirring music, or seen so many people so elegantly attired. In truth, everybody who was anybody was here, just as Lydia predicted. *May I not commit any gaffes tonight,* Evleen sternly resolved as she stood with the Trevlyns near a row of chaperones. Her conduct would be so impeccable Lydia Trevlyn would find not one little thing to complain about. At least she wouldn't have to worry about knowing the dances. In the ugly dress she was wearing, she knew there was little chance any man would ask her to dance.

"Don't forget your fan," Amanda whispered from behind her own fan.

Evleen held her fan clutched to her side. She considered placing it in front of her mouth as Amanda had done, but it was just too silly. She left it where it was.

Montague appeared and gave them both a warm greeting. Evleen knew she shouldn't ask, but couldn't resist. "And where is your brother tonight, Lord Eddington?"

"My brother has left for Tanglewood Hall, his estate near Abingdon."

Her heart sank. She knew she should not be disappointed, but she was.

"You will have to make do with me," said Montague with a supercilious smirk. "Would you care to dance?"

Not really. Not with this vain, overdressed fop, but what could she say? It was beyond her that he was actually Thomas's brother, the two were so different in so many ways. But this was the night she must be flawlessly correct, no matter what. She gave him her most gracious smile. "I would be delighted."

He led her onto the dance floor, but when the music began, she froze in dismay. *A waltz!* As her thoughts churned, Montague placed one hand on the back of her waist, while with the other, he held her arm straight out. He stepped forward to begin the dance, but she, not knowing which way to step, stood rigid, feeling at once both awkward and gauche. Panic swept through her as she looked around at all the graceful dancers floating by. *No use.* She would disgrace herself if she even made an attempt at the unfamiliar steps. Only one thing could she do, no matter how humiliating. "I . . . I am terribly sorry, Lord Eddington, but I don't know how to waltz."

"Would you care to try?" he asked. "I should wager one twirl around the floor and you'll catch on."

"I think not," she replied, knowing it would take more than one of Montague's twirls for her not to make a fool of herself. "Please, may we leave the floor?"

Montague appeared nonplussed, but only for a moment. "Quite all right, Miss O'Fallon. I shall return you to your chaperone. Perhaps later, when the orchestra plays something . . . uh, more simple, we shall dance."

Evleen could feel a blush of shame creep over her cheeks as Montague led her to the sidelines. When they arrived, he added to her humiliation when he proceeded to ask Charlotte, "Would you care to dance? It appears Miss O'Fallon, doesn't . . . er, care to waltz."

As if the whole world wouldn't know that socially inept Miss O'Fallon did not know how to waltz!

Numb with embarrassment, Evleen stood at the edge of the dance floor and watched as Montague swept Charlotte into his arms and whirled her away. As the two dipped and twirled to the strains of the lively waltz, she saw how skilled they were, how exceedingly graceful, thus making her mortification so much the worse.

She wondered why Lydia Trevlyn had misled her. Quickly, she found the answer. *To make a fool of me—discredit me in the eyes of Montague and all the rest.*

Evleen found a chair in a remote corner where she sat, wishing she could make herself invisible. The orchestra struck up another waltz, followed by a quadrille, which she also couldn't dance. She felt dowdy, clumsy, awkward, and awful.

It was going to be long night.

"Good evening, Miss O'Fallon."

Lord Thomas! Looking exceedingly handsome in his formal clothes, he stood before her, bending in a smooth little bow.

Startled, she leaped to her feet and blurted, "But I thought you weren't coming." She regretted her words instantly, not wanting him to know she thought of him at all.

"I changed my plans, obviously." His forehead furrowed in an inquisitive frown. "Why aren't you dancing?"

"I . . . have a headache." She hated to lie, but she'd be even further humiliated if he learned the truth.

"A headache?" he asked, obviously unconvinced. He smiled with beautiful candor and said, "You look lovely tonight. I cannot imagine why you're hiding in a corner. In fact, I would have thought you'd have captured every man's heart by now and become the belle of the ball."

"Obviously not." She knew he was just being polite because how could he think she looked lovely when her hair was awful and she wore an ugly dress? She knew she'd sounded cool, but her thoughts were chaotic as she tried to decide what to say next. If she was too friendly, he would ask her to dance.

"Do you realize we've never danced together before?" He

extended his hand. "Let us remedy that lamentable state of affairs right now, shall we?"

The orchestra struck up another waltz. Oh, no. How many times tonight could she die of shame? What to do? She did not want to be rude, but on the other hand, she most definitely did not want Thomas to witness her making a fool of herself.

"I do not care to dance with you, Lord Thomas."

For a fleeting moment, Thomas looked as if he had been struck. Quickly, his face became a mask. "Well, then," he said, obviously giving himself time to arrange his thoughts. He gave her a slight bow and with effortless grace continued, "Delightful to see you again, Miss O'Fallon. Good night. Have a pleasant evening."

As she watched his broad shoulders disappear into the crowd, Evleen wanted to cry, *Wait. Come back. I didn't mean it.* How terrible that she had allowed her pride to guide her feelings. She didn't know how she could feel any more miserable, as well as guilty, besides. She should simply have admitted to him she couldn't waltz, but she'd wanted to appear perfect in his eyes. *But how foolish. Such vanity.* She knew she shouldn't give a farthing what Thomas thought of her.

But aside from all that, even if she were skilled at waltzing, she should be searching for a rich man with a title, not a poor second son.

I'll get over him, she thought, as a lump rose in her throat. *I must.*

At last the orchestra played music for a country dance she recognized, and she realized she could dance to that. Even so, she was sorely tempted to remain safe in the sheltered corner until the ball was over. But she wasn't a coward, and she wasn't a quitter. She returned to stand by Lydia, who had earlier informed her a young lady must not stray far from her chaperone unless dancing. The orchestra struck up another country dance, which she knew she could do, and when a young blade asked her to dance, to her relief, she found she actually enjoyed it. It was hard to know how to handle her silly fan, though. She observed the other young ladies and noted how they would flutter their fans, occasionally bringing it to their faces, peering coyly at their partners over the top. *Such silliness. Not me, not ever,* she thought, and kept her fan to her side, occasionally raising it to let it rest on her right cheek. The gloves, too, were annoying. How she wished she could strip them off.

She was pleased that no waltzes or quadrilles had played for a time. She had been dancing every dance, with several different partners, when a florid-faced man of fifty or so, with a paunch and drooping eyelids, came up to Mrs. Trevlyn, eyed Evleen, and asked to be introduced.

Lydia demonstrated once again she could smile when the need arose. In fact, she appeared quite delighted. "This is William, Lord Corneale, Evleen," she said eagerly, signaling his importance by raising a significant eyebrow as she further commented, "Lord Corneale owns one of the largest estates in England and is recently widowed. Sir, this is Miss Evleen O'Fallon."

The older man bowed low to Evleen, all the time raking her body with lust-filled eyes. "Charmed to meet you, Miss O'Fallon. Where has a lovely girl like you been hiding?"

Evleen dipped a curtsey. After all that had gone wrong during the evening, she was relieved she didn't fall over. "I am delighted to meet you, sir."

Lydia assumed a simpering smile. "If you're wondering why her speech sounds a bit strange, Lord Corneale, our Evleen is fresh from Ireland. She's the sister of young Patrick, who is now heir apparent to my brother-in-law's estate. Just imagine, he was hidden away in Ireland all this time. Aren't we lucky we found him!" She turned fond eyes on Evleen. "And of course his darling sister."

Evleen almost laughed aloud. What could be more insincere than Lydia attempting to show her delight that her husband was no longer the heir? She wondered what Lydia was planning. It appeared she wanted to pawn Evleen off on this odious man. How could that be? she wondered. Lord Corneale was obviously a first son, apparently rich as Croesus. Surely Lydia would want to snare him for one of her daughters. The answer was obvious. First son or no, this man with the lascivious smile was just too odious.

"Would you care to dance, Miss O'Fallon?" asked Lord Corneale.

"Why, of course, I would be delighted." *Such hypocrisy.* She would rather be in Ireland digging potatoes than dance with this man.

Soon they were on the dance floor, she reluctantly on Lord Corneale's arm. He danced tolerably well, she'd give him that, but up close he had a musty smell about him, rather like an old tomb. She could hardly wait until the dance was over. When it was, she was starting off the dance floor when he quickly asked, "Would you care for a stroll in the garden, Miss O'Fallon?"

By the Saints, no. "Why, I . . ." As she searched for a suitable excuse, she lifted her fan to rest upon her right cheek.

His eyes lit. "Very good." Before she could think what to do, he took her arm and started to guide her from the dance floor.

She protested, "Lord Corneale, I didn't mean . . ." but he didn't seem to hear.

"Nothing like a stroll in the moonlight," he stated with great enthusiasm, and led her out the side doors to a balcony, where a wide expanse of formål garden lay below.

She was in for it now, she decided. Might as well go along and be polite. How he could have thought she wanted to step outside with him, she would never know.

They walked down a flight of stone steps to the garden below and started their stroll down a path barely lit by moonlight. "This is my favorite time of year for a garden," he remarked. "The daffodils and snapdragons are magnificent, would you not agree, Miss O'Fallon?"

"I can hardly see them in the dark," she answered bluntly. She was growing leery. As they strolled along, his breathing came faster and faster. Could it be his excitement over daffodils and snapdragons? She thought not. They passed a fountain, beyond which the path wound into a patch of darkness surrounded by high shrubbery. At the darkest spot, he halted. With a grunt, his arms went tight around her and pulled her close. Before she could utter a word, his wet, slimy lips pressed hard against hers. *Ugh!* She pounded his shoulders with her fist, but to no avail. She was suffocating. At last, desperate for breath, she shoved at him hard and managed to back away from him.

"Just what were you doing?" she demanded in a shaking whisper.

"Why, kissing you, my dear," he answered equitably, "just as you wanted me to."

"I wanted you to?" she asked, dumbfounded. "Just how did you decide that?"

"You said it with your fan, my sweet." He reached for her again. "Give me credit for knowing the signals."

His lips were about to descend upon hers again, but she managed to break from his grasp and duck away. "You are mistaken, sir," she gasped. Wanting only to remove herself as far as possible from such a disgusting man, she started down the path, but halted when she heard tittering, followed by hastily retreating footsteps.

Had they been seen and overheard?

She could have wept with dismay. Naive though she was concerning the rules of the *ton,* she strongly suspected that getting caught kissing a strange man in the dark corner of a garden constituted a major infraction. Even ignorance of the waltz would be a minor transgression in comparison. She shuddered to think what would happen if this got back to Lydia.

As she started back along the path, she reflected upon what a horrible night this had been, beginning early when she discovered not knowing how to waltz was akin to social suicide. Then she had insulted Lord Thomas, who would probably never speak to her again. Then her ignorance of the language of the fan had led her to signal the wrong message to Lord Corneale. All unknowingly, of course, but who would believe her? She doubted any of these stiff-rumped members of the Polite World would give her the benefit of the doubt.

And then the ultimate disaster—she and Lord Corneale had been discovered. She could only pray that whoever had seen them would not spread the news.

Sick with worry, Evleen reentered the ballroom. She remembered the fan, still clutched in her hand. *Fan language indeed,* she thought with deep irony. Resisting an urge to toss the lace-and-ivory root of her problems in the nearest waste receptacle, she wondered if there was a fan message for *Please, God, get me out of here. Let me go home to Ireland, and soon.*

Chapter 14

Lydia knew. They all did.

At the end of the evening, Evleen sensed Lydia's displeasure as they climbed into the carriage. She could tell from the thin, tightened line of Lydia's lips and the way her sharp nose kept twitching. Charlotte and Bettina had tiny smirks on their faces and kept casting Evleen furtive little glances. Amanda kept her eyes averted, as if she couldn't bear to watch the unpleasant scene that was sure to come.

"Well!" said Lydia the moment the groom closed the carriage door. "I can hardly believe what I just heard, Miss O'Fallon. When I think how your latest misstep will dishonor this family, I am scandalized and utterly appalled."

"What have you heard?" asked Evleen, sounding but slightly curious. Above all, she knew she must maintain her calm. Also, she must keep the skepticism from her voice because she very much doubted Lydia Trevlyn was truly scandalized. It was not difficult to read the woman's mind. Behind all that forced indignation, she was no doubt gloating over the social downfall of this Irish upstart she so very much resented.

But whether Lydia was scandalized and appalled or not, this was a horrible moment, and Evleen wished she were anywhere but here.

Lydia proceeded to describe her shock when she heard—she would not say from whom—that Evleen had been seen in the garden, wantonly kissing Lord Corneale.

"That is completely wrong," protested Evleen in a deadly calm voice. She tried to explain the true circumstances, but Lydia was bound to believe what she wanted to believe, and Evleen's efforts were hopeless, as she knew they would be. Charlotte and Bettina were equally set in stubborn disbelief.

Evleen could explain until dawn and her words would fall on three sets of deaf ears. *How I want to get home,* she thought, desperately trying not to let them see how upset she was, and how ashamed, even though she'd done nothing wrong. Although she seldom cried, she planned to retreat swiftly to her bedchamber the minute she got home. She would crawl into bed, pull the covers over her head, and let the tears flow. She wouldn't let her feelings show now, though. "So what do you intend to do?" she asked, pleased her voice was not shaking. "You can send me back to Ireland if you like. The way I feel now, I would be happy to go."

Her question further antagonized Lydia. "If it were up to me, I would send you back in a second, but it's not, is it? Since Lord Alberdsley appears to have a fondness for you, far be it from me to even suggest you leave." She released a weary sigh, as if the heavy burden of Evleen's deplorable conduct lay entirely on her shoulders. "I shall strive for tolerance, though God knows how sorely stressed I am. You come from a backward country. Naturally you do not know how to conduct yourself in polite society. What a pity you never learned your manners—"

"Or your morals," Charlotte interrupted with feigned indignation.

"Or how to dance the waltz," added Bettina with a giggle.

Evleen fought back a rush of bitter resentment. Why hadn't they warned her she should know the waltz and all the other dances? Why hadn't they offered to teach her? But such questions would be useless to ask. She was the intruder, thrust upon them. They had not wanted her in the first place. Most assuredly, they did not want her now.

By the time they arrived home, Evleen felt thoroughly desolate and heartsick. She planned to say a quick good night and hasten to her bedchamber, but before she could, Lydia declared she would say a final word. Forced to stand in the grand entryway, Evleen concealed her tears, clutched her fan, and grimly listened to Lydia's final admonition.

"We shall do what we can for you, but it's difficult at best to work with a girl who simply does not have the correct background. You cannot dance, politely converse, or even hold your fan correctly. You cannot sing, paint, or play the piano. In other words, you have no talent to speak of, which is a most deplorable lack, and, I think, an impossible situation for a young lady looking for a husband. Worse, though you claim otherwise, your morals are questionable. And you think you can be a member of the *ton*? Well, I think not."

As her two older daughters looked on, barely concealing their enjoyment, Lydia sternly advised, "You had best stay out of sight for the rest of the Season. If you cannot, if you *must* accompany us, *please* keep your mouth shut, and, as much as possible, just sit in a corner. I must admit, you're not a bad-looking young woman by half. You'll never find a husband in the upper ranks of our society, but perhaps . . . well, I cannot promise, but despite your deficiencies, you might find a husband of a lesser class. A well-to-do merchant, perhaps, or a vicar, or an officer in the navy or military, provided he's not a first son."

"Or a second," said Charlotte.

"Or a third or a fourth," Bettina added with great amusement, and they all, except Amanda, joined in her laughter.

Despite her misery, Evleen could almost laugh at the outrageous fate Lydia predicted for her. "I shall bear that in mind, Mrs. Trevlyn," she said solemnly, and with as much dignity as she could gather, left for her bedchamber.

"At least she didn't dance with Montague," Charlotte said when Evleen had disappeared from sight.

"Poor Montague," Bettina exclaimed. "Did you see how embarrassed he was when he found out she couldn't waltz?"

"Had to lead her off the dance floor," Charlotte said in disgust. "He could hardly wait to get rid of her. And to think, I was—well, I hate to admit this, but I confess I was slightly worried Evleen might try to steal Montague's affections."

"Hardly likely," said Lydia Trevlyn. "All that worry was for naught, although I shall confess I, too, thought the girl might be a threat." After a pause, her tightened lips relaxed into a broad smile. "But I most certainly was mistaken, wasn't I?"

The next morning, while Thomas was still floating in that murky, semiconscious state between deep sleep and wakefulness, his first thought was that something, he could not think what yet, was bothering him. The first thing he remembered was that he went with friends to Boodle's after the ball the night before—a rare occurrence. Ordinarily, he had no interest in gambling—a total waste of time and money, as far as he was concerned, but . . . he remembered now, he was trying to keep his mind off Evleen because . . . now he had it, she had rejected him last night.

I do not care to dance with you, Lord Thomas.

What a blow to his pride. Never in his life had he been so rudely dismissed. Come to think of it, no young lady had ever addressed him in such a manner. Wide-awake, Thomas swung his legs to the floor, sat up on the side of the bed, ran his hands through his wavy dark hair, and pondered. *Did I say something wrong? Do something wrong? No. As always, I was a perfect gentleman.* The fault was hers, not his, and why he, a man secure within himself with no need to feed his vanity, should be concerned about what some little chit from Ireland thought of him, he had no idea. His life was in good order. He had no need of her, or any woman.

Only . . .

A sense of loss suddenly assailed him. Somehow, for some reason he could not begin to fathom, he had thought she held a modicum of affection for him. Fool that he was, he had assumed she had experienced the same joy he'd experienced on the trip across Ireland. Never had he enjoyed a journey more. Conclonomaise . . . The Whispering Arch . . . had she forgotten that special look that had passed between them? It was a look full of unspoken desire, of tacit attraction, or so he had thought. More likely, he had been mistaken. That message of desire he'd read in those sapphire blue eyes was naught but a product of his wishful thinking.

But what about that kiss in the carriage the other night? Could it have been only his imagination that she had returned his kiss, and more than willingly? He didn't think so.

But you've got to stop thinking about her.

Whatever he thought, it didn't matter. The girl was seeking a good match, as was every girl, so who could blame her? He knew he was not a good match and never would be. For the first time in his life, he felt a deep resentment he'd been born a second son. If only he were Montague. He knew that if he were, he would lay his wealth and title at the feet of Miss Evleen O'Fallon.

Thomas went to the window, assailed by a terrible sense of bitterness as he gazed at the gardens below.

He was not Montague, he was a lovesick fool, and it was time to return to Tanglewood Hall and see to his horses. Why wait? He would leave today, as soon as he said his farewells.

Downstairs, he encountered Penelope at the breakfast table, just finishing eggs and ham and in a fine mood. "Good morning, Thomas," she said, beaming at him. "Did you enjoy the ball last night?"

"I most decidedly did not," he grumpily replied. "Just coffee," he said to the maid as he sat down. "I shall be returning to Tanglewood Hall today."

Penelope regarded him carefully. "I thought you planned to stay awhile."

"My horses—"

"In good hands, as you very well know what with your groom and stable boys." She cocked her head. "It's something else, isn't it?"

"You're being absurd again."

She ignored him. "Could it be Miss O'Fallon? Oh, my word." Her eyes went wide. "It is, isn't it? And after what happened last night . . . oh, dear."

Had something bad happened to Evleen? An uneasiness stirred within him, but he cautioned himself not to so much as blink an eye. "Really?" he asked with great casualness. "What about last night?"

"You cannot believe what happened to the poor girl. It seems she didn't know how to dance the waltz from what Montague told me. And then, as if that weren't enough, there was some ugly business involving Lord Corneale . . ."

When Penelope finished, Thomas smashed his fist to the table, causing his sister to jump and dishes and silver to rattle. "That randy old goat," he declared, near choking with indignation. "There is no way in the world she would have willingly kissed him. There's got to be an explanation."

"No doubt there is," Penelope said soothingly. "I, myself, would rather kiss a toad than the infamous Lord Corneale. Come to think of it, the man resembles a toad. But why are you so angry?"

"I'm not angry in the least." He ordered himself to calm

down. If he didn't, Penelope, with her keen perceptiveness, would guess the truth, if she hadn't already. He watched as her face lit. *Too late.* Could he not have one single secret from this perspicacious female?

"Ah-ha," she exclaimed. "You *do* have feelings for her, don't you?"

"They wouldn't do me any good. Her mother is insistent upon a good match."

"Aren't they all?" Penelope answered, conceding the point. "It's a shame, though. Miss O'Fallon might have a problem, considering her lack of polish."

"What are you saying?" Thomas asked, fighting back indignation. "Is this what we're about? Is there nothing more important in our lives than how a lady holds her fan? How she waltzes?"

"You misunderstand," Penelope replied with equal fervor. "Evleen O'Fallon is a charming, lively, beautiful young woman, and most certainly nobody's fool. If she wished, she could reach the pinnacle of social distinction. In essence, all she needs is a bit of dance instruction and a few pointers on how to hold her fan."

Thomas nodded in agreement. "One would think Mrs. Trevlyn and her daughters might have given her some pointers."

"Are you daft?" asked Penelope, bursting into laughter. "You think they should have helped her? I guarantee, Lydia Trevlyn is delighted over Evleen's social gaffes. Need I explain why?"

Montague. "No, I understand. But surely someone ought to help her . . ." An idea struck him. "Why not you?"

In deep thought, Penelope was silent a moment. "I didn't have the chance to speak to the poor girl, but I'm sure she must have been completely humiliated last night. Yes, I suppose . . ." Her expression brightened. "I'll do it! I know all the steps, and teaching her should be great fun. Besides, Charlotte and Bettina are just too snooty for words. I would love to see their faces when Evleen turns into Cinderella at the ball."

"Not a noble motive, Penelope."

"You don't understand women, Thomas."

He could tell from the firm set of his sister's jaw that she was not about to back down. But no matter. All he cared about was that Evleen would receive the help she needed. "Can you start right away?"

"This afternoon, if you like. I shall direct a note to Miss O'Fallon, explain what I'm planning, and invite her to take tea. Then, if she's agreeable, we'll have our first lesson."

"Fine. I'll be here. Perhaps I can help."

"I thought you could hardly wait to get back to your beloved horses."

He hoped his face wasn't turning red as he answered, "I have reconsidered. I've decided to stay in town."

Another silly English custom, Evleen thought as she sat in the Trevlyns' carriage and watched as the liveried footman approached the front door of the marquess's town house. She would have much preferred knocking on the door herself, but had been sternly informed, *It simply isn't done.*

"You sit in the carriage and you wait for the footman to knock," Lydia had admonished. "The footman gives your card to the butler. The butler takes the card to the mistress of the household, who then decides whether or not she is at home. Then the butler returns with the message."

"But how can she decide if she's home or not?" asked Evleen, bewildered. "If she's at home then she's at home, isn't she?"

Lydia threw up her hands. "You simply do not understand."

Evleen persisted. "But how could she be not home if she's home? How—?"

"Just do as I say," Lydia snapped, thoroughly exasperated. "And another thing—if you see the lady of the house peering at you from behind the curtains, you must pretend not to notice."

Such nonsensical rules. Such a silly, frivolous society. Still, when Evleen received Penelope's invitation to "take tea and discuss fans and waltzes," she deeply appreciated the generous and tactful offer. If she was to have even the slightest chance of fulfilling her promise to her mother, she must make amends for her miserable performance of the night before.

At tea, Evleen discovered that despite her lingering despondency over the previous night, she was enjoying herself. Thomas's sister was bright, pleasant, and stunningly attractive in her modish afternoon gown of yellow cotton batiste. Unlike the Trevlyns, she did not seem full of artifices. She also possessed a quick wit that, after the dullness of the Trevlyns, Evleen greatly appreciated.

"Where shall we begin your lessons?" Penelope asked when they'd finished tea.

"Anywhere," Evleen answered half humorously. "It appears I need improvement in all areas."

"Then let's do fans." Penelope unfurled and fluttered her ivory fan. "You see, you don't clutch it, you just hold it lightly." She placed the fan in front of her face and peered playfully over the top. "This means follow me." She placed the fan in her left hand. "Means I'm desirous of an acquaintance." She closed the fan and drew it across her forehead. "Means we're being watched."

A wry smile curved Evleen's lips. "How did I happen to say, 'Take me to the garden, Lord Corneale, and give me a big, sloppy, slimy kiss'?"

When they stopped laughing, Penelope remarked, "I'm not sure exactly how Lord Corneale got such a message, but perhaps . . ." She rested the tip of the fan on her right cheek. "Did you do something like this?" At Evleen's nod, she said, "Then that's likely what you did. In essence, it means yes."

For the next hour, Evleen practiced with her own fan, learned fast, and enjoyed herself in the bargain. It was good to laugh again, although she had never in her life spent such a frivolous afternoon. Back in County Clare, work and worry filled their lives. The money, the illnesses, the struggle to stay warm despite the damp, creeping cold left little time for such fancy-free fun.

Just as she was confident she'd mastered the language of the fan, Lord Thomas appeared in the doorway. Evleen caught her breath at the unexpected sight of him, standing there in that casual stance of his, with that lopsided grin on his dark, handsome face. "I thought you were leaving London today," she said.

"Obviously not," he replied. "Penelope has recruited me to help teach you the waltz."

She remembered the previous night and the callous manner

in which she'd rejected him. *What must he think?* "I'm sorry about last night."

"Say no more." He went to her and held out his hand. He signaled to Penelope, who had seated herself at the piano. "Play us a waltz, sister, slow if you please, and we shall have Miss O'Fallon waltzing in no time." He placed his hand around her waist. "Now, put your hand on my shoulder, don't look down, step back with your right foot, and off we go."

Soon she was waltzing. "You have a natural bent for it," Thomas declared after only minutes. Feeling herself move gracefully, in perfect time to the music, she knew he was right. *Such fun!* The remains of her blue funk disappeared. Later, when Montague came to see what all the commotion was about, he, too, waltzed her around the room and proclaimed she was a first-rate waltzer. "You'll do fine, Miss O'Fallon," he said, his eyes warm with admiration. "I shall claim all your waltzes at the next ball."

Thinking of Lydia's reaction if he did, her spirits dipped, but not for long. "We shall see," she said, giving him an enigmatic smile. Nothing could ruin such a delightful afternoon.

When she made ready to leave, she tried to express her thanks, but Thomas wouldn't hear it. "Come back tomorrow, Miss O'Fallon," he told her politely. "We shall learn the quadrille."

When Penelope was alone with Evleen at the front door, she asked hesitantly, "Er . . . that mud-colored gown? Will you be wearing it again to Lord and Lady Trent's ball next Friday night?"

"You needn't be polite," came Evleen's laughing answer. "Lord Alberdsley hired a dressmaker, and I've already been fitted. With any luck, at the next ball I'll have my own gown, not that hideous hand-me-down."

"Marvelous." Penelope clasped her hands with delight. "I have so enjoyed this afternoon."

"As have I."

"I have never met anyone quite like you." Penelope's warmth was sincere. "I predict that fair, fresh beauty of yours and that fiery Irish spirit will make you the belle of the ball."

Despite her new friend's encouraging words and her pleasurable afternoon, Evleen was struck by an odd twinge of worry. "I don't know that you're right," she said quietly, "but even if you are, what with one thing and another, I'm not sure being the belle of the ball is the best thing for me."

Penelope sighed heavily. "What you mean is, the more successful you are, the more jealous Lydia and her daughters will become."

"I suppose, but surely they would do nothing to harm me."

"Oh, no, no, of course not," Penelope quickly answered, but she didn't sound too convinced.

For several days in a row, Evleen was invited back to the marquess's elegant town house, where, after tea, the dancing lessons continued. Evleen found each visit delightful. She thoroughly enjoyed the music, witty conversation, and, most of all, the close proximity to a man whose company she found increasingly pleasurable. As for Thomas, at first she found his motives were obscure. He had been charming, yet distant. His manners were so impeccable she had begun to wonder if his passionate kiss in the carriage was simply a moment of playful lust, of no deep significance at all. She had about concluded he was helping her out of pity when, on the last day before the ball, she discovered otherwise.

They were standing together, having just concluded a dance, when Penelope briefly left the room. Ordinarily they would have broken apart, but some strange force kept them close together, facing each other, as if they were part of a tableau. When she looked into his eyes, she found him gazing at her with such a burning hunger she was taken aback. She was about to pull away when he swept her into his arms and kissed her fiercely. Before she could even think how to respond, he had broken off the kiss, clasped her arms, and firmly put her away from him. It was as if she were a forbidden pleasure, and he, after a momentary lapse, had regained his senses and did what honor decreed he should do.

"Sorry," he'd said, his breath coming fast. "Don't tell me that shouldn't have happened. I already know."

Before she could even begin to answer, Penelope had returned. If she noticed anything, she didn't say, and the lesson went on as if nothing had occurred. At the end, Penelope glowed as she said, "I have taught you all I know, Evleen.

You've done marvelously well. Just wait till they see you at the ball tomorrow night. The dandies will be falling all over themselves, trying to get a dance with you."

"That remains to be seen," Evleen answered cautiously, aware there was still so much that could go wrong. "You have been the most wonderful teacher, Penelope. I can't thank you enough."

"Evleen, you look magnificent and just so beautiful," exclaimed Amanda.

The night of Lord and Lady Trent's ball had arrived. As Evleen regarded herself in her mirror, she knew she looked the best she had ever looked in her life. *Magnificent and beautiful,* Amanda had said. She wasn't sure about that. Still, she knew she looked her best in the white silk ball gown adorned with clusters of pink roses, a wreath of pink roses in her up-swept hair, and a diamond and ruby necklace, a present from Lord Alberdsley. At least she could hold her head high and not run and hide, as she'd felt like doing in Charlotte's ugly dress. And perhaps, with a bit of luck, she wouldn't make a fool of herself this time.

When Evleen looked down from the landing and spied Lydia, Charlotte, and Bettina waiting in the front entryway, she could not resist a grand entrance. Sweeping down the stairs, head high, fan unfurled and held just so, she was secretly amused when an expression of astonishment crossed Lydia's face, followed by chagrin, followed by a mostly unsuccessful attempt to force her lips into the semblance of a smile.

"Well, Evleen, I must say you look quite presentable this evening," said Lydia. Almost choking, she managed to add, "I see the gown turned out tolerably well."

"Tolerably well?" asked Amanda, who had followed behind Evleen. "The gown is beautiful and so is Evleen."

Lydia awarded her youngest daughter a thinly disguised look of warning before she again addressed Evleen. "Bear in mind what I told you. Say as little as possible. Find a quiet corner if you can. I would hate to see you embarrass yourself again if someone should ask you to dance."

Amanda, the only one who knew of Evleen's dancing lessons, opened her mouth to protest, but Evleen gave her a quick nudge. "I shall heed your advice, Mrs. Trevlyn," she replied with the meekness of a scullery maid.

"Good. See that you do."

"And stay away from Montague," Charlotte, looking beautiful all in white, admonished. "He's close to proposing. I suspect tonight is the night."

"Of course," answered Evleen. *No problem there.* She didn't care a fig for that wastrel, Montague. Despite herself, though, she'd begun to think a good deal about Thomas. She pictured their kiss of the day before and a warm flood of excitement coursed through her veins. The desperate way he'd grabbed her—the hunger in his eyes—she knew he did care. And didn't she? Had she not found his closeness so arousing she'd momentarily forgotten the waltz, Penelope, and everything else except the exquisite joy of being in his arms?

Tonight, all she cared about was that Thomas would be there, that his eyes would light with admiration when he saw her, that they would dance every dance, spinning around the ballroom with eyes only for each other . . .

She caught herself and felt instant guilt. *But you won't feel guilty tonight,* she reminded herself sternly. Her pulse raced at the mere thought of being with him again. She was being selfish, of course, and less than honorable in ignoring her mother's wish, but her holiday from honor would last only the night. Tomorrow she would remember her promise to her mother, but tonight she would follow her heart.

"Look, Evleen," whispered Amanda, "everybody's staring at you."

They had just entered Lord and Lady Trent's ballroom. Evleen wondered what Amanda meant, but soon she knew. The eyes of nearly every man in the room were fixed upon her as she stood, gracefully fluttering her fan, surveying the crowd with a queenlike bearing.

A waltz began. Young Lord Edgemont, whom she'd met the other night, appeared before her. "You look beautiful tonight, Miss O'Fallon, would you care to dance?"

"She doesn't waltz," said Lydia.

"Oh, but I shall try," said Evleen.

All doubt concerning her ability to waltz faded quickly as

Lord Edgemont led her through a series of dips and twirls. Totally at ease, she followed gracefully, as surefooted as if she'd been waltzing all her life. Once or twice, as they whirled past Lydia, Evleen caught a glimpse of the look of incredulity on the older woman's face.

When the dance was over, Montague appeared and claimed the next one. For once, his sardonic expression was gone, replaced by one of admiration. "I see my brother taught you well," he commented.

"But where is your brother?" she asked, doing her best to make her question seem offhand.

"Left, finally, for his estate." He gave her a mocking smile. "I cannot imagine what kept him so long in town."

"Oh." Suddenly all pleasure left her. She felt hurt and deeply disappointed. Why hadn't he let her know?

"You seem downcast, Miss O'Fallon," said Montague. "I do hope the news about my brother hasn't ruined your evening."

Never would she let her feelings show. "Downcast, Lord Eddington?" She tilted her head back and awarded him a dazzling smile. "Never. I intend to have a wonderful time tonight and dance until dawn."

A quadrille followed. She would have danced it with Montague, but someone cut in. As the evening wore on, men were begging for her dances, showering her with compliments.

"Your eyes are like stars, Miss O'Fallon."

"I am struck by your throaty Irish laughter, Miss O'Fallon."

"You dance divinely, Miss O'Fallon. A fine country, Ireland, if it produces a girl as beautiful as you."

Montague kept returning, claiming as many dances as he could. "It seems you have captured the heart of nearly every man present tonight," he said as they waltzed and he held her as tightly as he dared.

Although she returned a dazzling smile and said thank you, Evleen found that what these strangers thought counted not one whit. All she cared about was that Thomas wasn't present.

She had another concern, too. From the sidelines, Lydia Trevlyn had been staring at her. As the evening wore on, her expression darkened, until now, as the last dance ended and Montague led her off the floor, it resembled a thundercloud.

Penelope caught her as she left the ballroom. "Sorry about Thomas," she said.

"Quite all right," Evleen answered with a forced smile, "although he did say he would be here tonight."

"He left rather abruptly." In deep thought, Penelope bit her lip. "I know him. I know something was bothering him, but I cannot think what."

Ah, how delightful the smell of oats and new-mown hay!
In the stables at Tanglewood Hall, Thomas took a whiff of the sweet air as he brushed the flanks of his favorite thoroughbred.

Why had he stayed so long in London? This was where his life would be, from now on. He would waste no more time making a fool of himself over a woman he couldn't have. No longer could he endure the shame of losing control of himself again, as had happened, however briefly, the other day.

No excuse. After the incident in the carriage, he had warned himself to stay away. But then she needed his help, and he had offered gladly, unthinkingly. But he hadn't thought ahead. He had not foreseen that with every dancing lesson, his longing for her would increase while his strict self-control decreased. Too many days of holding that soft, sweetly curved body in his arms had fanned his desire until the day before, like some clumsy oaf, he'd grabbed and kissed her with all the finesse of . . . he couldn't think what, but a clown at Haymarket came to mind. He had come to his senses quickly, of course, and made some stupid remark, but his actions made him realize he must remove himself as far as possible from Evleen O'Fallon. In the state he was in, to stay one more day in London was sheer folly.

At least he had preserved his honor. *A fine thing, honor.* Nothing counted more in this small, tight society in which he lived. Trouble was, honor would not warm his bed at night. *An increasingly lonely bed,* he thought with irony. And when he woke in the night, as he'd been doing lately, honor would not do one damn thing to ease his maddening, increasingly powerful longing for Evleen O'Fallon.

Chapter 15

Over the following weeks, a whole new world opened for Evleen. It seemed as if overnight she had become London's darling. It didn't matter that she hadn't officially come out, nor been presented at court. Men fought for her favors, extolling her beauty, melodious accent, and vivacious Irish charm. London's leading hostesses vied for the presence of "that delightful young lady from Ireland."

Lord Alberdsley crowed with delight. "We must have the dressmaker back. A popular young lady like you must have an ample wardrobe."

Properly chaperoned, she was escorted by eager beaux to Astley's Royal Amphitheater, where horses and clowns alike gave delightful performances; to Kings Theater, where she sat in awe of the actor Edmund Keen; to Green Park, where she and Patrick breathlessly watched a spectacular balloon ascension, the daring balloonists using a newfangled contraption called a parachute.

During all this, Evleen felt elated, yet torn. What a heady experience to be admired and sought after. Yet her newfound popularity did not come without a price, for the atmosphere around Alberdsley's London town house was decidedly cool. Lydia Trevlyn, hardly able to contain her jealousy, was now only barely polite. Bad enough that Evleen now outshone Charlotte, who had always been considered the great beauty of the family. Worse, despite Evleen's efforts to discourage Montague, he continued to pursue her, obviously enchanted with her Irish charm. He appeared to have forgotten Charlotte even existed, let alone that she was destined to be his bride.

At least Amanda was doing well. Much to the ongoing

surprise of her mother and sisters, she had blossomed and now had several suitors.

Thus far, Evleen had yet to meet a man she really liked, although she now had at least a dozen to chose from. Her mother was right. Too many men of the English nobility were vain, self-centered, and shallow—naught but worthless aristocrats who contributed nothing to the world but lived only for their own decadent pleasures. Evleen could not imagine being married to any one of them, regardless of how rich or how grand the title.

Meanwhile, Evleen had not heard one word from Thomas. Although she tried not to think of him, she often did. She concealed her thoughts from everyone, though, even Penelope, who had become a fast friend these past weeks. Often Evleen was tempted to ask Penelope the latest news of Thomas, but pride prevented her each time. With her sharp perception, Thomas's sister would guess immediately how much Evleen missed him and wanted him back. At least Evleen knew where he was. From Penelope's casual remarks she gleaned that Thomas had returned to his home near Abingdon, where he remained in excellent health and was devoting his time to breeding horses. It was obvious he wanted nothing more to do with her. Time after time she tried to convince herself she must forget him, but had not succeeded thus far.

She was having trouble sleeping nights. She could easily blame the excitement of her glittering new social life, but she knew otherwise. It was Thomas who kept her awake in those dark, silent hours when for the hundredth—the thousandth?—time she would relive that magical trip from Ireland when they'd exchanged that deeply meaningful look at the Whispering Arch; when she was seasick aboard the *Countess of Liverpool* and he'd cared for her so tenderly; when he, with the utmost generosity, had seen to it that Patrick got to ride in the "flying machine" across England. What fun they'd had! And then London, and that night they kissed in his coach . . .

Oh, Thomas, how could you leave and not even say goodbye? I thought you cared for me. Were those passionate moments in the carriage really just lust, as meaningless as Lord Corneale's kiss?

In dawn's clear light, after a few hours of fitful sleep, Evleen would always wake up to cold reality. Thomas did *not* care. Everything he'd done for her was out of pity and duty. But what of it? What was she thinking? Even if he did care, he was but a second son with a limited income, not even close to fitting her mother's requirements for the rich, titled Englishman she was supposed to find and marry.

She had written home that she now had her pick of rich Englishmen. Her mother's letters in return revealed how pleased she was, how eagerly she was waiting to hear who would be the final choice. Evleen suspected that one or two of her most ardent suitors were about to propose, but in the meantime, much to her great chagrin, there was Montague.

Nothing but trouble there. Montague had been doggedly pursuing her. He would not take no for an answer. How she would be able to handle his unwanted attentions she had no idea.

One day, another problem arose when Evleen, about to step into the drawing room, heard Patrick's voice and because of its imperious tone, stopped to listen.

"I said bring it now, and be quick," demanded Patrick, obviously addressing a servant.

"Yes, of course, Master Patrick," came the reply.

The butler. Evleen was horrified. Pierce, the white-haired butler who carried himself with supreme dignity, had been the family butler for more years than anyone could recall. Never had she heard him treated with less than the greatest respect, until now.

She waited until Pierce withdrew, then drew in a breath to regain control of herself and stepped into the drawing room where Patrick was playing a game by the fireplace. "What were you saying to the butler just now?" she asked with deceptive calm.

Pouting, Patrick said, "I asked for some sweets, and he said I shouldn't have them till I ate my lunch."

"He's absolutely right."

"He's not right." Patrick leaped to his feet and glared. "Pierce is only a servant. He must do as I say."

She was flabbergasted. "Who on earth told you such a thing?"

"Nobody had to tell me. Mrs. Trevlyn and Charlotte and Bettina yell at the servants all the time."

"Not Pierce they don't."

"Maybe not, but all the others."

That much is true, Evleen thought grudgingly. She was constantly appalled at the rude, unfeeling way the Trevlyn ladies treated their servants. "I cannot argue, Patrick, but are you a sheep? Mama taught us to be kind and courteous to everyone. She taught us to be strong and do what we know in our hearts is right, no matter what the consequences. You reveal a weakness when you follow what other people do and don't think for yourself."

"I don't care." Patrick crossed his arms over his thin chest and raised his chin. "I shall be the next Earl of Alberdsley, and everyone will have to do my bidding, even you."

"What?" Fury almost choked her. Her palm itched to slap that arrogant little face, but she had never struck Patrick, and, despite her rage, knew she never would. With a supreme effort, she quelled her hot rush of anger. Actually, she was as horrified at herself as much as at Patrick. *I should have seen this coming,* she thought with fearful clarity. While she'd been busy enjoying the delights of London, Patrick had changed from a bright, easygoing boy into a spoiled little prig who placed himself a cut above the rest. And all because of the indulgence of his grandfather. "Who do you think you are?" she asked, her voice shaking. "You must never talk down to the servants. Pierce may be a servant, but he's older than you, and wiser than you, and you will respect him, Patrick, or . . . or . . ."

"Or what?" Patrick defiantly demanded.

"Or . . . it's too terrible to tell you." She waited, expecting her little brother to blush with shame at her rare castigation, or perhaps even cry. Instead, he regarded her with brazen defiance. "I don't care what you say, Evleen, I'm the heir. I can do as I please, and people have to obey me."

In shocked silence she took the time to examine her red-haired little brother who had the face of an angel, but underneath, had developed the temperament of one of those worthless aristocrats she detested. Hard to believe that back in Ireland, Patrick had been an agreeable, even-tempered child without an arrogant bone in his body. But now . . . ?

Was having all this richness and privilege worth the trouble it caused? Perhaps they should just go back to Ireland. Evleen could almost laugh, thinking of how long it would take her mother to set Patrick straight. And going back would be good for her, too. She wouldn't have Montague chasing her about, nor suffer the unpleasantness of the Trevlyns. And perhaps she'd stop thinking about Thomas if she knew for certain she would never see him again.

But it was much too soon to think of going home. Besides, she realized all Patrick needed was a strong male voice to inform him of the error of his ways. *But whose voice?* Possibly Lord Alberdsley's, although considering the way he doted on the boy, she doubted he could administer the proper discipline. Regardless, Lord Alberdsley could be of no help now. He had returned to his estate and had not said when he would return. Walter was present, but weakling that he was, he could hardly be called a voice of authority.

There was only one man in all the world whom Patrick not only respected, but downright idolized. How ironic, she mused, that Patrick would not listen to his own sister, but if Lord Thomas were to tell him what to do, he would leap to obey.

If only Thomas were here!

And for many reasons, she mused, many of which had nothing to do with Patrick's transgressions.

Late on a warm evening in June, at the ball given by Lady Fitzgibbons at her palatial mansion on Bolton Street, Thomas, who had just arrived from Tanglewood Hall, stood by the side of the dance floor, gazing intently at the dancers.

"She's here, although I don't see her," said Penelope, who stood beside him.

He asked, "What makes you think I'm looking for anybody?"

Penelope tilted her pert nose. "Why the sudden visit to London? Aren't your precious thoroughbreds enough company?"

He shot her a teasing glance. "I prefer my horses any day to a certain nagging sister of mine." A force beyond himself pulled his gaze back to the dance floor. *Where is she?*

Penelope asked, "Did you know she's become the most popular belle in London?"

"Who?"

"You know very well who."

He deigned not to answer as he continued his search. Ah. She was dancing with Montague, a vision in a pale yellow silk dress, trimmed with silver.

"Lovely, isn't she?" remarked Penelope. He nodded briefly, careful he gave nothing away. "I know she's why you're here, Thomas. What do you plan?"

No use trying to fool her. "I want her," he said simply.

Penelope drew in her breath and clasped her hands together in a gesture of glee. "What wonderful news! Evleen and I have become fast friends these past few weeks. I so admire her for her honesty, her liveliness, her wit and charm, as well as—" Penelope's expression switched from ecstatic to doubtful. "Oh, dear. You want to marry her?"

"Of course. What did you think?"

"Oh dear." Penelope looked crestfallen.

Thomas laughed at his sister's sudden discomfort. "I know what you're thinking. I am far from being a prime candidate for her hand, aren't I? Second son, with but a modest income? On the face of it, my chances are nil."

"Montague is after her."

"With all due respect to my beloved brother, Evleen is far too smart to marry such a profligate."

"But you know her mother wants her to marry well."

"Never love an Englishman," Thomas quoted with a wry smile, "just marry a rich and titled one."

"Then how can you even think—?"

"I don't have a chance, unless she loves me."

"Does she?"

"That remains to be seen, doesn't it?"

Penelope lightly rapped his arm with her fan. "Oh, you can be so exasperating. Why didn't you tell me? I knew you liked her, but then when you left London all those many weeks ago, I thought you didn't care."

"Never fear, I care all right." *Care enough to risk getting soundly rejected,* Thomas thought but didn't say. Tanglewood Hall had been his retreat, a place where he had expected to find not only peace, but forgetfulness. In his ignorance, he had assumed he could easily erase those tormenting dreams of Evleen

and concentrate fully on breeding his thoroughbreds. Surely
Montague would marry. He would then proceed to present their
father with the heir he so keenly desired, and thus relieve
Thomas of any further responsibility. Only if Montague remained single, would Thomas consider taking a wife. Not Bettina. He had finally concluded he could not abide spending the
rest of his life with such a bubble-head. But if need be, surely
he could find some agreeable lady of modest means who would
be happy to marry a second son in reduced circumstances.

Such was his plan, but it contained a major flaw. His tantalizing thoughts of Evleen did not fade as expected. As time
went by, she increasingly haunted his dreams. When gossip
reached him that Evleen was now the toast of London, the jolt-
ing news caused the remnants of his forced, false serenity to
quickly evaporate. The thought of Evleen being cajoled,
charmed, wheedled, and deceived by a bevy of shallow London
dandies unleashed such a torrent of angst and apprehension, he
was forced to return posthaste to London.

She was finishing her dance with Montague, who looked be-
fuddled, he could tell, even in the distance. Although it was getting late, he still had plenty of time. He would get her alone
after supper, lay his heart at her feet, pride be damned, and see
what she said.

"Montague, you've had too much brandy," said Evleen as
the dance ended. She looked into Montague's face, now slack
from drink. "Take my advice and go home."

"Me, foxed?" Montague regarded her with blurry eyes.
"Ridiculous. I'm as sober as a vicar."

He staggered, ever so slightly, but enough for her to notice.
"You see? And whatever you do, don't try dancing again." Her
toe still smarted from where Montague had stamped upon it.

Montague replied, "I assure you, my wild Irish beauty, I am
totally in control. Matter of fact, I rather hoped you would take
supper with me."

"I think not." Disgusted, she tried to back away, but he took
her arm.

"You're so beautiful, Evleen," he said, his voice thick from
drink. His gaze dropped from her eyes to her shoulders to the

exposed top of her breasts where it lingered, frankly assessing. "Such beauty needs to be caressed, to be kissed, to be—"

"Oh!" Evleen cried, so revolted she pulled her arm away. "Go home and sober up, Montague."

As Evleen spun around and headed for the side of the room, she felt several pairs of eyes upon her. She felt mortified that the disagreeable scene had been witnessed by several people, but what could she expect? She and Montague had, after all, been standing in the middle of the dance floor.

She found Lydia Trevlyn staring at her with cold, questioning eyes. "What did you say to Montague?"

"Mrs. Trevlyn, Montague is extremely . . . *foxed* I believe is the way he put it."

"I can hardly believe that. Besides, was that any reason to be rude?"

"You did not hear what he said."

"I didn't need to hear." Lydia slowly shook her head, as if dumbfounded Evleen could do such a thing. " 'Tis beyond me how you could have shown such ill manners to the future Marquess of Wythe, and right in front of everybody."

Evleen wondered what a title had to do with an absolute boor, yet she maintained her calm. Let Lydia condemn her, she knew she had performed with admirable restraint. "I regret that you feel that way, but I did what I had to do."

Mercifully, the innocuous Lord Edgemont approached at that moment and asked her to dance. She swiftly said yes, thankful to get away from Lydia Trevlyn. He asked her to take supper with him, which gladly she did. Later, she was approaching the chaperones, girding for another confrontation with Lydia, when she heard a voice behind her that stopped her in her tracks.

"Wait, Evleen."

Thomas. Her heart leaped in her chest.

From close behind her, his breath warm on her ear, she heard, "Have you time for an old friend?"

Slowly, she turned, giving herself time to recover from her shock. By the time she faced him squarely, she had regained her composure enough to playfully remark, "He leaves, he doesn't say good-bye, he doesn't write." Jamming one gloved hand to her hip, she went on, "Some old friend, indeed."

Laughing easily, he remarked, "I hear you're the toast of London these days." He gave her a mocking bow. "Must be thrilling, all those men begging for so much as a glance, a dance, a smile."

Enough of silly banter, she thought. "I'm so happy to see you. How long will you be in London? I suppose you came to see the horses at Tattersalls?"

"Not really. I came to see you."

"Oh." At a loss for words, she noticed she'd been frenziedly and quite unconsciously fluttering her fan, a sure giveaway of her inner excitement. She snapped it shut and took a moment to collect herself. *I am so attracted to this man,* she thought, finally admitting the truth to herself. Judging from the intensity of his gaze, she hoped she might be receiving more than a casual answer to her next question. "And just what did you want to see me about?"

Thomas opened his mouth to answer, but was jostled by the pressing crowd. The continual noise had been loud enough, but now it was deafening, what with the murmur of the crowd, the announcement of the last dance of the evening, followed by the orchestra starting to play the last piece. Grimacing, he glanced about. "This is impossible. I do want to speak with you, Evleen. I shall call on you tomorrow." At her quick nod, he said good night and melted into the crowd.

Penelope appeared. "Where has my brother gone? I know he especially wanted to speak to you."

"We couldn't hear over all the din," Evleen answered, her voice raised. "He said he'd call on me tomorrow."

"Come with me," said Penelope. After she'd led Evleen to a relatively quiet corner, she asked, "You do know what it's about, don't you?"

"I'm not sure."

"I think you are."

No sense trying to fool Penelope. "I suppose I am, but . . ." Evleen frowned and bit her lip. "I am so confused. My mother thinks the most important thing in the world is for me to marry well."

Penelope raised her fine arched eyebrows. "We are all supposed to marry well, but that doesn't mean we must. I want you to listen to me. I don't care if I offend you or not, but there are things you ought to hear."

"Do go ahead," Evleen answered softly, not having the vaguest notion what her friend was going to say.

"I don't know what your true feelings about Thomas are, but I know what they should be. Of course, he is but a second son. Of course, he doesn't have a fortune. But a finer man never walked the face of this earth. He loves you, Evleen. He's going to ask you to marry him, and if you turn him down, I shall never forgive you."

"But I am in such a dilemma! My mother wants the best for me. I promised—"

"I am amazed. With all due respect, I cannot believe that a woman as strong and independent as you would not do exactly what she pleased instead of blindly following what she perceives to be what her mother wants."

"That's not so."

"Isn't it?" Penelope's eyes blazed with intensity. "Are you blind? Can't you see all that Thomas has done for you? Who escorted you clear across Ireland and comforted and took care of you when you got sick on the boat? Who found you and Patrick when you were lost and brought you home? Who saw to it that you learned the waltz, and all those other dances, and the language of the fan? Surely not the Trevlyns. And it wasn't my idea either, it was Thomas's. He cares for you, Evleen. Oh, you can find a rich man and a title easily enough, but can you find a man who's generous and kind and loves you with all his heart? I think not. And I think if it's true love you want, you'll use your own judgment and follow your heart, not your mother's wishes."

Penelope stopped for breath. "Oh dear," she said as a rueful smile crept over her face. "I didn't mean to be so vehement, I just wanted to let you know how deeply I felt."

"Quite all right," Evleen hastened to say, not revealing she was shaken to the core. "I value your opinion. My feelings for Thomas are . . . I'm just beginning to see . . . Rest assured, I shall think about what you said."

"Do," answered Penelope. She bid Evleen good night and turned away, leaving her in such a state of confusion she could only stand and stare, and consider Penelope's advice.

Follow your heart, not your mother's wishes . . .

Follow your heart . . . Of course. She loved Thomas. It was a moment of awakening that left her reeling. Suddenly, she felt wrapped in a blissful cocoon of euphoria. Thomas loved her. Tomorrow he would tell her so. Tomorrow he would ask her to marry him and with heartfelt joy she would accept because yes, yes, a million times yes! she loved him, too. Up until now, her mother's demands had come first. *Make me proud,* she had said, and Evleen, ever the dutiful daughter, had so wanted to abide by her mother's wishes she had never considered doing otherwise until this very moment. In all her heedful life, she had never understood the young girls who, in the name of love, had brought shame and disgrace upon themselves and upon their families because of some man. Had they no pride? How could they *do* such a thing? Now, for the first time, Evleen knew what a mad, heated, utterly irrational desire for a man could do. Nothing on earth compelled her to do what her mother said. Suddenly, it didn't matter what her mother wanted. Nothing mattered, except her passionate desire to be in Thomas's arms again, feel his lips on hers, and do those forbidden things that until now she could only guess about and dream about.

Evleen hated even to think how devastated her mother would be. Yet she knew Sinead O'Fallon was a reasonable woman, compassionate, and kind. Given time, perhaps she would forget money and titles and be proud to have for a son-in-law the kindest, most witty, most exciting man in all the world.

Outside, Evleen stood by the curb, clutching her light wrap about her, searching for the Trevlyns. All around departing guests milled about. The street was clogged with carriages and horses, the air filled with the cries of impatient coachmen who had picked up their passengers and were anxious to move from the curb.

To her surprise and disgust, Montague approached. And she thought she'd seen the last of him this night!

"Ah, my dear Evleen," he began, his voice even thicker than before. "Are you ready to apologize for your rudeness?"

"I shall apologize when hell freezes over, Lord Eddington."

"But see here . . ." As Montague rocked back and forth on two unsteady feet, his muddled mind groped for words. "Haven't you heard . . . uh, what a great catch I am? It would be to your advantage to be more friendly."

He reached for her. Repulsed, she backed away, just as Lydia and her daughters approached. "Leave me alone, sir," she coldly replied, too angry to care if the Trevlyns overheard. "You are most certainly not a great catch. You're nothing better than a cup-shot scapegrace, and I want nothing more to do with you. *Imeacht gan teacht ort!*"

Montague appeared taken aback. "And what does that mean?"

"It means, 'May you leave without returning.' "

Montague appeared nonplussed for a moment, then gave her an overelaborate and rather unsteady bow. He mumbled, "In that event, I shall bid you good night, but you haven't heard the last of me, my love," and disappeared into the crowd.

"How rude of you, Evleen," Lydia exclaimed.

"But, Mama, didn't you hear what he said?" asked Amanda.

Lydia ignored her daughter and glared at Evleen. "No lady of impeccable breeding would ever say such things."

For once, Evleen did not care to humble herself. "He deserved it, Mrs. Trevlyn."

Charlotte looked amazed. "I simply cannot understand how you could have talked to Lord Eddington that way."

Evleen ignored her. In uncomfortable silence they were waiting for their carriage when the sound of the frantic neighing of a horse came from up the street, followed by a shout of warning. There was silence for a moment, then horrified screams and more shouting. Men started running. With a sense of premonition and dread, Evleen ran, too, until, halfway up Bolton Street she saw a dark, still form lying partially beneath a coach and four.

She stood frozen. It couldn't be, but that form in the street lay so still. Her mind refused to accept the horrifying possibility, and yet she knew that only moments earlier she had been talking to Montague, telling him to leave and not return. And now . . .

In a daze, she heard a familiar voice call, "My brother!" and saw Thomas rush past and kneel beside the still figure. Just then Lydia and her daughters came to stand beside her. "It cannot be Montague," Lydia said in disbelieving horror.

"I'm afraid it is."

"Is he dead?"

Before Evleen could say she didn't know, someone shouted, "Eddington fell beneath the wheels. The poor devil's dead!"

Amanda looked stunned. Bettina started to cry. Charlotte, her hand pressed to her mouth, gasped in consternation. Her knees sagged, and she would have collapsed had not her mother and Evleen caught and supported her.

A grim-lipped Lydia looked to Evleen for support. "Help me. We must get my girls to the carriage at once."

"Of course." Evleen cast one more horrified look at the still body in the street and the small knot of people gathered around. Thomas was there. She longed to comfort him, but Lydia needed her.

With a heavy weight on her heart, she helped Lydia half carry a grieving, near-hysterical Charlotte back to their carriage, along with her stunned and horrified sisters.

"Montague, speak to me, speak to me. Oh, God." Thomas, kneeling in the street, held the body of his brother in his arms. *Montague was dead.* An unbearable wave of grief consumed him as he remembered the Montague of the olden days. In age, they were only two years apart and had been inseparable when they were young. Always the defiant one, Thomas had been saved from trouble many a time by his older brother. Now Thomas's heart cried out in anguish, not for the drunken wastrel Montague had become, but for that little boy who had always been staunchly loyal to his younger brother, always taking his side, fighting his battles.

He felt Penelope's presence beside him. "Is he gone?" she asked, tears choking her voice.

"He's gone," Thomas whispered, hard put to keep back his own tears. He laid Montague's lifeless body gently in the street, removed his coat and with care and reverence covered his brother's face. His own grief was nearly overwhelming, but sensing his sister's near hysteria, he drew her into his comforting arms.

A shaken coachman addressed him. "I'm not to blame, sir.

The gentleman wasn't looking when he stepped off the curb. Then 'e stumbled sort of an' fell directly beneath the wheels."

Someone in the crowd remarked, "Good grief. This changes everything for Linberry."

Did it? Thomas couldn't think beyond the realization that he had just lost his beloved, only brother.

The momentous consequences of Montague's death did not occur to Thomas until after his brother's remains had been removed, and he and Penelope were in their carriage, finally going home. Through her tears, Penelope asked, "Thomas, do you realize the import of this?"

"What do I care about import? Our brother is dead."

"But you must care. Think of it. Montague is gone and he didn't leave any heirs. That makes you the heir apparent."

Exhausted, not wanting to think, Thomas leaned back against the squabs. In the dim circles of light cast by passing street lamps, he could see his sister's anguished face. From outside he heard the familiar clip-clopping of the horses' hooves, and he thought how strange it was that anything could sound so ordinary on this extraordinary night. Soon, as he half listened, the stunning meaning of Penelope's words crept into his consciousness.

Yes, now he was the first son . . .
Yes, from this day forward he was Lord Eddington . . .
And yes . . .

He sat straight, hurtling back from his universe of grief into a new reality. No longer was he the insignificant second son. He was now Lord Eddington, who someday would become Marquess of Wythe and inherit one of the largest, most wealthy estates in all England.

"Do you not see what this means?" asked Penelope. "Your life is about to change, and most dramatically."

"Dear God," Thomas muttered. As a second son he had been in charge of his own life with nothing expected of him. But now he was the heir.

A new anguish seared his heart. Except for his dilemma over Evleen, he had been supremely happy with his life, just as it was. But what Penelope said was true, and he knew his life was about to change forever.

There was something else, too. It was a glimmering fact that he would tuck away in the back of mind until later when he could deal with it.

Evleen and the Trevlyns arrived home after a woeful carriage ride during which the Trevlyn girls worked through various stages of hysteria, particularly Charlotte, who appeared nearly prostrate with grief. It was not until they were all seated in the drawing room and Pierce had been instructed to bring them tea that Lydia said to Charlotte, "Do you realize Thomas is now the heir?"

"What do I care?" cried Charlotte. "Montague is dead, isn't he? My life is over."

She really did love him, thought Evleen with deep sympathy. How it was possible to love someone as selfish and self-indulgent as Montague was difficult to fathom, but Charlotte no doubt saw him through different eyes.

Lydia said gently, "Your life is not over, Charlotte. Just now you're overcome with grief, which is natural, but soon you'll be looking to the future, and that means Thomas."

"Thomas?" Charlotte asked in a vague way. With her lace handkerchief she dabbed at her eyes.

Lydia briskly nodded. "In case you didn't hear me the first time, Thomas is now Lord Eddington and will inherit his father's entire estate."

"Thomas is now the heir," Charlotte repeated in dazed wonderment. "I always did like Thomas."

Bettina said, "There was never anything wrong with Thomas, except he was a second son. But he isn't anymore, is he?" She brightened. "He has always liked me, you know. He greatly admires my needlework."

"So Thomas is the new Lord Eddington," Charlotte mused aloud, ignoring her sister. It was obvious she had finally grasped the full meaning of Thomas's new position in life. "Oh, Mama, do you think—?"

"So all is not lost, after all." A note of triumph, mixed with relief, filled Lydia's voice. "Montague was a fine man, God rest his soul, but he was into his cups a great deal of the time, whereas Thomas—"

"Thomas is everything Montague was not," said Charlotte

with growing enthusiasm. "I've always had the feeling he admired me."

Lydia shot her a look of disdain. "There are matters far more important than whether he admires you or not. Bear in mind, the marquess's fondest wish has always been that Northfield Hall and Aldershire Manor be conjoined. This is not the time to consider such matters, however I have not one doubt the marquess will expect Thomas to carry out his plan. Meanwhile, girls, we must summon Celeste at once. We must have suitable black clothing to wear to Montague's funeral. I suspect he'll be buried at Northfield Hall, so we shall be taking a journey tomorrow."

Montague's funeral, Evleen thought in despair. Little did she know when the day began how horribly it would end. She pictured her wardrobe, but there was nothing suitable. "I'm afraid I have nothing black to wear."

Lydia regarded her strangely. "You? Go to Montague's funeral?"

"Naturally I thought . . . well, yes, of course I shall go," answered Evleen. "Is there anything wrong?"

"You can go if you wish, of course," Lydia answered with an elaborate shrug. "Far be it from me to stand in your way, but I'd hardly advise it, considering feelings will be running high against you."

"Whatever do you mean?" Evleen asked, totally bewildered.

Charlotte spoke up. "She means those awful things you were saying to Montague. A lot of people heard you." She burst into a new fit of sobbing. "And now he's dead and you are the one responsible!"

Evleen was dumbfounded. "But that's ridiculous."

"Is it?" asked Lydia. "Can you deny you pushed Montague while on the dance floor? Many people saw you, Evleen. Of course, we shall try to stand by you." One corner of her mouth lifted in a halfhearted smile. "Even though that might prove difficult."

Still dumbfounded, Evleen declared, "I don't need you to stand by me. I have done nothing wrong."

Lydia appeared not to hear. "And then there's that business at the curb. You did say some terrible things to Montague. Surely you cannot deny it."

Evleen was aghast. "Are you trying to say I caused Montague's death?"

"Can you honestly say you had no part in it? That remark you made in Gaelic, telling him to leave and not return. In retrospect, do you realize how utterly vile it was?"

"But you don't understand." Evleen gave a choked, desperate laugh. "I mean, I said some things, but there were circumstances . . . didn't you hear what he said to me? Caused his death? That is beyond all reason."

Lydia answered, "Oh, you didn't personally shove him beneath the wheels, if that's what you mean, but it's clear your sharp tongue unsettled the poor man."

"Which is why he was so distraught he didn't watch where he was going," said Charlotte. Her eyes blazed with accusation. "It's all your fault, Evleen. You so much as killed him, and don't think for a moment the whole world doesn't know."

"That's not so, Charlotte," said Amanda, who up to now had remained silent. "Evleen is right. People don't know all the circumstances. We were standing right there, all of us, so surely you must have heard Montague saying those insulting things to Evleen. She was only defending herself. We need to tell people that. We need—"

"Hush, Amanda, you don't know what you heard." Lydia Trevlyn glared accusingly at Evleen. "Charlotte is right. We all heard the abominable things you said to Montague, and for no reason, other than your own vituperative motives."

"Utter nonsense," Evleen flatly declared. Up to now she had felt so confused and badgered she could hardly speak, but now she was getting angry. She stood up and declared, "You know very well, Lydia Trevlyn, Montague fell under that coach because he was foxed. That's the reason, pure and simple, and if you say otherwise, you are being hideously unfair."

Hearing Lydia's sudden intake of breath, Evleen knew she'd offended the woman, but she was too sickened and disgusted to care. Before Lydia could speak, Evleen raised a hand to silence her. "Montague is dead because of his own folly, and I'll not hear another word."

With firm steps, she strode from the drawing room, vastly relieved to escape an atmosphere reeking of reprobation, all directed toward her. She was about to mount the stairs when she heard Lydia's voice behind her.

"Wait a moment," the older woman called in a compromising tone. "I have something to say to you alone."

"And what might that be, Mrs. Trevlyn?" Evleen was hard put to keep the anger and resentment from her voice.

"We talked once, remember? I told you my daughters would always come first."

"I remember." Evleen wondered what the woman was trying to say.

Lydia raised her chin firmly. "I just want you to know I meant what I said—that I shall always put the best interests of my girls before anything and anyone."

The truth dawned. Evleen felt sick inside, but knew her only recourse was to confront the woman. "Mrs. Trevlyn, you have considered me a threat from the beginning. At first you thought I might 'steal' Montague. Now that he's dead, you're afraid I might do the same with Thomas, so you're willing to let untrue rumors circulate that surely will ruin my reputation. Am I not correct?"

Lydia Trevlyn's silence gave Evleen all the confirmation she would ever need.

"Then why are you even bothering to tell me? Is this some kind of apology?"

"Not an apology, but a warning." Lydia gave Evleen a long, withering stare. "You know Lord Thomas fairly well, don't you?"

"He accompanied Patrick and me from Ireland."

Lydia cocked her head. "Do you consider him attractive? I am only asking because—"

"You want me to stay away from him, don't you?"

"Exactly. He belongs to Charlotte now. I trust you understand."

In the face of Lydia's appalling warning, Evleen threw caution to the winds. Bitterly, she replied, "I understand all right. You said you put the best interests of your girls before anything and anyone. It is obvious you put them ahead of honor and integrity, as well."

Not wanting to hear another word, Evleen spun on her heel and left. Shocked, feeling totally isolated, she climbed the stairs to her bedchamber, wondering if there was any way she could set straight the Trevlyns' accusations. Amanda knew the truth, of course, but Evleen wasn't sure the girl could stand up for herself. The more Evleen thought, the more she realized there was nothing she could do. How could she prove Montague had been drunk and insulting when there were the high-and-mighty Trevlyns implying Montague was a saint, and his death was caused by that rude, selfish upstart from Ireland who had for no reason insulted him?

Her chances were nil, she concluded.

The brief period of euphoria Evleen had experienced at the ball was forever gone. *Ah Thomas, our dreams are shattered.* Evleen's heart ached as she perceived with fearful clarity that the sudden, tragic death of Montague had changed her life. The man she loved was not plain Lord Thomas anymore. *How ironic!* Her mother had wanted her to marry a rich and titled Englishman, and now Thomas was, but the barrier between them was higher than ever. As Lord Eddington, new heir of the Marquess of Wythe, he would be a different person, and feelings between them could never be the same.

Chapter 16

Evleen spent a sleepless, tortured night. Despite the Trevlyns' appallingly unfair accusation, she spent much of her time thinking of that pitiful dark form lying in the street and hearing Thomas's anguished cry. She felt so sick about Montague that tortured regrets assailed her.

True, he'd been obnoxious on the dance floor, but perhaps if she hadn't walked away . . .

True, he'd been intoxicated, but why had she made that terrible remark? If only she'd been kinder, more tolerant!

If only . . . if only . . .

But regrets would get her nowhere. Nor, she suspected, would any further protests regarding those horrible accusations that she was somehow responsible for Montague's untimely death.

And Thomas. What shall I do about Thomas?

In the morning, she yearned to stay in her bedchamber and hide, but she knew such a course would be a coward's choice. Feeling numb, she dressed carefully and went down for breakfast, head high but with a heart full of dread. Except for Amanda's smile, she was met by silent hostility at the breakfast table, until finally, as she sat picking at her food, Lydia asked, "So what will you do now, Evleen?"

"What do you mean?"

"Is it not obvious what I mean? Must I say it?"

Slowly, with great deliberation, Evleen set down her fork on the fine china plate. She lifted her crystal goblet and took a sip of water, then drew herself up. "I shall say this one more time. There is a misunderstanding about last night. I did not in any way cause the death of Montague."

Her words were met with stony silence. How unjust this all

was! But unjust or not, she realized she was helpless to prevent Charlotte from spreading lies or Lydia from backing her up. Evleen looked around the table and saw nothing but antipathy, except for Amanda, whose sympathetic eyes seemed to offer encouragement.

I do not have to stay here, I could go home to Ireland. She thought with a sudden awareness that there was no reason in the world why she should tolerate this treatment a day, an hour longer. And yet . . .

Her mother's words came back to her: *Make me proud.* She knew what she had to do. "You asked what I was going to do, Mrs. Trevlyn," she said. "My answer is, I shall continue on as before. I want to attend Montague's funeral and shall do so. As for Lord Thomas, he is a grown man who will decide his own future with no help from you or me."

Amanda, seated next to her, boldly whispered, "Good for you."

"We shall see," Lydia said in an ominous tone.

It was a veiled threat, but Evleen knew there was nothing she could do about it. She managed to smile and said, "Never fear, Mrs. Trevlyn, I wouldn't dream of interfering with your matchmaking." She shifted her gaze to Charlotte. "Lord Thomas is yours, Charlotte . . . if he'll have you."

Early the next morning, Thomas hastened to Northfield Hall, where his father, his gout worse than ever, was still confined to his room. Thomas had expected to break the sad news concerning Montague, but one look at his father's pale, drawn face told him he already knew.

"I've already heard, son," said the marquess in a stricken voice. "Bad news travels swiftly." He shook his head in disbelief. "Montague gone. I can hardly believe it."

"It was quick, if that's any consolation."

"None at all." The marquess heaved a deep, despondent sigh. "Ah, Thomas, there's no consolation in any of this. My first son dead . . ." He choked up, for a moment unable to continue. "At least I shall always know I did my best for him. The most excellent tutors, fine clothes, the grand tour, I don't know what more a father could have done. He had everything, yet you know how he chose to spend his recent—his last—years."

Tears formed in his father's eyes. Thomas had never seen him cry before, not even when his mother died. "Ah, Thomas, I loved him more than life itself, despite his weaknesses."

Thomas was hard put not to throw comforting arms around his father but he knew the gout would not permit it. Still, he could hardly bear to see his beloved father in such a state of grief.

As he watched, the marquess sat taller, seeming to try to pull himself together. An ironic smile touched his lips as he remarked, "So you're no longer the second son, Thomas. Have you considered what that means?"

"Do you think that matters to me now?"

"Not at the moment, but it will." The marquess waved his arm in an encompassing gesture. "All this will be yours now. The estate, my many properties, investments, titles—all yours."

"I would give them all up in a second if it would bring Montague back."

"I'm sure you would, but that won't happen, will it? So we must be practical." The marquess slanted a warning gaze. "The management of this estate is a tremendous responsibility. I wanted Montague to learn, but—" his shoulders slumped dejectedly—"I can only hope you will take your duties more seriously."

"You know I shall."

"You must marry soon."

Evleen. Was it less than a day ago they'd been carefree and laughing at the ball? When the excitement of their meeting had been almost palpable between them? He had said he would call, knowing she knew he would propose. Unless he was totally mistaken in his judgment of women, he was positive she would accept. But of course all that was before the death of Montague.

"I do plan to marry soon, Papa," Thomas said, "after the appropriate period of mourning, of course."

"Ah. Charlotte will make a fine daughter-in-law, and the perfect mistress of Northfield Hall."

"Not Charlotte, Father. I am in love with Evleen O'Fallon."

His father's eyes went wide. Aghast, he regarded Thomas. After a stunned silence, he declared, "Are you daft? Over my dead body will you marry that selfish, cold-blooded Irish tart."

Thomas was so stunned that for a moment he could not speak. "Why do you talk of her like that?" he finally asked.

"Because she's responsible for Montague's death and don't you tell me otherwise."

"That's absolutely absurd. Montague fell under that coach because he was drunk."

"That's not what I heard. Montague was distraught because of what that woman said to him. I heard that from a very good source, so you'll not dissuade me."

That much was true, Thomas thought disconsolately. Once his father made up his mind, nothing could change it. "You've heard lies. Evleen is guilty of nothing more than rejecting Montague's advances."

The marquess bristled. "Whether she's guilty or not isn't the point. In any event, Evleen O'Fallon would not make a suitable wife. Under no circumstances are you to marry her."

Thomas stared in disbelief at his father. "I am amazed. She's been the toast of London for weeks, and now you say she's not suitable?"

"There's no noble blood in her, not like Charlotte Trevlyn. Do you really want your children to be half Irish?"

Thomas was suffused with anger. "Now see here—"

Reaching toward his bandaged foot, the marquess flinched. "God's blood but it hurts," he cried in anguish.

Thomas's flare of anger instantly subsided. "I hate seeing you suffer. Is there anything I can do?"

"Don't marry that Irish girl."

"But you don't understand. I love her."

"I don't give a groat if you love her or not. You've been stubborn all your life. Always did what you pleased, even when you were a little boy. Now that you're grown there's been no controlling you. But now . . . Ah, Thomas," his father cried, gazing up at him with pleading eyes. "Can you not do this one thing for me? I'm old. I'm sick. My older son just died. How can you defy me?"

Not easily, Thomas thought as a lump rose in his throat. *But I must.*

"All that is true, sir, and I deeply sympathize, but you may as well know that nothing on this earth will prevent me from asking Evleen O'Fallon to be my bride."

Thomas braced himself, waiting for the eruption that was sure to follow his rebellious stand. But instead, with baleful softness his father remarked, "So you choose to defy me."

"You have never even met her. If you did, you would see—"

"I have no wish to meet her," the marquess snapped. "There's nothing I can do to dissuade you?"

"You can disown me if you like."

"Don't be ridiculous. You're my only son and heir now. Nothing will change that."

"Then I take it you're agreeable to my marrying Evleen?"

"We shall see, son."

"I want an answer now," Thomas demanded.

"I have no desire for any further discussion concerning that Irish girl."

What did Papa mean? Although Thomas had initially felt pleased that his father had appeared to capitulate, he felt a certain unease. Later, his disquiet grew the more he thought about it, the more he suspected this wasn't the end of his disagreement with an ever-stubborn, ever-domineering father, who, one way or another, nearly always managed to get his way.

In the small family burial plot at Northfield Hall, Montague, Lord Eddington, was laid to rest under the spreading branches of an ancient oak tree. Most of the black-garbed crowd attending had come up from London for the day. They remained a somber lot during the services. Afterward, inside the magnificent mansion, when servants passed among them serving refreshments, the atmosphere lightened considerably.

For Evleen, dressed in borrowed black, it had been a most difficult day. Not only did she grieve for Montague, she was in an agony of doubt over Thomas. Did he believe the rumors flying around? She had not spoken to him since before the accident. Now it seemed a lifetime ago when they were laughing at the ball. She recalled the urgency in his voice when he said he wanted to speak to her. Did he still? Today would he greet her warmly or would he blame her for Montague's death and cut her dead? As it was, she sensed a certain coolness among many whom she thought were her friends. Nobody had snubbed her completely, though, until she was given the cut direct by Lady Chatsworth, an old friend of the marquess. There could be no doubt. The elderly woman had ignored Evleen's greeting, stuck her nose in the air, and moved away.

"You must ignore her," said Amanda as she and Evleen stood together in the ornate drawing room. "She's a silly old lady who doesn't know any better. I shall go set her straight this instant."

"No, you mustn't," Evleen replied. "Your mother will strongly disapprove if you do."

"There are times when you must do what you know is right." Amanda flashed Evleen an admiring smile "You taught me that. You do not deserve such treatment, and I shan't allow it. Here I go. Wish me luck with Lady Chatsworth."

Evleen watched gratefully as Amanda moved away. Truly, the girl had changed of late. Evleen wasn't sure if she should take credit, but Amanda had recently discovered she had a backbone. Her new attitude showed in the way she held her shoulders back and the manner in which she looked people square in the eye.

Lord Thomas had been busy acting the host. Evleen had surreptitiously watched as, deeply grieved, yet alert to the comfort of his guests, he moved among the crowd, accepting condolences. Finally, he came to her. She held her breath, not knowing what he would say. What a relief when he took her hand in both of his and said warmly, "I'm glad you could come today."

He listened carefully as she told him how sorry she was about Montague. When she finished, she hesitated, wondering what more she should say, deciding it was best he know what was in her heart. "I know there have been stories going around, but—"

"But we shall pay no attention to them, shall we?" he said, a world of love, concern, and comfort in his dark eyes. He bent toward her and in a soft voice said urgently, "I must see you later, Evleen, after the guests have gone."

Someone interrupted. With a quick nod he moved away, but nonetheless she felt vast relief. He wasn't angry. *Thomas wants to see me.* Her heart filled with joy. She felt suddenly buoyant, and had to suppress an urge to laugh aloud, which most certainly would not be seemly at a funeral.

Not long after, the butler took her aside. "His lordship would like to see you, Miss O'Fallon."

Thomas's father? What could he possibly . . . ? She had met the marquess briefly when four male servants carried him down for his son's funeral. He had appeared to be in pain, and as soon as the services were over, was carried back upstairs. "He wants to see me now, this very minute?"

"Now, miss."

An oddly primitive warning sounded in her brain. This was not going to be good. With each step up the massive winding staircase, she grew more apprehensive.

"Do come in, Miss O'Fallon," said the marquess.

As Evleen entered the bedchamber and seated herself, her heart went out to the white-haired old man sitting with his bandaged foot propped upon a low stool. He had lost a son. He was obviously in pain. Thomas had mentioned once what a robust man of action his father used to be, but obviously not anymore.

Evleen offered her sincere condolences, then sat back to hear what the marquess had to say.

He wasted no time. "Were you aware my son wants to marry you?" he asked, fastening her with his piercing gaze.

She was taken aback and had to collect her wits before she replied, "I suspected as much, but I wasn't sure."

"And what will you say when he proposes?"

The effrontery! If this were anyone but Thomas's father, she would surely get up and leave. At least she readily knew the answer. "I would say yes. I love Thomas very much, although I have yet to tell him so."

The marquess cocked his head and examined her thoroughly. "You're pretty enough. Well-spoken, too, I see."

She'd had enough. He had a reason for saying all this, and she wanted to know what it was. "With all due respect, sir, what are you getting at?"

He wasted no time in replying. "Young lady, what I'm getting at is that I do not want Thomas to marry you."

This had not been a good day to begin with. Now the effect of the marquess's words seemed to her the final, shattering blow. Over the lump growing in her throat, she managed to inquire, "May I ask why?"

"Do not take this personally, Miss O'Fallon. You're a lovely woman, obviously well-bred, but you're not . . ." He appeared to be searching for the least hurtful word.

"Quality?" she inquired, hardly able to speak. A wave of bitterness struck her. "What you mean is, I am 'below your touch' as you English so quaintly say. Worse, I come from Ireland, that godforsaken land where only the lowliest of savages dwell."

"Now, now, I have no wish to insult you," the marquess replied indulgently.

"I am sure you don't, yet I don't hear you denying what I just said."

"The facts remain," the marquess stated firmly. "My son will soon inherit a vast estate. Surely you can see he must have a wife of impeccable breeding, not to mention unimpeachable propriety."

"Are you implying there's something wrong with my propriety?"

"I have heard the rumors."

"About . . . Montague?" His nod caused her to fling out her hands in simple despair. "I did not in any way cause the death of your son, but you won't believe that, will you?"

He squeezed his eyes shut a moment. She could see this horrid scene was as difficult for him as it was for her. In a deadly calm voice he said, "I wish you no harm, Miss O'Fallon, but the fact remains you are not . . . of our element. Please, I beg of you, do not marry Thomas."

She stood, stunned and sickened, her pride telling her there was only one course she could follow. "You have won, sir. Rest assured, I shall not marry your son."

Thomas was surprised to see Evleen coming down the staircase. There was only one reason for her to be upstairs—she had been talking to his father. He felt a flicker of apprehension that turned to consternation when he saw her stricken face. He asked quickly, "What is wrong, Evleen?"

"Nothing's wrong," she said.

Women. "Of course there's something wrong. Come, let us talk. I think the library is empty."

"No." Eyes cold and proud, she backed away. "We'll be having no need to talk, not now, not ever."

He was thunderstruck. "But see here—"

"It won't work, Thomas." She laughed bitterly. "Funny, isn't it? My mother wanted me to find a rich, titled Englishman. Well, now you are one, and much too good for a poor Irish peasant girl like me. Good-bye, Lord Thomas . . . oh, no, excuse me, it's Lord Eddington now, isn't it? Saints preserve us, you're a future marquess. Pardon me if I don't curtsey, but I'm Irish, so I don't know how."

"You're being ridiculous," he said, and reached out to her. "Please, we need to talk."

"I have nothing more to say." The gaze she leveled on him was full of anger, despair, and pride. "I am going home to Ireland, the sooner the better," she announced, then turned and hastened away.

Thomas watched wordlessly, knowing to go after her now would be sheer folly while she was in her current mood. *His father*. Thomas could guess what the marquess had said to her, but he needed to know exactly what had transpired. Driven by urgency, he sprang up the stairway, but came to an abrupt halt at the top. He must calm himself before he faced his father. Otherwise, God knew what might happen when he discovered what cruel words the marquess had employed to offend and enrage the only woman in this world he had ever loved.

Home to Ireland!

The words rang in Evleen's head as she slipped from North-field Hall without so much as a good-bye, and on foot hastened the mile to Aldershire Manor. Despite all the grief of these past few days—Montague's death, the lies that were told, and now this last horrible insult from the marquess—her heart lifted at the thought she was going home.

Patrick would stay, of course. She had done her best to change his arrogant attitude, and hoped she had. How she would miss him! Still, he was better off with his grandfather than he'd ever be in County Clare.

She would leave tomorrow, quietly, with as little fanfare as possible. As for Thomas, she hoped he understood she was going home, that nothing could stop her and that she never would return to England.

When she arrived at Aldershire Manor, she was met by

Pierce, the elderly butler, who had accompanied the family from London. He asked if he could speak to her alone.

"It's the young master, miss. You asked me to tell you if there were any further problems. Boys will be boys, and I hate to complain, but we've had another incident in which he's treated one of the servants abominably. If it were only me, I would not say a word, but when he shouts at a young footman who was only trying to please, it's quite out of line."

"Thank you, Pierce. You needn't say another word. The matter will be taken care of."

That settled it. She would not return alone to Ireland. She would take Patrick with her, back where he belonged.

Lord Alberdsley regarded Evleen aghast. "Your going back to Ireland is bad enough, but Patrick? How could you do such a thing after all I've done for the boy?"

"I know, sir, but you see . . ." For at least the third time, she explained to Lord Alberdsley her reasons for wanting to go home, although she was careful not to mention Thomas. "And I must take Patrick, at least for a while. Don't you see I have no choice, sir?" she cried. "Every day he's here I see him becoming more vain, arrogant, and selfish. Only the firm hand of his mother can set him straight."

Lord Alberdsley regarded her sadly. "You realize if Patrick doesn't stay, I'm within my rights to cancel that fifty pounds a year I promised your family."

"We managed without it before. We can manage without it again."

"Will you send him back to me?"

"Of course, when and if he mends his ways." She eyed him boldly. "You promised, sir, and don't forget, you said you'd pay our return passage."

"Hmm . . . so I did. All right then, go back to Ireland. Patrick's a fine young man. Let him listen to his mother. There's no doubt in my mind he'll mend his ways, and then you can send him back." He regarded her quizzically. "And you?"

"Never," she replied vehemently. "With all due respect, sir, I've had my fill of the *ton* and all their vain, silly, useless rules."

"You're aware you cannot journey to Ireland alone. You'll need a chaperone."

"No, we don't. We shall go by ourselves."

"Absolutely not," Lord Alberdsley said in a voice that brooked no further argument. "A young lady and a boy traveling clear across England and Wales, then crossing the Irish Sea, most certainly need protection. I shall send . . . by Gad, I know who can do it. My brother, Walter, will accompany you."

She knew further protest was futile. Besides, she liked poor, hen-pecked Walter well enough. "All right then, it's settled."

"When will you leave?"

"First thing tomorrow morning." She gave him a rueful smile. "You've been wonderful, Lord Alberdsley, and I much appreciate what you've done for us, but I know now England is not for me."

He returned her smile and nodded graciously.

Strange, she thought as she left the room, Lord Alberdsley was not nearly as upset as she thought he would be. Did he know something she did not? It was as if he didn't believe she really planned to leave.

Chapter 17

By dawn's first light, Evleen was packed and ready to leave. Even though doubts assailed her, she could hardly wait to remove herself from such a cruel, uncaring country and return to her beloved Ireland. She felt little joy, though. Her mother would be crushed that her eldest daughter had not found that rich, titled Englishman. And then there was Thomas. She felt an acute sense of loss, just thinking about him. In her heart she knew she could never love another man and doubtless would stay single for the rest of her days.

Downstairs, she found Patrick dressed, ready, and in high spirits. He had shown no great regret when she told him they were leaving England. "I shall miss Grandfather," he said, but then his eyes lit as he added, "I can hardly wait to see Mama and the girls again."

They ate a quick breakfast. Afterward, followed by a footman hauling their luggage, as well as Lord Alberdsley himself, they made their way to the marbled front portico, where Lord Alberdsley's coach awaited.

"I wish you godspeed on your journey," Lord Alberdsley said brightly after hugging Patrick and pecking Evleen on the cheek. "Patrick, always take pride in who you are. Never forget you are not simple Patrick O'Fallon, but Viscount Montfret, heir to my estate and title."

At another time, Evleen would have protested Lord Alberdsley's admonishment to Patrick. She would have ardently proclaimed that pride in one's inherited title was misplaced. Far better for Patrick if he took pride in his honor, integrity, and the manner in which he conducted himself, and that included his treatment of his so-called inferiors. But the old man meant well. He had been part of this stilted, vainglorious society all his life and knew no other. *Strange,* she thought again, how little upset he seemed. She had expected he would be distraught his grandson was leaving, but instead he appeared exceedingly cheerful.

"Where is Walter?" she asked.

"Er . . . you'll find your escort inside my coach. Er, good-bye, my children." With obvious haste, Lord Alberdsley retreated inside his mansion. *Surprising.* She would have thought he would stay to wave good-bye.

The footman opened the coach door. Someone was sitting there, she assumed Walter. She was halfway inside when she looked into his face and got such a jolt she gasped. It wasn't Walter, it was Thomas.

"You," she said, frozen.

He was sitting there grinning at her, one boot jauntily propped on the seat across. "Ah, good morning, Miss O'Fallon. Fleeing to Ireland, are we?"

She stepped back out of the coach and glared at him. "What are you doing here? Where is Walter?"

"Alas, Walter was busy, so I volunteered to take his place."

"You mean . . . oh no," she exclaimed. "Surely you're aware by now what your father told me. Why are you doing this? There's no point."

His grin disappeared. He sprang lightly from the coach and standing close, took both her hands. "You're making a mistake. Don't go. There's nothing we cannot work out."

She jerked her hands away. "I am indeed going to Ireland, but not with you. Patrick and I are quite capable of going by ourselves."

"That may very well be, but if you do go alone, it won't be in this fine coach. Lord Alberdsley insists you have an escort." He cocked an amused eyebrow at her. "Alas, it appears the only suitable escort available is me."

"I won't go with you!"

"Ah, but you will," he said smoothly. "I give you my word I shall be the perfect gentleman, just as before. Not only that, I promise I'll say nothing more to dissuade you from returning to your home."

"Please, can't Lord Thomas come?" begged Patrick, who had been listening wide-eyed.

"Well . . ." She felt herself weakening.

"Who knows the roads better than I?" asked Thomas. "Who knows how to get to Holyhead and find a ship?" An amused gleam filled his eyes. "Who else will take care of you when you're heaving over the side?"

"Oh, very funny," she retorted, unamused. He had a point, though. She could not picture Walter comforting her as Thomas had done. The timid little man would no doubt himself be heaving. Still . . .

"You and Lord Alberdsley plotted this together," she accused.

"Of course," he instantly admitted. "We don't want you to go, Evleen, but if you do, I promise, I shall be the perfect escort."

"Then . . . oh, all right, I suppose I must." *But I don't have to like it,* she told herself silently. She would be civil to him, and barely polite, but would keep her distance, mentally if not physically, and most certainly not indulge in any sort of personal conversation. "But I worn you, Lord Thomas, nothing on this earth can make me change my mind."

Thomas only smiled and had no answer.

Thomas remained true to his word on their trip across England. Always his charming self, he was helpful, courteous, and always amusing, but not one personal word crossed his lips.

Evleen remained aloof much of the day, constantly reviewing in her mind that terrible scene with Thomas's father. The coach was well past Shrewsbury before her curiosity got the better of her. "Why are you doing this, Lord Thomas?" she asked. Quickly, she corrected herself. "Lord Eddington, I mean."

"You need not be so formal," he replied. He was sitting across, so he was able to look her square in the eye. "Actually, 'Thomas' would do, if you could possibly bring yourself to be that informal."

"You have, answered my question, *Lord Eddington,*" she snippily replied.

"Ah, so that's the way it is," he said, amused. "Well, then, *Miss O'Fallon,* has it crossed your mind that I am here because I care enough to be concerned?"

"Totally unnecessary."

"Not unnecessary at all. According to Lord Alberdsley, you're a delicate flower who could not possibly be allowed to travel alone."

She bristled. "Delicate flower indeed." She noticed the mischievous gleam in his eye. "You weren't serious."

"Of course not. God help anyone who gets in your way."

"You are absolutely right," she replied, flinging the words at him. "There's never a need to worry about me."

"So true," he replied agreeably. "Actually, I foresee a marvelous future for you in Ireland."

"And what might that be?"

"You will marry that fine, upstanding Irishman, Timothy Murphy. You will have at least ten children—make that a dozen. You will live to a ripe old age and become the wizened old oracle of County Clare, dispensing sage advice far and wide. They'll be beating a path to your door. They—"

"I get the point," she said, not at all amused. Oh, he could be so exasperating! She knew she shouldn't bother to defend herself, but he needed to be set straight. "For your information, I shall never marry Timothy Murphy."

He raised a skeptical eyebrow. "Is that right? Then perhaps you and I should talk."

"You promised you wouldn't."

"I promised I would do nothing to dissuade you from returning to your home." He glanced out the window. "It would appear this coach is indeed heading west toward Ireland, just as you wished."

She took pains to conceal her rising curiosity. "Then say what you have to say."

"This is not the time nor the place." He replaced his mocking smile with a gentle one. "When it is, I shall let you know."

They crossed the Irish Sea on the *Union*, which pitched and rolled as much, if not more, than the *Countess of Liverpool*. Evleen found herself hard put to maintain her aloof attitude with Lord Thomas, especially when she was sick again, and he, all kindness and concern, was there to comfort her every mile of the way.

Back on land, Thomas hired a carriage in Dublin, which he

drove himself. They were nearly halfway across Ireland, near Athlone, when he made an unexpected turn and started down a familiar road.

"Are we going to Conclonomaise?" asked Patrick, full of enthusiasm.

"Oh, no, not now," cried Evleen. The closer they got to County Clare, the more anxious she was to see her mother.

"It will only take a few minutes," said Thomas. With a slight smile, he continued, "Indulge me."

The enduring silence of the ancient monastery grounds was broken only by the melodic chirping of the birds. Overhead, fleecy white clouds skittered about an azure blue sky as Evleen gazed down at the carved stone crosses dotting the emerald green setting of Conclonomaise. They were like silent sentinels guarding the centuries.

Since that terrible scene with Thomas's father, she had lived in her own little world of hurt and resentment, but gradually, as she gazed at the ancient ruins lying below her in the sunshine, her inner turmoil stilled, replaced by a marvelous feeling of serenity. "Just think, it was founded in 545 A.D.," she murmured. "It's hard to imagine, all those many years ago."

Thomas stood close by her side. "Here, I can think of Montague without feeling bitter at his wasted life. I know he's at last found peace."

Thomas has done so much for me, she thought with sudden clarity. The thought barely crossed her mind when another followed. *Even though he's grieving for his brother, he has taken the time to escort Patrick and me home to Ireland.* "How thoughtless of me," she told him. "I've been so sunk in my own troubles, I forgot how terrible you must feel."

"This is the least I can do. My father treated you abysmally."

"Yes, he did, but still . . ." She was silent for a time, putting her thoughts in order. "I'm so glad you brought me here. It's not easy to explain, but I'm thinking of all the people who've lived here over the centuries and how they've come and gone. They had troubles, too, but now, what does it matter? I stand here in awe. This place makes me realize how petty are my own concerns."

He nodded thoughtfully. "A hundred years from now all

those uncertainties of ours that loom so large today won't matter one whit."

So very true, she thought. Although she had been deeply wounded by the marquess's words, a year, six months from now, what would they matter? Aside from honor, the one thing in her life that truly mattered was her love for her family, and their love for her. And equally important . . .

Her heart swelled with newly discovered feeling. *My love for Thomas.* She smiled up at him. "I feel better somehow."

"You should," he replied. "Of your many admirable qualities, the one I admire the most is your faith in yourself. You *know* my father was wrong. You are *not* going to wallow in self-pity."

"I know, and I won't," she stated positively.

He took her hand. "Let's stroll, shall we? I want another chance at that Whispering Arch."

Patrick was off exploring when they reached the ruins of the cathedral and the Whispering Arch. "You stand here," said Thomas, placing her on one side of the arch. "And I'll stand here." He stood on the other side, and they faced each other.

Evleen's heart was pounding as she asked, "Would you mind telling me why you brought me here?"

He asked, "Do you remember what the old man said to us the first time we were here?"

"He said courting couples have been coming here for centuries. They stand, one on each side, whispering their words of love to each another."

"As I recall, you couldn't wait to inform him we were not courting."

"Which if you recall, we weren't at the time." As casually as she could manage, she softly asked, "Are we now, Thomas?"

He gave her a look so warm and compelling, so full of longing, it dispelled all doubts. "Of course we are."

She felt instant joy at Thomas's words, yet was suddenly beset with all the reasons why such a union would never work. "But your father disapproves of me."

"Not for long. Amanda is going to speak to him, if she hasn't already, and tell him the complete truth about Montague's death and that it was in no way your fault. My father will come round. If he does not, it's his loss, not ours. By the way, I'm amazed at the change in Amanda. Thanks to you, the girl has developed a backbone."

"That's all very well and good," she said, "but I hate to think of facing the Trevlyns again. You know how they dislike me."

"You will be happy to hear Walter and his family will soon be leaving Aldershire Manor. Before I left, I spoke to Lord Alberdsley. It seems he's booting them out. They'll be living on that estate Walter owns. There's a small manor house there. With a few servants they should be quite comfortable."

"Lydia Trevlyn will be miserable."

He gave her his lopsided grin. "Do you care?"

She grinned in return. "Of course not, except for Amanda."

"Never fear, Lord Alberdsley is giving Amanda her Season. The way she's changed, I'm sure the dandies will be swarming about."

Evleen was delighted. "Amanda will find her true love in no time." In the distance she saw Patrick and was reminded of yet another problem. "But then there's Patrick and his behavior—"

"Not a problem," Thomas interrupted firmly. "Lord Alberdsley has told me of the boy's arrogant conduct. It's quite normal, under the circumstances. All he needs is a firm hand."

"Which Lord Alberdsley will never use, I'm afraid."

"Nor should he. Grandfathers are meant to indulge their grandchildren, not mete out discipline. The firm hand will come from me." He gazed fondly at Patrick, playing in the distance. "We'll get along just fine." He swung his gaze back to Evleen. "All right, anything else? Or have we covered all your objections?"

She considered a moment. "I can't think of anything."

"In that case, it appears it's time to follow the old tradition." Thomas leaned a flattened palm against the arch, jammed his other hand into his hip, and jauntily crossed one boot over the other. He lowered his voice to just above a whisper and lightly said, "My dear Miss O'Fallon, in all my life I have never met a woman as beautiful, charming, witty, and entertaining as you, nor one as independent, if not downright obstinate. I love everything about you—the way your face lights up when you smile, the sound of your voice and that Irish brogue of yours, which, the madder you are, the thicker it gets. I want to hear it all the rest of my life. In fact, 'love' is hardly the word. I am mad for you. Will you marry me?" He took a deep breath and stared intensely, waiting for her answer.

"Must I whisper it?" she asked from four feet away, her heart racing.

"Tradition be damned." He stepped across the archway and swept her into his arms. "Say it as loud as you like."

"Yes, I will marry you," she cried, and would have said more but he crushed her lips with an eager, grateful kiss. Finally she pulled back enough to say, "I thought of something else."

"And what might that be?"

"I want a long, long visit with my mother."

"If you like, we shall post the banns in Galway and be married in Ireland."

"Mama would like that."

"Really? Didn't she tell you, never love an Englishman?"

Evleen smiled as she reached to kiss him again. "Mothers can be wrong."

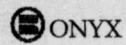

 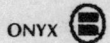

Dear Reader,

If you liked *You're What?!*, you'll love *The Pregnant Virgin!*

So many of you wrote requesting encore appearances from some of your favorite characters in my first two books—notably, the matchmaking septuagenarians Millie and Hazel—that I thought it was time to invite them (and a few others) back.

At Midtown Hospital in Detroit, love is right under the noses of our hero and heroine, Dr. Brad Darling and Ali Celeste, but it takes a little nudge from Millie and Hazel to make them see it and later believe that they can overcome the obstacles that threaten to keep them apart. One of those obstacles is the fact that Ali visits a sperm bank and then turns up pregnant after telling the hero that she's a virgin. Now, what man *wouldn't* have his doubts?

I hope you enjoy this one. I had a lot of fun writing it.

As always, I love hearing from you and welcome your letters.

Warmest regards,

Anne Eames

Anne Eames

You may write to Anne Eames c/o:
4217 Highland Road, Box #252
Waterford, MI 48328
For a response and an autographed doorknob hanger, please include a #10 self-addressed stamped envelope.

Dear Reader,

Spring is in the air…and so is romance. Especially at Silhouette, where we're celebrating our 20th anniversary throughout 2000! And Silhouette Desire promises you six powerful, passionate, provocative love stories *every month*.

Fabulous Anne McAllister offers an irresistible MAN OF THE MONTH with *A Cowboy's Secret*. A rugged cowboy fears his darkest secret will separate him from the beauty he loves.

Bestselling author Leanne Banks continues her exciting miniseries LONE STAR FAMILIES: THE LOGANS with a sexy bachelor doctor in *The Doctor Wore Spurs*. In *A Whole Lot of Love,* Justine Davis tells the emotional story of a full-figured woman feeling worthy of love for the first time.

Kathryn Jensen returns to Desire with another wonderful fairy-tale romance, *The Earl Takes a Bride*. THE BABY BANK, a brand-new theme promotion in Desire in which love is found through sperm bank babies, debuts with *The Pregnant Virgin* by Anne Eames. And be sure to enjoy another BRIDAL BID story, which continues with Carol Devine's *Marriage for Sale,* in which the hero "buys" the heroine at auction.

We hope you plan to usher in the spring season with all six of these supersensual romances, only from Silhouette Desire!

Enjoy!

Joan Marlow Golan

Joan Marlow Golan
Senior Editor, Silhouette Desire

Please address questions and book requests to:
Silhouette Reader Service
U.S.: 3010 Walden Ave., P.O. Box 1325, Buffalo, NY 14269
Canadian: P.O. Box 609, Fort Erie, Ont. L2A 5X3

The Pregnant Virgin
ANNE EAMES

Silhouette®
Desire®

Published by Silhouette Books
America's Publisher of Contemporary Romance

To my newfound family—
Lynne, Ken, Barbara and Keri—
who made me feel right at home.

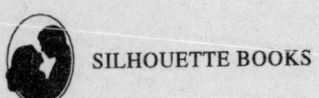 SILHOUETTE BOOKS

ISBN 0-373-76283-6

THE PREGNANT VIRGIN

Visit us at www.romance.net

Printed in U.S.A.

Books by Anne Eames

Silhouette Desire

Two Weddings and a Bride #996
You're What?! #1025
Christmas Elopement #1042
* *A Marriage Made in Joeville* #1078
**The Best Little Joeville Christmas* #1114
**Last of the Joeville Lovers* #1142
**The Unknown Malone* #1247
The Pregnant Virgin #1283

*The Montana Malones

ANNE EAMES

has been a Golden Heart finalist and Maggie winner, and her books have appeared on the *USA Today* best-seller list. This is her eighth novel for Desire.

Anne and her husband, Bill, live in southeastern Michigan with their pampered pooch, Punkin.

You may write to Anne Eames at: 4217 Highland Road, Box #252, Waterford, MI 48328. For an autographed doorknob hanger, please enclose a #10, self-addressed, stamped envelope.

IT'S OUR 20th ANNIVERSARY!
We'll be celebrating all year,
continuing with these fabulous titles,
on sale in March 2000.

Special Edition

#1309 Dylan and the Baby Doctor
Sherryl Woods

#1310 Found: His Perfect Wife
Marie Ferrarella

#1311 Cowboy's Caress
Victoria Pade

#1312 Millionaire's Instant Baby
Allison Leigh

#1313 The Marriage Promise
Sharon De Vita

#1314 Good Morning, Stranger
Laurie Campbell

Intimate Moments

#991 Get Lucky
Suzanne Brockmann

#992 A Ranching Man
Linda Turner

#993 Just a Wedding Away
Monica McLean

#994 Accidental Father
Lauren Nichols

#995 Saving Grace
RaeAnne Thayne

#996 The Long Hot Summer
Wendy Rosnau

Romance

#1432 A Royal Masquerade
Arlene James

#1433 Oh, Babies!
Susan Meier

#1434 Just the Man She Needed
Karen Rose Smith

#1435 The Baby Magnet
Terry Essig

#1436 Callie, Get Your Groom
Julianna Morris

#1437 What the Cowboy Prescribes...
Mary Starleigh

Desire

#1279 A Cowboy's Secret
Anne McAllister

#1280 The Doctor Wore Spurs
Leanne Banks

#1281 A Whole Lot of Love
Justine Davis

#1282 The Earl Takes a Bride
Kathryn Jensen

#1283 The Pregnant Virgin
Anne Eames

#1284 Marriage for Sale
Carol Devine

One

"**Y**ou're what!"

"I'm going to have a baby," Ali Celeste repeated, enjoying the shocked expression on her sister Lynne's face.

"But how did—I mean...I didn't even know you had a boyfriend!" Lynne looked as though she might hyperventilate at any second, so Ali put an end to the ruse.

"I said 'I'm *going* to.' I didn't say I *am*." She ate the last of her salad and pushed her plate aside.

Lynne leaned back in her chair, tapped her fingers against her chest and scanned the crowded cafeteria of Detroit's Midtown Hospital. Probably checking for eavesdroppers, Ali thought, unable to keep her smile in check.

"It's not funny," Lynne said, trying to sound annoyed, but her smile betrayed her. "You scared the hell out of me."

"Why's that?" As if she didn't know.

"Pregnant out of wedlock? Mom would roll over in her grave."

Ali laughed at her sister's choice of words. "Wedlock? Sounds like something out of the Middle Ages."

Lynne looked from side to side before she spoke. "Yeah, well, the principle still applies." She punctuated her point by pushing the last bite of sandwich into her mouth and shooting Ali her best frustrated-big-sister glare.

Ali averted her gaze to the novel sitting next to her plate and waited for Lynne to calm down. If only she could find a hero like the ones in her books. She sighed and wondered if she would have time to read a few more pages before her lunch hour was over.

Lynne tossed her napkin down and leaned her elbows on the table. "I thought you told me you were determined to be a virgin for Mr. Right."

"Yep. That's still the plan."

Looking more confused than ever, Lynne asked, "What are you up to, Alexis Marie?"

"Well, you know I work at the fertility clinic..."

"Of course, but what's—" Her eyebrows shot up and her eyes grew round. "No! You don't mean..."

"Why not? Maybe I can get some free samples." She knew this wasn't the case, but she was having too much fun teasing her sister.

"Get serious, Ali. Why would you want to use a sperm bank? You're still in your twenties."

"Not for as long as I'd like. And next month I can chalk up another year."

"Is that what this is all about? Birthday blues?"

Ali shook her head. "I never would have guessed I'd be this old and not even engaged. And don't give me that 'you're just a baby' look."

"But you are. You have lots of time left."

Did she? She used to think so. She stared at the blue painted ductwork overhead, and in her mind's eye years of fantasies paraded by—images of a strong yet sensitive man sweeping her off her feet. *Not* taking care of her, she reminded herself. Completing her was more like it. She could almost see his face, at least his eyes. They were always intense, sincere. And oh, so full of love for her.

She glanced back at the cover model on her book. *Ah, yes. Just like that.*

She mentally shook off the image and faced her sister again. "No offense, sis, but you and Ken thought you had a lot of time and look how long it took you to conceive." Ali leaned forward, deciding it was time to make her case. She didn't need her sister's approval, yet the months to come would be much easier if she could make Lynne understand.

"Lynne, you were nearly forty when you finally got pregnant. Remember the years of anxiety you went through, not to mention a chunk of money for treatments?"

Lynne nodded reluctantly. "How can I forget? If it weren't for Mom's estate I'd still be paying off loans...not that I'm complaining. Little Keri is worth every penny."

"I agree." She picked up her iced tea and pictured her two-year-old niece's kissable cheeks and smiled. If she loved Keri this much, how would she feel about a child of her own? As far back as she could remember she had delighted in playing with little ones.

No, there was no doubt in her mind that she was doing the right thing. She'd be a fool to wait for some fantasy man with dreamy eyes. Besides, what were the odds she would ever find one?

She set her glass down decidedly. It was time to take matters into her own hands, and she could sense her sister was weakening.

"Let's not forget Barbara. She wasn't as fortunate as you. Little Timmy is adorable and as loved as any child, but we both know adoption was her last resort when all else failed."

Lynne reached across the table for Ali's hand. "Sweetie, just because we had trouble doesn't mean you will."

"True. But I don't want to wait until the eleventh hour to find out. Besides, I haven't met a decent guy in over a year. In a blink of an eye I'll be thirty and still telling jerks to take a hike. Please, will you try to understand? I'd really like your support on this." Ali held her sister's gaze, hoping to telegraph just how serious she was about her decision.

Lynne squeezed Ali's hand, then on a long sigh, she let go and nodded slowly. "I can see you've made up your mind, so if it's my blessing you're looking for, you've got it."

It was all Ali could do not to let out a hoot and rush around the table to hug her sister. "Thanks, Lynne. It means a lot to me." She slouched in her chair, realizing she'd been holding her breath.

"Whew! I'm sure glad that's out in the open." She fanned a napkin across her face. "Now, what do you think Barbara will say?"

"Probably the same as I did. She'll put up a fuss before she acquiesces. Neither one of us has ever been able to say no to you, baby sister, and you know that."

Baby sister—that was the problem. At times she even wondered if her overpowering desire to have a child of her own was so everyone would stop viewing *her* this way. They always thought of her as a baby, even though she'd lived on her own for seven years now and had done all right for herself. Except in the men department. They were still an enigma.

She drank more tea and decided it was time for a new subject.

"Speaking of Barbara, any word about Tom's transfer back to Detroit?"

"She'd hoped before Christmas, but last time we talked she said it looked more like spring. I hope nothing slows things up again. We were kinda counting on doing some sort of job share. Something where I'd keep the little ones every other week while she worked and vice versa."

Maybe they could help with her little one, too, Ali thought. She would need reliable child care if she decided to return to work later. Fortunately her inheritance gave her the option.

Lynne glanced around the room, then leaned closer and whispered, "Have you even bothered to look around this hospital? Look at all the good-looking young men in this room alone. They can't *all* be married or undesirables."

Ali sighed, frustrated that "The Search," as it had come to be called, was again the topic of discussion. Reluctantly she scanned the area, not paying close attention. Good looks didn't mean much to her, anyway. And if the guy happened to be a doctor, there was a good chance he had a God complex. Experience had proven that point. If he was good-looking, too, forget it. He would probably have an ego the size of Saturn.

But Lynne had different ideas.

"Check out the tall, blond guy in the middle booth."

With a roll of her eyes, Ali looked. "He's got to be six-five if he's an inch. Just what I need. Someone fifteen inches taller than me. I get a stiff neck thinking about it."

"Okay," Lynne said, not sounding deterred. "What about the studious one in the corner...the one with the wire-rimmed glasses?"

"He's gay."

"Really?"

"No." She laughed. "I don't know. Maybe he is." She waved a dismissive hand. "Look, kiddo, do you think we could drop The Search...at least for today?" Lynne crossed her arms, resignation not being her strong suit, and Ali changed the subject. "Are you and Ken going to the Michigan-Michigan State game this weekend?"

Lynne shook her head slowly, looking somewhat annoyed. "Ken has to work. Wanna go?"

"Are you serious?" The game was one of the biggest rivalries of the football season and the weatherman predicted temperatures in the eighties, unusual for mid-September in Michigan. "You bet I do...assuming you won't try fixing me up with some guy in the stands. *Especially* if he's a doctor."

"This is still about Dad, isn't it? Come on, Ali. Let

it go. So he was a jerk who just happened to be a doctor. That doesn't make them *all* bad.''

"I might have agreed with you if I hadn't worked for that obnoxious group of surgeons at my last job.'' At least at her current job, doctor contact was minimal.

"Got a postcard from Dad last month,'' Lynne went on. "He and Tinkerbell are in Tahiti.''

Ali was surprised he was still with his toy bride. When he left her mom more than a dozen years ago for someone younger than Barbara and Lynne, Ali was sure it wouldn't last. It must be his money, she decided.

As young as Ali had been at the time, she could still remember how often her father had said this or that patient needed him, that he had to work late. While all along he was...

Poor Mom. Ali wondered again if Mom would be alive today if Dad hadn't broken her heart. She shivered and hugged herself.

"Doctors are the scum of the earth,'' she said, more for her own benefit than her sister's. "A necessary evil, maybe, but I wouldn't trust one any farther than I could throw him.''

Lynne shot Ali a derisive look before searching the room one last time. "Ooh, ooh. Table at four o'clock, just sitting down.''

Ali turned slowly, prepared for another glib remark...until she spotted him. Even in green scrubs his body looked hard and fit, well-worked muscles peeking from beneath short sleeves. Handsome didn't quite describe him. Yet the singular feature that held her attention was his eyes—so blue that even at a distance she couldn't miss them. He brushed a stray lock of jet-black hair off his forehead, then opened a napkin across his lap.

She was still watching when a second man joined the table. He said something as he sat down and the first man laughed aloud, dimples showing on either side of his drop-dead gorgeous smile.

"Well, well," Lynne said, bringing Ali's attention back to their own table. "You're not immune, after all." Then she chuckled. "Honestly, Ali, if you could see yourself. Sometimes I think you read too many of those romance novels." She pointed to Ali's book. "I can't tell you how many times I catch you with this faraway dreamy look on your face."

Ali hid behind her iced tea, feeling heat travel up her neck. What was the matter with her? Sitting here gawking at a total stranger. She set the glass down and said, "So...what's new with my favorite niece? Tell me everything."

Lynne smiled smugly before answering the question.

Ali knew she'd dodged a bullet this time, but she also knew that sooner or later The Search would crop up again.

"You're what!"

"Keep your voice down." Brad Darling glanced around the cafeteria, grateful no one seemed to have noticed his friend's overreaction.

"You heard me right." He pushed the stubborn stray hair off his forehead a second time.

"But why would you do...that?" Craig talked around the side of his juice glass as if he feared a lip-reader at the next table.

Brad chuckled softly. "Because it's quick, easy,

and pays really well, that's why. We weren't all born with a silver spoon in our mouth like you, Craig.''

"How many times have you…done it?" Craig asked. "For science, I mean,'' he added with a rueful smile.

"Actually, today will be my first. There's a fertility clinic in the professional wing next door. I'm going as soon as I finish this sandwich.'' He took a healthy bite and wondered if he'd been wise to confide in his friend. Confidentiality didn't concern him, yet the questions were bound to come. And they did.

"Aren't you afraid someone will recognize you?''

"For Pete's sake,'' he said, wiping his face with a napkin. "You make it sound like I'm about to commit adultery.''

"But you've got a reputation to maintain. You *are* a doctor—''

"Just barely.''

"Okay, so we're lowly residents. Still—''

"Look, I'm sure as hell not going over there wearing scrubs or a white jacket with my name on the breast pocket. I'll change first, go outside, then come in the separate entrance to the clinic. If someone sees me—'' he shrugged ''—they see me. But I don't plan to advertise.''

Craig laughed. "Good thing. I can hear the jokes already. 'Did ya hear about Brad's trips to the sperm bank? Yeah, I hear he's making money hand over fist'.''

"Very funny,'' Brad said, taking the last bite of his corned beef on rye before standing. "I gotta run. Catch ya later.''

"I'd say 'Don't do anything I wouldn't do' but—''

"I won't,'' Brad said, picking up his tray. "Since

I'm getting paid for it.'' He left Craig laughing and shaking his head as he strode out.

Brad wished he felt as self-assured and laid-back about the subject as he sounded. In truth, his sandwich was lodged in his chest and he could feel beads of perspiration forming on his brow. This wasn't going to be as easy as he'd made out.

Craig was right about one thing, though. The hospital grapevine would eat this one up if it got wind of it. He'd just have to be careful and make sure no one saw him.

Two

It was ten to one when Ali tossed her purse into her desk drawer and eagerly opened her novel. She tucked the book safely from view behind the tall countertop and continued where she had left off.

> She knew tonight would be the night. A fire crackled in the open hearth; candles flickered on every surface. He lifted his champagne flute to hers.
> "To the love of my life," he said, his eyes burning as bright as the fire, his gaze so intense she felt weak with love and desire.
> He set his glass down and took her in his arms, his eyes riveted on her mouth, his lips inching closer until—

"Darling," Ali heard, still in a daze.

"Yes-ss," she drawled, her eyes hooded as she slowly lifted her head.

"Brad Darling? I have an appointment?"

Ali stared at the handsome face, stunned for a moment to see the one and same man she'd been ogling in the cafeteria.

"Y-yes. Of course," she said, slamming her book closed and reaching for the top folder on the stack next to her. But when she glanced up again he flashed her his toothy smile and she could have sworn the air conditioning had stopped working.

Quickly she looked away and skimmed the contents of his file. "I see you've done all the preliminary work. Looks like everything's in order." Keeping her head down, she opened her appointment book. "How often do you plan to come?"

"*Excuse* me?"

"Once a week? Once a month?"

"Oh."

She heard him exhale and she thought he must be nervous. Not unusual. Especially for first-timers.

"Uh—" he tapped on the counter "—let's say once a week."

Eyes still down, she asked, "Is this day and time good for you?"

"Yes, yes. Fine."

"If you'll have a seat, someone will be with you shortly."

Out of the corner of her eye she watched as he passed her desk. His jeans were worn and tight, and she decided she liked this look better than the scrubs, although both packages were spectacular.

Damn. Why was she playing this game? After all, she was critical of guys who leered after women simply for their looks. Besides, she would never go out with someone who worked at the hospital. Especially not a doctor who probably thought he was God.

Aha! Now it all made sense. He was here in hopes of making *little* Gods—his contribution to mankind.

She pushed out of her chair and stuck the folder labeled "Darling, Brad" in the rack beside the closed door, admonishing herself for such shallow musings. Hopefully the technician would come out soon and usher the guy away.

But for some reason there was a delay and she heard Doctor Boy approach a while later. He stopped at the side of her desk and flashed her his Brad Pitt dimpled smile.

"Sorry to bother you. Any idea how much longer? I have to get back to work."

If his hair was blond he could double for her favorite actor, she mused, his question taking a beat to register. "Um…let me go find out what the holdup is." She stood, but he didn't back up, giving her little room to navigate. She stared at a dark tuft of chest hair peeking above the second button of his light blue shirt and waited for him to move. He stood there riveted and she let her eyes drift up to his.

Big mistake.

Too blue. Too intense.

The door to the back opened and they both turned toward it.

"Darling?" the technician asked.

"Yes," he said, then smiled at Ali one last time before he walked away.

Ali heaved a sigh and sat down. The book caught her eye, and she immediately grabbed it and opened the desk drawer. With one last look at the bare-chested hero on the cover, she shoved it into her purse. Maybe her sister had been right. At the very least, this wasn't the best place to read a romance novel.

Fortunately the phone rang, then other clients arrived, and Ali suddenly found herself very busy.

But when "Darling, Brad" sheepishly passed her desk a while later and headed for the exit, her gaze followed him.

And in that instant a seed of an idea began to take root.

Brad walked briskly around the exterior of the sprawling complex, muttering under his breath. What had gotten into him back there? Flirting with her like that. The last thing he needed was a personal relationship with someone who worked at the sperm bank he planned to visit every week.

Real discreet, guy. Real discreet.

He yanked open a back door and strode inside. So what if she's a knockout and built like a brick—

Forget it. Forget her.

He picked up his pace to the lounge and his locker. She could be the star of "Baywatch" with a Mensa IQ and it wouldn't matter. He didn't have time for a social life. At least not until his residency was over, and even then he would be hard-pressed to foot the tab for dinner and a movie.

With no one in sight he quickly changed back into his aqua scrubs, trying not to dwell on how long it would take him to repay one hundred and twenty thousand dollars in student loans.

Still, as the day progressed, Brad's worries about money were replaced by the image of the woman in the clinic. He would see a patient with blond hair and it would remind him of hers—long, thick and silky-looking. He wondered what it would feel like and how she would look with it mussed and falling in her face. Sometimes he'd catch himself and redirect his thoughts. Other times he'd simply smile and go with the flow.

When things slowed around midnight, he found an empty bed and settled in for a short nap. As usual the day had been long and grueling and he was beat. With a weary sigh he closed his eyes. And there she was again.

Ali called Michelle Singleton, a computer consultant who had helped her get the position at the clinic. She'd met Michelle at her previous job where the team of arrogant doctors had used Michelle's services. When Michelle gave notice that she wouldn't be working for them any longer, Ali asked Michelle's help in getting her out, too. A close friendship had been developing ever since.

As luck would have it, Michelle was free for lunch and she agreed to meet Ali in the cafeteria.

Ali arrived a few minutes early and staked out the same table she'd used with her sister the day before, except this time she sat on the opposite side. She tried to lie to herself as to why she did this, but she knew the truth. People were creatures of habit. Maybe that handsome creature would sit at his same table, too, and this way she wouldn't have to crane her neck to watch him.

Michelle placed her tray on the table a moment later and sat down. "How's the new job going?"

"Great. I owe you one."

The table behind Michelle remained empty and the
women ate and made small talk until Ali finally
worked up enough courage to broach the reason for
getting together.

"There's something personal I'd like to ask you,
but if you'd rather not discuss it, I'll understand."

Michelle wiped her mouth with her napkin and sat
back. "I can't imagine what would be so private, but
fire away."

"Your insemination," Ali said, not beating around
the bush. Michelle had confided her own trip to the
clinic a few years ago. Now Ali wanted more details.

"Oh, that." Michelle leaned forward and lowered
her voice. "No problem. What do you want to
know?"

Before Ali answered the question she said that her
mind was made up to do it and that she'd already
been to another clinic for a complete physical and
work-up.

"Good idea. If I had to do it over I wouldn't have
used the hospital's clinic, either. Too much breach of
confidentiality risk." Michelle whispered, "So this is
why you were so interested in that job! Smart girl—
learning all about things first. But do I detect a little
reservation in your voice?"

"It's going to sound silly—"

"No, go ahead."

"The father. Didn't it bother you that you didn't
even have a face or—" Brad Darling sat down at the
table behind Michelle and Ali stopped midsentence.

"Yes, it did," Michelle said.

Ali watched as he began to read a stack of papers
he'd brought with him, apparently not noticing her.
Ali ducked behind Michelle and picked up her water

glass, wishing again that maintenance would do something about the air. It was stifling.

"—so that's why I looked for a fantasy man."

Ali looked at Michelle, hoping she hadn't missed much. "Fantasy man?"

Michelle laughed and pushed away her plate. "It sounds pathetic, but every store I went into I looked at picture frames hoping to find just the right model's face behind the glass—someone who could seem real to me—the kind of man I'd be attracted to and go out with if given the chance."

"Did you ever find one?"

Michelle smiled. "Not in a picture frame. I met Kevin on a cruise—one that left the same day I was inseminated. And as they say, the rest is history."

Ali peeked around Michelle and caught "Darling" Brad staring at her, those damnable blue eyes boring into her, and she felt a pink tinge travel up her neck. He didn't smile or acknowledge her in any way. Maybe he was trying to remember where he'd seen her before. Or maybe he knew exactly where and that was the problem.

"Ali? Are you okay?"

"Uh…sure. Fine." She waved her hand in front of her face. "Just off in la-la land. I do that sometimes."

"Overactive imagination?"

"Something like that."

"Was that all you wanted to ask me?"

Was there anything else? Only one thing came to mind.

"I don't mean to sound like a wuss, but did it hurt?"

"More than I had anticipated, but not too bad…and it's over rather fast. A lot faster than the other end of the process, believe me. I'm sure you'll hear enough of those stories when your time comes."

When her time came. Not *if.* Michelle believed it would happen. Ali hoped she was right and that her sisters' problems wouldn't plague her, too. Over Michelle's shoulder she saw Blue Eyes leave the room, papers under his arm, empty tray in front of him. He had a confident yet not cocky gait, and again she noticed his narrow waist, long, lean legs and sinewy arms. And he had to be smarter than the average bear in his profession. Good genes, she thought. What more could she hope for?

"Do you have a time table in mind?"

He disappeared around the corner and Ali gave Michelle her full attention. She hadn't even told her sisters this, but Michelle had been so forthright it seemed okay to do. Besides, she'd been dying to tell someone. Who better than a trusted friend who'd been there?

Still she felt herself blush when she said, "Actually...any day now."

Michelle reached for her hand and squeezed it. "That's wonderful, Ali. I wish you luck. I know this is a very private matter for you, but if you ever want to talk again, I'm more than willing to meet you anytime. Just call."

"Thank you. I will." It was good to talk with someone outside the family who didn't see her as a child. Even though Michelle was closer to Lynne and Barbara's ages, she had never treated Ali as anything other than a peer.

They walked slowly to the tray deposit area and Ali was tempted to tell Michelle more—how she thought she had found the perfect fantasy father. But in the end she decided some things were better kept to one's self.

After work, in the privacy of her apartment, Ali went to her desk and found the long list of potential donors from the Midwest data bank. Retrieving her planner from her purse, she flipped to the memo section and read Brad's file number that she had jotted down at work. With fingers trembling she scanned the donor pages, searching for the unique number. On page five she found it. Next to it read: *five-foot ten inches, 175 pounds, blue eyes*—oh, yes, very blue eyes, she remembered—*and black hair. Field of work: medicine.*

Before she could change her mind, she raced into the kitchen and dialed the cross-town clinic. When the secretary answered the phone, Ali read her selection in a shaky voice and said to expect her later in the week, probably Thursday or Friday. She was assured all would be ready and waiting.

But it wasn't until Saturday morning, the day of the football game, that Ali discovered the time was right. She'd tested herself twice and come up with the same results both times: she was finally ovulating. Fortunately it was only 6:00 a.m. The clinic opened at seven. There was still time to make the game if she hurried. She called and said she was on her way.

Traffic was light as she drove I75 north to Royal Oak and she was making good time. Her stomach grumbled from lack of food, but there was no way she could eat. Her heart felt as though it were racing to keep up with the speedometer.

Finally she pulled into the clinic's parking lot, took

a few calming breaths and ran through everything again—family history of fertility problems, good men were hard to find, nothing wrong with wanting a face for the baby's father. She lingered on the last one. Michelle had felt the same way, so this wasn't unusual. And it wasn't as if she planned to hold the guy up for child support or anything. She didn't want a thing from him. Just a real person behind the sterile vial.

Lastly she thought about child care. She could ask her sisters for help if she wanted to return to work, or if she didn't, thankfully the income from her wise investments was large enough so she could stay home and be a full-time mom. The latter sounded most appealing. She closed her eyes and imagined the soft skin of her baby's cheek against her neck, the fresh scent of baby powder...and the beautiful sky-blue eyes of the father.

Yes, this was the right thing to do. Today was the day.

Three

Back in her bed midmorning, Ali wiped away another tear. All the way home she had cried. She was surprised there was anything left.

Everything had gone well. Too well. More like coldly efficient. Her hand circled her belly and she wondered what was going on in there. Maybe it had happened already. At the clinic they had warned her not to get her hopes up too high, that it often took a few tries. But they didn't warn her that she might feel so blue. In spite of all the facts she had collected, this wasn't how she had imagined things would happen.

Yes, she had wanted a baby, but always in her dreams there had been this wonderful man who adored her, who she loved with total abandon, whose arms would be wrapped tightly around her at a time like this.

She never felt so alone in her life.

She closed her eyes and tried to summon up the blue eyes, the dimpled smile. Only a vague blur, nothing in focus.

The phone on the nightstand rang. She let the machine pick it up. Then she heard Lynne's voice and she rolled over and grabbed the receiver.

"I'm just leaving the house. Pick you up out front in about twenty minutes." When Ali didn't respond immediately, Lynne said, "Are you all right?"

"Hmm? Oh…just a little sleepy."

"Well, go splash some cold water on your face and wake up. It's a beautiful day out. Wear something lightweight."

Ali replaced the receiver and gingerly lowered her legs to the floor. She knew she was being overly cautious, but she dreaded standing and walking around. She had a mad desire to stand on her head in the corner. She'd heard somewhere that it helped increase your chances.

Suddenly she laughed out loud at her weird musings. This was a day to celebrate, not to be maudlin. She'd been taking herself far too seriously and it was time that changed. She opened the closet bifolds and stared inside.

Lynne and the game would be a fun diversion…as long as she didn't tell her sister about this morning. No, before she talked to her sister about things again, Ali would wait until there was *real* news.

She found a short-sleeved maize pullover with University of Michigan stitched in blue over the breast pocket. She changed quickly and after tucking her top into a pair of jeans, she stood in front of the dresser mirror, meeting her eyes head-on.

Did she look different somehow? She told herself no and raced for the elevator.

But as she stepped into the lobby and strode out the door she felt as though a neon sign hung over her head announcing to the world what she had just done.

With two minutes left in the first half, Michigan was ahead by ten points. Ali turned to Lynne and said, "Think I'll head up to the concession stand before the line is too long. Can I bring you anything?"

"Hot dog with mustard and a diet Coke. Want me to come along?"

"Not unless you want to. I can manage."

"I'll stay here, then. Not in the mood to fight the crowd."

Apparently others had had the same idea as Ali; when she approached the concession all the lines were at least twenty deep. She queued up and scanned the crowd looking for familiar faces. With attendance exceeding one hundred thousand at every game there were many times she would never see a person she knew. It looked as if today would be one of those days.

"Ali?"

She turned at the sound of her name. Just behind her in the next line she spotted Michelle. She stepped closer and the two women embraced.

"I didn't know you were coming," Michelle said. "We could have driven together."

"I'm with my sister Lynne. Is your husband here?"

"Somewhere in this chaos."

"I'm glad he got some time off."

"Well, he's not totally off. He brought a couple of

young doctors with him. He's got his eye on one of them to sponsor as a surgical resident.''

The lines inched forward and they talked about the game and the beautiful weather, while all along Ali itched to tell Michelle about this morning. But the crowd had packed in tighter and there was no way their conversation wouldn't be overheard. She had a fleeting vision of the whole area falling dead still at the exact moment she uttered something such as "sperm bank," and she chuckled under her breath.

"If your sister isn't in a rush to go home, why don't the two of you join us for pizza after? We're going to the State Street Grill. We like to eat first and avoid the worst of the traffic jam."

"I'll ask her. Thanks."

Ali reached the head of the line and placed her order. Before she stepped away from the counter, Michelle said, "We'll never find each other later, so why don't you just come if you can. We'll save two extra seats."

"Okay. If we don't show, let's try for lunch early next week." Michelle nodded and turned in the opposite direction.

When Ali sat next to Lynne, she told her about Michelle's offer, and Lynne said it sounded like a good plan. They ate their hot dogs and only spilled half of their Cokes when Michigan scored again early in the third quarter. The band played another round of "Hail to the Victors," and Ali and Lynne shouted out the lyrics along with the rest of the packed house.

It was just as far to the car as to the restaurant, so Ali and Lynne decided to walk. The sidewalks were teaming with fans, all regaling each other with high-lights of another big win.

The excitement was infectious and Ali lifted her face to the sun and smiled. What a glorious day. Great weather, great game, great company. And most of all, she very well may have realized one of her life's big-gest dreams. Now she wondered why she had in-dulged in such a melancholy morning.

"Penny for your thoughts," Lynne said just outside the restaurant.

"Oh, just enjoying this perfect day." Lynne opened the door and Ali followed her inside. "Can't wait for you to meet Michelle. I know you'll like her." And Ali couldn't wait to meet Michelle's hus-band. She'd heard so much about Kevin.

The room was elbow to elbow, televisions blasting replays of the game over the din of the crowd. In the back corner Ali spotted Michelle waving her arm and they inched their way through the press of bodies to the rectangular-shaped table along the wall. At one end of the table was a distinguished-looking man she assumed was Kevin. There was gray at his temples with smile lines at the corners of his eyes. His face was tanned, warm and very open. She could see why Michelle—

The two young doctors across from Michelle turned in unison and the air rushed out of Ali's lungs.

Him! *Oh, no. Not today.*

Never one to be shy, Lynne had already slipped into the seat next to Michelle and was introducing herself, which meant there was only one seat left at the end of the table. Next to…him.

Michelle introduced her husband and the two young men, Craig and Brad. Ali smiled and choked

out an appropriate response as she met each man's
eyes. But when she came to Brad she saw a hint of
anxiety on his face, leaving her no doubt that he recalled exactly where they had first met. Thankfully
her sister cut the awkward moment short.

"Ali tells me you two have twin preschoolers. That
must keep you busy."

Michelle looked at Kevin lovingly and then back
to Lynne. "Yes, they do. But we're lucky to have
such wonderful sitters. Gives us a break now and
then. Their grandmothers are probably spoiling them
rotten this very moment."

"Both of your mothers are at home with them?"

"Well, not exactly. My mother died before Abe
and Abbie were born, and Kevin's mom lives in Europe. We've sort of adopted a pair of elderly sisters
as grandmothers." Michelle laughed and took
Kevin's hand. "We met them on a cruise the same
day we met each other, and they've been in our lives
ever since."

Kevin chuckled. "Millie and Hazel are quite the
characters. They volunteer at the hospital. You're
bound to run into them someday." He shook his head
and chuckled again. "And believe me, you'll know
them when you do."

Kevin and Michelle took turns telling about the re-
lentless matchmaking efforts of the older sisters on
their cruise, but Ali found it difficult to concentrate.
She munched on pizza crust and stared straight ahead,
feeling Brad's eyes fixed on her. Mercifully the conversation drifted to work and he became engaged in
a long discussion with Kevin. Finally she felt the tension ease.

With his face turned toward the other end of the

table, Ali studied Brad's pleasing profile. She loved how strands of unruly shiny hair fell across his forehead, giving him a relaxed, uninhibited look. And of course there were his eyes, every bit as powerful as she remembered. They were watching Kevin's face now. Intense, thinking, processing, never drifting. She liked a person who kept eye contact while conversing. So many didn't. She liked—

She liked everything she saw. And the nearness of him was driving her crazy. How absurd this whole thing was—her sitting here, acting calm, cool and collected, while at this very moment she may be carrying this man's child.

Yet as absurd as it seemed, her imagination ran full steam ahead. She wondered if they might go out sometime...if he danced. If maybe—

If maybe she was crazy. She could hear it now. *I'd like you to meet my date, Ali. She works at the sperm bank where I make donations.*

The waiter came with the check and Kevin picked it up. Everyone had thanked him and they were finishing their drinks when Craig, who had been fairly quiet, looked at his watch. "Gee, it's later than I thought."

"Got a hot date waiting?" Brad teased.

"As a matter of fact, yes. But that's not what I was thinking. I was thinking it's going to be dark before we get home."

"Don't worry. I'll protect you from the boogeyman."

"Gee, thanks. But it's your old lady I was thinking of."

Ali felt everything inside her go rigid and cold.

And Craig's explanation to Kevin and Michelle did nothing to ease her disappointment.

"Sally will be sitting in the window watching for him when you drop him off. Just wait and see."

"You're just jealous you don't have anyone waiting for you at home." Everyone laughed as they stood and gathered up their belongings. Everyone except Ali and Lynne, who was looking sympathetically at her sister.

Ali stood, feeling numb, and pushed in her chair. She hated men calling their wives "old lady." It showed no respect. At the very least Brad could have corrected Craig by using a more endearing term. She sighed. Who was she kidding? It wasn't *what* he'd called his wife that bothered her most. It was the fact that he *had* one.

She lagged behind the others as they made their way to the exit, not wanting anyone to see her face. Tears burned at the back of her eyes. Why had she assumed he was single? The clinic certainly didn't require it. She swallowed hard and told herself it shouldn't matter that he was married. She had never planned to have a relationship with the donor anyway. He was strictly a face for the father.

Yet as everyone said their goodbyes and walked their separate ways she realized how much she had hoped for more.

"Wouldn't you know?" Lynne said, stepping up the pace back to her car.

"What?"

"Brad. I was getting all excited for you, thinking maybe here was a good one. Then the 'old lady' remark. I'm feeling frustrated for you, sweetie." She put her arm around Ali's shoulder as they walked.

Ali shrugged, trying her best to seem unfazed. "Easy come, easy go."

They got into the car and Ali found a classical radio station and reclined her seat-back. After twenty minutes of talking about little Keri, Lynne fell silent and Ali was relieved. She was tired of sounding light-hearted. She didn't have to pretend with Lynne; she could have told her the truth about the source of her emotional pendulum today. But she felt too vulnerable to hear any reproach in her sister's voice. Besides, she had her pride. If she gave voice to her sadness right now, it would be tantamount to admitting she'd made a mistake.

She hadn't, she lectured herself. She would be a good mother and surround her baby with love and affection. That was what this morning was about. That was *all* it was about. If she had made any mistake, it was in letting her imagination run rampant with thoughts of Brad.

If only he'd remained a stranger. But sharing a meal with him, knowing each other on a first-name basis, having mutual friends...

No! She'd just have to put him out of her mind.

But after Lynne dropped her off and Ali was alone in her apartment, she stood in front of the floor-to-ceiling window facing the Detroit River and wondered if after today Brad would continue coming to the clinic. She wondered if his wife knew he was a donor. She wondered if he had been as uncomfortable tonight as she had. But most of all, she wondered what he was thinking now.

With Saturday night traffic slowing to a crawl just outside Greektown, Brad and Craig thanked the Singletons and said they would walk the rest of the way.

Brad lived closest, in a bare-bones, one-room walk-up just off Monroe, a couple of blocks straight ahead and less than a mile from the hospital, which was convenient since he couldn't always count on his old clunker of a car to start. Most days he preferred walking home, anyway, a chance to clear his head. It wasn't always possible to leave work behind, especially when there were critical or terminal patients.

But today he'd been lucky. Morning rounds were uncomplicated; everyone was stable. He'd been able to enjoy the game and for once not worry. Everything had been perfect—the weather, the game, the company. Until after, when—

He shook his head and tried to clear thoughts of Ali from his mind. What a sick twist of fate that she would keep crossing his path this way. First at the clinic last Monday, which had provided him with enough stimulation to get the job done, and then later in the week in the cafeteria. It had been hard to take his eyes off her both times. Now again today. Each encounter with her added another layer of unwanted attraction.

"Hey, you got that stressed-out look on your face again. It's Saturday night." Craig punched his shoulder. "Lighten up, guy. Let's go find us a party."

"Don't you have to work in the morning?"

"Negative. You?"

"Some of us have to keep the place going."

They walked a ways without talking, stepping around slower moving pedestrians, and Brad thought he was home free. Craig hadn't mentioned Ali once.

"So what did you think?"

Damn. "About what?"

"Ali, man. You do have a pulse, don't you?"

Brad shrugged and hoped he looked unimpressed. "She's okay, I guess. I don't know. She didn't have much to say."

"Who cares? Did you look at her? I mean *really* look at her?" Craig let out a low wolf whistle. "The way that old alma mater lettering stretched across her breast pocket. I thought the stitching was going to pop any second. Wow. And what a face! That blond hair looked like it could be natural, too. And those eyes! Elizabeth Taylor, eat your heart out. I've never seen such violet eyes."

Brad laughed in spite of himself. "Maybe you should ask her out."

"Huh. I don't think she knew I was there. She only had eyes for you, my man. Sad, but true."

"What are you talking about?"

"I watched her watching you all through the meal. She barely ate, poor girl."

"Give me a break."

"I'm serious. She was really checking you out. So why don't *you* ask her out?"

"Don't even start."

"What are you? Some kind of monk? I can't remember the last time I saw you with a woman. Third year med school?"

Brad walked faster and ignored the question. They both remembered how *that* had worked out—an ambitious redhead with eyes on the brass ring.

"Give me one good reason why you shouldn't give Ali a call."

"I'm too busy."

"Never stopped me. I work as many hours as you do."

"Then I don't have your energy." Nor your money. A simple fact that Craig had never had to face. Dates cost. Still, he knew neither time nor money was the true reason to avoid Ali.

"Come on, man. Ya gotta have some fun."

"I do. Today was fun." Most of it.

Craig stopped at the intersection and faced him. "I could find out where she works. Maybe you could—"

"It isn't going to happen, so forget it." He turned away and eyed the traffic light impatiently.

Craig didn't move when the light changed. "I detect there's more to this story. Am I right?"

Brad stepped off the curb and Craig stopped him. "Well? Am I?"

Brad let out a long breath and backed up onto the sidewalk. There was only one way to shut Craig up and that was to tell him the truth. "Okay. But I don't want to hear 'I told you so.'"

"What? What?"

Brad leaned closer and whispered, "She works at the clinic."

"What clinic?" Craig said loudly, catching the interest of a passing couple.

Brad gave him a bugged-eyed stare and a few seconds to figure it out.

"No! You don't mean—"

Brad nodded, wishing this would be the end of the subject, but knowing sooner or later Craig would bring it up again.

Craig just stood there shaking his head, until finally he said, "Sure you don't want to hang out with me tonight?"

"Positive."

The light turned green again and they crossed the street. "What a waste," Craig mumbled under his breath.

Brad wished he could disagree. But he couldn't. It had been a long time since he'd been attracted to someone. All through dinner he had felt an undercurrent of something going on between them. And the one time he had accidentally brushed her leg under the table he'd felt his pulse quicken. The mere closeness of her had generated more heat than his rusted radiator on the coldest night. Strange. They had barely spoken to each other, yet—

Craig stopped in front of Trapper's Alley. A few nurses from the hospital standing just inside saw him and came running out. Brad called good-night over his shoulder and kept walking, glad to be alone with his thoughts. If he was going to spend the evening debating what to do about Ali—

Wait a minute. What debate? Was there a choice?

Okay, maybe. In either case, he much preferred the quiet privacy of his Murphy bed to sort things out than on some ear-splitting dance floor.

He rounded the last corner to his building and had a sudden image of dancing with Ali. He could almost feel her—

A wino staggered out of an alley and Brad nearly knocked him down. After righting the guy, Brad apologized and went on, telling himself to get a grip.

Across the street, framed in the first-floor picture window, he saw his landlady rocking away, watching the world go by. When she spotted him she smiled a gap-toothed smile and waved a gnarled brown hand.

Her door to the hall was open, so he called out to her as he climbed the stairs.

"Good night, Sally."

"You in for the night?"

"Yes, ma'am." He smiled.

"That's a good boy."

The old lady could sometimes be a pain, but he knew she cared about her building and her tenants.

There was a lot to be said for that.

Four

At lunchtime on Monday Ali ate at her desk and in spite of earlier misgivings, read more of her novel, feeling envious of the heroine who had found the man of her dreams.

Man of her dreams.

Every time she closed her eyes these days there was only one man in Ali's dreams. And he had an appointment here in fifteen minutes. She had half expected him to cancel, but now that the time had drawn near, it didn't look as though he would.

She put her book away and rested her chin on her fist. He was married, she reminded herself, so there was no hope for a relationship. Still, she closed her eyes and remembered his perfect face smiling down at her. Ah...

She opened her eyes and nearly fell off her chair.

Brad was leaning on the counter, smiling down at her. She blinked, trying to separate fact from fiction.

He was still there. And instantly she felt a pleasurable tension running through her.

"Sleeping on the job?" he asked, a playful tilt to his head. She looked at her watch, stalling for time.

"I was just…just—" *Damn.* This was so awkward. She had to stop all this fantasizing! At a loss for words, she simply said, "You're early."

"I know." He looked around as if to be certain they were alone. "I was hoping we could talk a little."

"About what?" *That you're married? Or that I might be pregnant with your child?* Anxiety won out over pleasure as she wondered how she was going to face this man week after week.

"Well, first I wanted to thank you for not saying anything at dinner the other night."

She told herself to relax. He was just being nice. "No problem. Besides, it's nobody's business."

Suddenly he was the one to look ill at ease. "I don't know why coming here is so embarrassing. I'm a doctor, for Pete's sake. It's just that…well, I was wondering if maybe you—"

Another client approached the counter and signed in. Then the phone rang and she mouthed "I'm sorry" before Brad shoved his hands into his pockets and walked toward the chairs along the wall.

By the time she had finished the second call she heard someone moving behind her and swiveled in her seat. It was the technician looking for Brad's folder. She walked over and handed it to him and he ushered Brad off.

It wasn't until some time later, after he had left the

clinic, that she remembered what he had started to say. *I was wondering if maybe you—*

If maybe what? *You'd like me to father your child? Why, yes. That would be very nice, thank you.*

Another client stopped at the counter and she wiped the smile off her face. She had to do something about this imagination of hers. It was going to get her into trouble someday. Maybe it was time she switched to horror fiction.

On Thursday, Ali stopped in the hospital gift shop to check out the new arrivals. They always had the cutest seasonal decorations and infant clothes. She was trying to decide whether she liked the papier-mâché ghost or witch the best when she glanced up and saw Brad in the next aisle.

He looked up and a warm smile lit his face. "Hi," he said, looking sincerely glad to see her.

"Hi," she said, praying he wouldn't notice how very glad she was to see him.

He was holding a small pair of blue overalls that, after looking at the price tag, he put back on the rack.

She hadn't even considered that he might have children. For some strange reason she'd hoped hers would be the first. He looked up at her again and she did her best to hide her thoughts.

"For your son?" she asked.

He laughed. "Oh, no. Not me. Just looking for a little something for one of my patients. Delivered my first baby today." He beamed as if he were the proud father himself. "Eight pound healthy boy. Any suggestions?"

She didn't know how much he wanted to spend and wasn't comfortable asking, but since most residents she'd met were broke she pointed to a blue-trimmed terry bib with an attached pacifier. "This is usually a safe bet."

He picked one up and said, "Great. Thanks." Then, turning to face her, he shifted his weight from one foot to the other. "Look, Ali...I'm not very good at this, but would you like to do something tomorrow night?"

She stared at him, not believing her ears. She'd been sitting right there after the game when he'd talked about his wife. What did he think she was?

She headed for the door, not even dignifying the question with an answer. "Excuse me. I have to get back to work."

"Wait a minute." He was right on her heels. "I know I'm out of practice, but what did I say wrong?"

She spun on him. "It's not what you said. It's what you left out."

"I don't follow."

"Let me give you a clue. It starts with w-i and ends with f-e." She started to turn, but he caught her elbow.

"You think I'm married?"

He was a good actor; she had to give him that.

"Pizza after the game? Your 'old lady' waiting for you at home?"

He let go of her arm and started to laugh. "You mean, Sally?"

"Yes, Sally."

"She's my sixty-five-year-old landlady. A very protective and dear lady who watches over me like a hawk, that's all."

She gave him a sidelong look, wanting to believe

him, but afraid he'd soon dash the hope and excitement building behind her rib cage.

He drew an X over his heart and held up a palm. "Honest. I wouldn't lie about something like that."

Ali folded her arms and let a smile slip across her face. "What *would* you lie about?" His dimples reappeared and by the quickening of her pulse she knew she was in trouble. Big trouble.

"Nothing with you. I have a feeling I'd never get away with it."

"Smart man."

"So, what about it? I was thinking if the weather is nice we could take the People Mover down to Hart Plaza and listen to a little jazz, watch the freighters go up the river. You know…your basic cheap date."

She was flirting with danger and she knew it. He was simply The Face, she reminded herself. It wouldn't be wise—

"Sounds terrific. I'd love to."

They firmed up the details and went their separate ways, with Ali doing her best to act as though this was no big deal. It wasn't until she entered the next wing that she realized she was holding a witch in one hand and a ghost in the other, neither paid for. She raced back to the gift shop and made good on her purchases, then somehow got through the rest of the afternoon.

That night, though, she found herself obsessed with Friday's date. She laid out half a dozen outfits on her bed, finally deciding on casual navy slacks and a two-piece powder-blue sweater set. She debated whether to wear these to work or to take them in a bag and change afterward, since he was meeting her there. Decisions, decisions. Now she knew why she didn't date. It drove her crazy.

In the end she wore the outfit to work, but at quarter to five, with her stomach in knots, the phone rang and it was Brad.

"I'm really sorry, Ali. I'm going to have to ask for a rain check. There's been a three car pileup on the Lodge Freeway. Serious injuries. I don't know when I could get away."

"I understand," she said, hoping he didn't hear the disappointment in her voice.

"Unfortunately I'm on call the rest of the weekend."

"Such is the life of a doctor." She shrugged and remembered another doctor who often called and canceled.

"E.M.S. is just pulling up. Gotta run."

She listened to the dial tone for a moment and then slowly replaced the receiver. What a fool she'd been to allow herself to get her hopes up. But she had no doubt he was telling the truth.

This time.

Yet memories of other times when she'd heard her mother crying into her pillow in the next room came back to haunt her. How many birthdays and anniversaries had her mother spent alone? And how many of Ali's recitals and basketball games had her father missed? For that matter, how many had he ever made? She couldn't remember a one.

She locked up her desk and left the clinic, feeling sadder but wiser.

Maybe Brad had fathered her child. Maybe. But it was best she remembered that doctors weren't meant to be dads.

After a fitful night's sleep Friday, Ali spent most of Saturday at her sister's playing with little Keri. Lynne didn't ask, and Ali didn't volunteer that she had already made a trip to the sperm bank. Nothing may have come of it, anyway. It was bad enough that she was watching the calendar and counting the days; she didn't need Lynne being anxious for her, too.

But later that night, alone in her bed, Ali had to admit she was indeed anxious. Anxious to know if she was pregnant. Anxious to know if she was being too hard on Brad, if anything could develop between them. And even anxious about Monday and seeing him again. She wondered if he would ask her out again or if he would act aloof, sending signals that his first invitation had been impulsive and that she shouldn't expect another.

The weekend was long, her mind never quiet. When the alarm sounded for work on Monday morning she felt as though she hadn't slept a wink.

At the office she unlocked her desk, deposited her purse and then read over the notes left by the weekend secretary. She made a pot of coffee, grateful that she had a few minutes to herself before the first client. When the coffee had dripped through, she poured herself a cup, returned to her desk and opened the appointment book. The first thing that caught her eye was that the standing appointment for one o'clock had been erased.

Brad had canceled.

She told herself it could have been for any of a hundred reasons, that she shouldn't take it personally, but logic didn't help. Emotions had ruled the weekend and had tagged along today to torture her some more.

She drank her coffee and stared off into space.

Even when she was awake, Brad's face was only a blink away. She hadn't realized how much she had wanted to see him today. Blue Monday took on a whole new meaning as she finished her coffee and indulged in a moment of self-pity.

The first client arrived and Ali lowered her eyes as soon as she greeted him, feeling moisture pushing at the back of them. It was her own damn fault, she lectured herself. She had let her fantasies carry her away and now she had to pay the price. Next time, she told herself, walking briskly to the coffeepot for a refill, she would know better.

In the meantime she would go out to lunch today and avoid the cafeteria and any chance of running into Brad. She'd pack her lunch the rest of the week.

On Thursday, however, she forgot her brown bag on the kitchen counter and didn't realize her mistake until noon, so she decided to risk the cafeteria. After carefully scanning the crowded room and seeing no sign of Brad, she chose a window seat in the atrium area, far from the center of the room where she had first spotted him.

She finished her soup and salad in peace and pulled out her book. A chapter later, the scraping of the chair across from hers brought her eyes up from the page.

And smack-dab into those unfathomable blue eyes.

"Mind if I join you?"

It was obviously a rhetorical question, since he'd already sat down, dimples competing with the flash of perfect white teeth. She finished her ice water in one long swallow, feeling his eyes lingering on hers while she wondered if there might be some kind of inoculation to make herself immune to this man.

"I'm really sorry about last Friday..." he started.

She flipped the back of her hand. "No problem. Completely understandable." That's it, she told herself. Act indifferent. She was a strong, independent woman. She could handle this hunky guy and not submit to his charms.

She tapped at her watch. "Oops. Time's up. Gotta get back to work." There! She'd done it. She stood and picked up her tray.

"So...want to try again for this Friday?" he asked.

She took a fortifying breath and let her shoulders drop.

"Okay."

Five

————

He was placing far too much significance on one little date, Brad thought, making a last notation in the tall stack of charts beside him. He tossed the pen down and slouched back in the chair. Maybe it had been a mistake to ask Ali out. What if they really hit it off? What could he offer her? Very little that required money. Definitely not a lot of time. So why was he doing this?

He pushed out of the chair and went to his locker to change. He knew why, and that's what bothered him. He had this overpowering need to be with her, to find out what made her tick.

It had been years since he'd been attracted to a woman the way he was to Ali. Still, he should be careful. The last time this happened had been a near disaster. If he had stayed with Valerie he would have been bankrupt by thirty. She had no compunction about running up her credit cards, falsely assuming that he'd be making big bucks soon and would bail her out.

Yet there was a discernible difference with Ali. Her eyes reflected intelligence and character, and he suspected a quirky sense of humor, too. But if he thought it was only her mind he was interested in, he would be lying to himself. An unmistakable chemistry sparked between them every time he saw her. And instead of telling his libido to take a hike, he found himself wondering if he shouldn't stop by the pharmacy for a supply of foil packets.

He shrugged out of his white jacket and wondered what kind of a lover Ali would be—shy or assertive? Hard to read. Then he pulled a blue crewneck sweater over his button-down shirt and chuckled at his own ramblings. He was getting way ahead of the game. She'd given no clue she was interested in a relationship—physical or otherwise. In fact, she'd almost seemed jumpy around him.

Why was that? he wondered, walking down the hall leading to the clinic. He shrugged as he rounded the last corner and decided some things were better left undissected. Besides, it was about time he just kicked back, relaxed, and had a good time.

But when he saw Ali standing at her desk and bending to retrieve her purse, nothing inside him felt relaxed. Her pants fit snug across a perfectly rounded backside. Her waist was small, especially in contrast to her more than ample bustline, which when she turned he noticed was outlined nicely in a lavender sweater, a shade not unlike the eyes that were watching him approach.

She smiled a shy smile and he was a goner. At that

moment she could have had anything she wanted from him. His firstborn child, if he had one.

He approached cautiously, probably about the way a man would go to his own hanging. Now he remembered why it had been so long since he'd dated. The tension between them was nearly palpable.

"Hi," he said, suddenly not knowing what to do with his arms and hands. He reached up and drummed his fingers on the counter in front of her.

"Hi, back," she said, looking as nervous as he felt.

Finally he heaved a loud sigh. "Having fun yet?"

A small laugh burst from her glossy pink lips. "I don't do this often."

"That makes two of us."

The night-shift secretary breezed into the reception area and Brad took Ali's elbow and led her to the exit. She smelled of wildflowers and a warm spring afternoon and something far more dangerous—the scent of a woman who could mean more to him than he was prepared to handle.

"Hungry?" He let go of her arm and opened the door.

She glanced at him, then straight ahead. "A little."

He smiled down at her, hoping she remembered this was to be a cheap date. "I know this great kiosk that serves the best hot dogs and vinegar fries."

She smiled. "Sounds perfect."

It was a mild October evening, sixty-ish with only a hint of a breeze, so Brad asked, "Mind walking to the People Mover? Or we could take your car, if you'd like. Mine's at home."

"It's a beautiful night. Let's walk." She hesitated, then added, "I'm embarrassed to say this, but as long as I've lived downtown I've never ridden the People Mover.''

"Really? Well, then, you're in for a treat.'' And one he could afford. A couple quarters in the turnstile each way and they could ride the unmanned rail all night.

They sauntered toward Greektown, his hand closest to hers itching to reach out, a magnetic pull as alive as the frenetic birds that flitted from one golden-leafed tree to the next. From the corner of his eye he watched her take it all in—the noisy birds, the honking drivers impatiently fending their way home, the graffiti on an occasional abandoned building. She seemed fairly relaxed now and he tried for the same.

"Have you always lived in the area?'' Real original, but it was a place to start.

"My parents had a home in Grosse Pointe. I lived there with my mom...until she died.''

"I'm sorry.''

"Me, too. I miss her.''

"And your dad?'' Immediately her posture told him he'd touched a sore spot.

"Traveling the world with his child bride.'' There was a bite behind her words that verified his suspicions. They crossed the street and before he could change the subject he saw Sally waving in his direction.

"Speaking of wives...'' He nodded his head toward the large picture window.

"Sally?''

"Sally. And it looks like she's motioning us over.'' He took Ali's elbow and whispered an aside. "We'll make it quick, but be prepared. Never know what she's going to say.''

Sally greeted them at the door, smiling from ear to ear. "I'm so glad ya happened by. Did I tell ya the plumber's comin' in the mornin' and the water'll be shut off a spell?"

Brad shot a knowing smile at Ali and said, "Yes, Sally. You told me when I left for work." And she knew it, too, the sly old fox. She wasn't kidding him for a second.

"I don't believe I've met yer lady friend here." She thrust out a wavering hand. "Name's Sally Williams."

"Ali Celeste. Nice to meet you, Sally."

"Likewise, I'm sure." Then she turned to Brad. "Glad to see ya havin' some fun for a change, boy." Back to Ali, she added, "Ya know, as long as this boy live here I never see 'im with a lady. I was beginning to wonder." She winked and then let loose with one of her raucous laughs.

Brad ducked his head and turned Ali toward the door. "Night, Sally."

He could still hear her laugh from across the street, and he caught a smirk on Ali's face.

At the entrance to Trapper's Alley, the closest access to the overhead rail, Brad opened the door and stepped back for Ali to pass. Before she did, she gave him a hint as to what he was in for.

"By the way, my father? Just so you know, he was a very busy and successful doctor." She walked ahead and he followed, accepting the challenge she'd laid down for him: prove to me all doctors are not the same. Why he wanted to prove this to her was beyond him, but he knew he did.

They took the escalator to the third floor and he stood behind her, admiring the view. Beneath the

form-fitting pants he couldn't help but notice the outline of high-cut bikini panties and he wondered what
color they were…and if he would find out—

Not smart, he lectured himself. Not the way to
prove he wasn't just another lecherous doctor interested in a personal survey of her body parts. Likewise,
he didn't think Ali Celeste was a woman to be tam-
pered with. Not just because of the thin veneer of
anger toward doctors he'd just discovered, but something else. She had the air of a woman who held virtue in high esteem, someone who didn't seek security
or validation in the arms of a man—doctor or otherwise.

They reached the top floor and passed half a dozen
shops until they came upon the gate. He leaned
around her, deposited the coins, and she passed
through. He followed behind her and then, without
thinking, took her hand and led her to the platform
outside.

"It should be along any second," he said, hoping
he was wrong. The current traveling through his fingers, up his arm and to his chest was like nothing
he'd ever felt. Touching. Such a simple thing, but, oh,
so powerful.

Brad laced his fingers through hers and noticed she
didn't resist. She also didn't look at him or say a
word, and he wondered what she was thinking. He'd
give anything to crawl inside that beautiful head of
hers and read her thoughts.

Ali couldn't believe how good and natural his hand
felt in hers. It had happened so quickly she hadn't
had time to think, which was just as well. If she had
avoided his touch, look what she would have missed.

She wanted to squeezed his fingers tighter in hers, yet she didn't want to appear overeager. Was it too much to hope for that the train would never show?

She turned her face away from him, pretending to watch for their ride. Her breathing was irregular and she prayed he didn't notice. It wouldn't do for him to know how much his touch excited her, how it stirred something primal that challenged her beliefs in purity and patience. She hated to think what a kiss might do.

No, she didn't. She relished the thought. And if she were truthful, she longed for the moment.

She felt vibrations on the platform and soon the tram slowed to a stop in front of them. Its doors slid open and a stream of harried commuters pushed out. Brad released her hand and rested his on her back, guiding her inside and to the nearest seat. He sat beside her and folded his hands in his lap. Immediately she missed his touch.

They left the station and Ali stared at Brad's long fingers, as if willing them back to hers. When they didn't move, she let out a sigh and watched the streets of Detroit whiz by.

He didn't talk much, she noticed, which was okay, she guessed, as long as he wasn't bored. If anything he seemed a little distracted. Perhaps a sick patient. Perhaps fatigue.

Perhaps she worried too much.

She shifted in the plastic seat and so did Brad, the end result bringing their thighs side to side.

He didn't pull away.

Neither did she.

At the next station the tram glided to a stop and her weight shifted forward, flattening the side of her breast against his arm. Before she could move, he eased his arm around her shoulder and gazed down at her with his killer smile.

"Enjoying the ride?"

"Uh-huh." Brilliant conversationalist, she was.

"Good." He squeezed her shoulder and left his arm around her.

Too soon they reached the Renaissance Center, forcing her to leave her cozy seat and the warmth of the man beside her. As they stepped out, he reached for her hand and this time she took it with a squeeze and a slow smile.

He led her through the maze of circular towers to the lower level and then outdoors where they crossed to the adjacent Hart Plaza. A few kiosks, remnants of summer, lined the riverfront. Behind them, in a sunken amphitheater, the sounds of lazy jazz carried over the water.

They strolled to the railing overlooking the Detroit River and Canada beyond, and the world around them faded away. Lights from Windsor Casino glistened in the still waters and Ali struggled to focus on the view, all the time distracted by the man whose thumb slid slowly up and down her own. A passing freighter sat low in the water, some of its crew waving to those on shore.

Brad turned to her, still holding her hand. "Thank you," he said, looking far more relaxed than earlier.

"For what?"

"For luring me out here."

She chuckled. "You're the one who asked me. Did you forget?"

He shook his head. "I may have done the asking, but you provided the motivation." He squeezed her hand and turned his baby blues loose on her. "All work and no play. I'm afraid I've become a dull boy."

Not hardly, she thought. "Then I guess I'm just what the doctor ordered."

He laughed and touched her cheek. "Remind me to thank that doctor...whoever he is."

"Or she," Ali said, lifting her chin.

"Or she," he said with an agreeable smile. Just as quickly his smile faded and his eyes zeroed in on her mouth. He inched closer and she closed her eyes, feeling as though her heart might jump from her chest. But then she felt his lips on her forehead, soft and moist, and she suppressed a groan. Too soon for more, she told herself, feeling disappointed nonetheless.

Brad tugged her around in front of him and, pressing her back to his chest, wrapped his arms around her. Never had she felt so secure yet frightened, coddled yet vulnerable. And she wouldn't trade the moment for anything. They fit perfectly, she thought, his chin nestled beside her head.

"Hungry yet?" he said after a while.

"No hurry."

"Mmm, good. I like this."

The music swelled behind them and he began swaying slowly from side to side, taking her with him, his breath growing warmer against her cheek. After a moment he whispered, "Ah, Ali Celeste...my celestial angel of mercy...a little slice of heaven you are."

She laughed nervously. "I've never been called an angel before. Maybe you should talk to my sisters."

"And what would they tell me?"

"Oh, probably that I'm a little too headstrong and independent for my own good."

"Why would they say that?"

She couldn't tell him the most recent example that came to mind. Although someday soon she might have to. But for now she wouldn't let anything ruin the delicious night. "You'd have to ask them," she said evasively, giving a quick shrug and changing the subject. "While we're on the subject of names, I have to ask—"

She hesitated and he said, "What?"

"Do you ever get teased about yours?"

"Why? What's so funny about Brad?"

She nudged him with an elbow. "You know what I mean."

"Yes." He laughed, sending a puff of warm air through her hair, teasing her senses a little more. "All the time. But probably not as much as my uncle who's a minister. Can you imagine being called 'Pastor Darling'?"

She laughed long and hard, feeling some of her tension ebb.

He took her hand and started for the kiosks. "I'm ready for some artery-clogging fries doused in vinegar. How about you?"

"Famished," she lied, food the furthest thing from her mind.

They ate in the amphitheater, listened to more jazz, and people watched, and all the while Ali felt a mix of emotions. Only two weeks ago Brad had simply been The Face of the donor. Now, in one short evening, he had become so much more. He was kind and warm, not at all pretentious or arrogant as she'd prejudged. And if he was impressed with his good looks, he didn't show it. This should be good news, she told herself.

As long as she wasn't pregnant with his child. How could she ever explain that?

She was merely a couple of days late. A little longer and she would have to use one of those test kits.

She finished the last of her fries and felt the full weight of her dilemma. If she *was* pregnant and she kept seeing Brad, when would be a good time to tell him? And how would he feel when he learned the child was his?

She knew how she'd feel. Trapped. He hadn't asked for this. It wasn't fair to—

"Warm enough?" He wrapped his arm around her shoulder and ran his hand down her arm. "You're shivering. Maybe we should head back before it gets colder."

She glanced up at his gentle and handsome face. "Are you on tomorrow morning?"

"Afraid so."

"Then maybe we should."

He looked disappointed as he took her hand and guided her up the steps. While they waited for their ride, she held onto his arm and smiled up at him. "I've had a lovely time tonight. Thank you, darling Brad."

He bent and brushed his lips on hers—over before it began—and her heart soared.

"Me, too, Angel Celeste." He flicked the tip of her nose playfully. "Think we might try this again?"

"Sure," she said too quickly, sounding as if she'd attached about as much importance to another date as the offer of another hot dog. That wasn't at all how she felt. God forbid he should see through her, because the bald truth was she felt too much—far more than the average commitment-phobic male could handle.

But then, she asked herself, what was average about Dr. Darling?

Six

No call came Saturday or Sunday and neither did Ali's period. She didn't know which created the most angst. She told herself one or both probably meant nothing. Nonetheless, at work Monday, she beat a path in the carpet leading to the rest room to check on things, and by twelve forty-five she was ready to throw her watch into the trash basket if she looked at it one more time.

Five minutes later Brad strolled in, dimples and all, and Ali's stomach did another somersault. He wore a Detroit Tigers baseball cap with the brim tugged low over his eyes, a sweatshirt with the sleeves cut off and faded jeans with holes in the knees.

He never looked sexier.

"Hey, good lookin'. Like the disguise?" He leaned on the counter and leveled his big blues on her.

"Is that what you call it?" She laughed, as much from nerves as anything.

"I'm getting a little paranoid about seeing someone I know here. This way I can pull the cap lower if I have to." He demonstrated for her.

"You already know someone here—me," she reminded him.

He raised the brim again. "That's different."

He had a way of holding her eyes that made her feel naked, as if he could read her thoughts, which she hoped to hell he couldn't.

"I've been meaning to ask you—do you ever get to see the results of this place? I mean...you know. People who couldn't otherwise have children. The happy ending."

"Occasionally, yes. Sometimes I fill in on the other side when someone's out sick."

"It's good to imagine happy couples benefiting."

"It's not always couples." Now why had she said that? Everything had been going fine.

"Hmm. I guess I hadn't thought about that. Are there a lot of single women who use this kind of place?"

"The number's growing every year." She had to do something quick to change the subject. This was a little too close for comfort. For once she wished the phone would ring. Anything.

Unable to concentrate, she glanced down the open corridor in front of her desk and suddenly she heard wheels rolling closer. A pair of blue-haired elderly women were pushing a gift cart.

Brad let out a low groan, pulled his visor down and retreated to the chairs along the back wall.

Ali looked back at the approaching women and

wondered if Brad knew them. They were each turned out in crisp pink pinafore aprons and sensible white walking shoes, which squeaked on the tile floor when they stopped in front of the counter.

"Hello. My name is Millie. This here is my sister Hazel. We're candy stripers with the hospital auxiliary." They both smiled, heads bobbing slightly.

Ali stood and leaned across the counter that separated them. "Alexis, but most call me Ali. Nice to meet you." She sat back down, a candy bar catching her eye. "I didn't realize a cart came into this wing."

Millie leaned over the counter and whispered, "Actually, this isn't our normal route. But those old geezers on Three East are tighter than a new girdle. Lucky to make a couple bucks for the auxiliary over there."

"That's right," Hazel piped in. "Besides, Sister and I like being around younger folks, anyway. And over here they don't try pinchin' our butts, either."

Millie threw her sister a disgusted look, then turned back to Ali. "You must be fairly new here. Tell us about yourself, dear. Are you married? Any little ones?"

"Millie! Mind your own beeswax."

Ali laughed, warming instantly to this eccentric little pair and grateful for the diversion. "Nothing to tell, I'm afraid. I'm single."

"A pretty little thing like you? What's wrong with men these days?" Millie lowered her voice again and with her head motioned to the young man seated against the wall, his long legs stretched out in front of him, arms crossed and chin on chest. "Maybe you're working in the right place." She wiggled her thin, penciled eyebrows. "My, my. From what I can see of him under that cap he's a handsome one."

Then she frowned and stepped back from the counter, reading the sign that clearly labeled this a fertility clinic. She looked from the sign to the man and back, trying to puzzle it out while Ali struggled to keep a straight face.

"Shh!" Hazel said. "Lower your voice or he'll hear you."

Ali eyed Millie and Hazel as if just seeing them for the first time. "Wait a minute," she said. "You must be *the* Millie and Hazel. The ones from Michelle's and Kevin's cruise."

"Why, yes," Millie said. "You know the Singletons?"

"Michelle is a friend of mine. In fact, she helped me get this job."

"Well, well. Small world, isn't it?" Millie said just as the phone rang and Ali answered it.

As she penciled in an appointment, she glanced up. The sisters were giggling between themselves and Ali was afraid to guess about what. As much as she liked the pair, she worried for Brad that they may recognize him and she knew he wouldn't be happy about that. Maybe buying something would get them moving.

Before she even hung up the phone Ali wagged a finger toward a candy bar. Hazel handed it to her and took the money, seeming pleased with her bit of commerce. As soon as Ali replaced the receiver she thanked Hazel and was about to walk over to the file cabinet when Millie's eye suddenly went wide and her mouth dropped open.

She recovered quickly and under her breath said, "Now I get it. Oh, my. Oh, my, my, my."

"What?" Hazel whispered. "What do you get?"

Ali kept her head down, busying herself with the myriad forms spread across her desk, not quite sure how to handle the conversation unfolding in front of her.

"I bet he's here to...you know."

"No. I don't know. Tell me."

"Oh, honestly, Hazel. You can be so dense." She whispered in her sister's ear.

"Oh, my!" Hazel giggled, then covered her mouth with her freckled hand. Holding up her index finger, she turned back to the cart and started riffling through magazines. Mercifully the door behind Ali opened and she heard Brad's footsteps retreat down the hall.

"Oh, phooey!" Hazel said, turning a moment too late. "I thought maybe I could sell him this." She held up a *Playboy* magazine and Millie gave her a hard elbow to the ribs before grabbing the handle to the cart.

"Can't take you anywhere, Hazel." Millie rolled her eyes and glanced back at Ali as she started down the hall to the next office. "Nice meeting you, sweetie. We'll stop by again."

Ali waved and waited until they were out of sight, then ducked her head behind the counter and laughed out loud. The phone rang and she dug deep for a somewhat professional-sounding voice. Realizing it was her sister, she laughed again as she relayed the story of Hazel and Millie. She neglected to mention who the handsome client was, however.

With no one else in need of her attention Ali lingered on the phone, thinking it was time she talked to Lynne about her current state of affairs. She finagled an invitation to dinner and was just hanging up when Brad paused at her desk.

"That was a close one. Nice old ladies, but they have a reputation for playing hardball when it comes to matchmaking." He took his cap off and ruffled his hair, making him look as though he'd just climbed out of bed.

When she didn't say anything, he continued. "Barring any emergency, I have Thursday night off. Want to do something?"

Was it good for him to know she was almost always available? Should she play hard to get? Damn, she hated this whole dating game thing.

"If you're busy, maybe—"

"No, no. Thursday's fine. Why don't I cook?"

"Never turn down a home-cooked meal." He rapped on the counter twice. "I'll call you later about details." He smiled and raced off.

Ali stole one more peek at his handsome face, then quickly refocused on the paperwork in front of her, admonishing herself for such shallow musings. Even though a voice at the back of her head said it was more than his looks that attracted her, she dismissed such a notion. It was this donor business that had her so confused. If she didn't think there was a possibility that she was pregnant by Brad, would she be lusting after him the way she was?

The answer was loud and strong.

Turning back to her work she did her best to ignore it.

Ali cut tomatoes and dropped them atop the salad while Lynne took a large loaf of garlic bread from the oven and began slicing it.

"Have any plans for your birthday Thursday?" Lynne asked.

"As a matter of fact, I do."

Lynne hiked an eyebrow in Ali's direction.

"I don't want you to make a big deal over this, but I actually have a date."

"Anyone I know?"

"You met him after the game. Brad."

"But I thought—"

"We were wrong." Ali explained about Sally and then how Brad had asked her out when they bumped into each other in the gift shop, omitting any mention of the clinic.

When she fell silent, Lynne said, "You've done it, haven't you?"

There was no point playing games. She'd come for a little TLC and this was as good a time as any. "Yes. The morning of the game."

Lynne looked stunned and a little hurt. "And you didn't tell me?"

"I-it was a strange day for me. Sorry, sis. And...well, I thought I'd wait until there might be more to discuss."

Lynne slapped her knife down and turned, eyes wide with excitement. "You mean—"

"I don't know." Ali kept tossing the salad, feeling embarrassed all of a sudden. "I was thinking of buying one of those test kits."

"I have one under the sink in my bathroom. Bought it a little prematurely some time ago." She dried her hands on a dish towel and took Ali's hand. "Come on. The lasagna needs to cool a few minutes, anyway."

Ali let herself be towed down the hall to the master

bedroom and into the bathroom, alternately feeling excitement and worry. But at least she wasn't alone this time.

Lynne rummaged under the sink and came up with a water-stained box. "The pipes leaked on it before we got the drain fixed, but I'm sure the inside's okay." She opened it quickly, acting as nervous as Ali felt.

"The directions are smeared but the kit seems fine. All you have to do after you use it is wait a few minutes to see if the strip turns blue." She took Ali by both shoulders and smiled at her lovingly. "Want me to wait in the bedroom or should I go back to the kitchen?"

"Wait," Ali said, nudging Lynne out the door. "I'll hurry."

But when she joined her sister on the edge of the bed a short time later, there was no need to reveal the results. Her face must have reflected it because Lynne wrapped her arms around Ali and rocked her from side to side. "I'm sorry, sweetie. Maybe next time."

Ali let her sister comfort her while she thought about next time. Would she go through this for years as her sisters had?

Lynne handed Ali a tissue and she dried her eyes before giving her nose a good blow. "I was so sure because I skipped a period. I should have remembered—"

"Ah, yes. 'The Celestial Curse' as Mom used to call it. We've all had many skipped months and even more when we didn't ovulate. Strange breed, we Celeste women."

Ali straightened and pulled herself together. She'd been overly optimistic that the first time would work.

She would just have to try again and again, if need be, until she reached her goal. Anything worth having was certainly worth the wait, she told herself, pulling her sister back into her arms.

"Thanks for being here, sis. It means a lot to me."

"What are sisters for?"

They returned to the kitchen where Ken was lifting Keri into her high chair and it was all Ali could do not to cry. She put up a brave front throughout dinner and while cleaning up afterward, but as soon as the dishwasher was loaded, Ali made her excuses and went home.

She brushed her teeth, washed her face and slipped into a long flannel T-shirt before finally climbing between the cold sheets. She rolled to the opposite side of the bed and stared into the darkness. Tears slipped from the corners of her eyes, wetting her hair and pillow and she let them flow, feeling as blue as the day she had been inseminated.

When the tears had run their course she wondered if there might be a message in all this somewhere. Could God be telling her to wait a little longer? That perhaps Brad was the man she never thought she would find? That maybe she could have his child the old-fashioned way? She mulled on this awhile. She'd never been one to believe in coincidence. Her mother had always said God had a plan for everything, that to everything there was a season.

She rolled onto her back and in the moonlight she saw the first snow of winter drifting slowly past her bedroom window. On a long sigh she closed her eyes as her limbs dipped deeper into the mattress and the troubles of the night were replaced with loving blue eyes and a reassuring smile.

Seven

At her apartment window Thursday night, Ali watched a freighter pass and worried about Brad's imminent arrival. Was it wise to have him here so soon? She loved her home, but there was no way she could afford to live here if it weren't for her inheritance—a fact she'd forgotten was best kept under her hat as long as possible. Previous dates had fallen into one of two categories: those who were suddenly too interested in her money or those whose egos couldn't deal with her having more of it than they had.

She wanted to believe Brad was different, that he didn't fit into either category, but it was too soon to tell.

She walked back to the kitchen to check on the roast when the phone rang. She groaned aloud, knowing full well who was calling, and shut the oven door.

After explaining the current crisis, Brad asked, "How late is too late?"

"Dinner won't be ready for another hour." Time she had hoped they would have had getting to know each other better. But maybe this was just as well. She had an idea.

"Would it be easier to eat at your place?" she asked.

"I forgot to bring a change of clothes. I would've had to run home and change first, anyway. That would give us more time. Sure you don't mind?"

"Not at all."

"Great. I'll call Sally and tell her to let you in."

After packing everything into a wicker picnic basket Ali drove over to Brad's place and Sally stepped out into the hall as soon as she spotted her.

"Mmm, mmm! Somethin' sure do smell good."

"Hi, Sally. Just your basic pot roast."

Sally winked before she hauled herself up the stairs ahead of Ali. "Never met a man yet who don't love pot roast." She unlocked the door and swung it open. "Here ya go. Have a nice evenin', now."

"Thanks, Sally." Ali closed the door and turned to face the single room. It was about what she'd expected. The small galley kitchen along with a door next to it leading to a bathroom consumed about a third of the space, the balance left to a threadbare brown sofa, a small Formica-topped table and two chrome-legged chairs in front of the only window, and a Murphy bed that had been left down and unmade. On the wall opposite the window stood an exercise bench with a cracked black vinyl seat and a number of weights stacked at each end of the suspended bar.

She set the basket on the counter, feeling drawn to the rumpled sheets. After hanging up her coat she walked over and sat tentatively on the edge of the bed. She felt bold for invading such a private space, but she couldn't resist. She gave the mattress a couple of test bounces, then flopped on her back, throwing her arms out to her sides. For a moment she followed a hairline crack in the ceiling until finally she closed her eyes and pulled the sheets to her face. They smelled of soap and aftershave, the same musky male scent she had noticed sitting next to him on the People Mover. She remembered the feel of her hand in his, the brief touch of his soft lips, the swell of her breast against his arm. How she longed for more of the same.

She remembered the unfinished roast on the counter and sat up with a start. Bounding off the bed she put the covered pot in the oven, turned it on and set the timer. Then she looked around again. Should she make the bed and put it up? This would certainly send the right signal when Brad got home.

It *was* the signal she wanted to send, right? Yes, she told herself halfheartedly as she made the bed and lifted it to the wall. With hands on hips she spun around the small space and noticed a portable CD player in the corner near the window. She selected a CD, inserted it and adjusted the volume, her mind on fast forward. Again she wondered if he danced and she could almost feel him pressed against the length of her, swaying slowly to the music.

Growling in frustration Ali rushed back to the safety of the kitchen, where she busied herself finding plates and utensils, napkins and even a candle, which she placed in the center of the small table once it was set.

When all was ready, she sat on the sofa and perused a stack of medical journals on the floor alongside, pretending she wasn't at all nervous and that she did this sort of thing all the time.

But when she heard footsteps on the stairs her heart raced. She felt as though she were a young bride waiting for her husband to come home from work. It was all she could do not to run to the door and plant a big kiss on those luscious lips.

Brad approached the door, his shoulders sagging as he ran his hand over the dark stubble on his cheeks. He thought he must look as energetic as he felt. But simply knowing who waited inside boosted his spirits, and he pushed the problems of the E.R. behind him, squared his shoulders and opened the door.

"Wow! It smells great in here," he said, shrugging out of his jacket and hanging it on the hook by the door.

He tried to keep the devilish smile from his face, but when she walked toward him he gave up the charade and handed her the single long-stemmed red rose he'd been feebly trying to hide. "Happy Birthday, Ali."

She took it from him, surprise registering on her beautiful face as she held the flower to her nose. "How did you know?"

"On my way out I ran into Michelle. I told her you were cooking dinner for me and she said to wish you happy birthday. Why didn't you tell me?"

She shrugged, looking embarrassed. "I didn't want

you to feel you had to buy me something." She felt one of the velvety petals. "But thank you. It's beautiful."

"Let me see what I can find to put it in." He opened and closed a few cupboards before going to the refrigerator where he found a nearly empty bottle of wine. He uncorked it, took a whiff and then making a face drained the contents down the sink. After rinsing it out he filled it with cold water and carefully threaded the thorny stem down the neck of the bottle.

"There. That problem's solved. But now we don't have any wine for dinner."

"That's okay. I'm not much of a drinker, anyway. A couple glasses and I'd be too sleepy to drive home." She laughed and turned her back on him to check on the roast, and he thought he noticed a pink tinge traveling up her neck.

He watched and wondered if she'd always been this nervous around men. Regardless, he found it rather refreshing. So many women he knew made no bones about what they were after and often it had nothing to do with getting to know him as a person; it was more what he could give them, either in bed or future luxuries. With Ali he sensed neither was high on her list of priorities.

He looked around her as she forked the meat. "Pot roast?" Brad said, standing close behind her. "How did you know? It's my favorite." She closed the oven and he placed his hands on her waist and turned her around, in an instant lost in the depths of her violet eyes. "Gosh, it's been too long since I've had some." Damn! That hadn't come out right. He hoped she knew he meant pot roast.

She was staring up at him, almost expectantly.

He ran a hand over his rough chin. "Do I have time to shower and shave?"

She averted her eyes. "Y-yes. Sure, go ahead." She turned and pulled a platter from the cupboard, looking very much at home, and suddenly he felt more at home here than he ever had. Until now it had simply been a place to crash. "I'll hurry."

When he stepped out of the bathroom a few minutes later the food was on the table, along with the rose and the flickering light of a candle he had forgotten he had. Classical music flowed softly from the CD player, and silhouetted against the window was the woman who had transformed his pathetic digs.

She turned and he walked toward her, taking both her hands in his. "Thank you," he said, inching closer, his hands moving to her arms and trailing down her silky blouse.

"You haven't even tasted it yet," she said, her eyes on his mouth.

He could feel her breath on his face and when she licked her lips he pulled her to him, her body meeting his halfway. This time the kiss wasn't quick. She opened to him and his tongue slid hungrily inside. And when she groaned he felt the press of swollen flesh against his zipper.

His senses were drunk with the crescendo of music, the steaming platter on the table beside him and the warm, intoxicating feel of the good woman in his arms.

With all the strength he could muster he set her away from him and smiled down at her, his breathing jagged. "I've been wanting to do that for a long time."

Her gaze didn't waver. "Me, too." Almost shyly she took his hand and seated him in a chair at the table. "But now it's time for other pleasures."

She walked around the table, sat down and took her time unfolding a paper napkin across her lap. She was perfect, he thought. Everything about her was perfect. And the best part was she didn't seem to know it.

She dished them each a plateful of mouthwatering food and he refocused his attention. The meat was tender and juicy and he emitted sounds of approval as he savored every bite. "I can't remember the last time I ate so well. This is terrific."

She looked pleased, though he noticed she was only picking at her own food.

"Aren't you hungry?"

She pushed a potato around with her fork and said, "I guess I tested enough earlier that it took the edge off my appetite." Then she flashed him a big smile. "But don't let me stop you. Eat up."

And he did. Right down to the last morsel.

Afterward he helped her clear the table, insisting that she leave everything for him to clean up in the morning since he had the late shift tomorrow and would have plenty of time.

He took her hand and walked her to the sofa where he angled himself to face her. "Ali—" he started, then paused to gather his thoughts. "This has all been a very pleasant surprise."

"Dinner?" she asked, looking uncertain.

He smiled. "That, too." When she lowered her head he lifted her chin with his finger and waited for her eyes to meet his. "You're a very special lady, Ali—"

"But?" she interrupted, more than a hint of suspicion crossing her face.

"But what do I have to offer you?" With a sweep of his arm he motioned around them. "Certainly not money...and even less time."

"Maybe I should leave." She started to stand, but he tugged her back down.

"Please...don't be angry."

She glared at him. "Look. I'm a big girl. If you don't want to see me, just say so."

He couldn't help but let out a small laugh. She couldn't be further from the truth. "Don't want to see you?" He shook his head, still not believing she could think that. "In a perfect world I'd like to see you every day, to end each day just like this." He saw her face soften and the words passed his lips before he could stop them. "And much more."

He ran his fingers down her cheek, its soft creaminess pushing his limits of self-restraint. "There's nothing I'd like more than to make love to you this very second, to kiss every inch of that beautiful body of yours, to hear you whisper my name in the morning—"

"Brad, I—"

"But I won't push you, Ali. I just wanted you to think about what you were getting into. And if you decide this isn't for you, I'll understand." She suddenly looked as though she might cry, so he tried to lighten things up.

"I'd be devastated and sulk for months, of course, but I'd try to understand." He smiled and was rewarded with a small smile back. "Do you still want to leave?"

She blinked hard and shook her head.

He let out a loud sigh. "Good." Then he braved the next subject. "There's no good time to talk about these things, but...well, I just wanted to remind you that I was tested before I started visiting the clinic. And I haven't been with anyone since. For that matter, it's been years."

He waited, hoping she would volunteer her history and they could be done with it. Even in the dim lighting he could see her cheeks coloring. "I know this isn't very romantic, but better now than...I mean just in case—"

"Brad—" She looked away, then back. "I—I'm a virgin."

He knew his face must have registered shock. He'd heard about women her age waiting, but he'd never expected to—

She lowered her eyes and he said, "I'm sorry. You just stunned me for a moment." He took a calming breath and braved the all important question. "So, Angel Celeste, where do we go from here?"

At hearing his playful tone Ali perked up and lifted her chin a notch. "Wherever the road may lead."

"You sure?"

"I'm positive."

"But slowly...at your pace."

She exhaled loudly. "Then I think I'd better go...now." She brushed his lips quickly with her own and stood. He followed her to the door, wanting another kiss, but not daring.

She retrieved her coat from under his and without looking back said, "I had a wonderful birthday, Brad. Thank you."

Eight

For the next month, by tacit agreement, Brad and Ali avoided each other's apartments, opting instead for long walks at lunchtime or evenings along the riverfront.

On one blustery Tuesday, snow gusting against the windows, they braved lunch in the hospital cafeteria—something they had avoided, hoping to sidestep gossip.

Ali studied Brad's relaxed face as he watched the snow, and in spite of a chill coming off the glass she felt a warmth wash over her. At quiet moments like this she wondered if she should tell him about her one and only trip to the cross-town clinic. It had been two months now, the same length of time she had known Brad.

Still, something made her hesitate. He really didn't need to know, and it would open up an issue she wasn't ready to share with him yet—her desire to have a child. The last thing she wanted was for him to think he was merely a means to an end. Or worse, that his lack of funds might prevent her from fulfilling her dream in the foreseeable future.

Besides, since coming to know him, her goals had been altered. She wanted more than a baby now.

He looked back at her and smiled a lazy smile, knowing there was no need to fill the silence with words. She had grown comfortable with his lingering looks, and he with hers. Well, comfortable wasn't always the way she felt, as was the case now as he reached for her hand and her heartbeat quickened. He started to speak, but stopped abruptly at the sound of squeaky shoes coming closer.

Ali turned to look and suppressed a groan.

Brad shifted in his seat and said, "Uh-oh," under his breath.

"Why, Ali, dear! Hazel and I haven't seen you in ages!" Millie didn't hide her curious stare at Brad's name tag on his jacket pocket. She tapped a finger on her cheek a moment before her eyes went round. "You're the young man who's been working with Dr. Singleton, right?"

Ali watched Brad force a smile. "Yes, ma'am."

"I knew you looked familiar."

Hazel nudged her sister aside and smiled at Brad. "My name's Hazel and this is Millie. We're very good friends of the Singletons, you know," she said, sounding proud.

"Nice to meet you Hazel, Millie."

Millie quietly assessed the young couple a moment and then nodded her head suddenly as if she had come to an important decision.

"Ali—" she began, hooking her elbow behind her sister's and pulling her close. "Hazel and I were wondering if you could do us a big favor."

Ali felt the snare being set and braced herself.

"We have these two tickets to see the *Nutcracker Suite* at the Fox this Thursday and sadly we can't make it."

"We can't?" Hazel interrupted, her forehead wrinkling.

Millie jabbed an elbow into Hazel's ribs. "Ouch," she said, looking crossly at her sister. Then recovering quickly, she said, "Oh! No, we can't. So unfortunate."

"So," Millie continued, "I know it's Thanksgiving Day, but we were hoping maybe you could go. It would be a shame to waste them." Then she turned to Brad. "Did I mention there are *two* tickets?"

Brad picked up his water glass and eyed Ali over the rim as if to say "I'll let you handle this one. Please!" Ali bit the inside of her cheek to keep from laughing. These two were about as subtle as a train wreck, but adorable and well-intentioned just the same.

"I'd love to go," she said finally. Then to protect Brad the best she could from the unrelenting pair, she added, "I'm sure I'll find someone to join me. Thank you very much."

Millie's gaze ping-ponged between Ali and Brad another beat, then she winked and turned her sister around with her. "You two have a nice time."

As soon as they were out of earshot Brad leaned closer. "It will be all over the hospital before sunset."

"Oh, I don't know," Ali said, chuckling. "They

might like to play matchmaker, but somehow I don't see them engaging in idle gossip.''

"I hope you're right."

"Would it matter so much if word got out?"

"Maybe not," Brad conceded. "I'm just trying to avoid the locker-room kind of talk. Some of the guys can be pretty crude in voicing their assumptions."

Ali smiled, loving this protective side of Brad. He wasn't worried about himself, just what others might say about her. She gave his hand a squeeze. "We haven't talked about Thanksgiving, but if you have time I'd be happy to make a turkey and all the trimmings. I could cook it on Time Bake so it would be ready after the play."

"Aren't you going to your sister's?"

"They went out to California to be with Barbara and her family." Brad curled the tips of her fingers over the side of his hand and her temperature went up another notch.

"Craig owes me a favor. Let me see if we can swap days. But you don't have to go to all that work. We could just go to the play and raid the refrigerator."

"I don't mind. In fact I'd enjoy it."

"You mean, I'm finally going to see *your* place?"

She couldn't put it off much longer. "Yes."

Brad picked up his tray and held out Ali's chair. But before she stood he whispered near her ear, "I have to warn you, gorgeous…I don't know how much longer I can keep my hands off you. You sure you want me alone in your apartment?"

Her breath caught in her throat and she glanced up at him. "Yes, I do. Very much."

They walked to the tray deposit area without another word, and Ali knew exactly what she had led Brad to believe.

The crowds that had lingered in downtown Detroit after the annual Thanksgiving Day Parade had thinned considerably by the time Brad and Ali exited the Fox and caught the People Mover back to her place.

Brad held Ali's hand as they talked about the play and the grandeur of the restored old theater all the way to her apartment door, where the strong aroma of roasting turkey made Brad's stomach growl.

Ali preceded him inside and he came to an abrupt stop in the doorway. "Wow! I don't know what I expected, but this is elegant." Ali took his coat and hung it in the entryway closet, seeming pleased with his praise.

He walked to the glass wall with its view of the Detroit River and Windsor. "And this view!"

When he looked over his shoulder he saw Ali already busy in the kitchen. He joined her there and about half an hour later he found himself mashing potatoes while she made gravy. In no time at all they were seated at an elaborately preset glass-topped table enjoying another of Ali's masterpieces. Except just as before, he noticed she wasn't eating much.

"Never did like my own cooking," she volunteered, and he let it go at that.

But after the table was cleared he said he thought she looked a little pale and he felt her forehead. Finally, after she put away leftovers, he turned her toward the living room and told her he would clean up, that she should just relax.

When he had finished loading the dishwasher he

noticed that she was reading the *Wall Street Journal*. He wiped the counter and smiled in her direction. "She cooks, she follows the stock market...what other secrets is she keeping from me?"

Ali met his eyes briefly, then buried her face behind the paper. "Wouldn't you like to know?" she said, and even though he knew she was kidding, he thought he detected a slight strain in her voice. *Was* she hiding something?

Not for the first time he stole a furtive glance around the apartment. How could she afford this place? She couldn't be making that much at the clinic.

Without putting the paper down, she said, "In case you're wondering, wise investments is the answer."

"You mean, you really know how to play the market?"

"I'm not a day trader, if that's what you mean. I'm more into long-term gain. But if you do it right, the dividends are a nice supplement to your regular income."

"When the day comes I have a dollar to spare, I'll have to give it to you." She gave him a faint smile and returned to her reading.

He wondered how many supplemental dividends it would take to afford all of this and a new car, too. He hated playing games with her, but memories of Valerie still lingered. He had to be sure.

"You know, I don't even own a single credit card."

She turned the page and didn't look up. "I have two. One I use, the other I keep in my desk as backup just in case."

"How high's the interest on those things these days?"

"I don't know. I pay the whole balance every month, so there isn't any interest."

"Smart girl." He'd worried needlessly. Ali was as guileless as a newborn babe. He should have known he could trust her, that she could never have ulterior motives for seeing him. Now he felt guilty for doubting her.

"You feeling any better?" he asked.

She set aside the paper and turned toward him, resting her chin on folded arms across the back of the sofa. "Yes. Much." She gave him a shy smile. "I—I think I was just overly excited about..." She lowered her eyes. "Tonight."

He knew what she was referring to, and though they had both danced around the subject all day, his own excitement was nearing fever pitch. Yet looking at her now, pale and nervous, he wondered if they were rushing things, if she was truly ready for the next step.

He was about to ask her but when she curled her index finger, luring him over, he dropped the dish towel and went to her. She draped her arms around his neck and pulled him closer, initiating the first of what he hoped would be many kisses before the night was over. Her lips were warm and inviting and there was no mistaking the permission they gave him. Another kiss, deeper this time, and he slipped his arm under her legs and stood, lifting her off the sofa.

Her eyes fixed on his and he saw a frightened look pass over her face.

"You trust me, don't you?" he asked, carrying her down the short hall.

She nodded slowly, biting her bottom lip.

"I'd never hurt you, Ali. Any time you want me to stop, just say so, okay?"

"Okay."

He laid her gently on the bed, then curled on his side next to her, light from the kitchen seeping into the room. When he bent over to kiss her, he could feel her trembling. Slowly, gently, he tugged her sweater over her head and tossed it aside. Her chest rose and fell rapidly, her full breasts straining against a thin lacy restraint. He released the front hook and simply stared at her, eventually letting his gaze meet hers.

"You're so beautiful, Ali." She just watched him and waited. But when his finger circled one nipple, it went taut and she closed her eyes on a groan. He lowered his mouth to her other breast while his hand trailed to the button at her waist. Almost impatiently she raised her bottom and he freed her of her skirt and everything else except a pair of black high-cut bikini panties. He ran his hand over her mound and between her thighs, feeling dampness through the silky fabric.

Raising his face to hers he waited for her to open her eyes, then he kissed her greedily as his hand crept under her panties and he slipped a finger inside her.

She groaned into his mouth and squirmed beneath his touch, but when his thumb worked her most sensitive spot she tore her lips from his and called out his name.

"Oh, Brad." She arched her head back and he saw her grip the sheets on both sides of her.

"Let it go, sweetheart. Don't hold back." He rubbed his thumb faster and harder, lowering his mouth again to her breast, his tongue flicking over her. Her breathing came in loud, short bursts and he felt himself straining against his fly. Then with a long shudder her body went limp beneath him.

She opened her eyes and looked at him, seeming embarrassed. He straddled her now and kissed her gently. When he hunkered back she sat up and worked the buttons of his shirt, pushing it off his shoulders and helping him lift his T-shirt over his head in rapid succession.

Shyly she stared into his chest. "Brad, I—I—"

He kissed her forehead and tucked a wild strand of hair behind her ear. "You can say anything, Ali. Let's not be awkward with each other."

She braved a quick glance, her cheeks flushed. "I never even had brothers. I—I never—"

"My sweet, sweet innocent Ali." He feathered light kisses against her hair and took her hand in his. Guiding it down, he pressed it against him. Her fingers trembled beneath his as she slowly traveled the length of his firmness, eliciting a moan from deep in his throat. And when she unzipped him and he filled her hand, she gasped.

He gritted his teeth and fought for control. Then quickly he rose from the bed and shed the rest of his clothes. As an afterthought he fumbled in his pants' pocket for a foil packet. When he started to open it, she stilled his hand.

"Do we have to?"

"Is it safe? I mean—"

She kissed him and slipped quickly from the bed, holding a pillow modestly in front of her. "I'll make sure."

Brad breathed deeply, waiting for her to return from the bathroom, both surprised and turned on with the idea that she was prepared for tonight. Obviously she had wanted this moment as much as he had.

She returned to bed and blood pulsed through his veins once again. But when she stretched out next to him and he kissed her, her lips quivered.

"Ali? Is everything okay?"

She stole a quick peek down the length of him. "It's just that …you're so big," she said, not looking him in the eye. "Will it…I mean—"

He pulled her to him and chuckled softly in her ear. "Oh, my angel. You do wonders for a man's ego." Then kissing her long and deep, he added in a husky voice, "Trust me. We'll fit just fine." His fingers trailed over her tummy and found their mark again.

When he thought it was time, he pushed her knees wider with his own. With one arm wrapped tightly under her waist, he opened her with his swollen flesh, nudging himself ever so slightly into her tight recesses, sheathing himself with her moist silkiness. He fought the urge to drive into her. He could feel Ali tensing and he slowed.

"Relax, sweetheart. There might be a little discomfort, but only for a moment."

Her eyes were closed tight, her bottom lip between her teeth, but soon she began to move with him as his thrusts grew deeper and deeper, until finally he surged forward, hoping to break her quickly with a minimum of pain.

But then he realized he had penetrated her completely. Nothing had stood in his way. His brain registered the fact, but soon passion replaced confusion as Ali ground her hips into his, lifting herself to meet his every thrust.

He crushed his mouth against hers and rode her hard now, her breathing as hot and labored as his own, their tongues imitating the rhythm of their slick bodies.

Suddenly he pulled her closer, his body racked with spasms, and he flowed into her. Still breathing hard he kissed her neck and breast. "Ali, Ali, Ali." Her hands traveled up and down his spine, spreading their newfound intimacy, making it linger, and he knew he would love her again before the night ended.

In the predawn gray of morning Brad slipped from beneath Ali's sheets, picked up his clothes and headed for the bathroom. He had less than an hour to shower, dress, and grab the rail to work. His mind started to engage under the cold spray, but he hurried along, not liking the dark mood that threatened. As soon as he was dressed he kissed a drowsy Ali goodbye and jogged to the Renaissance Center and the closest gateway.

Only when he took his seat on the tram did he allow the doubts to take shape. Next to her, in the warmth of her bed, nothing but loving her and holding her close had seemed important. Now, in the cold, hard face of morning, with Ali miles behind him, he couldn't help but ask himself questions. He hated thinking anything bad about her and he fought it as long as he could, but still, some things just didn't add up.

First, her apartment. Even if she did invest well, it took money to make money. She said her mother had never worked outside of the home before she died, and Ali also said she was estranged from her father, so it seemed unlikely that he was supplementing her income. If she wasn't in debt up to her eyebrows, then where did the money come from?

When he couldn't figure that out, his mind drifted to their lovemaking. She said she was a virgin, and she seemed so innocent. Yet there had been no physical evidence, nor even an explanation for the lack of it. He supposed there could have been an accident of some kind. Those things did happen.

He pushed his hair off his forehead and leaned back against the window. He despised these nagging doubts. Was it his history with Valerie haunting him again, or was Ali being less than forthright with him? If it was the latter, what did she have to hide?

And finally, he wondered, stepping onto the platform at his exit, what type of protection had she used before they made love? Or had she been less than honest about that, too? In the heat of the moment he hadn't given it a second's thought. Now he wished he had.

He ran the remaining blocks to the hospital, trying to convince himself he was overreacting, that he may have just found the most wonderful woman in the world, that the only reason he felt uneasy was that everything had been too perfect. But once he caught his breath inside the locker room he knew with absolute certainty that there was more to Ali Celeste than she had let on. Like it or not, his instincts never lied. She was hiding something.

Nine

Ali pulled the covers closer, missing the warmth of Brad by her side. The scent of his aftershave on the pillow lingered, as did the unfamiliar scent of their lovemaking.

She turned on her back and smiled at the ceiling. She had finally done it. And it had surpassed even her most vivid dreams.

She reached down and gingerly touched the swollen flesh between her legs. Never could she have imagined something so delicious. There had been some discomfort, as Brad had warned, but nothing compared to the ecstasy she'd felt when he filled her. Already she longed for the next time and the next time and the time after that. She knew she would never again feel complete without the nearness of him.

She glanced at the clock on the nightstand: 8:15.

She rolled over lethargically and snuggled under the covers. She had the day off and could sleep until noon if she wanted. Maybe she would. She never seemed to get enough sleep these days. She made a mental note to buy some vitamin B the next time she went shopping. Her energy level wasn't what it used to be. Then she thought of Brad and their lovemaking and how very little sleep she had gotten. No wonder she was exhausted.

She closed her eyes and pictured him there beside her and hoped that he would call before the day was over.

But when Brad finally did call after seven that evening it didn't go as Ali had expected. He thanked her for yesterday in a rather formal if not abrupt fashion, and then told her that he would be staying at the hospital all weekend. There was no mention of talking later or when they might see each other, which left her shaken and confused.

She took a long bubble bath after Brad's call and tried to rationalize things. He had no doubt worked very hard today after having very little sleep. He may have been calling her between seeing very sick patients and he didn't have time for small talk. And after last night he probably assumed she knew they would see each other again as soon as possible.

She shook her head slowly from side to side and sunk lower in the water. No, something was wrong. There was no mistaking the coolness in Brad's voice.

Ali cupped her hands and filled them with bubbles, watching them as they popped and disappeared. And then she thought of Brad vanishing from her life just as easily and she cried.

* * *

Before she even took her coat off Monday morning, Ali flipped open the appointment book and saw the erased line next to one o'clock. She had suspected Brad would cancel, but the reality of it cut through her like a knife. The insecure part of her wondered if her inexperience in the bedroom had been the turnoff. Yet at the time everything had seemed just as special for him as it had been for her.

She dropped down into her chair and buried her face in her hands. What had she done to turn him away? Did she seem too eager for a relationship? Had she somehow telegraphed her readiness for marriage and a family? Was that it? Were things moving too fast for him?

She sprang out of her chair and raced for the coatrack in the corner, growling in frustration. When would she ever understand men?

For the next few days Ali packed turkey sandwiches and ate at her desk, not wanting to run into Brad in the cafeteria. She didn't want to appear as though she were chasing him. If he wanted to see her, he knew where to find her.

But by Friday, with no leftovers for lunch, Ali had reached her boiling point. The cafeteria was as much for her use as his; she'd be damned if she'd hide her face another day.

With no clients left to attend to, she switched the phone to the answering service and headed for lunch ten minutes early. Her stride was long and determined, as if she dared him to cross her path.

She went through the line and then scanned the room for an empty seat. He was nowhere in sight.

There was a table in the atrium so she strode over and claimed it.

There. That was easy, she told herself. Mentally, she felt in charge, but her stomach had other ideas. It was queasy again, so she opened a packet of soda crackers and munched on one before starting her salad. After drinking some hot tea she felt a little better and pulled out her book and read as she ate. At least in her novels there was a happy ending.

She was almost finished when she heard the scraping of the chair across from her. She looked up and there he was. This time he didn't even bother to ask if he could join her; he simply sat down and stared at her.

"Hello," he said, acting about as engaging as a cobra.

She packed her book in her purse and started to stand.

"Wait," he said, reaching across the table and holding the edge of her tray. "Can we talk a few minutes?"

"About what?" She wasn't going to make this easy for him.

"Look, Ali...you're a very special person." She rolled her eyes. "I guess I'm just not ready for—"

"Let me guess. 'A relationship.' How typical." Between clenched teeth she leaned closer and whispered, "And I suppose you didn't know this before Thanksgiving night."

"It's not like that."

"Oh, no? Then what changed your mind that night? Come on. I'd love to hear it." She knew she was being bitchy, but she couldn't help it. "Hey, if you're worried about hurting my feelings, don't hold back.''

He ground his teeth, then said, ''All right, since you asked.''

She leaned back and folded her arms. This had better be good.

''Your apartment.''

''What about my apartment?''

''You're living above your means, and—''

''Hold it right there. Who says I am?''

''Ali, come on. Your job can't pay well enough to—''

''No, it doesn't. I told you I have investments.''

''Yes. And you told me you've been on the outs with your father for years, so who gave you the money to invest in the first place?''

''Why, you sexist pig!'' Her raised voice brought curious stares from neighboring tables. She took a deep breath and let it out before she continued. ''Not that it's any of your business, but my mother was a genius at investing, far better than my father. She taught me everything I know about managing money—which I do very well, thank you very much—and she also left me enough in her will to get me started.''

The look in Brad's eyes softened and she could see that he was sorry. He reached across the table for her hand, but she pulled it away. The misunderstanding may have been cleared up for him, but it was far from over for her.

''Tell me,'' she started, cocking her head to one side, ''how *did* you think I afforded my lifestyle?''

''I told you. I thought you were living beyond your means, that you were probably in debt.''

"So now I'm a liar, too?"

"Ali—"

"I told you I paid my charge cards off every month, that I didn't carry a balance. If this is all a matter of trust, *Darling*—" she leaned on his name heavily "—then maybe you have some old baggage to deal with that has nothing to do with me." She waited for some kind of retort, but instead he hung his head, looking as though she'd hit the mark.

When he didn't say anything Ali leaned closer and said, "Well, Doctor, while you're wallowing in the past, you just blew a shot at the best future you could have had." With that she pushed out her chair, stood, and walked away.

Whatever pleasure Ali had taken in telling Brad off slipped away as the lonely weekend stretched slowly by. On Sunday afternoon, while paying her bills, she looked at the calendar and realized what else was bothering her. She'd been using the ovulation test kit nearly every day and still nothing. Even for her wacky system this was strange.

By the following weekend she decided it was time for another kind of test kit. She drove the short distance to the drugstore, made her purchase and drove home, thousands of twinkling Christmas lights along Jefferson Avenue doing nothing to cheer her.

Now, sitting on the side of the bed and staring at the results, her mind refused the truth that stared back at her.

She was pregnant.

She should be celebrating, she told herself. This was what she wanted.

But not like this.

All she wanted to do at the moment was escape into a deep sleep. She lay back and curled onto her side. And as soon as she closed her eyes, there he was again—the face of the father. Except Brad was no longer just a face. He was a man she had been close to, closer than any man ever. And not just physically, she realized. Somehow he had worked his way into her heart. Even worse, she knew he was very much lodged there, even now that all was lost.

Before a tear could fall, Ali shoved off the bed and went to the spare bedroom where she had stored Christmas decorations. She busied herself the rest of the day and night, assembling the artificial blue spruce and decorating it. Christmas carols burst joyfully from the stereo and occasionally she even sang along and pretended all was well.

But in the end, with nothing left to do, she sat on the sofa, a warm mug of hot chocolate cradled in her hands, and thought brokenheartedly of what might have been.

On Wednesday, Michelle agreed to meet Ali for lunch at the Coney Island restaurant near the hospital. Part of her wanted to tell Michelle about the baby, but Ali knew she couldn't talk about it yet without crying, so she decided to wait.

She was just starting to relax and enjoy herself when Michelle said, "You didn't forget about the Christmas party at our place Saturday night, did you?"

Actually she had. Instantly she wondered if Brad might be there.

"You're coming, aren't you?"

Ali forced a smile. "Of course. Can I bring anything?"

"A date, if you'd like." She raised and lowered her eyebrows a couple of times, leaving Ali to wonder if Michelle had Brad in mind. Had she heard rumors?

"Well?" Michelle said.

"Thanks, but I'll be coming alone."

Michelle eyed her over the rim of her coffee mug, looking as though she hoped for an explanation. When none came, she abandoned the subject and they talked of Christmas shopping and safer topics until it was time to leave.

But when Ali returned to work, Christmas was the last thing on her mind.

Would he be there Saturday?

How should she act if he was?

And perhaps most important, she thought with a wicked smile as she drove home, what should she wear?

She laughed out loud for the first time in weeks and shook her head. Man, how could she have let herself get so down? It wasn't like her to be so deep in the pits. And it wasn't like her to give up without a fight. If her new goal had been to have the baby *and* the father, then why had she given up so easily?

So they had an argument.

So he acted like a jerk.

So what? She'd be lying if she said she didn't still think of him day and night.

She parked her car, ran inside and punched the elevator button twice, hoping to hurry it along. As soon as she entered her apartment and shrugged out of her coat, she raced to the bedroom closet and started pulling things out and spreading them across the bed.

Something Christmassy, yet sexy, she thought. She stripped down to her underwear quickly and chose a short, green-beaded dress first. Standing in front of the full-length mirror behind the door, she smoothed it down and tugged at the side zipper. When it didn't budge she took a deep breath and it finally slid up. She felt like a stuffed sausage and looked like one, too.

She stared at herself in disbelief. When had she gained this weight? She certainly hadn't been over-eating. Her hand rested on her stomach. It couldn't be the baby yet, could it? No. It had to be the dry cleaners. The dress must have shrunk.

She slipped out of it and found a long burgundy-velvet dress with an empire waist and low neckline. It fit perfectly, showing off one of her better assets, if she did say so herself.

She piled her hair high on her head and then with a laugh let it tumble down.

"Watch out, 'Darling' Brad. Here comes Ali Celeste."

Ten

Kevin Singleton had no sooner taken Ali's coat and bussed her cheek than she spotted Brad in the living room to the left of the foyer. He stood tall and looked extraordinarily handsome in a black pin-striped suit, white shirt and red tie—attire she was surprised he even owned, much less something in which he appeared completely comfortable. A new side of the man.

She tried not to stare at him as Michelle hooked her arm and led her to a spacious and elegant dining room. A large sterling-silver punch bowl graced the center of a beautifully decorated table loaded with trays of canapés, finger sandwiches, petits fours and every imaginable treat for the palate. Angled in the corner was a portable bar with a black-tuxedoed bartender busy at work.

Michelle stopped at the table. "Would you like a

cocktail, eggnog, or some of this non-alcoholic punch?'' She gestured at the ornate bowl.

''Punch, please.''

Michelle gave her a sidelong look, one eyebrow arched. ''Can't tempt you with something a little stronger?''

Ali smiled. ''I'm not drinking these days.'' If there had been a loudspeaker, her words couldn't have been more clear.

Michelle pulled Ali into an instant and tight embrace and whispered into her ear, ''I'm so happy for you, sweetie.''

Ali whispered back, ''I haven't told anyone yet.''

''I'm flattered, then.'' She poured a cup of punch and handed it to Ali. ''Would you like to eat a little something now or should I introduce you around?''

''I'm really not hungry just yet.'' She took a sip of the tangy punch and let Michelle take her down the hall to the library.

''By the way, if you need a good doctor,'' Michelle said, ''I highly recommend Dr. Wilson. He's on staff at Midtown, very well-respected, great bedside manner. I had some problems carrying the twins and he had all the answers.''

''Thanks. It's still kind of early, but I'll give him a call when the time comes.''

Someone spirited the hostess away and Ali drifted through the crowd of the sprawling Tudor home, offering holiday greetings to a few casual acquaintances and taking in all the decorated nooks and crannies. She stopped short of the living room, though, purposely not orchestrating a meeting with Brad. It would happen in due time.

A couple of towheaded little ones poked their heads

around the archway leading to the kitchen and Ali went to them, pleased with the chance to meet Abe and Abbie at long last. They were all decked out in red velour jumpers over white turtleneck sweaters and she wanted to squeeze them.

To think that someday soon....

Brad stepped up to the table for some hors d'oeuvres, and glancing casually to the left found who he was looking for. Ali was hunkered down in front of the twins, talking animatedly with them. They giggled at whatever she had said, and he thought what a natural she seemed with children. He guessed she had plenty of practice with the niece and nephew she'd mentioned, yet he knew that not every woman was that at ease with children, and the fact that Ali was left him with a strange sense of pride.

He bit into something he couldn't quite identify and continued to watch her, not sure why he felt proud of a woman who would just as soon spit in his face as say hello. He had positioned himself in front of the fireplace in full view of the door, hoping she would see him and come over. Was she waiting for him to take the initiative or had she planned to avoid him altogether?

Before he could make up his mind whether or not he should risk the long walk to her, Millie and Hazel clamped a hand on each of his arms.

"Dr. Darling!" Millie sang out.

"It's so good to see you, dear boy," Hazel said.

They engaged him in small talk as he surreptitiously eyed the hallway. Unfortunately or fortunately—depending on what happened next—the sisters turned him toward the hall just as Ali approached.

"Oh, my. Ali, my dear. You look absolutely stunning! Doesn't she, Sister?"

"Oh, yes. And I love your hair that way...all piled up on your head. Just beautiful."

"Thank you, ladies. You look lovely yourselves."

The sisters demurred then giggled before Millie said, "It was very thoughtful of you to send a thank-you note for the tickets."

At this Ali caught Brad's eye and smiled. Looking away she said. "We enjoyed them very much."

Millie glanced back at Brad, looking as if she wanted to say "Aha! I knew it," but she just smiled a satisfied smile instead. "Well, you two have a lovely evening now. Hazel and I were just making the rounds."

"We—Ow! Oh, yes. We were. Goodbye." They waved their diamond-clad fingers and hurried away, leaving Ali laughing as she turned to face Brad.

Brad let out a soft whistle and said, "Wow!" as he looked Ali up and down.

"Like it?"

"That doesn't quite describe it. But I like what's in it even more." He might be pushing things, but he couldn't help himself. It was true.

"Was that meant to sound as lecherous as it did?"

"Promise not to call me a sexist pig?"

She laughed easily, no sign of the residual anger he had expected.

"Promise."

"Then, yes. I could say more, but you might throw your punch in my face." She stepped closer and the familiar scent of her was intoxicating.

"No, I won't. Say it."

He let his gaze drop to her deep cleavage. "You

look good enough to eat." Then his eyes came up to meet hers, where they lingered as he struggled for the right words. "Ali...I'm so sorry. You were right. I had some old baggage to deal with."

She slanted her head. "And did you?"

He pushed his hair off his forehead. "God, I hope so."

"So do I. I'd hate to think it would get in the way again." She turned up the wattage on her smile and it was all he could do not to take her in his arms and kiss her until she couldn't see straight.

"Did I just win a 'Get out of jail free' card?"

"Let's just say you're on parole." She leaned into him and kissed his cheek, her breasts pressing against his chest. He caught her by the shoulders before she could back away and kissed her hard on the mouth.

He released her sooner than he wanted and he saw the shocked expression on her face.

"Aren't you afraid of what people might think?"

"Do you think there's a soul here who hasn't already figured it out?"

She trailed a hand down his cheek and looked at him so tenderly that he wanted to say things he had no right to say. At least not here, not yet. But sometime soon when she trusted him again.

"Does this mean we can leave together?" she asked, letting him know it was her wish.

"Whenever you're ready," he said, holding her hand.

"I'm in no hurry. I just wanted to know."

He kissed her on the ear. "Well, now you know."

He would have left that very moment, had she asked. She didn't, however. And it didn't take long for him to figure out that she wanted to slow things down a bit, to make sure everything was as it should be.

So an hour and a half later when she offered to drop him off at his place before she drove home alone, he was disappointed, but not surprised.

The surprise wouldn't come for another two weeks.

A fellow resident had traded Hanukkah for Christmas Eve, giving Brad this special night off. So now he sat in Ali's living room with his arm around her, and looked at the recently opened packages under the tree.

"I'm sorry I couldn't get you more, Ali."

She turned slightly and gazed up at him. "Don't be silly. This is the richest Christmas I've ever had." She cupped his chin and looked at him earnestly. "You've given me so much more than can be put under that tree."

"You're sweet for saying that," he said, feeling inadequate nonetheless.

Her face grew more somber and he sensed something was on her mind. He was about to ask her what, when she looked as though something had crystallized behind her eyes, as if a decision had been made and she was about to share it. He waited patiently, not having a clue as to what it could be.

"Brad...what's this season all about?"

"The commercial side or spiritual?"

"Spiritual."

"You mean, the birth of Jesus?

"Yes." She smiled sweetly. "The birth of a baby that would change all time."

An alarm sounded in his head. "Ali—"

She took his hand and guided it to her belly, where

she held it and closed her eyes, a single tear streaking down the side of her nose. Brad lost all feeling in his limbs. His heart raced as his mind went into denial.

"I'm happy about this, Brad. Everything will be okay."

He simply stared at her, suddenly seeing a stranger sitting next to him. She sounded as if she had wanted this all along, that it was part of the plan. There were no histrionics, no excuses. Just a calm, smiling woman.

Telling him she was pregnant with his child.

When he said nothing she opened her eyes and her smile disappeared. "Please, Brad. Don't be upset. I want this baby."

He was afraid to speak. Afraid if he opened his mouth he would vent the rage building inside him. Finally he took a deep breath and turned away from her. "Did it even occur to you that I might not?"

"Yes," she whispered, sounding disappointed.

He pushed off the sofa and paced in front of the window, wishing he could ram his fist into the glass. "For Pete's sake, Ali. I can't even buy you a decent Christmas gift or take you to a nice restaurant." He spun on her and stopped. "It will be years before any of that changes."

He raked his hair back with both hands, wanting to take her by the shoulders and shake her. Then he remembered the night they had made love, how he had wanted to use protection and she had stopped him.

He sat down again and glared at her. "I asked if it was safe, remember?" She nodded, and despite his resolve he shouted at her. "So what did you do in the bathroom? Comb your hair?"

"I—I used an ovulation test kit."

He slapped his thighs and stood again. "Oh, great. The rhythm method. Perfect. Well, you see how well that works."

When he turned back, Ali was standing. "Maybe you should leave," she said, her voice wavering.

He stepped closer to her, his chest heaving. He wanted to take her in his arms, which only made him angrier.

"I'm not asking anything from you, Brad. I was hoping maybe—"

"That maybe we could get married and live happily ever after? Ali, wake up. This isn't one of your romance novels. I barely have two nickels to rub together. And you see how little time off I have. It's not enough for you, let alone a child."

Without another word she walked to the door, her eyes on the floor, the silence as thick as the carpet beneath his feet. He grabbed his coat out of the closet, not wanting to go, unable to stay.

She opened the door and looked at him with the saddest eyes he had ever seen.

"I didn't want things to be like this," he said, feeling an obstruction at the back of his throat.

"Neither did I," she said, and closed the door softly behind him.

Ali spent Christmas Day at Lynne and Ken's. Barbara and Tom were in from California and the two little ones, Timmy and Keri, were a delight as they tore into their brightly wrapped packages, predictably finding more entertainment in the myriad boxes left behind.

Throughout the day Ali thought about next year when she would have a child of her own. As sad as she felt about Brad, she relished her secret and refused to get in the pits again. Screwy hormones or not, she had allowed herself to get down before; she wouldn't again.

Besides, in the deep recesses of her heart, she hadn't given up on Brad. She even understood his reaction last night. Maybe when he got used to the idea…

No, she scolded herself. She wouldn't place all her hopes on that. After all, her original plan was to have a baby and raise it herself. If that's what happened, so be it.

But after dinner, once the men and children were in the family room and the sisters were alone in the kitchen, Ali couldn't keep her secret another moment. She had decided today would be the day to tell them, a Christmas bonus of sorts. Now that it was time, though, her well-rehearsed words escaped her and she chose an uncircuitous approach instead.

"I'm pregnant," she said softly.

Lynne, who had been washing crystal, and Barbara, wrapping leftovers, stopped what they were doing and turned to her with mouths agape.

Ali kept drying the goblet in her hand and smiled, waiting for the shock to pass. Then they were all over her, hugging her and kissing her and rocking her between them.

"You must be so excited," Lynne said, brushing a tear away.

"I can't believe you really did it," Barbara said, shaking her head and laughing all at the same time.

Lynne took her hand and led her to the breakfast nook in front of the frosty bay window, where the three of them sat and giggled, reminiscent of younger years. After Lynne blew her nose, she said, "What a surprise. I didn't even know you went back to that place."

Ali averted her eyes and both sisters read the body language.

"Alexis?" Barbara began. "Is there something you're not telling us?"

Ali heaved a sigh and leaned back in her chair.

"Oh, no. Don't tell me," Lynne said. "The doctor... What was his name?"

"Brad." She knew it would all come out sooner or later and she was glad it was now. She had never kept secrets from her sisters and she didn't want to start.

"Who's Brad?" Barbara asked Lynne.

"He's a young resident at the hospital where Ali works. She's been dating him." Lynne said.

"A *doctor?*" Barbara said incredulously. "She's dating a doctor?"

"Hey, you guys," Ali finally interjected. "I'm sitting right here. You can talk to me about this, you know."

"Okay," Barbara said, facing her. "What's this Brad got to do with it?"

"He's the baby's father," Ali said, an unexpected pain shooting through her. This was a happy day with happy news, she reminded herself. She had to keep a rein on her emotions.

"Can I assume you don't mean through artificial insemination?" Lynne asked, seeming a little stunned.

"Yes," she said, hoping she wasn't in for a lecture. Barbara and Lynne exchanged a look that didn't escape Ali.

"I know, I know. But I thought he was the one."
Her voice cracked midsentence and she swallowed
hard.

"And he's not?" Barbara asked.

"The jury's still out."

Simultaneously they each took one of Ali's hands
and squeezed hard, and that was the end of her self-
control.

Once Ali regained her composure, Lynne said,
"Are you sure you're pregnant? I mean...have you
been to see your OB yet?"

Ali sniffed and wiped her eyes, coming away with
a tissue smeared with mascara. "I thought I'd wait
until I was a little further along. I just used one of
those home pregnancy tests."

"I don't know if I'd totally trust those do-it-
yourself things," Barbara said. "They're not always
foolproof."

"You have a point," Ali said. "I trusted my ovulation kit and it was wrong. I used it the day I—"
she glanced up sheepishly "—you know. And it said
I wasn't ovulating."

Lynne frowned. "So one of the tests has to be
wrong. Either you *were* ovulating that day...or you're
not pregnant now."

"Oh, I'm pregnant," Ali said, certain that she was.
"My body feels different and my waistbands are already getting tight."

They agreed with her that a woman knows these
things, and soon the subject shifted to baby showers
and fixing up the spare bedroom and all the joyous
things Ali had ahead of her. And the day passed with
more laughter than tears.

Later, on the way home, Ali counted her blessings,

still feeling the glow of her sisters' tender loving care. She was glad everything was out in the open. Well, almost everything. She pulled into her parking spot, shut off the ignition and thought of the one omission—she hadn't told them she'd used Brad's sperm before they had started dating.

She shrugged and got out of the car.

What difference could that make now?

Eleven

The next four weeks were the longest of Brad's life. How many times had he reached for the phone to call Ali? Yet he hadn't. He needed time to sort things out and curb his temper.

It was Thursday night and a mid-January sleet pelted against Brad's apartment window. He added weights to the steel bar, returned to the bench and pumped iron until beads of sweat burned his eyes and his arms began to quiver. With a heavy clank he nested the bar in place and swore.

How could she do this to him? Was it her plan all along? He had just convinced himself Ali was nothing like Valerie, then look what she pulled. Maybe she didn't need his money—or future money, as the case may be—but she obviously wanted something from him. But what? Simply to snag a husband? Was that why she let herself get pregnant? She had to have *let* it happen, after all, since he'd had the damn foil packet half open when she stopped him.

He wiped his face with a towel and swore again. He'd been over and over it again and again to no avail. Some way, somehow, she had deceived him. Yet she seemed so self-sufficient and self-assured, not at all the type who needed a husband just for the sake of having one.

He threw the towel down. Nothing made sense.

But then, when had anything about women made sense to him? Maybe he should stick to *fixing* human hearts rather than *understanding* them.

This line of thinking made perfect sense, he thought, going to the refrigerator for a Coke. He'd always been far more interested in cardiovascular medicine than psychiatric.

He took a healthy swig of soda and let his mind drift back to earlier today when Kevin Singleton had called him into his office. If it weren't for Ali's news, they would be celebrating this very minute. It wasn't every day that a guy is told he's the front-runner for a surgical residency sponsored by one of the Midwest's top cardiologists. If he didn't screw up in the months ahead, the job would be his by summer.

But he hadn't even told Craig yet. In his current mood, Brad thought it was wise to keep it to himself, at least until he got a better handle on things.

He finished the Coke and tossed the empty into a recycle bin under the sink. With a resigned sigh he folded his arms and leaned against the counter. There was only one way to handle things. Like it or not, he had to talk to Ali.

He paced to the phone before he could change his mind. It was ten-thirty and she answered on the third ring, sounding drowsy and far too sexy. Images of her in the bed they shared floated up, but just as fast he pushed them down.

"We have to talk," he said.

"Okay," she said tentatively, clearly waiting for him to say when and where.

Not his place, not hers, certainly not the hospital. Someplace away from downtown, very public, maybe even noisy where they couldn't be overheard—someplace he could dart in and out without much notice.

"Ever been to Alley Cat on Woodward in Royal Oak?"

"Been by it."

"I get off early Saturday night. Could be there around nine."

"Want me to pick you up?" she asked.

"I'll meet you there."

"Okay."

The silence stretched and he could hear her breathing. *Damn,* but he wanted to keep her on the phone, to hear the sound of her voice.

"Fine," he said, disgusted with himself. "See you then."

Saturday night, fifteen minutes late, Brad found the nearest parking space a block away and ran to the door of Alley Cat, wishing he hadn't left his coat behind. But when he pushed through the entrance a gust of hot air greeted him.

He'd heard this place did a brisk business, but he was surprised to see an elbow-to-elbow crowd. He'd wanted someplace public and crowded, but this was absurd. He'd have to shout to be heard. A vision of Ali screaming the word "pregnant" just as the band went on break and the room quieted brought a smile to his face, one that disappeared quickly when he thought of the gravity of what he had to say.

A tall urban cowboy with a big Stetson and bolo tie nudged him out of the way and Brad stumbled slightly to the right. Regaining his balance he threaded his way to the long bar where a tall, fair-haired bartender was pouring drinks with both hands and talking with patrons. He smiled when he noticed Brad step up to the bar.

"Howdy," he said. "What can I get ya?"

"A draft would be fine." Brad glanced at the name tag—Jake Alley. "You own this place?"

"Yep," he said proudly. "Bud okay?"

"Perfect. Man, you really pack 'em in here."

"That's the idea," Jake said before moving down the counter. Brad looked around, still not seeing Ali. Jake returned with a mug of beer and Brad plopped down a five and waited for change.

"Hey, cowboy. What you doin' in this neck of the woods?"

Brad turned with his mug and nearly spilled it down Ali's denim shirt. She wore jeans and boots, and looked right at home. "Thought you'd never been here."

"I haven't. But it doesn't take a rocket scientist to know the appropriate outfit." She looked him up and down, lingering on his running shoes. "Well, at least you're wearing jeans."

He was about to debate the relevance when he noticed the mug of amber brew in her hand. She started to raise it to her lips and he caught her wrist. "You shouldn't be drinking that stuff now."

She gave him a sidelong look, then smiled. "It's non-alcoholic."

He let go of her. "Oh." He glanced around, wishing there was a table to put between them. This close proximity and her all-too-familiar perfume was sidetracking him, making him forget he had an agenda and that he should stick to it.

"I don't suppose you have a table?" he asked.

"Afraid not." She was eyeing him over her mug, as much as saying "The ball's in your court."

A guy at the microphone said, "Okay, folks. We got a new number to teach you. Here's a chance for all you first-timers to learn a few steps. Come on down. Don't be shy."

Ali looked from Brad to the dance floor and back before she hooked an arm behind his elbow.

"Oh, no." He shook his head vigorously. "Not me," Brad said, digging in his heels.

Ali released her hold, took his mug and deposited it alongside hers on the bar. "Jake." The bartender turned. "Okay if we leave our drinks here a few minutes?"

"Sure thing."

She took Brad's hand and started for the dance floor. Her fingers laced in his felt so damn good he forgot for a moment he was angry with her. And the next thing he knew he was in a row with others, stepping to the right, stepping to the left, kicking and turning. His shoes didn't shuffle and stomp like the others, but he doubted anyone noticed.

The instructor picked up the pace and it was all he could do to keep up. He looked at Ali and worried. Leaning into her he said, "You sure you should be doing all this strenuous stuff?"

She tucked in her chin and eyed him as much as to say, "You've got to be kidding." When she saw that he wasn't, she said, "You're a doctor. You have to know it's okay."

"It's different when—" The line turned and his back was suddenly to her.

She leaned over his shoulder and said, "When you're the father?"

The father. He didn't like the tingle of excitement these simple words evoked. The line changed direction again and Ali messed up a step. Brad wondered if she did it on purpose to make him feel better. She laughed and kept going and he found himself doing the same. It was that or get run over by the six-foot-five wrestler type on the other side of him.

They finished practicing the steps as the music started and Brad was swept along with the crowd. He wasn't even a fan of country-western music, he chided himself. How on earth had he let this happen? He flubbed a step and scrambled to find his place, laughing despite himself.

Just as fast as one number ended, another began and Brad kept stepping and stomping and laughing, and so did Ali. Suddenly the band shifted gears and a slow number began. Before he could regroup, Ali stepped into his arms and cuddled close. It was then he threw in the towel. To hell with his agenda. She felt good. Real good.

While others two-stepped around the perimeter of the floor, Brad held Ali close and stayed in the center, her body molded to his, swaying slowly to the music. He could cut himself at this moment and he doubted he would bleed. The sum total of his blood supply had been summoned to the area south of his belt. For the life of him he couldn't think of a single reason for not holding Ali in his arms. There wasn't any blood left in his brain *to* think. That was the problem.

But when another fast number started he finally took her hand and led her back to the bar where they collected their drinks.

Ali smiled at him and said, "You wanted to talk to me?"

He took a long swallow and motioned to Jake for a refill. "Yes, I did." She inched closer, a slightly smug look on her face. "And stop trying to distract me," he added, smiling down at her.

She stood so close he could feel her breath on his neck. "Oh? Am I distracting you?"

"More than that, and you know it."

Her eyes danced with mischief. "Should I be sorry?"

He wiped the smile off his face. "I don't know. Should you?"

She stopped smiling, too. "What do you mean?"

"Did you lay a trap for me, Ms. Celeste?"

She made a humphing sound and backed away. "Oh, right. I always dreamed of a life with a doctor and losing my virginity to a man who would walk away the morning after and never look back." She took a swallow of her drink, the expression on her face one of hurt more than anger. Maybe she *hadn't* intentionally gotten pregnant, yet she sure didn't seem troubled by it, either.

He waited for her to look back at him. "Ali...I care about you. I truly do. But—"

"But you don't want to be saddled with a wife and kid. Fine. I'll manage." She finished her drink and slapped the mug on the counter. "So what did you want to tell me tonight?"

"I want to help you."

"How?" She was all business now.

"Well, child support, for one."

"I don't need your money." She folded her arms and glared at him. "What else?"

"Whether you want it or not, it's my responsibility and I'd like you to hear me out." She drummed her fingers against her elbows and waited. "If we could agree on a fair amount, I thought maybe we could keep a running account of the balance and then after I start making some real money, I could make extra payments each week until the debt is paid."

"Until the 'debt is paid'? You make this sound like another of your student loans."

"Ali, be reasonable. I'm just trying to help."

"Well, you're not. You're making it worse." She was grinding her teeth, yet in spite of her angry tone, he noticed tears teetering on her lower lashes.

"Speaking of money," she said, lifting her chin, "I hope you didn't stop your visits to the clinic just because of me."

"I didn't. I mean...well, I'm still going. On Saturdays."

"Oh," she said, her voice dropping.

"On second thought, maybe I could give you that money," he said. A tear escaped and she brushed it quickly from her cheek. He opened his arms to comfort her, but she stiff-armed him in the chest.

"Let me repeat, Brad. I don't want your money. And I sure as hell don't want your pity." On that note she turned and pushed her way through the crowd, toward the exit. He slapped more money on the counter and ran after her.

Through a hole in the crowd he spotted her at the door, yanking her coat from the rack. She kept moving, never looking back. Brad bulled his way through couples blocking his path and ran out the door. He pivoted on the sidewalk, looking for blond hair blowing in the frigid winds, or a car moving in the lot, anything.

Nothing.

He beat his hands against his arms and stomped his feet to keep warm, his eyes ever busy. Snow impaired his vision and he watched as an unfamiliar car spun out of control on the icy road in front of him.

Damn. Ali shouldn't be driving on a night like this. He gave up his search and raced to his car. Sitting behind the wheel, he pumped the pedal and cursed out load.

"Well, Darling. You sure handled that one well."

The rear end of her car spun dangerously close to the next lane and Ali let up on the gas. With both hands gripping the steering wheel she regained control and then let out a loud sigh of relief.

Stupid, stupid, stupid. She'd let that man rattle her again. Why had she thought if he just saw her again he would soften his position? He wanted to be a father about as much as he wanted to double his student loans.

"Money," she said with disgust. Everything seemed to be about money. She had more than enough and he had none. If it were the other way around would it be such a problem? Probably. Then he would think she was after him for his.

Maybe it was time to accept Plan A. Even though
her original plan of having a child and raising it by
herself was an okay one, she had to admit Plan B
would have been better. If only she hadn't allowed
herself to get so carried away, to hope for more. Her
body ached for the nearness of him, even now. And
one little slow dance had only fueled that need. It felt
so natural, so right to be in Brad's arms. They fit so
perfectly. She remembered another time, another fit,
and her vision started to blur again.

The windshield wipers struggled to keep up with
the heavy snow and Ali slowed to a crawl, her mind
searching for a thread of hope. Something still bugged
her about this money issue and she couldn't quite put
her finger on it.

She thought about it all the way home until she
reached her apartment and made a careful turn off
Jefferson, stopping when she pulled into her parking
spot.

And then it hit her.

Thanksgiving. Her apartment. He had assumed she
was living beyond her means. Even when she had
assured him she wasn't, she hadn't really told him
how well off she was. Past experiences had taught her
not to. Maybe it had been a mistake not to tell Brad
the rest. What irony if he thought she was after his
future earnings. Could this be part of the "baggage"
he'd referred to? Perhaps someone else had been too
impressed with the income he could one day provide.

Almost laughing she sprang from the car, knowing
exactly what she would do. It might not work, but it
was certainly worth a shot.

Twelve

Energized by her new idea, Ali arrived early for work on Monday morning, went right for the hospital directory and found the name Michelle had recommended: Dr. Lawrence Wilson, Obstetrics and Gynecology. She thought a moment, then dialed the number. It was only the first of February and she was barely two months along, but she was eager to have her findings confirmed.

The secretary answered and Ali asked for an appointment.

"Have you seen Dr. Wilson before?" she asked.

"No. This will be my first visit."

"For OB or GYN?"

"OB," Ali said, feeling as strange and excited as she always did whenever she thought about truly being pregnant.

"Doctor likes to allow more time for the initial visit. How far along are you?"

"Two months."

"Oh, then we have some time." Ali could hear the flipping of pages, and then the secretary asked, "How's two weeks from today at four thirty?"

She was hoping for sooner, but this would work. "Fine."

Ali gave her name, address and insurance information, then hung up just as the first client of the day signed in.

The day raced by, busier than usual, giving her little time to think about Brad and her idea, but later, once she was home, he was the only thing on her mind.

She stood in front of her bedroom closet and shed her too tight-fitting pants, along with panty hose she swore she wouldn't ever wear again. She eyed her comfortable long terry robe, then changed her mind. Before she could lose her nerve she rushed to the phone on her nightstand and punched in Brad's home number, half hoping he wouldn't be there so she would have an excuse to procrastinate a little longer.

She was about to hang up on the fourth ring when Brad answered, sounding winded.

"Did I call at a bad time?"

There was a pause and Ali's heart raced. Was there another woman with him?

He exhaled loudly and said, "No. Just let me catch my breath. I was at the bottom of the stairs talking with Sally when I heard the phone ring."

She let out a breath of her own, still feeling tense. Even the sound of his voice and breathing excited her.

She'd never felt this way about a man. What was it about this one that left her tongue-tied?

"I—I was wondering…if it's okay—" *Damn! Spit it out, Celeste.* "I'd like to come over."

"Now?"

"Yes."

"Okay."

"See you in about a half hour." Ali hung up the phone and raced back to the closet, trying not to get too excited. What she had to tell him might make no difference at all.

But then again, it could.

Something loose and comfortable, she told herself, sliding hangers left to right. A simple, long-sleeved, cotton-knit dress caught her eye and she slipped it from the hanger. Perfect. No waist, mid-calf and not in the least bit sexy. They had business to discuss. Certainly he wouldn't think she was there to seduce him wearing this. Just to be sure she put on a pair of matching purple slouch socks and a pair of beat-up white sneakers.

Twenty-five minutes later, Ali stepped up her pace from the parking garage to Brad's building, telling herself she was shivering from the cold rain and not the prospect of facing the man who had become too important to her.

Sally smiled and waved enthusiastically as Ali passed the big picture window. Ali waved back and then marshaled her courage as she mounted the steps.

Brad heard her and opened the door. "Hi," he said, stepping back for her to pass.

She stood riveted in the doorway. With a towel draped around his neck, he wore thin blue nylon shorts and nothing else. The black hair on his chest glistened; the loose strands on his forehead were wet. Ali's breath hitched in her throat.

He tugged her inside and shut the door behind her. "I was just working out." He gestured to the weight bench. "It helps me release tension." He took her coat and hung it over his, looking far more relaxed than she felt.

Ali clutched her big leather bag, knowing she must look like a fragile octogenarian fearing a purse snatcher, yet she couldn't help but think of the papers inside and worry whether she was doing the right thing.

"Would you like a cola or anything?" He went into the kitchen and took one out for himself, popping the top and waiting for her answer.

"N-no, thank you." She wished he had more clothes on. He wasn't making this easy. As always, his eyes were locked on hers, never straying.

"Come on. Let's sit down." He positioned himself at one corner of the sofa, turned sideways and crossed his legs.

She didn't know what she had expected, but certainly not this, not after the way she'd stormed out of Alley Cat. He actually seemed glad to see her.

Ali stepped out of her wet shoes by the door, then moved to the opposite end of the sofa, as far from his nearly naked body as she could. He smiled at her and waited patiently, which she found most disconcerting.

"I—I've been thinking about things," she began. "And, well…there's a lot we don't know about each other…that maybe we should."

"What do you want to know?" He draped his arms over the back and end of the sofa and widened his smile.

His simple question caught her off guard and she struggled for an answer. She knew what she had come to tell him, but yes, there were things she would like to ask him, as well. Finally she chose what she thought would be a safe place to start. "Tell me about your family."

"One older sister, Mary Beth. She and her family live in Florida. My dad died several years ago and my mom's been living with Mary Beth since her stroke." He took a sip of cola, and she could see he was debating whether to tell her something else.

"Dad was a truck driver until his sight got so bad he had to retire early. Mom used to do a little sewing work out of the house. Things were always tight, but we had everything that really mattered. When I start making more money I plan to send some down to them. Mary Beth's husband doesn't make much and they've been shouldering all of Mom's care and expenses."

Another piece of the puzzle fell into place. No wonder he was so concerned about money, as if his student loans weren't enough.

"What about you?" he asked. "Tell me more about your mother."

"Mom was a full-time homemaker—a great one, too. She was a gourmet cook and even though she could afford help, she always cleaned the house and did everything herself. I found out later that she had invested every spare dollar she could. Like I told you before, that was her real talent...that and being a mother. I couldn't have hoped for more in that department."

"But the same wasn't true for Dad, right?"

She hadn't planned to talk about her father, but

now that Brad had asked, she thought it might help if she did. "I overheard him tell a colleague once that I was a mistake...you know, a change-of-life baby. And that's pretty much how he treated me."

"Oh, Ali," Brad said, and shook his head with such a tender look on his face that it brought tears to her eyes.

She let out a sardonic chortle to hide her pain. "Funny thing...he was an OB-GYN. The births of other babies lined his pockets, while I, on the other hand, was merely an inconvenience." She realized she was making herself out to be a martyr and she changed her tone. "Anyway, he was never around. Worked nights and weekends or played golf when he didn't. Mom never complained. She defended him right up till the end...when he ran off with that woman...someone whose age was less than her bra size, not to mention her IQ, though Mom would never say that."

Brad nodded as if everything made sense now. "And so all doctors are pond scum."

She allowed a small smile. "I thought so, yes."

"Past tense?" he said, dimples bracketing his mouth.

"Well...yes." His smile was warm and too adorable.

"I like this getting to know each other business."

He drank more cola and seemed to be waiting for her to keep the ball rolling. She hated to risk ruining the mood, but there was no better time to ask. "You said you had some old baggage to deal with—"

"Ah, that." He took a moment to gather his thoughts. "Her name was Valerie. It was a long time ago...when I was still in med school. I should have seen the warning signs when she introduced me as Dr. Darling long before I earned the M.D. Whenever I'd worry about all the new clothes she seemed to have or the new car or whatever, she'd assure me she made good money and got everything on sale, that I shouldn't worry.

"Then one day she forgot her purse at my place…and well, I'm not proud of it, but I snooped. Turns out she had more than twenty charge cards. A couple of past-due bills showed balances in the high five figures. When I confronted her about it she said, 'What's the big deal? You're going to be filthy rich someday and we can pay everything off then.' I don't think she ever understood why that didn't sit well with me.

"Anyway, I haven't dated much since. The couple times I did, my dates always wanted to know what I would be specializing in and I could imagine a calculator working in the back of their heads."

It was Ali's turn to nod her head. "So when you saw my apartment—"

"Exactly."

This was the cue she'd been waiting for. She opened her purse and pulled out a manila envelope. "Brad—" Already his blue eyes were smiling at her, saying he knew she was different from the others. Perhaps she didn't need to do this, but she had come this far. "I've done my best to conceal whatever money I have…probably for the same reasons you're leery. I don't want someone looking past me for my money. I've never shown anyone this, except my broker. But I thought it might help if you knew." She handed him the envelope and he took it, a crease furrowing his brow.

"What is this?"

"Just look it over. Take your time." She stood and walked to the kitchen for a glass of water as he opened the envelope and pulled out the contents. Leaning against the counter she watched as he flipped through the pages of her portfolio and his mouth dropped open.

Finally he let out a low whistle. "Ali! There's over a quarter million dollars here!"

"Most of it my mother left me, but I've been able to add a decent amount." She walked around the sofa and sat back down. "I told you she taught me a lot about the market."

His look was incredulous. "But, Ali—" He ran his fingers through his hair and simply stared at her.

"So," she said, trying not to appear smug, "do you still think I'm after your money…or that I have some romantic notion about the medical profession?"

He shook his head slowly. "No…on both counts." He slid over and returned the envelope. "Thank you for trusting me with this."

"You're welcome," she said, putting the envelope back in her purse and setting it aside. When her hands were free, he captured them in both of his.

"Is there anything else you want to ask me?"

Was there? With Brad touching her, it was difficult to concentrate. "I don't think so." His eyes left hers for just a moment, but long enough that she thought something was still on his mind. "How about you?"

He opened his mouth to speak, then stopped.

Ali squeezed his hands. "Brad, you can ask me anything."

"This is awkward," he started. "When we made love…"

"Yes?"

"Well, you said you were a virgin, so I was expecting—"

Ali nodded. "Oh, that." She hadn't planned to tell him about her visit to the clinic tonight, but perhaps now was the time. She took a deep breath and began. "The doctor broke it when—"

Brad cupped a hand over her mouth. "I'm sorry. I never should have brought it up. I trust you, Ali." He lowered his hand and slid closer. "Thank you for coming tonight, for telling me everything."

Ali reached for her purse and started to stand, but he caught her wrist and stopped her.

"You're not leaving, are you?"

"I'll let you get back to your workout."

He didn't let go of her. "Stay. Please?"

She studied his handsome face. "All right, but please finish your workout."

"While you watch?"

"I guess so," she said, eyes cast down as she felt her cheeks grow hot with embarrassment.

He laughed, then so did she. He didn't have a clue how sexy he was in those shorts or what fantasies she already had about that narrow black bench.

"Okay, then. Let's get on with it." He took her hand and tugged her off the sofa, leading her over to the weights. Then he lay down on the bench and flashed her a smile. "You could help, you know."

"How?" She was truly stumped as to what she could do.

"When I get tired it's difficult to keep my back flat. I tend to arch it, which isn't good. Why don't you sit on me?"

From the corner of her eye she gave him a dubious look. "What are you up to, Darling?"

"Exercise. What else?" His grin said more.

She didn't care what he was up to, so she hiked up her dress and straddled his waist. "Like this?"

His dimples deepened. "Perfect." Then he reached overhead and gripped the steel bar. He took a few deep breaths and expelled them before he hoisted the heavy bar.

Ali watched the muscles straining in his arms and chest. He had a physique that rivaled any cover model's.

He lowered the bar and it clanked in place. Then he lifted it again as she traced the ridges and planes of his beautiful body. He said nothing and kept pumping, but under her she knew she felt something else. She carefully shifted her weight, the thin fabric of her panties growing moist as she slid slowly down the firmness of him. Brad groaned and the weights clattered to a halt. His hot hands trailed slowly up and down her inner thighs and she let out a groan of her own.

She looked down and saw the familiar swell of him and her heart beat faster. With a light, feathery touch she traced the bulge in his shorts until his hand pressed hers down harder. With more audacity than she thought she possessed, she lowered his waistband and stared at his perfection.

Brad sat up and cupped her face in his hands, his mouth suddenly on hers, his tongue mating with hers in a way she wanted other parts to do. She kissed him back with such hunger that it left no doubt what she wanted.

His hands trailed down to her breasts and he

worked her nipples through her clothes. Then, without removing her panties, his fingers pushed the narrow strip of fabric to one side and dipped inside her. When she thought she could take no more, he lifted her bottom and slid himself gently inside her.

He took her weight and let her inch down him at her own pace. He filled her so totally, so perfectly, that she wondered how she had managed to go so long without him. But when he thrust his hips into her, all thought was replaced with pure ecstasy.

With his arms wrapped tightly around her, he lowered his back to the bench and took her with him, their mouths exploring each other once again. The kiss was long and wet and punishing, desperate in its need for more, never satisfied. Finally, Ali pulled back, gasping for air, and Brad kissed her neck and whispered in her ear.

"You drive me crazy, Angel."

Then he started to pull out of her and she was confused. But only for a moment. Barely inside her, he rubbed the ridge of himself over and over her, dipping a little deeper, then returning to the same tender spot, until finally silver streaks scattered behind her tightly closed lids and an uncontrollable shudder left her weak and breathing hard against his chest.

Brad moved deeper and faster and she floated on a blissful sea of total abandon. With his hands clutching her bottom, he drove into her one last time and she felt him go rigid beneath her. His breathing was as labored as her own as he held her tight.

Then suddenly he sat up, taking her with him and arching his back. "This bench isn't as comfortable as it was a few seconds ago." He kissed her forehead then hugged her to him. "Oh, Angel. I'm just glad you came over."

"Me, too." She kissed him playfully on the shoulder, then retreated to the bathroom. When she came out, Brad was leaning against the counter drinking some water. He handed her the glass and she downed what was left, feeling completely void of fluids. He refilled the glass and slipped an arm around her shoulder.

"I have to be back at the hospital in less than an hour."

"Oh. Then you'd probably like a little time alone to rest."

"No. Please stay." His eyes traveled down her and stopped at her stomach. He set the glass aside and turned her toward him. He stared at her waist and frowned before his warm hand came to rest on her belly. "You're starting to show already."

Ali glanced down, enjoying his intimate touch, knowing that just below was the child he had given her.

"Isn't it a little early?"

"Is it?"

He shrugged. "Not my specialty. What does your doctor say?"

She picked up the glass and drank a little more, wondering how he truly felt about the baby. "I haven't seen him yet. I have an appointment with Dr. Wilson in two weeks."

Brad took her hand and smiled at her. "By the looks of things, I'd say we don't need him to confirm you're pregnant."

Ali smoothed her dress over her belly, surprised that it indeed was obvious. "Maybe I've been eating too much lately. I always put on a couple pounds during the holidays.'' She looked up at Brad and winked. "Speaking of which...I'm famished. Let's go get a pizza. My treat.'' And maybe in a public place with a table between them they could talk about what lay ahead for them and the baby.

Brad laughed and circled his arms behind her. "This dating a rich woman has its advantages.'' He kissed her once lightly on the mouth, then came back for a slower, deeper one. "Mmm...you taste good,'' he said, leaning closer. Into her ear he whispered, "Don't you have anything at home in your refrigerator?''

His mouth returned to hers before she could answer. She felt herself melt against him and mumbled, "Uh-huh,'' as she wrapped her arms around his neck.

"I could wait and eat later at the hospital.'' He kissed her neck, one hand kneading her breast.

"Could you?'' she whispered, her breathing already jagged.

He unzipped the back of her dress and raised it over her head, releasing her bra a second later. He looked at where her panties should have been and she said, "They're history. I left them in the bathroom.''

He chuckled as he stepped out of his shorts. "I think you should leave the socks. They turn me on.''

Feeling brazen, she gripped him in her hand and stroked his silky firmness. "Oh, is that what did this?''

He lifted her and carried her to the sofa.

"Most definitely. It had to be the socks.''

Thirteen

Just past midnight Brad pulled Craig aside in Exam Room Three. "I'm in the mood for a pizza. Wanna go half?"

"Sounds great. I gotta gash to the forehead in One and dementia in Two. All I have to do is get Psych down here and stitch up One. Should be done in plenty of time."

"Everything but anchovies?"

"And peppers. Can't handle them, either."

"Gotcha."

Brad placed the order and was suddenly swamped again. By the time he joined Craig in the lounge, a quarter of the pizza had disappeared.

"Man, am I hungry." Brad laid into a slice as Craig plunked a can of Coke down in front of his friend.

"You can see how I waited for you."

"Mmm-hmm," Brad mumbled, his mouth already full. Well into his third piece, he decided it was time for a little fishing expedition.

"You worked with Wilson for a while, right?"

"Yeah. Top-notch guy. Really knows his stuff. You're not thinking of going into Obstetrics, are ya?"

Brad shook his head and kept eating.

"Good. The hours are crap and malpractice insurance for OBs is right through the roof."

Brad wiped his mouth with a napkin and avoided Craig's eyes. "Someone said she's going to Wilson, so I was just checking." He took a swallow of Coke, decided to go for broke, and asked the question that was really bugging him, even if it led to other questions. How he'd kept Craig in the dark about Ali this long was a mystery.

"How far along before the patient usually starts to show?"

Craig leaned back and rubbed his stomach. "Hmm. I saw more third-trimester patients than first. Is she heavy or trim?"

"Trim."

"Oh, I'd guess by four months, some sooner, some later."

"As early as two and a half?"

He shrugged. "If she had another kid not long before, she might pop out fast. Yeah, it's possible." Craig folded his arms and gave Brad a sidelong look. "What's this *really* about, guy?"

Brad felt the need to talk with someone and Craig was the logical choice, but still he dreaded his friend's sure reaction.

"You gotta swear you won't breathe a word."

Craig leaned forward, elbows on knees. "Okay, okay. I swear."

Brad tossed an unfinished piece of pizza back into the box, his appetite suddenly gone. He let out a long sigh and looked over his shoulder to be certain no one else was around. Back to Craig, he said, "It looks like I'm going to be a father." He could have said he was considering a sex change and Craig's expression couldn't have appeared more stunned.

"I didn't even know you were dating!" he said when he recovered. "Anyone I know?"

"Ali," he said, and took a swig of Coke.

Craig hiked his eyebrows. "When did this start?"

"Soon after we met."

"And you're just now telling me?"

"Well, it's been on and off. Right now it's on." He picked off a piece of pepperoni and braced himself for a lecture.

"Hey, man, I know you haven't dated since the Stone Age, but didn't they have little foil packets back then?" He ran his fingers through a tangle of unruly red hair and looked as though the problem was his. "You're a doctor, man. And a broke one, to boot. How did you let this happen?"

Brad could hear himself saying the same thing if the situation were reversed, so he took the criticism on the chin. "How or why is a moot point, wouldn't you say?" He stared at his shoes and waited for the inevitable.

"Wait a minute. You say she's two and half months and already showing? How do you know—"

Brad shook his head. "I know." She couldn't have faked such innocence. Now he wished he hadn't brought up the subject.

"So...ya gonna marry her or what?"

"The subject hasn't even come up."

"But ya gotta know she's thinking it. What woman wouldn't?"

He was probably right, but until tonight the pregnancy hadn't seemed real. It had even occurred to him that Ali could have been wrong, that when she saw a doctor he would tell her she wasn't pregnant, after all. But when he took a close look at her belly...

The beeper on Craig's belt went off. He looked at it and stood. "Gotta run." He paused and said, "Get rid of the doubts, guy. Go with her to see Wilson." Then he patted Brad on the shoulder on his way out the door. "We'll talk later, okay?"

"Sure."

Alone in the lounge Brad thought about what Craig had said. Surely other new fathers went with their wives for the first exam. Problem was, Ali wasn't his wife and she might not want the gossip. But the gossip would come either way. An unmarried woman working at Midtown? Sure grist for the mill.

He was paged a minute later and before he knew it the sun had come up on another morning. At seven-fifteen he wandered down to the cafeteria for breakfast and a much needed cup of coffee. He read the paper and killed time until seven-fifty when he headed down the hall to the clinic.

Ali was just coming through the door and her face lit up when she saw him. He looked around and, seeing no one, went to her and held her tight. "Morning, beautiful."

"This is a pleasant surprise."

He kissed her quickly and stepped back, seconds before a pair of nurses rounded the corner and eyed them suspiciously. When they passed, he said, "I'm on my way home, but wanted to catch you first." He leaned closer to her ear. "Guaranteed sweet dreams this way."

Ali smiled as they walked behind her desk and she hung up her coat. He noticed she wore a loose-fitting jumper and he remembered Craig's suggestion. Before he could debate his decision, he asked, "What would you think about me going with you to see Wilson?"

She bit her bottom lip in that adorable way of hers and once again he felt guilty for his duplicity.

"You want to do that?" She seemed genuinely touched.

"Yes."

"I'd love for you to go with me."

A client approached her desk and Brad stepped out of the way. "Good." She gave him a sweet smile before he turned and walked away.

The day had finally come and Ali was a nervous wreck. It was after four and the last client was still in the back. Ali had cleared things with her boss to leave early for her four-thirty appointment with Dr. Wilson, but now the final minutes dragged on.

She was eager to see the doctor, especially since she had been feeling strange for about a week now—nothing painful, just an occasional fluttering that concerned her. Lynne had had a miscarriage at about this stage and Ali couldn't help but worry that something might be wrong. More than ever, she was happy Brad would be with her. Just in case.

She chastised herself for having negative thoughts and, checking her watch again, focused on Brad's interest in the baby instead. They still hadn't talked about the future, but she thought the mere fact that he wanted to accompany her today was a good sign.

Besides, they had plenty of time. There was no reason to rush things.

At four twenty-five the last client left. Ali locked her desk, grabbed her coat and caught the elevator to the fourth floor. When she walked into the waiting room Brad was already there reading an article in *Parenting* magazine, and her heart skipped a beat. She could never see him without this reaction, but here, like this...

She had to blink hard to keep from crying—which seemed a common occurrence these days.

He looked up as she approached and his killer smile made her insides turn to mush. She wondered if he had any clue what effect he had on her.

"Hi," he said.

"Hi. Let me sign in. I'll be right back." She could feel his eyes on her as she crossed to the counter. She completed the necessary paperwork and shortly after they were escorted to a room.

The nurse handed her a paper gown and turned to Brad. "Would you like to wait in the doctor's office until the exam is complete?"

Ali interrupted. "Is that necessary? I was hoping he could stay."

"If you'd rather—"

"Yes." As an afterthought she glanced at Brad and he nodded.

"Okay, then. The doctor will be right in."

Ali turned her back to Brad and stripped quickly, feeling a little self-conscious. She slipped into the gown and Brad tied it at the neck for her.

"Very sexy," he whispered.

She laughed, expelling some of her mounting tension. She didn't know why she was so nervous. He was her lover, the baby's father, and even a doctor. Nothing was about to happen that he hadn't seen before. Still, there was a vague uneasiness that was growing with every passing second. So much so that by the time Dr. Wilson entered the room Ali was about to scream.

"Ali, I'm Dr. Wilson. Nice to meet you."

She took his hand. It was dry and his shake was firm yet gentle. She started to relax a little. He turned to Brad and glanced down at his name on his breast pocket.

"Dr. Darling! We've met before, haven't we?"

"Yes, some time ago. I'm a friend of Craig Miller's."

"That's it. And how's Craig doing? I was sorry to lose him to E.R."

"Great, great."

Wilson looked down at the chart in his hand and then shared a look between the couple. "So, Dr. Darling…your interest in this is—"

"I'm the baby's father."

The simple admission brought another lump to Ali's throat.

Thankfully the doctor made no judgments and quickly asked her a few questions. She told him of her irregular periods and ovulation problems and then about the strange way she'd been feeling recently, which caused a look of surprise to cross Brad's face. She hadn't wanted to alarm him unnecessarily.

Finally, Wilson buzzed for a nurse to come in while he examined Ali. Brad walked to the head of the table and Ali reached back for his hand. He squeezed it and then stroked her hair gently as Wilson made small talk with her and did his job.

Finally she heard the snap of his latex gloves as he removed them and tossed them into a wastebasket. He tugged the sheet down over her knees and patted them.

"You can sit up now, Ali."

The nurse left and the doctor stayed seated on the stool at the end of the table.

Ali studied his face and felt her heart race. Something was wrong. She thought Brad must have seen it, too, because he came alongside the table and put a hand on her shoulder.

"Well," the doctor started, "everything looks good."

"But?" Ali asked, and she felt Brad's fingers dig deeper.

"But you're not two and a half months pregnant."

She stared at him, not knowing what he was saying. She *had* to be pregnant. She was so certain—

"No, I'd say more like *four* and a half."

Brad's hand dropped from her shoulder.

"B-but—"

"With your irregular cycle it was an easy mistake to make. And those flutters you mentioned? Well, my dear, that's your baby reminding you he or she's there."

The doctor stood, all smiles, not having a clue as to the impact of his news. "I'll schedule you for an ultrasound next week. Then you'll see just how big your little one really is. In the meantime, you two have to decide whether you want to know the sex of the baby then. Depending on the positioning, we'll probably be able to tell.''

When neither of them said a word, Wilson said, "Do either of you have any questions?"

Ali couldn't look at Brad. What must he be thinking?

She shook her head at the doctor and with his hand on the doorknob he said, "When you come out, the nurse will give you a booklet that addresses the basics—vitamins, exercise, diet, what to expect at different stages. If you have any questions or problems, feel free to call me anytime. Otherwise I'll see you in a month." He nodded goodbye to Brad and left the room.

For what seemed an eternity Brad didn't move or speak until Ali found her voice. "I know how this must look, but I can explain—"

He stepped around in front of her and glared at her. "I'm sure you can. You're very convincing, Ali. You had me fooled every step of the way."

She watched his jaw muscles flexing and she wanted to reach out to him. "Please, Brad, I—"

"Don't," he interrupted. "Nothing you can say will change the facts. You led me to believe I was the only one, that I was the father. Obviously neither is true."

"But—"

"I know you want this child and I'm sure you'll be a good mother."

He glanced at the door and she knew he would be walking through it soon. "Brad—"

He looked back at her one last time, the hurt in his

eyes so apparent that she couldn't control the tears any longer.

"Goodbye, Ali. I wish you luck."

He slipped from the room quietly and she buried her face in her hands.

Fourteen

Ali spent Saturday night alone in her apartment. After several breathless bouts of racking tears she called Lynne and told her everything.

As always, Lynne offered up a healthy dose of TLC and in the end extracted a promise from Ali that one way or the other she would tell Brad the rest of the story. Regardless of the outcome, he deserved to know the truth.

She hung up feeling a little better and made herself a cup of herbal tea. When she sat and drank some of the hot liquid her body finally began to relax.

And then she felt the fluttering.

She set the tea down and pressed both her palms against her belly and waited. There it was again, a little stronger. Her smile turned into giggles and then to tears of joy. This was what she had wanted all of her life. A child to love and nurture and call her own.

Almost an hour passed with Ali still sitting at the table, feeling the life inside her and wishing Brad was here to share this moment. And while she sat there she decided how she would tell him the rest of her story. There would be no more unexpected visits to his apartment; nor would she bother him at work. She would explain everything in a letter the best she knew how and then let the chips fall where they may.

She wasn't fooling herself; she wanted Brad in her life. Yet she wasn't going to hold a gun to his head. And she wasn't going to hang all her hopes on him coming around and wanting more anytime soon. Even if all he wanted was to see their child later, she would be grateful for that and never stand in his way.

But Lord, how she prayed he would want much more.

Over the next three nights Ali wrote and rewrote her letter. Friday morning, when she thought she could do no better, she sealed the envelope and mailed it to Brad's apartment on the way to work, assuming he would receive it in the morning. Now the worst lay ahead—waiting and wondering what he would do with the new information, and trying not to stand by the phone.

Late Saturday night, after twenty-six hours on duty, Brad climbed the steps, let himself in and flopped on the sofa, where he stayed until Sunday morning when the pager on his belt vibrated, summoning him back to the hospital. He slept there that night and would have the next if he hadn't needed fresh clothes.

Close to midnight Monday he stopped at his mailbox at the bottom of the steps and extracted a couple day's worth of junk fliers mixed with a few envelopes that he hoped were also junk and not more bills. Once inside his apartment he dumped the whole pile next to the sink, thinking he'd feel better after he had something to eat and a shower.

There was tuna fish salad in the refrigerator. He made a sandwich and found some stale chips and ate both propped against the counter. He stared at the pile of mail, not in the mood to deal with it, until he noticed the edge of one envelope with something handwritten on it.

Curious, he pulled it out and opened it. Without skipping to the end of the multipage letter he knew who the sender was. A part of him wanted to wad the whole thing into a tight ball and send it sailing across the room. A bigger part made him read on.

When he had finished he stood there stunned.

Could she be telling the truth? Or was she a pathological liar with more imagination than Hollywood?

He slammed the letter down and headed for the shower, wide awake now and furious. He stepped under the spray without waiting for the water to warm and swore out loud.

How in the hell was he supposed to know the truth? If he waited until the baby was born and tests proved he was the father, then he would have missed these important months with Ali and she may never forgive him. Yet if he believed her and she was lying, he would be devastated later.

Last Monday at Wilson's office had been painful enough. He had given up fighting his feelings for Ali, but he hadn't realized how real the baby had become to him—only for the rug to be pulled out from under him so unexpectedly.

"Damn that woman!" he shouted, turning off the

water and yanking back the curtain. What was he going to do now?

The weekend had been the longest two days of Ali's life and by Monday night she was certain Brad must have received her letter and rejected her explanation.

Work was her salvation and thankfully she found herself busier than usual. And in the evening she began reading from the stack of child-care books she had purchased, using a Hi-Liter, making lists of things to purchase, and in general relishing every detail.

It was only when she went to bed that she couldn't control memories of Brad. Thursday night, with another long weekend fast approaching, she tossed and turned, unable to fall asleep.

If only she had told him earlier, she thought, maybe he would have believed her. She remembered she had started to tell him the night she had gone to his apartment, but somehow the conversation had gotten diverted.

On and on a litany of what-ifs churned in her head until the alarm sounded and she staggered into the bathroom. She considered calling in sick and returning to bed, but today was the ultrasound and already the excitement of seeing actual pictures of her precious little one gave her the burst of energy she needed.

Somehow she got through the next eight hours. And now, at day's end, Ali was lying on the hard examining table, staring at the blank monitor to the left of her and waiting for the doctor to come in.

Behind her she heard the door open and she turned to greet Dr. Wilson.

Brad shut the door behind him and took a tentative step closer. Ali fixed on his conflicted face and held her breath.

He looked at the monitor, refusing to meet her eyes. "I don't know if I should be here or not," he began.

She wanted to say it was enough that he was, but was it? She didn't know what to make of this unexpected appearance.

Before anything else could be said, Dr. Wilson swept into the room. "You two ready for some interesting movies?" He opened a tube of jelly and Ali shivered as he spread the cold goop over her belly. Without waiting for an answer to his first question, he asked another.

"How are you feeling? Eating and sleeping okay?"

Ali averted her eyes. "I feel fine," she said, deliberately avoiding any mention of sleep.

"Good, good." He turned to Brad. "You can see better if you come around the table by Ali's head."

Out of the corner of her eye Ali watched as Brad took Dr. Wilson's suggestion. She wondered if the doctor would find it strange that she and Brad weren't speaking to each other, nor were they touching. But when the doctor started working an instrument over her belly as if it were a computer mouse, all of her attention went to the screen of strange shapes and jiggles.

"Uh-huh. Just as I thought. You're about twenty weeks along, Mom." Suddenly he lifted the instrument and said, "Oops."

A fistlike grip constricted Ali's heart. "What? Is

something wrong?'' Brad moved closer and took her hand.

"I didn't mean to alarm you," Wilson said, sharing his smile with the two of them. "The baby is positioned so that you can clearly determine the sex. I forgot to ask you if you want to know."

Ali let out a loud sigh of relief and she heard Brad do the same. She had vacillated back and forth on the doctor's question all week, but if it meant not seeing pictures today, she knew she couldn't wait.

She braved a look at Brad. "I want to see." She didn't need his permission, but she was hoping he would agree.

He held her gaze with those intense blue eyes of his and she knew he was asking questions of his own. *Could he trust her? Was this really his baby?*

She didn't so much as blink, hoping he had found his answers.

Squeezing her hand, he turned to the doctor. "Yes. Let's have a look."

The doctor lowered the instrument and began rolling it again. Pointing to the screen he said, "This is the head. And here's the heart."

Brad's thumb worked the back of Ali's hand and she found herself overcome with emotion. Moisture blurred her vision. She sniffed and with the back of her free hand dried her eyes.

Dr. Wilson traced a finger down a long line. "This is the umbilical cord, which means this—'' he pointed to a smaller line just below "—is not." He glanced up and smiled. "Looks like you have yourself a boy in the making."

Brad's thumb stilled on Ali's hand and she gazed up at him. His eyes, also brimming with moisture, were trained on the screen. Tears escaped from the corners of her eyes as she tightened her hold on Brad. Finally he tilted his head back before looking down at her. And in that instant she knew that regardless of whatever else might happen, they now shared a bond that would never be broken.

A son. A helpless little boy who would someday soon rely on the two of them to provide all his needs.

"I can print out a couple pictures, if you'd like."

Ali nodded, unable to speak. She watched the shapes on the screen, what looked like little arms and legs continuously moving, and it seemed her heart might burst through her chest. If the baby hadn't seemed real before, it did now.

She was going to be a mother.

And the man who held her hand would be a father.

With this reality she suddenly realized something else—how very selfish her thinking had been. She had been so blinded with her desire to have a baby that she hadn't thought enough about what she would be denying her child if he didn't have a father as part of everyday life.

Well, she told herself, feeling fiercely maternal, there was still time to change that. Pride be damned. If there was any way she and Brad could be the traditional parents this baby deserved, she would find it. It may take time and patience to make things right, but she had plenty of both when it came to their child.

Dr. Wilson handed them each a black-and-white picture. "Take your time and enjoy. If you have any questions I'll be right outside." He left and the room grew silent.

Ali stared at the picture in her hand and struggled

to find the right words for Brad. She couldn't let this moment slip away without reaching out to him.

"Brad, I—" Her voice sounded hoarse and she cleared her throat. "I swear to you...I'd even take a lie-detector test if you wanted...this is *your* son."

"Ali—"

She heard the wariness in his voice and she interrupted. "I'm sorry I didn't tell you about the insemination earlier. I didn't mean for it to be a secret. Honest."

He turned around and sat on the edge of the table, looking for all the world as though he wanted to believe her. She took a deep breath and said what her heart told her. "I—I think I fell in love with you the first time I saw you."

He looked surprised at her bold declaration and for a moment she wondered if she'd made a mistake in telling him. But then she remembered her new resolve and she stopped worrying about herself. There was someone far more important to consider.

"This baby needs you, Brad. *I* need you."

He shook his head at her last words. "You don't *need* me, Ali."

"Okay. Maybe 'need' is the wrong word. I *want* you."

He stood slowly and set her hand down gently beside her.

"You deserve a husband, Ali. The kind of man who comes home for dinner every night, who has the weekends off." She shook her head from side to side, but he kept talking. "Someone who can contribute to the household income, who isn't so deep in debt."

She could feel him slipping away and she found herself growing angry with his resistance. "If it makes you feel better, you could pay half the rent on my place. And if the student loans bother you that much I could pay them off tomorrow and we could be done with it.''

His mouth settled into a tight, straight line. ''How do you think that would make me feel?''

''Try relieved,'' she said stubbornly.

He ground his teeth a moment then said, ''I haven't even accepted the fact that this is my child and already you want me to take your money. You can't buy me, Ali. No matter how much you want a husband and father for your child.''

''You arrogant bastard.'' She felt tears streak down her cheeks and she wiped them away angrily. ''I'm not trying to buy anyone. I was simply trying to solve a problem. Excuse me if I offended your delicate ego, Dr. Darling. Try not to trip on it on your way out the door.''

He glared down at her, looking as though he would like to strike her. Without saying another word he left the room, slamming the door behind him.

Ali sat up, wiped the gel from her belly and dressed in a flurry. She placed her precious photo inside her purse and practically ran down the hall, taking the steps instead of the elevator to the first floor. She continued her pace to her car and then pounded on the steering wheel all the way home, wishing it was Brad's puffed-up chest instead.

It wasn't until she was seated at her kitchen table with a glass of apple juice that she calmed down and realized what she had done.

She stared at the photo in her hand and then traced the outline of her baby. ''I'm sorry, little guy. I guess I have a lot to learn about patience, don't I?'' She drank some juice and felt a wave of regret for her harsh words.

"I think we're going to have to give your daddy some more time to think about things. He's really a good man, you know. And even if he hasn't admitted it yet, I think he loves us, too."

Fifteen

It was the end of March and a late snow blanketed the city. When the snow turned to ice on the freeways, traffic accidents added to the patient load of slips and falls and gunshot wounds, and every cubicle in the emergency room was filled, with more gurneys lining the hallways.

Brad worked through the night Friday and finally finished his charts at nine on Saturday morning. He was exhausted and badly in need of a shower and shave and a good night's sleep, but something had thrummed through him all night long, keeping the adrenaline flowing.

Today he would deal with that something once and for all.

He jogged the few blocks to Trapper's Alley, hopped the People Mover to the Renaissance Center and then ran the rest of the way to Ali's apartment.

There was no energy to rehearse his words, let alone sort them out. It didn't matter. She'd just have to indulge him.

He pounded on the door, still breathing hard from his run. He knew she would be looking through the peephole in her door any second now and he set his face in a no-nonsense look. He started to knock again when the door swung open.

She wore a long chenille robe with the sash tied above her bulging middle and he couldn't help but stare at her changed body. Her hair was sleep tousled, and she looked sexy, even at six months pregnant.

He brushed by her without an invitation, putting her appearance out of his head.

"Would you like some coffee?" she asked, seeming too calm about his unannounced visit. He had hoped for an element of surprise. Instead she acted as though she'd been expecting him.

"No," he said curtly. She poured herself a cup and sat on the sofa, motioning with a sweep of her hand for him to join her. He ignored her gesture as well as her serene smile, choosing to pace in front of her instead.

He strode the length of the showcase window and turned back before he spoke. "You've ruined it for me, you know." He glanced at her, looking for some sign of anger, but she merely sipped at her coffee and eyed him evenly. He continued pacing, refusing to be affected by her cool demeanor.

"I used to love my work. I gave every waking moment to it and never resented a second." He pushed the hair off his forehead and paused to glare down at her. "Now I'm distracted all the time. I think of you and wish I was here. Damn it! I can't even lift weights anymore without thinking of you. Nothing…absolutely nothing…is the same now. I find no peace. Anywhere!''

Ali simply sat there, poised and quiet, infuriating him further.

"Okay, look—" He inhaled deeply and blew out a loud breath. "I've come to a decision."

"Yes?"

He sat on the edge of the sofa as far from her as he could. "I'd like us to try to work things out…no matter whose baby it is. The baby will be yours and that's enough for me." He watched her now and waited, her face inscrutable.

"I see," she said. She set her mug on the table in front of her and folded her hands in her lap.

"'I see'?" he repeated. "Is that all you have to say?"

"That's kind of you, Brad, but it's not enough."

He sprang from the sofa and thrust his arms out to his sides, letting them drop with a slap to his thighs. "What do you want from me, Ali?"

She looked up at him patiently. "Everything."

"Can you be a little more specific?" The woman was driving him crazy.

"To begin with, total trust. If our relationship isn't based on that we may as well build castles in the sand."

"I trust you," he said, ready to explode.

"If you did, you wouldn't be questioning the father of this baby." She ran a hand tenderly over her belly. "I told you you were the father, but still you doubt me. Maybe you even think I slept with someone else, which I never did."

"And how in the hell am I supposed to know that

for sure without blood tests? Tell me." He started pacing again, no resolution in sight.

"I had hoped you knew me well enough to know that I would never lie to you about something so important...about anything, for that matter. I had hoped in your heart you would know the truth."

With effort she pushed off the sofa and walked toward the door. Her hand rested on the knob, sending the clear message that she would like him to leave.

Brad growled and strode to the door. "I came here hoping we could come to an understanding. At the very least your son deserves a father."

"*Our* son, Brad," she said, correcting him. "Yes, he does. But I'd rather raise him alone than with a man who didn't trust his mother."

Brad fought the urge to shake some sense into her...and another urge to forget words and pull her to him, kissing her as she'd never been kissed before.

Through clenched teeth he said, "It won't be easy raising a son alone. You're going to regret this someday, Ali."

The cool look in her eyes softened. "I already do, Brad. But for our baby I have to be strong. I can't compromise on something so fundamentally important. Every child deserves unconditional love, and if the father isn't sure about things...well, it just won't be right."

Brad pounded his fist against the door and she flinched. "Damn it, Ali, under the circumstances don't you think you're asking an awful lot of me?"

She nodded, her eyes growing shiny. "Yes, I am."

She opened the door slowly and Brad stared at her for the longest time, his breathing labored, head pounding. Then he turned on his heel and left.

Ali took her coffee mug to the kitchen and rinsed it out, forcing herself not to dwell on Brad's surprise visit and glad that her day would be busy. She had just enough time to shower and dress before Lynne picked her up for lunch and then shopping.

Today she would buy the baby's crib and other large items she needed for the nursery. Nothing, not even Brad, would detract from the joy of this special day.

He still had time to come around, she told herself, slipping out of her robe. But once in the shower, she let the tears flow, knowing she would feel better if she didn't hold them in. And after a few minutes she did feel better. In her heart she knew that holding out was the right thing to do. For all three of them.

She only prayed that she wasn't holding out for the happy ending that may never come.

The baby shower at Lynne's a month later was everything and more than Ali expected. Barbara and her family had moved back in time to be there and she and Michelle struck up an instant friendship. Both of Ali's sisters were enamored with Millie and Hazel, who had dropped so many hints that they wanted to be included that Ali had made sure they received an invitation.

A few cousins and old friends rounded out the cozy group, all of whom were oohing and aahing over all of Ali's gifts while Lynne handed each woman a piece of cake and Barbara refilled coffee cups.

But it wasn't until everyone had left, except for Michelle and her sisters, that Ali was given one of the biggest surprises of the day.

Michelle sidled up next to Ali as she wiped a

counter down and said, "I have a proposition for you, if you're interested."

Ali didn't have a clue. "About what?"

"I don't know what your plans are for work after the baby, but I could really use some help with my business. I'm getting referrals I'll have to turn down unless someone wants to help me." She smiled, having made her point obvious.

"Me?" Ali was surprised and more than a little excited.

"You're familiar with a lot of the systems I set up. You're especially good at database work and I could teach you web design, too, if you'd like."

She wasn't all that crazy about her job at the clinic and it wasn't the most stimulating experience she'd ever had. It had definitely outlived its purpose.

Ali fired off a rapid succession of questions and learned that about twenty hours a week was all that would be required, and best of all she could work at home and be with the baby. When Michelle stated the hourly fee she had in mind, double what Ali was making at the clinic, the deal was made. Ali decided she would give a two-week notice Monday morning.

At least that was the plan.

Brad had no sooner fallen asleep Monday morning than his beeper vibrated. Without sitting up, he opened one eye and squinted at the E.R. number and the emergency code added to the end.

He groaned and struggled to an upright position, questioning whether he would be of any value to anyone as tired as he felt. This thing with Ali had deprived him of the little rest he got, to the point that he felt like a zombie and prayed he wouldn't make a mistake in his diminished capacity.

After splashing cold water on his face, he hiked the short distance to Midtown Hospital and soon after punched the button that opened the doors to Triage. Craig saw him coming and pulled him aside.

"What's so urgent you had to drag me back here?" Brad said, sounding as irritable as he felt.

"I thought you'd want to know—Ali's in Number Eight."

Brad ran down the hall without waiting for an explanation, not sure what he would find. He yanked back the curtain with such force that Ali raised her head off the pillow with a start. Then she settled back and he could see she'd been crying. Even now her bottom lip quivered and she bit it.

Brad clasped her hand in his and rubbed her arm. "What happened?"

"I—I think the baby's coming." A tear rolled down from the corner of her eyes. "Brad...it's way too early."

"Shh. Try to relax, Ali. It could be a false call. These things happen all the time, you know."

She stared at him, wanting to believe him.

"What does Dr. Wilson say?"

"I just got here. He hasn't been in yet."

"Any bleeding?" he asked gently, running a proprietary hand over her belly, his heart racing. She shook her head. Suddenly he felt something beneath his fingers and he went very still.

"What?" she said, looking alarmed.

"I felt something."

Ali nudged his hand aside as she felt for herself. Then she relaxed against the pillow again. "I think it's a foot. He does that all the time.'' She smiled sweetly at Brad and it was all he could do to control the mix of emotions surging through him.

''This is a very good sign,'' he said, holding her steady gaze. Then finally, feeling like a jerk, he admitted to himself what he had known for some time. This woman was not a manipulator, nor a liar. The baby that moved under his hand was his. He'd never been more sure of anything in all his life.

He let go of Ali's hand as he used both of his to feel the son whose life he prayed would not be cut short. Worry gripped his chest and heart as chapters from prenatal textbooks flashed through his head.

''Let me go see what's holding up Wilson. And we'll get a fetal heart monitor hooked up just to be sure. I'll be right back.'' He started to turn and Ali gripped his arm.

''You believe me, don't you?''

Brad bent down and kissed her lips softly. ''Yes, Angel. I'm sorry I ever doubted you. Now let me go so I can get some help for our son, okay?''

She nodded, tears streaming down her pale cheeks, and he darted from the room.

Wilson was already in the hall studying her chart and Brad practically accosted him. ''How about a monitor? Want me to get one? I'll get it. Be right back.''

Wilson stopped him. ''Hey. Slow down. One's already coming. Why don't you go wait in the lounge and try to relax. I'll come talk to you when I'm finished examining Ali.''

''But I—''

Wilson grabbed an arm and turned him around.

"Look, Brad, I've got a job to do, and quite frankly, Dad, you're in the way. Now go."

Brad did as he was told, but he didn't like it. He wanted to be with Ali and their son.

He dropped heavily into a plastic chair at a long table in the lounge and buried his head against his folded arms, trying to slow his heart rate, desperately searching for the calm under pressure he had come to expect of himself.

This time it wasn't there.

This time it was different.

He prayed with simple words, words that, like a mantra, replayed over and over. *Please, God, save our son... Please, God, save our son... Please, God, save our son.*

He felt a warm hand on his back and jerked upright, turning his head. Craig stood next to him, concern written on his normally mirthful face.

"Has something happened? Is Ali—"

Craig sat down. "I don't know a thing, guy. Wilson's still with her. Just thought you could use a little company. Are you all right?"

"I'm fine," Brad said, exhaling a long breath. "I'm just worried about Ali and our baby."

Craig smiled and looked askance at Brad.

"If there's anything amusing right now, I sure wish you'd let me in on it."

"Suddenly it's 'our' baby. When did you come to this conclusion?"

Brad pushed out of his chair and headed for the coffeepot, filling a cup before he turned to face his friend. "I don't know. I just know it's true." He shook his head. "I haven't a clue how we're going to work this out, but somehow we have to. And soon.

No matter what happens to—'' He couldn't put voice to his worst fears. "The timing might stink, but another Ali will never come along."

"Man, you got it bad," Craig said, chuckling.

"Maybe I can get a loan against future earnings. Maybe Singleton can give me a letter or something I can take to the bank."

Craig's pager went off. He slapped Brad on the shoulder and said, "Good luck, man. Let me know if there's anything I can do."

Brad drank his coffee and was about to refill the cup when Wilson came in. His smile seemed genuine, his body language was relaxed, and Brad released a breath.

"The baby's fine, Brad. Looks like Ali has a simple case of intestinal flu. Easy to mistake all the cramping. She's running a little fever, so we'll admit her and keep her overnight…push liquids, keep the monitor on the baby. But I'm sure she'll be fine. Probably go home tomorrow."

"Thanks, Doctor," Brad said. Then feeling a little embarrassed he added, "About earlier, I—"

Wilson waved a hand. "Doctor or no doctor, when it's your kid you're a father first and a doctor a distant second. Don't give it a second thought."

He breezed out of the room and Brad fell against the counter and offered a prayer of thanks. It was time to regroup. He had a lot of making up to do with Ali and if she was up to it, maybe now was the time to start.

But where? And then he remembered what he had said about a possible loan. He had the day off.

Maybe...yes! He dumped his cup and raced back to Ali's bed where he found her sound asleep. Perhaps by the time he returned, he would have the good news he wanted.

Sixteen

———

After a frustrating hour with the hospital credit union and an equally nonproductive visit to the bank where he kept a checking account with a whopping three-digit balance, Brad returned to the hospital feeling defeated.

He stopped at Patient Information and got Ali's room number and then trudged down the hall to the elevator, deprived of sleep as well as solutions, the latter taking a greater toll.

On the third floor Ali sat propped up in her bed drinking a glass of Gatorade, her eyes bright. "Hi, handsome," she said with a smile he hadn't seen in ages, one that warmed his sagging spirits.

He tried not to let his fatigue and depression show as he went to her and hugged her tight. "You had me worried. How are you feeling?"

"With the exception of frequent trips to the bathroom—which isn't all that unusual these days—I feel much better.''

He stepped back and felt her forehead. ''Still a little warm.''

''Not so bad,'' she said. ''As long as I know the baby's okay, I can handle anything. I was just so worried.''

''I know, sweetheart.'' He sat on the side of the bed and held her hand.

''Did you mean it earlier when—''

He kissed her cheek and she fell silent. ''I have so much lost time to make up for.'' He glided his hand over her belly, hoping to feel some movement, but nothing happened this time and he was disappointed.

Before he could say more, Ali's eyes widened as she stared past him. He turned to see a huge bouquet coming through the doorway, almost floating in of its own accord. But then it came to rest on the side tray and Millie and Hazel stepped from behind it.

''Oh, they're just beautiful,'' Ali said, her cheeks suddenly flushed. And Brad mentally kicked himself for not thinking to bring her anything. What a clod she must think he was.

''You really shouldn't have. My goodness. I've never had such a big arrangement. Thank you both so very much.''

''You're welcome, dear,'' Hazel said before Millie started dragging her out the door.

''We'll leave you two lovebirds alone,'' Millie said, sharing an approving smile with the young couple. ''Be back later, dear. Toodle-oo.''

Ali leaned to one side of the bed and sniffed the flowers. ''They are such dears, aren't they?''

Brad couldn't meet her eyes.

"Brad? What's wrong?"

"I'm the one who should have brought you flowers."

She reached for his hand and returned it to her belly. "You've given me a far more precious gift. And now that you know this is your son...well, everything is perfect."

Except he couldn't afford flowers, let alone the ring and future she deserved, at least not for a couple of years.

"Why so glum?" she asked.

"Every time I picture the three of us crammed in my little apartment...with you and the baby alone a lot...I see you miserable."

"Who says we have to live at your place? What's wrong with mine?"

He shook his head. "I can't afford it, Ali. And I can't have you supporting us."

"It won't be forever." She ducked her head down, forcing him to look at her. "Later you'll be making big bucks and I'll let you pay all the bills, if it will make you feel better."

"You make it sound like it's no big deal."

"It isn't."

"Ali, you just don't understand—"

"No, I don't, Brad." There was no mistaking the annoyance in her clipped words.

He had to make her see his side. "The surgical residency under Singleton is practically a shoo-in. In two years we could have the big wedding I'm sure you always dreamed of and then—"

She sat higher in the bed and pushed his hand away. "Let me get this straight. You want me to give up a perfectly good two-bedroom apartment to simply *live* with you?'' Her look was incredulous.

''Just until I can afford—''

''Get out!'' she shouted.

''Ali, come on—''

''Unless you want to be wearing this vase on your head, I suggest you leave.''

''I know you don't feel well. This was a bad time to—''

''Now!'' she yelled, reaching for the flowers.

He held up his palms and got off the bed. ''Okay, okay. I'll come back later and we'll talk.''

She folded her arms tightly under her breasts and stared out the window. ''Don't bother.''

Brad turned and left the room feeling worse than when he'd entered. And making matters even more difficult, he bumped straight into a pair of eavesdropping sisters. He gave them a disapproving look, but they didn't seem fazed.

''What is the matter with you, young man?'' Millie wagged a bony finger inches from his face.

''I beg your pardon?'' he said, pushing her hand away.

''Indeed you should.''

''You should beg Ali's pardon, too,'' Hazel piped in. ''We didn't mean to overhear, you know, but we couldn't help it. We were just waiting to see Ali and things got kinda loud.''

Millie was in his face again. ''Tell me something. If you were already making lots of money and Ali wanted to wait a couple years to pay off her debts, how would you feel…what with a little one coming anytime now, hmm?''

''That's different—''

"Why? Because you're a man and you always have to make more to feel comfortable?"

"You tell him, Sister!"

Millie backed Brad against the wall. "Don't you know that if money can fix it, it isn't a problem?"

"That's right." Hazel nodded vigorously.

"Now cancer, that's a problem. Or Alzheimer's."

"Or ingrown toenails," Hazel added, and Millie gave her a disgusted look. "Well, they hurt."

If he thought it wouldn't encourage them, Brad would have laughed. Despite his mood, it was difficult to take offense with this well-meaning if not eccentric twosome.

"Anyway," Millie continued, "if it's money you got your shorts in a knot over, we could loan it to you and you could pay us back when you're a successful cardiologist."

Brad slanted them a disbelieving look.

"We know you'll be working with Dr. Singleton soon. The whole hospital knows it."

"Dr. Singleton hasn't offered me—"

"Oh, pshaw," Millie said, waving a hand. "Simply a formality and you know it."

"So what about the loan?" Hazel said.

"It's very generous of you, ladies, but I don't think you realize how big a debt—"

"How big?" Millie pressed.

He couldn't believe he was talking about this standing here in the hallway, but he could see they were hell-bent on a conclusion, so he thought answering the question would be the easiest way out. "Over a hundred grand."

The sisters looked at each other and began to laugh.

Then Millie said, "Is *that* all? Petty cash, young man."

Hazel tapped a finger on his chest and looked at him sternly. "You're a fool if you let Ali get away. A good girl like that don't come along every day, you know."

Millie fished a card from her apron pocket. "Here's our number. Call us when you come to your senses. By the way, we were thinking a balloon note with no payments for three years, longer if you need it. Oh, and we won't say a word to Ali about this. She needn't know where the loan came from unless you want to tell her." She pressed the card into Brad's hand, then the pair brushed by him and headed for Ali's room.

Brad sagged against the wall, his mouth agape. He didn't quite know what to make of the offer. A part of him wanted to be offended over them sticking their noses in where they didn't belong. Another part wondered if they were loony tunes and even had that kind of money.

But the biggest part said he was far too exhausted to make a rational decision. A few hours' sleep and he would rethink things and see Ali again.

He told Ali's nurse where to find him if there was any change in her condition, and then he went in search of an empty bed, still unable to shake the angry look he'd seen in Ali's eyes.

She had to know how he felt about her. Surely she—

With a mental thump to the forehead he suddenly realized he had never told her—not in the words any woman would want to hear.

He found a bed and dropping onto it he muttered aloud, "Darling...you are one stupid jerk."

Shortly after dawn Brad was reading Ali's chart when a call came down from Singleton's office that Dr. Darling was to go up immediately.

Brad punched the elevator button and thought about the past few days. Had he done something wrong? He'd been so tired and distracted lately he could have overlooked something. Yet by the time he reached the doctor's secretary and identified himself, nothing had come to mind.

"Doctor's expecting you. He said to go right in."

Kevin Singleton stood and extended a hand across his desk before motioning to Brad to have a seat.

"I know how busy you are, so I'll come right to the point." He rocked back in his leather chair and steepled his fingers, seeming to take Brad's measure before he continued.

"If you're still interested in the surgical residency, it's yours."

Brad sat there nonplussed. He hadn't expected to hear one way or the other for a few months. And then he wondered why the offer came now.

"Thank you, Doctor. Yes, I'm most definitely interested. But—"

"But?" Kevin leaned forward and rested his elbows on the desk.

"I have to ask...does this have anything to do with—"

"—with your being the most talented candidate I've had in years?" He smiled kindly. "Nothing else counts, Brad. You're the man for the job. If the timing is good, all the better."

Brad puffed out his cheeks and expelled a long stream of air. "I don't know what to say."

Kevin stood. "I do." He reached across the desk for another shake. "Congratulations."

Brad pushed out of his chair, overwhelmed with the unexpected good news. "Thank you, Doctor. I can't tell you how much I appreciate this."

Kevin clasped his other hand on top of Brad's. "We'll talk details later. I just thought you'd like to know."

It was all Brad could do not to kick up his heels as he strode back to the elevator. When one didn't come quick enough he ran down the stairs, knowing the first person he had to tell. But when he got to her room the curtain was pulled around her bed and his heart leaped to his throat.

He paced outside, tempted to go in, but forcing himself to wait. He tried to hear what was going on. Nothing.

With his hands jammed into his pockets he felt the business card placed there last night and he knew with certainty what he would do after he saw Ali. He passed by the door again and prayed. *Please, God, don't let anything be wrong.*

And then Wilson pushed the curtain back and Brad could see he was smiling. "The baby's fine, Ali. You can go home now, but it might be best to take the rest of the week off."

Brad released a long breath and walked in. Wilson clapped his shoulder as he passed, the ever-present smile fixed on his face.

"She's all yours, Dr. Darling."

Brad hoped Wilson was right. Was she? By the

piercing look in her eyes he could see he had his work cut out for him.

"How do you feel?" he said, moving within striking distance.

She crossed her arms. "Fine."

"Mind if I sit down?" he asked, beginning to lower himself onto the side of the bed.

"Yes. As a matter of fact, I do. I'd like to get dressed and go home, so just tell me whatever it is you have to say."

"Okay." He glanced out the window and then back. He hadn't had time to rehearse and it would probably come out all wrong, but it was time to cut to the chase.

"I love you, Ali, and I want to marry you."

She stared at him for the longest time before the set of her mouth relaxed. Then she said, "Okay. You can sit down now." There was a glint of a smile in her eyes.

He took her hand in both of his. "Ali Celeste...will you marry me?"

"When?" she said, looking a tad suspicious.

"In as many days as it takes to get a license." Still she wasn't celebrating.

"Is this because of the baby?"

"Oh, Ali. You have to know I'm crazy about you. Maybe this is happening a little faster than I expected, but no...I didn't ask you because of the baby. I can't imagine a life without you."

At last she flung her arms around his neck and he felt tears wet his cheeks—his or hers, he wasn't sure.

After a moment she said, "We can live at your place till things get better. I don't care. I just want us all to be together."

He sat her away from him, relishing the next part of his news. "I don't think that will be necessary."

"What do you mean?"

"Singleton offered me the job this morning."

She squealed and pulled him to her again, laughing and crying at the same time. "Oh, Brad. That's wonderful. I know how much you wanted it. I'm so proud of you." Then she sat back and looked confused. "But how does that change things...I mean for now?"

"I'm getting a balloon loan. No payments for three years. By then it shouldn't be a problem." He loved the look of joy on her face and the fact that at last he had been the source of it. "Now. About the wedding. When and where, Angel?"

She gave him an impish grin, then said, "If it's okay with you, and you can get the time off, how about two weeks from Saturday? Michelle has offered their home and Millie and Hazel said they'd help me with the arrangements."

It was Brad's turn to be surprised. "You had this all worked out?"

"Well," she said, color rising in her cheeks. "You know...just in case."

He threw back his head and laughed as he cradled her in his arms.

Seventeen

"**I** look like a beached whale," Ali said, staring at her full-length reflection in Michelle's bedroom mirror.

"No, you don't," Lynne said, fussing with Ali's veil. "You look beautiful."

"I'm fat."

"No, you're not. You're eight months pregnant."

Ali turned sideways and groaned at her profile. "Even the baby doesn't like this dress. He's been complaining for over an hour."

"He probably wishes you would stop worrying about everything and relax."

"Maybe," she conceded.

Barbara entered the room and closed the door behind her. "Everything's ready downstairs. Are you, baby-sister?" She rushed over and gave Ali an air kiss so as not to spoil her makeup. "You look absolutely radiant."

"I've been telling her that for an hour, but she doesn't believe me."

Ali felt the tears welling up again and she grabbed a tissue before her mascara could run. "I'm so glad you're both here. I just wish Mama was."

"She's here, sweetheart," Lynne said, and Barbara nodded.

Ali smiled, realizing they were right.

Barbara headed for the door. "I'll go down and tell them to start the music, okay?"

Ali took a deep breath and let out a nervous laugh. "Okay."

When they heard the baby grand piano begin the familiar music, Lynne preceded Ali down the long winding staircase trimmed in white satin ribbon and gardenias. Halfway down Ali wished she had gone to the bathroom one more time. The pressure low in her belly was fierce, making her feel as though she were carrying a sack of potatoes upside down and that it was about to burst any second.

But then she saw Brad's handsome face, his intense blue eyes riveted on hers, his tender smile saying how much he truly loved her, and she forgot all about her physical discomfort. This was the day she had always dreamed of...the man she thought she would never find. She had to be the luckiest girl in the world.

And as they stood before the minister, amid the heady scent of white roses and in the presence of all those they held dear, they faced each other and the vows began.

Brad spoke loudly and clearly, his voice steady and

sure. Ali drank in each word, memorizing each moment, and then it was her turn.

She arched her back, trying to relieve the pain she'd felt there off and on all morning. She repeated after the minister, her breathing now coming in short bursts. Beads of perspiration wet the hair on her forehead and she felt the room begin to spin. She clutched at Brad's hand with both of hers as she slipped the ring on his finger.

Somewhere in her haze she heard, "You may kiss the bride."

Brad leaned forward just as Ali bent and clenched her belly. "Oh, no. Oh, God."

Brad took her by the elbow. "What is it?"

She lifted the hem of her dress and they both stared at the telltale stains on her satin shoes and the carpet below. "My water broke." A contraction brought her to her knees and she cried. "Oh, Brad. It's too soon."

"Oh, my," Hazel said. "She's going to have the baby right here." Hazel swooned and Millie pointed her toward the door.

"Oh, no, you don't," Millie said. "No passing out on me this time. You already did that trick at Michelle's wedding." She ushered her sister outside for some fresh air, while the minister looked dazed.

"Here, you need to sign the license," he said.

Ali started to stand when another contraction hit her, this one harder than the first. She held tight to Brad and scribbled her name on the line right under his. Looking up at her new husband's worried face, she felt hot tears streak down her cheeks. "Should they be so close?"

Brad pivoted to Craig. "Get your van and bring it

to the front. Someone call Bon Secours and tell them we're on the way.''

Ali wiped her face with both hands and said, "Not Midtown?''

"Sorry, honey. There isn't time.'' To Kevin he said, "Call Wilson and tell him to meet us there.''

Brad helped Ali to the nine-passenger van and settled her onto the middle bench seat. Kevin came running out with his black bag in hand and said, "Wilson's on the way.''

"Great.'' Brad looked from Ali to Kevin. "In case we don't get there in time—''

"What do you mean 'in case we don't get there in time'?'' Ali cried, then fell back with another sharp pain.

"Don't you think you should ride back here?'' Brad finished.

"Have you ever delivered?'' Kevin asked.

"Once. A few months ago.''

"That's as often as I have…and a lot more recent. I'll drive.'' He ran around to the driver's side.

Craig stood alongside the van. "Should I wait here?''

"No!'' Ali yelled. "Get in the front.'' She didn't have time for subtleties. And all of a sudden doctors weren't such a bad thing. The more the merrier if this baby couldn't wait.

Another pain seized her, this one more fierce than the others. Ali swore under her breath and lifted her head. "Can we get this show on the road? Please!'' She motioned hurriedly for her sisters to get in the back.

"Are you sure?'' Lynne asked.

"Yes, yes. Hurry up,'' she said, not meaning to

sound so gruff. They both scrambled into the rear seat.

Michelle handed Brad a stack of clean towels, slammed the door and the van barreled down the side street and turned south on Kercheval.

Ali's breathing started coming in short pants. She glanced at Brad whose eyes didn't mask his fear.

Suddenly she felt the urge to push. Rising up on her elbows she gritted her teeth so hard she thought they might break. Beads of sweat trickled down her forehead and under her neck.

"She's crowning," Brad yelled to Kevin. The van careened around another corner and Ali gripped the back of the seat to keep from falling. She felt Lynne's hand on hers, holding her tight, while Craig gave Brad instructions and Barbara said she thought she might be sick.

Ali couldn't stop panting now as the urge to push grew stronger. She bore down hard just as the van screeched to a stop in front of the emergency entrance.

"That's it, sweetheart. One more time."

Ali lifted herself onto her elbows and gave it all she had until she heard Brad say, "Here he is, Mama." He held the red squirming infant high for Ali to see before she fell back against the seat.

What happened next seemed a blur. Craig helped Brad cut and clamp the cord seconds before hospital personnel wrapped and whisked the baby inside. Ali felt herself being carried to a gurney, feeling dazed, excited and worried, all the time clutching at Brad's hand.

"Is he okay? Is he big enough?"

"He's beautiful, Ali. Not as big as some, but big enough."

She was lifted from the gurney to a bed. "You sure?"

He kissed her forehead. "I'll go pay him a visit and be right back."

Brad had no sooner left than Dr. Wilson rushed in. The attending physician was delivering the placenta when Wilson came around the side of the bed. "I see you didn't need me, after all," he said, taking Ali's hand and smiling.

He looked from the white flowers in her hair to the now-rumpled wedding dress and chuckled. "I guess congratulations are in order…in more ways than one. Bet you won't ever forget this day!" He glanced at the pager on his belt. "Looks like you're not the only one. Let me make a call and I'll be back to check on you before I go." He patted her knee and left as Brad strode in pushing an isolette.

"Look who's here to see you," he said, not hiding his pride. The nurse finished with Ali and left the new family alone. Ali pushed the button on her bed and raised the head higher as Brad brought their son alongside.

"Oh, Brad." She stared down at the tiny infant swaddled in a blue receiving blanket and her heart felt too big for her chest. "He *is* perfect, isn't he?"

"I tried to tell you."

"How much does he weigh?"

"Surprisingly, just under five pounds. I'd hate to think how big he would have been if you'd gone full term."

She longed to hold her little one in her arms, but for the moment she was content to touch him through the portholes and watch the love and joy on his father's face.

After a while Ali asked, "What happened to my sisters?"

"I think Barbara's still passed out in the van."

"Oh, dear," she chuckled. "And Lynne?"

"Breathing into a paper bag last I saw her."

Ali held her stomach and laughed out loud. "Will life always be like this?"

"As long as I'm married to you, Ali Darling, I'm betting on yes."

Ali Darling. Mrs. Ali Darling. It didn't get better than this.

"And how long do you suppose that will be?" she asked, wiping away happy tears.

"Married to you?"

She nodded and stroked the back of his hand, feeling as though she would burst from joy.

"Oh, I'd say a few more babies and fifty years or so."

"What then?" She smiled.

"Maybe by then it will be safe to renew our vows."

Exhausted, Ali fell silent while Brad inched closer. "You know...I never got to kiss the bride," he said.

Gently he lowered his mouth to hers and Ali thought his lips never tasted sweeter. And when the kiss ended, his intense look of love reached deep inside her and squeezed her very soul...in a way words alone never could.

"Thank you, Ali," he whispered. "For our beautiful son...for being my wife...but most of all, for never giving up on me."

She touched his cheek, still finding it difficult to

believe she had found this great man, that he was hers alone to love...today, tomorrow...always.

She brushed more tears from under her eyes until slowly they tore their gazes from each other and looked back at their precious child. Wild tufts of black hair shot in every direction. Ali beamed.

"He looks just like his daddy," she said, and turned back to see a sheen settle over her husband's eyes.

"Yes, he does, doesn't he?"

*   *   *   *   *

Look for the next book in
THE BABY BANK,

HER BABY'S FATHER,

*by Katherine Garbera,
on sale April 2000,
only from Silhouette Desire.*

is proud to present

Where love is measured in pounds and ounces!

A trip to the fertility clinic leads four women to the family of their dreams!

THE PREGNANT VIRGIN (SD#1283)
Anne Eames March 2000

HER BABY'S FATHER (SD#1289)
Katherine Garbera April 2000

THE BABY BONUS (SD#1295)
Metsy Hingle May 2000

THE BABY GIFT (SD#1301)
Susan Crosby June 2000

Available at your favorite retail outlet.

Where love comes alive™

Looking For More Romance?

Visit Romance.net

Check in daily for these and other exciting features:

Hot off the press

View all current titles, and purchase them on-line.

What do the stars have in store for you?

Horoscope

Hot deals

Exclusive offers available only at Romance.net

Plus, don't miss our interactive quizzes, contests and bonus gifts.

PWEB

Continuing in April from

Silhouette® Desire®

SECRETS!

the compelling series by
Barbara McCauley

They're back!
The Sinclair brothers now have their own
stories…with plenty of hidden passions,
hidden promises and deepest, most desirable
secrets imaginable!

Don't miss:

CALLAN'S PROPOSITION (SD #1290)
in Silhouette Desire this April
and
GABRIEL'S HONOR (IM #1024)
coming to Silhouette Intimate Moments in August

*Watch for more **SECRETS!** to be uncovered in 2001!*

Silhouette®
Where love comes alive™

Look Who's Celebrating Our 20th Anniversary:

Celebrate 20 YEARS

"Silhouette Desire is the purest form of contemporary romance."
—*New York Times* bestselling author
Elizabeth Lowell

"Let's raise a glass to Silhouette and all the great books and talented authors they've introduced over the past twenty years. May the *next* twenty be just as exciting and just as innovative!"
—*New York Times* bestselling author
Linda Lael Miller

"You've given us a sounding board, a place where, as readers, we can be entertained, and as writers, an opportunity to share our stories.… You deserve a special round of applause on…your twentieth birthday. Here's wishing you many, many more."
—International bestselling author
Annette Broadrick

Celebrate the joy of bringing a baby into the world—
and the power of passionate love—with

A BOUQUET OF BABIES

An anthology containing three delightful stories
from three beloved authors!

THE WAY HOME
The classic tale from *New York Times* bestselling author

L I N D A
HOWARD

FAMILY BY FATE
A brand-new Maternity Row story by

PAULA DETMER RIGGS

BABY ON HER DOORSTEP
A brand-new Twins on the Doorstep story by

STELLA BAGWELL

Available in April 2000, at your favorite retail outlet.

Silhouette®
Where love comes alive™

SILHOUETTE'S 20TH ANNIVERSARY CONTEST
OFFICIAL RULES
NO PURCHASE NECESSARY TO ENTER

1. To enter, follow directions published in the offer to which you are responding. Contest begins 1/1/00 and ends on 8/24/00 (the "Promotion Period"). Method of entry may vary. Mailed entries must be postmarked by 8/24/00, and received by 8/31/00.

2. During the Promotion Period, the Contest may be presented via the Internet. Entry via the Internet may be restricted to residents of certain geographic areas that are disclosed on the Web site. To enter via the Internet, if you are a resident of a geographic area in which Internet entry is permissible, follow the directions displayed on-line, including typing your essay of 100 words or fewer telling us "Where In The World Your Love Will Come Alive." On-line entries must be received by 11:59 p.m. Eastern Standard time on 8/24/00. Limit one e-mail entry per person, household and e-mail address per day, per presentation. If you are a resident of a geographic area in which entry via the Internet is permissible, you may, in lieu of submitting an entry on-line, enter by mail, by hand-printing your name, address, telephone number and contest number/name on an 8"x 11" plain piece of paper and telling us in 100 words or fewer "Where In The World Your Love Will Come Alive," and mailing via first-class mail to: Silhouette 20th Anniversary Contest, (in the U.S.) P.O. Box 9069, Buffalo, NY 14269-9069; (In Canada) P.O. Box 637, Fort Erie, Ontario, Canada L2A 5X3. Limit one 8"x 11" mailed entry per person, household and e-mail address per day. On-line and/or 8"x 11" mailed entries received from persons residing in geographic areas in which Internet entry is not permissible will be disqualified. No liability is assumed for lost, late, incomplete, inaccurate, nondelivered or misdirected mail, or misdirected e-mail, for technical, hardware or software failures of any kind, lost or unavailable network connection, or failed, incomplete, garbled or delayed computer transmission or any human error which may occur in the receipt or processing of the entries in the contest.

3. Essays will be judged by a panel of members of the Silhouette editorial and marketing staff based on the following criteria:

   > Sincerity (believability, credibility)—50%
   >
   > Originality (freshness, creativity)—30%
   >
   > Aptness (appropriateness to contest ideas)—20%

   Purchase or acceptance of a product offer does not improve your chances of winning. In the event of a tie, duplicate prizes will be awarded.

4. All entries become the property of Harlequin Enterprises Ltd., and will not be returned. Winner will be determined no later than 10/31/00 and will be notified by mail. Grand Prize winner will be required to sign and return Affidavit of Eligibility within 15 days of receipt of notification. Noncompliance within the time period may result in disqualification and an alternative winner may be selected. All municipal, provincial, federal, state and local laws and regulations apply. Contest open only to residents of the U.S. and Canada who are 18 years of age or older, and is void wherever prohibited by law. Internet entry is restricted solely to residents of those geographical areas in which Internet entry is permissible. Employees of Torstar Corp., their affiliates, agents and members of their immediate families are not eligible. Taxes on the prizes are the sole responsibility of winners. Entry and acceptance of any prize offered constitutes permission to use winner's name, photograph or other likeness for the purposes of advertising, trade and promotion on behalf of Torstar Corp. without further compensation to the winner, unless prohibited by law. Torstar Corp and D.L. Blair, Inc., their parents, affiliates and subsidiaries, are not responsible for errors in printing or electronic presentation of contest or entries. In the event of printing or other errors which may result in unintended prize values or duplication of prizes, all affected contest materials or entries shall be null and void. If for any reason the Internet portion of the contest is not capable of running as planned, including infection by computer virus, bugs, tampering, unauthorized intervention, fraud, technical failures, or any other causes beyond the control of Torstar Corp. which corrupt or affect the administration, secrecy, fairness, integrity or proper conduct of the contest, Torstar Corp. reserves the right, at its sole discretion, to disqualify any individual who tampers with the entry process and to cancel, terminate, modify or suspend the contest or the Internet portion thereof. In the event of a dispute regarding an on-line entry, the entry will be deemed submitted by the authorized holder of the e-mail account submitted at the time of entry. Authorized account holder is defined as the natural person who is assigned to an e-mail address by an Internet access provider, on-line service provider or other organization that is responsible for arranging e-mail address for the domain associated with the submitted e-mail address.

5. Prizes: Grand Prize—a $10,000 vacation to anywhere in the world. Travelers (at least one must be 18 years of age or older) or parent or guardian if one traveler is a minor, must sign and return a Release of Liability prior to departure. Travel must be completed by December 31, 2001, and is subject to space and accommodations availability. Two hundred (200) Second Prizes—a two-book limited edition autographed collector set from one of the Silhouette Anniversary authors: Nora Roberts, Diana Palmer, Linda Howard or Annette Broadrick (value $10.00 each set). All prizes are valued in U.S. dollars.

6. For a list of winners (available after 10/31/00), send a self-addressed, stamped envelope to: Harlequin Silhouette 20th Anniversary Winners, P.O. Box 4200, Blair, NE 68009-4200.

Contest sponsored by Torstar Corp., P.O. Box 9042, Buffalo, NY 14269-9042.

ENTER FOR
A CHANCE TO WIN*

Silhouette's 20th Anniversary Contest

Tell Us Where in the World
You Would Like *Your* Love To Come Alive...
And We'll Send the Lucky Winner There!

Silhouette wants to take you wherever
your happy ending can come true.

Here's how to enter: Tell us, in 100 words or less,
where you want to go to make your love come alive!

In addition to the grand prize, there will be 200
runner-up prizes, collector's-edition book sets
autographed by one of the Silhouette anniversary
authors: **Nora Roberts, Diana Palmer,
Linda Howard** or **Annette Broadrick**.

DON'T MISS YOUR CHANCE TO WIN!
ENTER NOW! No Purchase Necessary

Silhouette®
Where love comes alive™

Name:

Address:

City: State/Province:

Zip/Postal Code:

Mail to Harlequin Books: **In the U.S.**: P.O. Box 9069, Buffalo, NY
14269-9069; **In Canada**: P.O. Box 637, Fort Erie, Ontario, L4A 5X3

PS20CON_R